Sticks & Scones

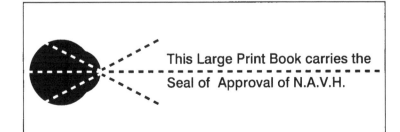

This Large Print Book carries the
Seal of Approval of N.A.V.H.

Diane Mott Davidson

Sticks & Scones

Waterville, Maine

Published in Large Print by arrangement with Bantam Books, a division of Random House, Inc., in the United States and Canada.

The text of this Large Print edition is unabridged.
Other aspects of the book may vary from the original edition.

Set in 16 pt. Plantin.

Printed in the United States on permanent paper.

ISBN 1-56895-1973 (lg. print : sc : alk. paper)

To John William Schenk,
a stupendously talented and fabulously
creative chef and caterer.
Thank you.

ACKNOWLEDGMENTS

I wish to acknowledge the assistance of the following people: Jim, J.Z., and Joe Davidson; Jeff and Rosa Davidson; Kate Miciak, a fabulous editor; Sandra Dijkstra, an incredible agent; and Susan Corcoran and Sharon Lulek, both unequaled publicists.

For help in Great Britain, I am particularly indebted to the marvelous staff at Books for Cooks in Notting Hill; to the equally brilliant staff at Hampton Court; to Julie Cullen, Director of Catering for Cliveden, Taplow, and Maidenhead, in the National Trust; and to David Edge of the Wallace Collection.

I was also greatly aided by my friend Julie Wallin Kaewert, who intrepidly drove on the left side of the road for our great adventure into English castles, abbeys, hotels, bookstores, and gourmet restaurants.

In addition, I am thankful to the following people: Lee Karr and the group that assembles at her home; Carol Devine Rusley, for encouragement and friendship; Lucy Mott Faison, who once again provided sisterly aid by testing and retesting the recipes at low altitude; John William Schenk and Karen Johnson, who once more took time to answer numerous catering questions; Katherine Goodwin Saideman, for her close readings of the manuscript; Shirley Carnahan, Ph.D., instructor in Humanities at the University of Colorado, for her helpful tips on all aspects of medieval history and castle life, and for her insightful reading of the manuscript; Dr. Michael Schuett, Attending Physician, Emergency Department, Porter Hospital, for insight into emergency procedures; Chuck Musser, meat department, Albertson's Grocery Store, Evergreen, Colorado, for advice on the steak pies; Richard Staller, D.O., Elk Ridge Family Physicians, for medical details; Meg Kendal and Daniel Martinez, M.D., Denver-Evergreen Ob-Gyn Group, for all manner of medical background; Francine Mathews and Mo Mathews, for their extremely helpful historical input; Kay Bergstrom; Triena Harper, chief deputy coroner, Jon Cline, coroner's investigator, Chris Bauchmeyer, Deputy District Attorney, all of Jefferson County, and John Lauck, Criminal Investigator, District Attorney's Office, First Judicial District of Colorado, all of whom provided key information; Paula Millsapps, for offering banking background; Webster Stickney, philatelic agent, Harmer Schau Auction Galleries, for providing outstanding stamp-collecting expertise; Deputy Troy Murfin, Jefferson County Sheriff's Department, for details on statutes; and as always, for his wide-ranging knowledge and his wonderful ability to articulate it, Sergeant Richard Millsapps, Jefferson County Work-Release Program, Lakewood, Colorado.

Wounds of the flesh a surgeon's skill may heal,
But wounded honor's only cured with steel.

—"THE ART OF DUELLING," BY
'A TRAVELLER.' LONDON, 1836

LABYRINTH DONOR'S APPRECIATION LUNCH

Hyde Chapel, Aspen Meadow, Colorado
Monday, February 9, noon

Chicken Croquettes, Dijon and Cranberry Sauces

◆

Winter Salad of Chèvre, Figs, Filberts, and Field Greens
Port Wine Vinaigrette

Shakespeare's Steak Pie

◆

Steamed Green Beans with Artichoke Hearts

◆

Elizabethan Manchet Bread, Butter

◆

Chocolate Marble Labyrinth Cake

◆

Merlot, Sparkling Water, Teas, and Coffee

CHAPTER 1

Nighttime noises are torture. When a midnight wind shrieks through our window jambs, or footsteps clomp past the house, I think, *It could be anything.* Once a snowbank slid from our roof and thundered onto the deck. I awoke, heart pounding, convinced I'd been shot.

It isn't logical, of course. But living with terror for seven years had not made me the most rational of thinkers, least of all when roused from sleep. A sound could be anything? *No.*

It was *something.*

When I awoke at four o'clock on Monday morning, February ninth, those years of dread were long over. Still, I was certain I'd heard a tiny scraping noise, like boots chafing against ice. *Think,* I warned myself. *Don't panic.*

Heart pulsing, throat dry, I waited for my brain to clear, for the sound to come again. My husband Tom was out of town. Even when he's at home, noise rarely interrupts his slumber. Tom is a big hulking cop, and isn't afraid of much.

I shifted in the chilled sheets. The temperature outside was close to zero. Frigid air poured through tiny leaks in our bedroom windows. The noise had come from outdoors, from below, of that I was fairly certain.

Now all was quiet. No sound emanated from Arch's room down the hall. Two months from turning fifteen, my son slept so soundly even a howling blizzard would not rouse him. On the first floor, our bloodhound, Jake, was not growling or pacing in his enclosed area next to the kitchen. These were good signs.

Maybe I was imagining things. I'd gone to bed too late, after cooking all evening for today's catered event. And I was stressed out, anyway. In December, our family life had been in an uproar. My in-home commercial kitchen had been shut down, and Tom and I had ended up involved in a homicide case at a nearby ski area. To make things worse, on New Year's Eve, right after the official reopening of my kitchen, I'd catered my first party in months. It had gone very badly.

Wait. Another unmistakable scrape was followed by a tiny *crack*. It was like…what? Elk hooves shattering ice? A pine bough creaking under its burden of snow? Like…someone opening a suitcase across the street?

Who unpacks bags at four in the morning?

Henry Kissinger said, *Even a paranoid has real enemies.* With that in mind, I decided against getting out of bed and peering out a window. My eyes traveled to the bedside table and I reached stealthily for the portable

2

phone. In addition to being paranoid, I some-times suspected I was an alarmist, or, as the ninth-grade tough guys at Arch's school would say, a *wimp*. Now, I bargained with myself. One more sound, and I would speed-dial the sheriff's department.

I shivered, waited, and longed for the heavy terry-cloth robe hanging in my closet, an early Valentine's present from Tom. *Caterers need to rest after cooking, Miss G.,* he'd said. *Wrap yourself in this when I'm gone, and pretend it's me.*

Of course, I would have much preferred Tom *himself* to the robe. For the past week, he'd been in New Jersey working a case. There, he reported, the weather was rainy. In Aspen Meadow, I'd told him in our evening calls, each day had brought more snow. Arch and I had made a morning ritual of shoveling our front walk. But daytime temperatures in the mid-thirties had melted our man-made snowbanks, and the nightly freezes trans-formed the sidewalk into a sheet of ice.

So. If someone *was* on our sidewalk, he or she was on a *very* slippery slope.

I propped myself up on my elbow, yanked up the bedspread, and listened intently. In the neon light cast by the street lamp outside, I could just make out my own reflection in our mirror: blond curly hair, dark eyes, thirty-four-year-old face just a tad round from an excess of chocolate. It was a face that had been happy for almost two years, since I'd married Tom. But now Tom's absence was an ache.

3

Back in my old life, my ex-husband had often stumbled in late. I'd become used to the drunken harangues, the flaunted infidelities, the midnight arguments. Sometimes I even thought his girlfriends used to follow him home, to stake out our house.

Of course, I absolutely believed in *Tom's* fidelity, even if he had been both secretive and preoccupied lately. Before he left, he'd even seemed low. I hadn't quite known how to help. Try as I might, I was still getting used to being a cop's wife.

Five minutes went by with no sound. My mind continued to meander. I wondered again about Tom. Six A.M. on the East Coast; was he up? Was he still planning on flying back this morning, as he'd promised us? Had he made any progress in his investigation?

The case Tom was working on involved the hijacking—on a Furman County road— of a FedEx delivery truck. The driver had been killed. Only one of the suspected three hijackers had been arrested. His name was Ray Wolff, and he was now in the same cell block as my ex-husband, Dr. John Richard Korman. The Jerk, as his other ex-wife and I called him, was currently serving a sentence for assault. During Arch's weekly visit, John Richard had boasted to his son of his acquaintance with Ray Wolff, the famous killer-hijacker. How low things had sunk, I thought, when a father reveled in his own criminal infamy.

I shivered again and tried not to think of the threats my ex-husband had sent from jail.

4

They'd been both implied and overt. *When I get out of here, I'll set you straight, Goldy.* To Arch, he'd said, *You can tell your mother your father has a plan.* I guess I wasn't surprised that those tiny signs of remorse John Richard had shown at his trial had all been for the benefit of the judge.

I jumped at the sound of a third, louder crack. Downstairs, Jake let out a tentative *woof.* I hit the phone's power button as an explosion rocked our house.

What was that? My brain reeled. Cold and trembling, I realized I'd fallen off the bed. A gunshot? A bomb? It had sounded like a rocket launcher. A grenade. An earthquake. Downstairs, glass crashed to the floor. *What the hell is going on?*

I clutched the phone, scuttled across the cold floor, and tried to call for Arch. Unfortunately, my voice no longer seemed to be working. Below, our security system shrieked. I cursed as I made a tripping dash down the unlit hall.

The noise had been a gunshot. It had to have been. Someone had shot at our *home.* At least one downstairs window had been shattered, of that I was certain. *Where is the shooter now? Where is my son?*

"Arch!" I squawked in the dark hallway. Dwarfed by the alarm, my voice sounded tiny and far away. "Are you all right? Can you hear me?"

The alarm's wail melded with Jake's baying. What good did a security system do, anyway?

Alarms are meant to protect you from intruders wanting your stuff—not from shooters wanting your *life*. Yelling that it was *me*, it was *Mom*, I stumbled through my son's bedroom door.

Arch had turned on his aquarium light and was sitting up in bed. In the eerie light, his pale face glowed. His toast-brown hair had fanned out in an electric halo, and his hastily donned tortoiseshell glasses were askew. He clutched a raised sword—a gleaming foil used for his school fencing practice. I punched the phone buttons for 911, but was trembling so badly I messed it up. Now the phone was braying in my ear.

Panic tensed Arch's face as he leaned toward the watery light and squinted at me.

"*Mom*! What was *that*?"

Shuddering, I fumbled with the phone again and finally pushed the automatic dial for the Furman County Sheriff's Department.

"I don't know," I managed to shout to Arch. Blood gurgled in my ears. I wanted to be in control, to be comforting, to be a good mother. I wanted to assure him this was all some terrible mistake. "Better get on the—" With the phone, I gestured toward the floor.

Still gripping the sword, Arch obediently scrambled onto a braided rug I'd made during our financial dark days. He was wearing a navy sweat suit—his substitute for pajamas—and thick gray socks, protection from the cold. *Protection.* I thought belatedly of Tom's rifle and the handgun he kept hidden behind a false wall in our detached garage. Lot of good

6

they did me now, especially since I didn't know how to shoot.

"We'll be right there," announced a distant telephone voice after I babbled where we were and what had happened. Jake's howl and the screaming security system made it almost impossible to make out the operator's clipped instructions. "Mrs. Schulz?" she repeated. "Lock the bedroom door. If any of your neighbors call, tell them not to do anything. We should have a car there in less than fifteen minutes."

Please, God, I prayed, disconnecting. With numb fingers, I locked Arch's door, then eased to the floor beside him. I glanced upward. Could the glow from the aquarium light be seen from outside? Could the shooter get a good purchase on Arch's window?

"Somebody has to go get Jake," Arch whispered. "We can't just leave him barking. You told the operator you heard a shot. Did you really think it was from a gun? I thought it was a *cannonball.*"

"I don't know." *If any of your neighbors call...* My neighbors' names had all slid from my head.

The front doorbell rang. My eyes locked with Arch's. Neither of us moved. The bell rang again. A male voice shouted, "Goldy? Arch? It's Bill! Three other guys are here with me!" Bill? Ah, Bill Quincy...from next door. "Goldy," Bill boomed. "We're *armed*!"

I took a steadying breath. This was Colorado, not England or Canada or some other place

7

where folks don't keep guns and wield them freely. In Aspen Meadow, no self-respecting gun-owner who heard a shot at four A.M. was going to wait to be summoned. One man had even glued a decal over the Neighborhood Watch sign: *This Street Guarded by Colts.* Although the county had sent out a graffiti-removal company to scrape off the sticker, the sentiment remained the same.

"Goldy? Arch?" Bill Quincy hollered again. "You okay? It doesn't look as if anybody's broken in! Could you let me check? Goldy!"

Would the cops object? I didn't know.

"Goldy?" Bill bellowed. "Answer me, or I'm breaking down the door!"

"All right!" I called. "I'm coming!" I told Arch to stay put and tentatively made my way down the stairs.

Freezing air swirled through the first floor. In the living room, glass shards glittered where they'd landed on the couch, chairs, and carpet. I turned off the deafening alarm, flipped on the outside light, and swung open the door.

Four grizzled, goose-down-jacketed men stood on my front step. I was wearing red plaid flannel pj's and my feet were bare, but I told them law enforcement was en route and invited them in. Clouds of steam billowed from the men's mouths as Bill insisted his companions weren't budging. As if to make his point, Bill's posse settled creakily onto our frosted porch. The men's weapons—two rifles and two pistols—glinted in the ghostly light.

Bill Quincy, his wide, chinless face grim, his broad shoulders tense, announced that he intended to go through the house, to see if the shooter had broken in. I should wait until he'd inspected the first floor, he ordered, pushing past me without further ceremony. Bill stomped resolutely through the kitchen and dining room, peered into the tiny half-bath, then returned to the hallway and cocked his head at me. I tiptoed behind him to the kitchen. He shouted a warning into the basement, then banged down the steps. If the intruder was indeed inside, there could be no mistake that my neighbor intended to roust him out.

Jake bounded up to Arch's room ahead of me. Scout, our adopted stray cat, slunk along behind the bloodhound, his long gray-and-brown hair, like Arch's, turned electric from being suddenly roused. Following my animal escort, I silently thanked God that none of us had been hurt, and that we had great neighbors. The cat scooted under the bed used by Julian Teller, our former boarder, now a sophomore at the University of Colorado. Arch asked for a third time what had happened. I didn't want to frighten him. So I lied.

"It just...looks as if some drunk staggered up from the Grizzly Saloon, took aim at our living-room window, and shot it out. I don't know whether the guy used a shotgun or a rifle. Whatever it was, he wasn't too plastered to miss."

My son nodded slowly, not sure whether to

believe me. He shouldn't have, of course. The Grizzly closed early on Sunday night.

I stared at the hands on Arch's new clock, a gift from his fencing coach. The clock was in the shape of a tiny knight holding a sword, from which a timepiece dangled. When the hands pointed to four-twenty-five, a wail of sirens broke the tense silence. I pushed aside Arch's faded orange curtains and peeked out his window. Two sheriff's department vehicles hurtled down our street and parked at the curb.

I raced back to Tom's and my bedroom and slid into jeans, a sweatshirt, and clogs. Had someone unintentionally fired a gun? Was the damage to our window just some stupid accident? Surely it couldn't have been deliberate. And of all the times for this to happen...

I started downstairs. Today was supposed to herald my first big job in five weeks, a luncheon gig at a Gothic chapel on an estate dominated by a genuine English castle. The castle was one of Aspen Meadow's gorgeous-but-weird landmarks. If things went well, the castle-owner—who was hoping to open a conference center at the site—promised to be a huge client. I didn't want *anything* to mess up today's job.

Then again, I fretted as I gripped the railing, I was a caterer married to a cop, a cop working on a case so difficult he'd been forced to search for a suspect two thousand miles away. Perhaps the gunshot had been a message for Tom.

Outside, the red-and-blue lights flashing on snow-covered pines created monstrous shadows. The sight of cop cars was not unfamiliar to me. Still, my throat tightened as I wrenched open our front door. Bill and the other gun-toters looked at me sympathetically.

Why would someone shoot at the house of a caterer?

I swallowed hard.

Did I really want to know?

CHAPTER 2

Two cops trod up the icy path to our door. The first was tall and decidedly corpulent, the second short and slight, with a dark mustache set off by pale skin.

"Mrs. Schulz?" asked the tall one. "I'm Deputy Wyatt. This is Deputy Vaughan."

I nodded and shook their hands. I remembered both of them from the department Christmas party, which was actually held three days before New Year's, since Christmas and New Year's themselves are always high-crime days. While the impromptu posse, three neighbors plus Bill, looked on curiously, I thanked the cops for responding so quickly.

Wyatt, who had dark, intelligent eyes, addressed me in a low, terse voice. "We're going to secure your house. Then we'll need to talk to your neighbors." He took off his hat, revealing a head thinly covered with dark brown hair. "After that, we'll want to talk to you."

I let him in while Vaughan stepped aside and talked quietly to the men on the porch. With most of the front window missing, it seemed silly to shut the door firmly behind Wyatt. But I did anyway. Amazing how old habits die hard.

Once I'd turned on the living-room lights, Wyatt stepped toward the window. He frowned at the glass fangs hanging from the casement. Frigid air poured through the hole. The deputy gave a barely perceptible nod and began to move through the house.

Arch's music wafted down from upstairs. Unrhythmic thumps—Jake's tail hitting the floor—indicated the bloodhound had stayed with him. Now *there* was a recipe for comfort: rock and roll, plus a canine companion.

The icy February air made me shiver. I headed to the kitchen, where I could close the hall door against the chill. There, I could also turn on the oven. My oven was to me what Arch's music was to him.

But heating the oven wasn't enough. My mind continued to cough up questions, and I moved nervously from one window to the next. Who shot at us? Why would someone do such a thing? Outside, flashes of the police car lights blinked across the snow-sculpted yard. Should I call Tom now, or should I wait? Would they assign this case to him?

In the basement, I could hear Wyatt's

scraping shuffle as he moved from Tom's office into the storage room, bathroom, laundry room, closets.... The hole in the window meant I could just hear Vaughan's low murmur on the front porch, interspersed with responses from one or the other of the neighbors. How much longer would they leave me here? Could the shooter be inside? Impossible. But might he not still be somewhere outside? Unlikely, I reasoned.

I hugged myself as cold air streamed under the door between the kitchen and the hall. How was I supposed to work in my kitchen today if it was so doggone cold? And anyway, a hot oven wasn't going to make me feel any better unless I actually put something into it. Something hot and flaky, something you could slather with jam and butter, or even whipped cream....

Again the gunshot echoed in my ears. I couldn't stop trembling. Where were the cops? Why was it so cold in here?

I needed comfort. I was going to make *scones*.

I felt better immediately.

I heated water to plump the currants, powered up my kitchen computer, and rummaged in our walk-in refrigerator for unsalted butter. I'd done a great deal of research on English food for the catering stint I was starting, and what I'd learned had been fascinating. Scones had first been mentioned as a Scottish food in the sixteenth century. Since that meant the Tudors might have indulged in the darling little pastries, my new client was desperate for a good recipe.

Intriguing as the notion of the perfect scone might be, the ability to concentrate eluded me. Fretting about how long it might take to get our window repaired, I smeared a stick of butter on the marble counter. When the gunshot blast reechoed in my brain, I forgot the stopper for the food processor. A blizzard of flour whirled up to the ceiling, then settled on my face. When I coughed and jumped back, my elbow smacked a carton; a river of heavy whipping cream *glug-glug-glugg*ed onto my computer keyboard. I was cursing mightily when Wyatt and Vaughan finally pounded into the kitchen. Surveying the mess, their eyes widened.

"I'm cooking," I told them, my voice fierce.

"So I see," said Wyatt. He cleared his throat. "Umm... Why don't you have a seat for a minute?"

I shut down the computer and unplugged it, turned the keyboard over to drain, turned off the food processor, and wiped the flour from my face. Without missing a beat, Wyatt launched into his report. Thankfully, he'd found nothing amiss—no sign of forced entry, no strangers lurking in closets or under beds. Investigators and techs, he assured me, would be along in no time to process the scene.

I offered them hot drinks. Both declined as they settled at our oak kitchen table. I fixed myself an espresso, picked up the dripping cream carton, and poured the last of the white stuff into my coffee. *Fortitude,* I reminded myself. The kitchen air was like the inside of a refrigerator. I should have put on two sweatshirts.

"I remember you," Wyatt said, a mischievous smile playing over his lips. "And not just because you're married to Tom Schulz. You're the one who's gotten kinda involved in some investigations, right?"

I sighed and nodded.

Vaughan chuckled. "Seems to me we've ribbed Schulz about that a time or two. We asked him, why don't you just give her a job?"

Didn't these guys care about our shattered window? Why weren't they digging bullets out of my living-room wall? Or searching for footprints in the snow? "Thanks, guys," I replied. "I've got a job. A business. Which this incident is not going to help. And I also have a son who needs to be protected," I reminded them grimly.

Getting serious, the deputies fired questions at me. What had I heard? When? Why was I so sure it was a gunshot? Had I actually seen anything out the window? Had Arch?

Warmed by the coffee, I gave short answers while Wyatt took notes. But I faltered when he asked if any member of our family had received threats lately.

"There was something involving the department about a month ago," Wyatt prompted me, when I didn't immediately answer. "You're the caterer who turned in the Lauderdales. New Year's Eve? Child abuse, right?"

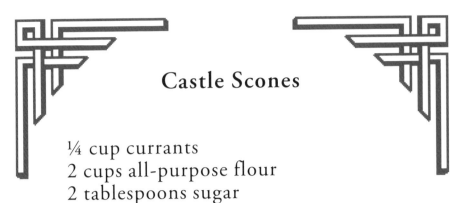

Castle Scones

¼ cup currants
2 cups all-purpose flour
2 tablespoons sugar
1 tablespoon baking powder
½ teaspoon salt
4 tablespoons well-chilled unsalted
    butter, cut into 4 pieces
1 large egg
¼ cup whipping cream
½ cup milk
2 teaspoons sugar (optional)
butter, whipped cream, jams, curds,
    and marmalades

Place the currants in a medium-sized bowl and pour boiling water over them just to cover. Allow to stand for 10 minutes. Drain the currants, pat them dry with paper towels, and set aside.

Preheat the oven to 400°F.

Mix the flour, sugar, baking powder, and salt in the bowl of a food processor fitted with a steel blade. With the motor running, add the butter and process

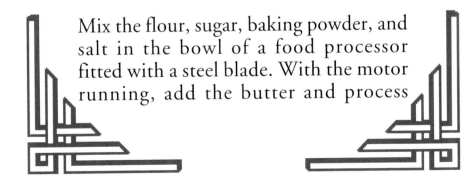

until the mixture looks like cornmeal. In a separate bowl, beat the egg slightly with the cream and milk. With the motor still running, pour the egg mixture in a thin stream into the flour mixture just until the dough holds together in a ball.

On a floured surface, lightly pat the dough into 2 circles, each about 7 inches in diameter. Cut each circle into 6 even pieces. Place the scones on a buttered baking sheet 2 inches apart. Sprinkle them with the optional sugar, if desired.

Bake about 15 minutes, or until the scones are puffed, golden, and cooked through. Serve with butter, whipped cream, and jams.

Makes 12 scones

"Yes," I replied. "I turned in Buddy's-your-buddy, the Jag's-in-the-bag Lauderdale. He shook his baby daughter until the poor child passed out."

Wyatt looked up from his notebook and scowled. "You were doing a party there, isn't that what I heard?" he asked. "Big party, even though the guy's facing bankruptcy or something?"

Or something. Buddy Lauderdale's rumored financial difficulties had been widely reported, along with his arrest. According to the whispers, dutifully conveyed in the newspapers, the new, expanded Lauderdale Luxury Imports, situated near the fancy new Furman East Shopping Center, was about to go belly-up.

Buddy Lauderdale, fiftyish, swarthy, and boasting a full head of newly plugged hair, had scoffed at the rumors. With his ultrachic, fifteen-years-his-junior second wife Chardé, Buddy had thrown an extravagant New Year's party to show the world *just* how rich and confident he was. And I'd been booked to do the catering, thanks to the recommendation of Howie Lauderdale, a star sophomore on the Elk Park Prep fencing team. Sixteen-year-old Howie, who'd befriended Arch, was the product of Buddy's first marriage. Naïvely, I'd thought the father would be as nice as the son.

All had gone well on New Year's Eve, I recounted at the cops' prompting, until about eleven-thirty, when Buddy and Howie had put on a fencing demonstration for their guests. Unfortunately, Patty Lauderdale, the cute-as-a-button one-year-old daughter of Buddy and Chardé, had started to wail just as the demonstration began. Buddy had ordered me to take the baby away, which I had. In the kitchen, I'd rocked, cooed, and sung to the screaming Patty, all to no avail. The child should have been in bed, of course, but the parents had wanted to show her off to their guests. Impatient with the racket, Buddy had stormed into the kitchen. In the presence of no other adult but me, he'd grabbed little Patty from my arms. Over my protests, he'd shaken that poor child until she choked, her eyes rolled back in her head, and she lost consciousness.

So yes, I'd called the cops. Patty had been removed from the family home for a week. After an investigation, the Lauderdales, who had no priors, had been cleared of child abuse. Little Patty, reportedly still undergoing neurological tests, had been returned to her parents. But I've learned to suspect the corrupting power of money, influence, and lawyers. Through friends, I'd heard that the Lauderdales had sworn they were going to *get Goldy*. They insisted that good old Buddy had just been trying to be a good parent. And they also claimed that their name and their business had been irreparably harmed by my call to law enforcement. A hysterically toned *Mountain Journal* article, discussing the incident and my own history of spouse abuse, had not helped the situation. Beside the article had been two pictures. The first was of Buddy

Lauderdale from his Jag's-in-the-bag TV commercials, where he wore a hunting outfit, toted a rifle, and had a large bag slung over his shoulder. The second was of him being led away from his home in handcuffs.

"Heard from the Lauderdales lately?" Wyatt asked now.

I shook my head, but my heart sank. Unfortunately, Chardé Lauderdale was designing and implementing the makeover for the interior of Hyde Castle, where I would be catering later in the week. Chardé had also overseen the redecoration of Hyde Chapel, where I would be working later today. Make that, where I was *hoping* to work later today, if I could find a place to cook that had heat, ovens, and windows without bullet holes.

"Do you know of any recent threats made against Tom?" asked Vaughan.

I sighed and said no. If anyone had threatened *him*, I reminded them, there ought to be a record of it at the department. The hijacking-homicide case that had taken Tom out of state involved a heist from a Furman County store named The Stamp Fox. One of the envelopes in the hijacked delivery truck—the main target of the thieves—had contained collectible stamps worth over three million dollars. The Stamp Fox had been shipping the stamps in a plain FedEx envelope to a philatelic show in Tucson. So much for transmitting valuables incognito. When the FedEx driver resisted, he'd been shot dead.

"Tom's supposed to come back today," I told

Wyatt and Vaughan. "He's been looking for a local fellow who's been connected to the delivery-truck hijacking. Name's Andy Balachek."

"Isn't Balachek the kid with a gambling problem?" demanded Wyatt. "Stole his dad's excavation truck and then sold it? Got involved with Ray Wolff?"

I nodded. This, too, had been in the papers. Andy Balachek's friendship with Ray Wolff, the infamous hijacker now behind bars in the Furman County Jail, had proved costly to the naïve twenty-year-old. As one of Wolff's known associates, Andy had been questioned. The night of the hijacking, Andy's father had had a heart attack. Then Tom had arrested Ray Wolff, who'd left a fingerprint on the steering wheel of the hijacked FedEx truck, at a storage area on the county line. Wolff, vowing revenge, had spat in Tom's face before being led away in handcuffs.

I knew, but I was not sure that Wyatt and Vaughan knew, that Andy Balachek had confirmed the department's suspicions of his partnership with Ray Wolff. A few days after the theft, Andy had contacted Tom, requesting Tom communicate with him via e-mail. Andy was interested in a plea deal. The county D.A. had told Tom to string Andy along. Fearing his father was not long for this world, and needing to clear his conscience, Andy had been the one who'd tipped Tom off to Wolff's visit to the storage area. Then Andy had e-mailed Tom saying that he'd gotten a stake and was heading for Atlantic City. And off Tom had gone—to find him.

"Any other problematic cases Tom might have mentioned?" Deputy Vaughan persisted. "Somebody else have an ax to grind with him?"

I frowned and thought back to the e-mail account Tom had been forced to set up on his computer at home, because Andy Balachek had insisted he wouldn't send any correspondence directly to the sheriff's department. It had been out of character for Tom to take so much time to work at home. But he had, until he'd packed up for New Jersey. No, I didn't know whether Tom was working on other *problematic* cases. What I did know was that he'd been working too hard.

"Did he mention threats from Balachek?" asked Vaughan.

"When Balachek e-mailed Tom that he was leaving the state, Tom immediately got approval from Captain Lambert to go looking for him."

Vaughan raised his eyebrows, as in, *That's it?*

"And you, Mrs. Schulz?" asked Wyatt. "Aside from the Lauderdales. Anyone else you know might want to take a shot at you? Or your son, for that matter?"

Wyatt scribbled as I told him that Arch's father, my ex-husband, was being considered for parole, actually an early release, because of his so-called "good behavior." I added that serving less than five months of a three-year sentence didn't seem like much of a punishment for beating the daylights out of a woman. No, I told them, John Richard wasn't in jail for assaulting *me*. Or his other ex-wife, my best friend, Marla Korman. Not this time. I added that the idea of the Jerk being a model prisoner was an oxymoron on the order of fat-free butter. I told both deputies that John Richard could be out of jail anytime. But I was supposed to receive a notice from the Department of Corrections before that happened.

I fell silent. Wyatt and Vaughan studied me. The coffee was no longer hot; my teeth were chattering. Wyatt got up and called to the team who'd arrived and begun working in our living room. A policewoman brought in a quilt. I thanked her and wrapped myself up in the thick handmade comforter, sewn by county volunteers for crime victims.

"Any neighbors who might pose problems?" Wyatt's partner asked patiently. "Those guys outside look a tad trigger-happy." Was that a hint of a grin on Wyatt's face? I gushed that our neighbors were all terrific. The last time a neighbor had shot at anything, it had been a woodpecker. But he'd really *hated* that bird; his skirmishes with it were the stuff of neighborhood legend. And anyway, after he'd fired, the woodpecker had flown away, unscathed.

"Are there any other folks," Vaughan pressed, "any other clients, you might have had trouble with?"

"Ordinarily," I replied, "my clients only get upset if I don't show up." My throat closed. What was I supposed to do about the lunch? The bullet-smashed window made it too cold to do the crucial last part of the necessary food-prep here at home, unless I could quickly find a repairman to put plywood over the window. I *had* to honor my luncheon commitment at Hyde Chapel. If I wasn't able to get the window fixed, could I do my cooking in the castle kitchen? Would the Hydes want me to arrive at the castle before sunup? Gooseflesh pimpled my arms, and I sighed.

Wyatt closed his notebook. The phone rang. I bolted for it, hoping it was Tom.

"Goldy, it's Boyd," said the gravelly voice of Sergeant Boyd, one of Tom's closest friends in the department.

"Oh," I said, trying to hide my disappointment. "Did you hear about the—"

"It's why I'm calling," he interrupted. Boyd had a no-nonsense attitude that was complemented by his barrel-shaped body and unfashionable crew cut, all of which I had come to cherish. Tom trusted his life to Boyd, as did I. "Listen," he said now. "I want you out of there."

"I'm thinking about it," I protested. "I'm also thinking our window just needs some plywood—"

"Forget it. Your security system needs to be rewired and the house may not be safe. I've already talked to Armstrong." Sergeant Armstrong, who worked with Boyd, was another friend and ace investigator. "We want you to *get* out and *stay* out until Tom gets back. It is *not* safe there. You and Arch can hole up in my spare bedroom if you want. Armstrong's family is willing to have you, too."

I thought of the minuscule kitchen in Boyd's bachelor apartment, and of the chaos Armstrong's six children wrought wherever they went. "Thanks. I don't—"

"We'll get your window fixed, don't worry. And your security system, too. But we need to find out who did this to you."

"Okay," I agreed reluctantly, knowing Tom would want me to do whatever Boyd recommended. "I'll...make some arrangement."

"Good. Talk to you later."

I thanked him, hung up, and told the deputies what Boyd had said. Both seemed relieved. After all, the house would be too cold and too dangerous to stay in, at least for that day. So what other impromptu arrangement was I supposed to come up with? What friend can you call at four-thirty in the morning, to ask for refuge and a large kitchen?

During the current remodeling of her guest bedroom, my best friend Marla Korman—who always claimed that the Jerk had married her for her inherited fortune, which she'd refused to share with him during their brief marriage—had staked out a suite at Denver's Brown Palace Hotel. I knew Marla would have welcomed me, even at that ungodly morning hour. But the sixty-five-minute trip back from downtown Denver to Aspen

25

Meadow, to cater at Hyde Chapel between ferrying Arch to and from school, was simply not feasible. Plus, the Brown probably wouldn't look kindly on yours truly invading their restaurant kitchen.

Reluctantly, I realized that whatever I decided, I would soon have to call the Hydes—Eliot and Sukie—proprietors of Hyde Castle. The Elk Park Prep fencing coach, Michaela Kirovsky, doubled as a caretaker at the castle. She had mentioned to Arch that the couple who owned the castle would not mind if both of us stayed there while Tom was gone. Staying there, Michaela had kindly suggested, might even make my upcoming castle catering jobs easier for all concerned. But it was far too early to call the Hydes. And I didn't know how impromptu Michaela Kirovsky's invitation had been. Maybe the Hydes didn't want their caterer underfoot. Their caterer and her *son*, I reminded myself.

What would Tom want us to do? I had no idea. I had stayed in the home of clients before, when my ex-husband had been making threats, and before our house had a security system. But those clients had been relatives of Marla's. Working for Eliot and Sukie Hyde was purely a business arrangement.

Without enthusiasm, I made a decision: I'd just have to pack up my son, myself, and all the food, drive to the castle gates, and give the Hydes a ring from my cellular. If they said they wouldn't have us, then I'd have to come up with another plan.

As Deputy Wyatt sent out a newly arrived pair of deputies to canvass my neighbors, the video team arrived. I went upstairs to pack a few things and asked Arch to do the same. My son announced that the first thing we had to do was find someone to take care of Jake and Scout. I called Bill's wife, Trudy—their lights were all on, so I knew she was up—and made arrangements for our pets. It would only be until I could come up with a repair plan, I assured Trudy, trying to sound confident and also apologetic, for calling at this hour. But she was wide-awake and glad to help. In fact, it seemed as if all the folks on our street were up. They were either entertaining neighbors in their kitchens, clomping up and down the icy sidewalk, or sipping coffee on the curbs while exchanging theories on the shooting. The incident at our home had turned into a predawn block party. Welcome to the mountains.

I tossed my pj's, toothbrush, and a work outfit into a suitcase, then reentered the kitchen just as Wyatt finished interviewing the canvassing team. The deputy's face pinched in dismay when I asked if any of my neighbors had seen anything. One woman—the wife of one of the gun-toters—had reported hearing something moving on the ice-slickened street. After the gunshot, she'd glanced out her window and made out someone bundled into a bulky coat hustling away from our house. Judging from the person's muscular build and swaggering stride, she thought the figure was that of a man. The person she'd glimpsed, she insisted, had had a rifle tucked expertly under his arm.

"We'll keep working on it," Wyatt reassured me, in a kindly voice. "By the way, I called Captain Lambert. Since the department employs your husband, and this may be connected to an official inquiry, we'll handle finding a janitorial service to clean up the glass and an electrician to redo your security system. The department will have the window replaced, too," he added.

I thanked him and, trying to smile, asked if bulletproof glass was available.

Wyatt's reply was humorless. "We'll look into that. And Mrs. Schulz? We'll need to know where you're heading."

"I'm going to show up a little early at a client's house.... I have a booking today at Hyde Chapel, by the estate," I replied. Wyatt copied the Hydes' number from my client directory. "If that doesn't work out, I'll give you a call—"

"*The* Hydes?" Wyatt asked suspiciously. "They live in that big castle up on the hill? *Poltergeist Palace*?"

"I've heard it called that," I said. "But I don't truck in ghosts."

He frowned. "The chapel you're working at is that one down by Cottonwood Creek where people used to have weddings? Looks like a little cathedral?"

"The Hydes gave the chapel to Saint Luke's," I told him, "but they're still involved in running the place. I'm...just starting to work for them," I added, wondering at Wyatt's sudden interest. My paranoia engine must have been in overdrive, though, because Wyatt merely grunted.

Just after five-thirty, Jake was ensconced, but not happily, at Bill and Trudy Quincy's house. Trudy had promised to take in the mail, monitor the cleanup and window repairs, and care for Scout the cat, who'd refused to leave his post under Julian's bed. Arch and I tucked two suitcases into the back of the van Tom had bought me for Christmas. My chest felt like stone. I hated leaving our house.

I filled a carton with my mixer, blender, favorite wooden spoons, and assorted culinary equipment. In our walk-in refrigerator, I'd already assembled the ingredients for the steak pies and chicken croquettes, plus their accompanying sauces. After transporting those boxes to my van, I packed up frozen containers of homemade chicken stock and frozen loaves of manchet bread—the sort eaten by Tudor royalty, Eliot Hyde had informed me—and fresh beans and field greens, along with almost-ripe dark Damson plums. Last, I packed two fragrant, freshly stewed chickens.

A chicken in every pot, Herbert Hoover had promised, when speaking of the delights of the prosperous household. What would Hoover have said about being forced from one's home, clutching the cooked birds in a box?

CHAPTER 3

My new van chugged the short distance to Main Street. There, darkened shop windows and ice-crusted pavement mirrored the gloomy glow from our town's rustic street lamps. Exhaust-blackened heaps of snow clogged the gutters. A rusty van and what looked like an old BMW were parked across from the bank. Both had a forlorn look about them. I prayed that no homeless people were sleeping in those vehicles on this frigid morning. Not only did our small mountain town have no motels, it also possessed no shelters. The occasional homeless person who attempted to brave the winter at eight thousand feet above sea level usually gave up and hitchhiked to California.

My tires crunched up to the icy curb. On the north side of the street, the Bank of Aspen Meadow's digital numerals blinked that it was three below zero at thirty-eight minutes after five. Beside me, Arch scrunched down in his jacket. Heat poured from the humming engine while I stared up at the sky and tried to plan what to do next.

Furry, impenetrable clouds obscured the stars. The light of the rising sun would not begin creeping over the mountains for nearly an hour. I tugged my hat down over my ears and struggled to work out the logistics of a predawn appearance at Hyde Castle.

I'd first visited the Hydes during a freezing,

mid-January fog. At the time, I'd been grateful for Sukie Hyde's call. Ever since the unfortunate New Year's party at the Lauderdales', I'd been low. When the police had refused to bring an assault case against me—Buddy had claimed I hit him when I tried to wrench little Patty away from him—the Lauderdales' lawyer had begun calling me, threatening civil suits. Self-proclaimed friends of the Lauderdales had either snubbed me or scolded me for dragging the name of a longtime Saint Luke's Episcopal Church and Elk Park Prep supporter through the mud. Forget *low*. Until Sukie called, my mood had been *subterranean*.

I'd known Sukie casually for the past two years, through Saint Luke's. A widowed Swiss émigrée, she had married the reclusive Eliot Hyde a little over a year ago. Her call to me in January had been to announce that she and Eliot intended to turn his family castle into a retreat center for high-end corporate customers. They'd been remodeling the castle for months, and now Eliot was eager to move ahead with his plans for historic Elizabethan meals—meals that would eventually be served to conference clients. Was I interested?

I practically choked saying, *You bet, yes, please, absolutely, I adore history and the food that goes with it!*

I was desperate for the booking; I was also curious to see the lavish work on the castle redo. Rumor had it that Eliot and Sukie had already spent several million dollars. Everyone in town knew that Sukie was a cleaning and organizing whiz. And good old Eliot Hyde must have thanked his lucky stars, rabbit's feet, and four-leafed clovers when Sukie's reputation had proved true.

When Sukie first arrived in Aspen Meadow, the story went, she was bored. Her husband, Carl Rourke, had owned a successful roofing company that many local high-school students, including Julian, had worked for. Sadly, Carl had died on the job, in a freak electrical accident. After a year of widowhood, Sukie's loneliness had made her restless. Figuring her obsessive tidiness ought to be worth something, she'd advertised to work as a personal organizer.

Her first and last client was Eliot Hyde. Never married, virtually penniless, Eliot was a former academic who had retreated to the castle he'd inherited after being denied tenure at an East Coast college. The castle itself, built in Sussex, had been bought by Eliot's grandfather, silver baron Theodore Hyde, on a trip to England in the twenties. Belonging to a line of earls, the castle had been uninhabited since the time of Cromwell. Like the parvenus making social splashes with their enormous palaces in Newport, Rhode Island, silver-baron Theodore had apparently hoped his castle would give him the social cachet of an *actual* baron. He had the castle disassembled in England, then he hired a team to reassemble the royal residence in Aspen Meadow. He dammed up Fox Creek that flowed down the hill to the castle, to make a moat. He hired a fleet of servants to keep the place sparkling. Among his employees were a Russian fencing-master to teach him historic martial arts, and a butler to bring him tea and scones each day at four o'clock.

Unfortunately, Theodore and his wife Millicent had disliked tea and found fencing exhausting. The butler quit; the fencing-master, Michaela Kirovsky's grandfather, became the castle caretaker. The Hydes, meanwhile, decided that what they really liked was collecting old European buildings. Once the castle was in place, they purchased a thirteenth-century French chapel that was a mini-version of Chartres. That Gothic jewel had been painstakingly reconstructed not far from the castle, on the Hydes' sloping forty acres below Fox Creek and above Cotton-wood Creek, the wide body of water that runs through Aspen Meadow. Then, before their dreams of purchasing a ruined abbey could be realized, Theodore and Millicent had both been killed in a railroad accident.

Their only son, Edwin—facing a Depression economy, played-out silver mines, and no financial assets aside from his parents' estate—had tried to turn the castle into a hotel. This failed, as did mounting Aspen Meadow's first and last circus on the castle grounds. After hiring ranchers to cart away mountains of elephant manure, Edwin and his wife had been reduced to charging for tours of the castle.

Their son, Eliot, had returned to the castle

almost nine years ago, after his parents' death and his own failure in academia. At thirty-nine, he hadn't accumulated much in the way of savings, and those had drained swiftly away as he, too, struggled to make a living from giving tours and renting out the French chapel by Cottonwood Creek, now christened Hyde Chapel. By the time Eliot hired Sukie to organize the place, he'd stopped the tours and sunk into a depression. Income from renting the chapel was down, and stories in town had him living like a hermit in one room of his castle.

The family of the fencing-master, meanwhile, had been offered one whole wing of the castle rent-free, as long as they remained the caretakers. It was in their palatial fencing loft that young Michaela Kirovsky's grandfather and father had taught her to fence, a skill that subsequently provided income for her, when she became the fencing coach at Elk Park Prep.

Beside me, Arch was fast asleep.

There was more to the tale of Eliot Hyde and Sukie Rourke. In fact, the months-old series of events were now routinely chronicled by townsfolk over coffee and doughnuts. Oddly, *You can't be too clean* seemed to be the moral of the story.

When then forty-seven-year-old Eliot hired thirty-five-year-old Sukie, she had crisply informed him that she would not work in the castle as long as the stench remained from the castle's medieval toilets. Unfortunately, these thirty-three so-called "garderobes"—actually

34

ancient narrow bathrooms corbeled out over the castle walls—had not been cleaned before leaving England. Also central to the Sukie story was an acknowledgment of one of the flaws of medieval military architecture: Each garderobe had its own shaft into the moat. Those shafts had proved a convenient, if messy, mode of entry to attackers of Richard the Lionheart's Château Gaillard on the Seine, but Sukie hadn't cared about old tales of invaders. Back in medieval days, each castle garderobe shaft emptied into a cesspit or the moat itself, both of which had been periodically cleaned out. But the medieval folks had not cleaned the garderobe *shafts*. Ever. After all these years, they still stank.

Yes, the story went, medieval courtiers had tossed down herbs, straw, and old letters to absorb some of the filth, but the latrine stench invariably sent foul smells throughout the castle. The British construction folks who'd taken the castle apart eighty years earlier to be shipped here to America had pulled down the shafts in sections. And the shafts had also been reassembled that way, much to Sukie's disgust.

So: For Sukie's first order of organizing business, she'd had each and every garderobe and shaft disassembled to be cleaned and disinfected.

And *then*.

Think of flushing things down the toilet, I'd said to Arch, when Sukie's subsequent discovery made national headlines. You might flush down things that made you angry, like a dunning bill for canceled phone service, or a Dear John letter from someone who'd sworn to love you forever. Or…say you received a letter from the government denying you guardianship of your beloved, orphaned nephew. That denial made you *so* enraged, you threw that bureaucrat's epistle down the toilet shaft, where it…stuck….

In 1533, that was just what the Earl of Uckfield had done. His petition to raise his wealthy nine-year-old nephew, the orphan of his ultrarich brother-in-law, a duke, had been turned down by the monarch. In a fury, the earl had flung that letter down one of his garderobe shafts. And that was where the missive had stayed for over four centuries. It had taken a compulsively clean Swiss woman, ordering that the shaft be *scrubbed,* before the discovery was made.

The letter denying the earl custody of his nephew had been signed by Henry VIII. It bore the king's initials, H. R., and his royal seal.

The letter sold for twelve million *pounds* at Spink's, a leading London auction gallery. Eliot had immediately married Sukie, christening her his twenty-million-dollar woman. After their honeymoon, he announced to the media, Sukie would be embarking on a cleaning expedition of the other thirty-two garderobe shafts in the castle.

She hadn't found anything else.

Eliot hadn't minded.

The day after Sukie's call, I'd gone to Hyde

Castle. Once seated in the imposing living room, I drank tea and ate stale, mail-ordered scones, made tolerable only by heaping tablespoons of homemade strawberry jam, Eliot's one and only specialty. With great fanfare, tall, handsome Eliot Hyde brewed our tea. Eliot dressed like an F. Scott Fitzgerald character; for tea, he wore herringbone knickerbockers and a silk scarf. When he brewed the tea, there was no dumping of hot water over a teabag. No: Eliot tossed his silk scarf over his shoulder, removed the lid from a bone china teapot in the shape of a prissy-faced English butler, cleared his throat, and meticulously, s-l-o-w-l-y poured boiling water over Golden Tips leaves. Then he covered the pot with a cozy. Finally, he asked Sukie honeykins, as he called her, to time the steeping.

Good tea, bad food, I'd reflected, as I sipped the dark brew moments later. *I'm going to love this place.*

I'd told them yes, February was almost completely open for me. My son was in school every day. And I could hire Julian Teller, our former boarder, to help with the catering, as he was taking only a half-load this semester at the University of Colorado. Plus, I added, Julian had toured the castle during his time at Elk Park Prep, and knew his way around.

I'd listened to their food proposals, nodded, and written up a contract. Eliot's ideas sounded awfully work-intensive, but focusing on paying work, instead of on the Lauderdales, their bloodthirsty lawyer, and their Jaguar-driving

37

cronies, was a welcome relief. In the end, Eliot and Sukie had booked Goldilocks' Catering for two events. First would be an Anglophile lunch in appreciation of the big donors who'd paid for the new marble labyrinth set into the floor of Hyde Chapel. The second was an Elizabethan feast that would double as the end-of-season banquet for the Elk Park Prep fencing team. Eliot had been quick to clarify that the Tudor upper crust had only seen a *feast* as a grand meal. A *banquet,* on the other hand, had been an elaborate dessert course served later, often in a charming banquet-house not unlike our modern gazebo. These days, the terms *feast* and *banquet* had become synonymous, alas. In any event, Michaela Kirovsky wanted to hold her team's banquet at the castle. For the opportunity to test feast-giving in their Great Hall, Eliot and Sukie were picking up half the tab.

Eliot, meanwhile, would continue working, planning, and publicizing, to ready the castle for opening as a conference center.

"That's my dream," he'd informed me, although his dark brown eyes looked unexpectedly sad. Above the creamy silk shirt and scarf, he had a beautifully featured, smooth-shaven face, framed by long, wavy, light brown hair. If my catered events went well, he added, we'd work out further bookings featuring historic English food.

I'd set aside any hesitation. My only other February commitment was making cookies and punch for the Elk Park Prep Valentine's Day

Dance. The chapel lunch had been scheduled for today, Monday; the Elizabethan feast, for this Friday. I'd asked Michaela Kirovsky if the fencing team wanted swordfish. Her white hair had jounced around her pale face as she laughed at my suggestion. No swordfish, Eliot had protested. The recipes he wanted me to test on the students and their parents were more of the English court variety. So I'd ordered veal roasts, to be served with a potato dish, a shrimp dish for those Catholics who'd rejected Vatican II, a rice dish, a plum tart...and Eliot and I would come up with the rest of the details this week.

Okay. Back to the present, to five minutes to six, to be exact. The sun would be rising soon on a day which found Arch and me temporarily homeless. *Time to get moving.*

To get to the castle, the van would have to pass through antique gates that were over half a mile from the castle itself. Those gates, bearing the Hyde coat of arms and several other painted shields Sukie had unearthed in a Denver antique shop, had been open when I'd visited three weeks ago. Were they electronically armed before sunup? I had no idea.

I stared again at the bank's digital clock. The van was becoming warm. If I waited too long, the cooked chicken would begin to spoil. After the first question of catering: *How does the food look?* there is always the second consideration: *How does it hold up?* Because you were never going to get to the third question: *How does it taste?* if it had all turned moldy green.

With sudden decisiveness, I made a U-turn on Main Street and followed ice-carved Cottonwood Creek as it flowed eastward. Every now and then, spotlights from a cabin lit up the creek. On the patches of ice, fallen snow lay strewn like spills of popcorn. Steam rose from the trickle of the creek that had not frozen.

Just beyond a Texaco station, I slowed. A lighted sign on the left side of the road indicated the entry to county-owned Cottonwood Park. This meant I was getting close to the castle. On my left, the heavily forested hills of the park rose steeply from the road. On the right, the creek was now invisible. I pressed the accelerator resolutely and the van chugged forward.

A moment later, headlights glared in my rearview mirror. I skidded onto the shoulder. We were just over half a mile from the castle. When someone shoots your window out, everything is suspect. Arch, who'd awakened, checked the side view. The vehicle passed us at a noisy clip and roared on eastward, down the canyon.

"We're on our way to Hyde Castle," I said to Arch.

His face within his jacket hood became wary. "Poltergeist Palace? That's where the people want you to fix the historic food?"

"Exactly. Let's hope they're awake." I frowned. First the cop, now my son. Did everyone except me believe in ghosts? "Why exactly is it called Poltergeist Palace?"

"Jeez, Mom, don't you know? The ghost of the earl's nephew, that the famous letter was about? After his uncle told him he couldn't stay with the uncle's family, the kid got sick. He died of pneumonia. Anyway, he's supposed to run around the place at night, carrying a sword."

"Does he hang out in the kitchen?"

"I don't know. Michaela's been telling us about the Great Hall, where the banquet will be on Friday night," Arch went on. "We're going to do a fencing demonstration before we eat."

I powered up the cellular and pressed in the Hydes' number. Sukie, sounding only slightly groggy, answered on the second ring. I tried to make our plight sound humorous. Not fooled, she asked in a hoarse, concerned voice where we were. Heading east, I told her, along the creek. She consulted with Eliot, then came back. When she was less than fully awake, her accent was more noticeable. *Ze gates arh oh-pen,* she announced. I should take care on the driveway, she cautioned, as it was long, winding, and not well lit. She gave me the security-pad code for the castle gatehouse—the imposing, twin-towered entrance to the castle itself—and said please to come immediately. I was profusely thankful.

As Arch and I passed through the quiet canyon, a light snow began to fall. To our right, Hyde Chapel appeared, its two spires silhouetted by a street lamp. The chapel had its own bridge across the creek, which looked romantically inviting in the darkness. Maybe *that* was where the earl's ghostly nephew was now hanging out.

A few moments later, I turned at the paved castle driveway and drove over another old bridge spanning Cottonwood Creek. More grim coats of arms had been wired to the high iron fence that circled the castle property. With my new concern for security, I would have to ask the Hydes about how they kept undesirables out of their castle. Hearing the details of my shot-out-window story, perhaps Eliot and Sukie would reconsider their kind invitation.

The driveway wound past spotlit boulders, tall, creaking lodgepole pines, stands of white-skinned aspens, thickets of chokecherry bushes, and blue spruces in perfect Christmas tree shapes. When the van suddenly thudded over a large rock, I reminded myself to drive more carefully, or risk becoming part of a not-so-scenic overlook.

We followed the twisting drive upward until my headlights illuminated snow-crusted boulders marking the first parking area. At the edge of the lot, a one-lane wooden causeway beckoned. Beyond the bridge rose the castle itself.

I gulped. My previous visit had taken place during the day. In the predawn darkness, the stone fortress, built in medieval military style and rooted into a forested hillside, looked far less inviting. Spotlights carved out the

42

façade's four crenellated towers, the high, arched gatehouse, and the widely spaced, narrow windows from which, centuries ago, archers had rained arrows down on their enemies. Snow spiraled onto the steaming moat. Above the water, creamy patches of fog drifted across the tower tops and into the trees.

Arch said, "Suppose they'd let me have my birthday party here?"

I grunted a negative as our tires thumped across the planks of the causeway. To keep the moat water from freezing, Sukie had ordered the installation of aerating pumps. That way, fish and wildfowl would make it through the winter. I smiled. Wealthy folks were always telling me how much they cared about the environment.

My cell phone bleated. Rather than risk driving off the causeway, I braked and put the van in parking gear. Arch peered down at the ducks huddled around one of the aerators.

"Good God, Goldy, where the *hell* are you?" Marla Korman's voice sounded even more husky than usual. "I called your house and got some cop."

"I'm at the Hydes' castle. Or just about there," I corrected. "It's a long story." Long or no, Marla would want to hear it. "A couple of hours ago, somebody shot out the picture window in our living room. There's glass everywhere, and the cops wanted us out."

Marla, usually a late sleeper, was silent. No matter the time of day, though, once she started talking, my friend rarely stopped.

Below us, the causeway swayed slightly. Steam from the moat clouded our windows.

"Where's Tom?" she demanded, her voice urgent.

"About to leave New Jersey. I'm going to try to reach him as soon as I get settled. We're here because Arch and I needed a place to park until we get sorted out. I didn't want to bother you this early."

She groaned. "We should be together."

So all of us could be in danger? "Look, Marla," I said, "thanks. But you don't need to worry. Tom will be back late this morning. Everything is going to be fine."

"Listen." She lowered her voice to a murmur. "Is Arch with you?"

Suddenly I felt my son's eyes on me. "Of course."

Marla said, "The parole board met Friday, Goldy. The Jerk's out."

CHAPTER 4

I stared at the twin clouds of mist coiling upward from the moat's aerators. *It can't be true.*

"You there, Goldy?"

"I was supposed to get a letter...."

"You're on the victim notification list?" She took a swig of something, probably orange juice. Marla never faced crises without food and drink. "I'm not on the list, but I told my lawyer to stay on top of John Richard's petition for early release. Your notification is probably in the mail."

"Lot of good that does me now."

Marla said, "If you can't come down here, I'll drive up to the castle after I get dressed. I can be there in ninety minutes. Wait at the gate for me."

There was a whirring in my ears that didn't come from the cell phone. "No, Marla, please. Thanks, but don't come this early—" I faltered. I thought again of the noise that had awakened me. I'd heard a footstep on ice, but had it been a familiar one? Crack, gunshot, splintering glass. "Marla, did you tell the cops at our house? About him?" I glanced at Arch, who was pretending not to listen. He had fixed his eyes on one of the spotlit corner towers, tall granite drums where lookouts had once been posted. "Marla, did you tell them?" I tried not to hear the anxiety in my voice.

"Of course not. *I* didn't know why the cops were there, and they sure weren't about to tell *me*. All they'd say was that you were alive. So I had to talk to you."

"I'd better call them back," I said.

Marla started to say something, but the line cracked and blurred. Dog*gone* it. The Department of Corrections had notified us when John Richard had first petitioned for early release. I'd appeared before the parole board in January, giving all the reasons why an early release was a very bad idea. Dr. John Richard

Korman should serve at least the minimum—eight months—of his two-year sentence for assault. The Jerk believed he should serve no more than four months, and had cited his behavior as a model prisoner, which included using the Heimlich maneuver on another inmate who'd been choking on a hot dog.

Just in case the board did give him early parole, I'd obtained a temporary restraining order, to go into effect the moment his release took place. Then, if John Richard wanted to keep me in the dark about his plans, we could go before a judge and decide on parameters for visitations with Arch. But for the Jerk to be presented with a temporary order to keep away from me—just as he was about to taste freedom—probably wouldn't sit very well. Had it sat so badly he'd felt it necessary to aim a gun at our house?

"Goldy—" Marla's voice crackled, then vanished.

I stared at the moat. Bizarrely striped ducks—offspring of discarded Easter ducklings breeding with the wild variety—huddled by the aerator. They looked as miserable as I felt.

"Mom!" Arch protested. "I'm *cold*!"

"Can you hear me?" Marla demanded so loudly that I winced. "Where exactly are you two?"

"I told you, we're sitting outside Hyde Castle. I have a job here today."

"Get inside. *I'll* call the cops about the Jerk. Then I'll phone my lawyer and anyone else I can find. After that, I'll come up. Isn't

46

the church having a luncheon at Hyde Chapel today? I think I got an invitation."

"Yes. It's a thank-you lunch for the people who paid for the labyrinth stones installed in Hyde Chapel. I'm doing the cooking."

"I gave that fund five thousand bucks. Save me some cake."

She signed off. I stared glumly at the three coats of arms hanging over the gatehouse entranceway. Each represented a baron and his soldiers, Sukie had told me, medieval protectors of one section of the fortress. *That's what I need,* I thought, as I pressed gently on the gas. *A militia for each part of my life.* The van resumed its slow rumble across the wooden bridge.

"Mom? Is Dad out?"

"Yeah." I kept my tone light. "Did you know he was being released?"

"I wasn't sure. He hasn't called me yet." Arch spoke guardedly. "Viv said he might be out soon."

"Viv knew he was getting out," I repeated, for clarification.

Viv Martini, a slender, striking, twenty-nine-year-old sexpot, was John Richard's current girlfriend. He'd met her in jail, where she'd been the girlfriend of another prisoner, until John Richard had exerted his charms on her. Or so Arch had reported. I'd seen Viv a few times. She wore her platinum hair David-Bowie-style, had breasts the size of cantaloupes, and sported a reputation of having slept with every rich, shady guy in the county.

When Viv and the Jerk had become an item, I figured they deserved each other.

"Listen, Mom." Arch's voice became earnest. "Dad *wouldn't* have shot at us. He's no good with guns. He tried to learn early last summer, but every time he shot at a target, he missed by a *zillion* yards. Viv offered to teach him again, when he got out, but he said no. You know how Dad is when he can't do something. He quits and says it's dumb."

The tires made a rhythmic *whump whump whump* over the causeway's planks. I wondered, of course, why John Richard would even think he *needed* to learn to use a firearm.

The castle gatehouse loomed before us. Unlike the later gatehouses of manor houses, Eliot had solemnly informed me, the fortified entry of medieval times is the built-in entrance to the castle itself. The Hyde Castle gatehouse featured two portcullises, those massive wooden grilles raised to let in friends, and lowered to keep out foes. One stood at the front entry, the other could be lowered over the gatehouse's rear entry facing the courtyard. This was in the event that enemies breached the rear, or postern, castle gate. When that happened, Eliot had concluded with pride, the castle inhabitants holed up in the gatehouse itself.

A hundred feet in front of the gatehouse, two single-story stone garages mirrored the contours of the twin towers of the gatehouse. To anyone looking straight at the immense stone façade from the bridge, the garages were indistinguishable from the castle itself. Inside

48

the garages, six parking spaces had been marked out for vehicles. I accelerated over the last part of the bridge, pulled into a garage slot next to Eliot and Sukie's matching silver Jaguars—*hmm*—and cut the van's engine.

The thought of lugging my boxes all the way to the kitchen on less than three hours' sleep was more than I could bear. Perhaps there was a hidden pulley system that delivered orders. At least I hadn't been forced into the humiliation of using the servants' entrance, as I had at the Lauderdales' modern monstrosity in Flicker Ridge. The castle did not have a separate entry for servants, Eliot had loftily informed me, because the castle's status as military outpost meant all the needs of the grand medieval household had to be met within the walls. *Think self-sufficiency,* he'd concluded, as he'd knotted the silk scarf with a flourish.

Arch and I jumped from the van. Dwarfed by the spotlit portcullis, we walked gingerly over the frost-slickened gravel. One of the Hydes must have registered our presence, for the portcullis rose smoothly even before we arrived. Behind the portcullis stood two formidable wooden doors.

I glanced at my son as our boots cracked across the icy gravel. *Did Viv offer to teach you to shoot, too?* Unfortunately, Viv was also an accomplished tae kwon do practitioner *and* fencer. Feeling more inferior than I cared to admit, I had signed up for the free weekly fencing lessons Michaela Kirovsky had offered team parents. I told myself it was to keep up with Arch, but deep down I suspected it was to keep up with Viv. Which I couldn't do, as it turned out. My first three lessons, I'd suffered claustrophobia from the mask, thighs so sore I'd been unable to walk, and confidence so shattered I'd dropped out of class.

Come to think of it, could Viv have shot out our window? Why would she do that?

A speaker on the security keypad beeped. The massive doors creaked open.

"Gol-dy!" Sukie Hyde's cheery, familiar voice made a ringing echo on the ancient stones. "You're here!"

"Yes, we are!" I called back with what I hoped was a self-assured voice. "Thanks for having us!"

Sukie, wearing a full-length, forest green coat, cooed at Arch and me as she bustled toward us. "Look at you two!" she exclaimed. Worry furrowed her rosy-cheeked face as she assessed us for damage. Looking younger than her late thirties, unpretentiously cheery and always happy to see you, Sukie was plumply appealing, like one of those happily voluptuous women painted by Rubens. Her wavy golden hair drifted out in all directions, giving an incongruously disheveled air to the superbly organized gal beneath. "Welcome to Hyde Castle. Eliot and I were *so* shocked to hear what had happened! Imagine, your windows shot at!"

"It was only one window," I assured her. "The food's in the back of the van, if you'd like me to bring it in."

Sukie beamed and said Michaela could do that.

"It could spoil," I started to protest.

"Don't *worry* about it, Gol-dy." Sukie's voice was richly comforting, like vanilla custard. "Please, you have just had a terrible shock. Soon there will be warm coffee cake in the kitchen," she said. "Come on, both of you, we will get you some hot drinks. I am making the coffee cake myself. From a mix, of course," she added with a giggle.

I smiled in spite of myself. Sukie could make the castle as tidy as a Swiss hotel, but she could not so much as toast bread. She had what we in the food biz gleefully call a *cooking block*. According to Marla, Eliot abhorred the kitchen, too, except for the jams and jellies he made in the middle of the night, when he couldn't sleep. Well, at least he wasn't canning okra. Before Sukie had changed Eliot's life, he'd subsisted first on frozen dinners, then SpaghettiOs, and finally, just when Sukie came into the picture, enormous casseroles of beans and rice. These cheap repasts were not, of course, suitable for the suddenly wealthy. Nevertheless, the Hydes soon wearied of eating out. On my first visit, I'd brought Sukie and Eliot a dinner to tuck into their refrigerator and reheat. They'd found my culinary powers awesome, and their praise had warmed my heart.

At the far side of the entryway, new plate-glass doors looked out on the courtyard. Sukie switched on spotlights and drenched the

51

interior space in a blaze of glory. The previous summer, a landscaper had followed Eliot's directions for planting a Tudor garden. Eliot had used the strawberries and chokecherries for his jams. But it was all I could do to keep from laughing when Eliot had gone on to tell me they'd given the cabbages, cucumbers, radishes, parsnips, and even the freshly grown herbs to Aspen Meadow Christian Outreach, since neither he nor Sukie knew what to do with their cornucopia of ripe goodies. In the spotlights, the geometric layout of ice-burnished twigs sparkled.

To surround the courtyard, Theodore Hyde had replaced the crumbling interior walls with an Italianate arcade made of new Colorado granite. The lights illuminated dazzling silver rapiers set beneath the support for each arch. Above the arcade, more spotlights, their lenses tinted hues of orange and pink, bathed new stone walls and courtyard-facing windows with a welcoming glow.

"Wow!" Arch exclaimed. "They've done a lot since the sixth grade came here for a tour." He craned his neck to gaze up at the arched ceiling of the gatehouse. "Check it out, Mom, those things haven't changed." He pointed upward. "*Meurtriers.* Otherwise known as murder holes."

"*What?*" Overhead, at the intersection of each arch, holes pierced the ceiling.

"You see," my son went on, "even if the enemy could get across the moat and through whatever barbican or outer defense was set up, they'd still have to get through the gate-house." He pointed back at the entry portcullis. "So if the attackers rammed the portcullis to get into this space, the castle's warriors poured boiling oil down on the bad guys through those holes." He announced this with a fourteen-year-old's relish for violence.

"Let's go," I said hastily, as Sukie disappeared through another pair of glass doors. I preferred to associate boiling oil with doughnuts and French fries, thank you very much.

Now twenty steps ahead of us, Sukie was either turning off another security system or rejiggering a thermostat. I shuddered to think of the electric bills generated by heating and lighting these vast spaces. I hated even more thinking how to tell Sukie and Eliot that their security system might have to withstand a visit from the Jerk.

Arch tugged on my elbow. "How many times have *you* been here?" he demanded, his voice just above a murmur. "Did she talk to you about the...earl's nephew?" Ever wary of being dubbed a wimp, Arch was reluctant to use the word *ghost*.

"I've been here once, and nobody talked to me about spirits," I whispered back. "At some point, you can ask the Hydes about it. Just not today, okay?"

He frowned, but joined me in following Sukie as she bustled down a dazzling rose-and-gray marble hallway. The marble, too, was from Colorado, Sukie had told me, and had been picked out by Chardé Lauderdale as the basis for the interior color scheme. Flickering electrified candles atop gleaming brass wall sconces lit our way as we walked down a plush carpet runway patterned with gold medallions on a royal-blue background. Arch stopped to touch one of the reproduction leaded-glass windows. Then he eyed a threadbare tapestry depicting a maiden patting her unicorn.

"Do you think the Hydes will let Dad visit?" he asked.

"I don't know. Probably you'll go to his place, once we get things worked out."

Arch was silent. I looked around. On our right, a twentieth-century spiral staircase led up to a doorway into the gatehouse, put there, Eliot had told me, by his thoughtful grandfather. Old Theodore did not want his caretakers traversing the cold stone entryway to get to their apartment, once they finished nighttime kitchen duty. Personally, I would have preferred an escalator.

Ahead of us, Sukie swept through more glass doors beneath another archway. The doors opened into the living room. But on my tea-visit, "living" in this room had seemed unimaginable. The room looked more like the lobby of a grand hotel than a place where people would actually snuggle down for conversation or reading. The vast space featured a polished dark wood floor covered by Oriental rugs in rich hues of scarlet, royal blue, and gold. Couches and wing-back chairs upholstered in floral and paisley chintz, the shades chosen to match the rugs, sat beside massive antique tables of mahogany and cherry. The effect was impressive. No matter what else you said about Chardé Lauderdale, the woman knew what she was doing in the decorating department.

Our boots made a *shh-shh* noise as we shuffled over the sumptuous carpets. I touched the cellular in my pocket. The moment we were situated, I promised myself, I would call Tom's hotel.

"You're a member of the fencing team, right, Arch?" Sukie trilled over her shoulder. "When your teammates come to our banquet this week, you'll be able to show them around. We have an indoor pool, now, on the ground floor west of the postern gate, if you want to go for a swim."

Arch mumbled, "Okay." He hated to swim. He said, "Miss Kirovsky has been telling us about her collection of royal memorabilia. I'd really like to see *that.*"

I exhaled. At least he hadn't requested an interview with the phantom of the young duke-apparent.

"Then ask her, my dear," Sukie replied graciously as she paused by one of the glass doors. "And perhaps Michaela could take you to school today, after she unloads your mother's equipment."

I felt a tad confused, as I hadn't realized that Michaela was regarded as a general servant in addition to caretaker *and* local fencing coach. But it was too early in the day to delve into the particulars of the Hydes' household arrangements.

While Sukie held open the door, Arch turned to me and asked softly, "How will Dad even know I'm here?"

"I'll call the county lawyer, all right?" I was not about to call John Richard's attorney, that pompous nerd responsible for mailing child support payments from John Richard's fat hoard of cash, the result of the sale of his ob-gyn practice. Dealing with the Jerk's attorney was like being forced to eat...well, that historic but unappetizing food: *pottage*. It was not something I chose to do.

A hint of desperation threaded through Arch's voice. "Look, Mom, I know you don't want to see Dad. But I promised him we could get together as soon as he got out. It's what he said he wanted more than anything. So could you please find him? Please?"

"I told you I would, hon. Just not this sec, okay?"

Sukie waited politely until my son and I had finished our whispered conference. In tense silence, we went through yet another set of glass doors, which Sukie said they had installed as insulation against the cold. The need for insulation quickly became evident when we entered the tower. An arctic blast made us all pull our coats tightly around us.

Unlike the hallway, the corner drum tower was not newly lined with marble. Frigid air poured through slits in the gray stone—more narrow openings used by archers.

Sukie pointed to a smaller, covered stone cylinder on the tower floor. "This was the castle's original well, Arch. Do you know why they placed the well inside the castle, instead of outside?"

I knew she was trying to be nice, to make Arch feel welcome. I was not sure it was working. Arch frowned, as if deciding whether to indulge Sukie with an answer.

"Actually," he said finally, his voice raised over another sudden cold wind. "I do know about castle wells. People living in the castle had to have their water supply inside the fortress walls, in the event of siege. They didn't want the enemy poisoning their drinking supply. Do you use it for the castle's water?"

"Oh, no," Sukie answered, apparently delighted with his interest. "Eliot's grandfather had a new water system put in, and Eliot's father used insurance money to get the whole plumbing system upgraded, after Fox Creek flooded in '82."

She gestured for us to go through the door she'd opened to the next large space, the dining room. Here, the walls had been painted a creamy yellow, which was the perfect complement for the lime, pink, and cream Persian rug, walnut dining-room table and chairs, and large matching buffet and glass-fronted wine cabinet, one of the two places Eliot kept his jam supply. No doubt, this furniture was also gen-yoo-ine antique, the kind Tom, but not I, could have dated and placed.

"And this is the buttery, Arch," Sukie

explained. "Or at least it used to be. Bottles of ale were kept here. The wine cellar was underneath. Next door to the buttery was the stillroom, where they made preserves, and next to that was a bedroom. We combined all three rooms for the dining room and kitchen. Eliot makes his jams in the kitchen, since the stillroom is kaput. Wait until you taste his goodies. Your mother loved them."

"I did indeed," I murmured, as we entered the kitchen. I had been in this grand cooking-and-serving space on my earlier visit. Four electrified chandeliers provided the lighting. Glass-fronted maple cupboards with painted porcelain handles rose above a shiny backsplash of blue-and-white Delft tiles. A maple corner cupboard was also crammed with jars of preserves. Overhead, an immense, hook-studded iron rack hung from the ceiling. From each hook dangled a darkened pot or roasting pan, some of them massive enough to roast a flock of geese. One wall boasted framed photos and reproduction signs from English taverns. Along the other wall, cozy embers glowed in one of the two stone hearths. In spite of the flickering electrified candles, shadows filled the kitchen's corners like smoke.

Arch's insistent voice cracked next to my ear. "I have to get ready for school. *Now,* Mom."

"I'm sure we'll be going to a place where you can change in a minute," I said quickly, feeling my irritation flare. But he was right. Sukie's leisurely early-morning guided tour of her castle was getting on my nerves, too.

58

Arch glared at me. "When?"

I squared my shoulders, shot him a reproving look, and asked Sukie, who was donning heavy pot-holder mitts, "Is Michaela—Miss Kirovsky, that is—coming over here? I mean, to the kitchen?"

"Any minute, just...agh!" Sukie had pulled open her oven door, and a cloud of black smoke billowed out. Somewhere nearby a smoke alarm started shrieking. "Oh, *dammit!*" she hollered. Dropping the pot holders, she pulled out the charred coffee cake with her bare hands. She immediately let go of the pan and screamed bloody murder.

"Eeoyow! Hilft! Mutti!"

"Cold water!" I cried. "Now! Now!"

She didn't move. I tugged her to the sink, where I ran cold water over her hands while murmuring comforting words. Tears streamed down Sukie's perfectly made-up cheeks. When I was sure she was going to stay put, I grabbed two folded kitchen towels and picked up the offending coffee cake pan from the floor. One of the first things I'd learned working in a professional kitchen was not to dump smoking food into the trash. I tossed the coffee cake under a second faucet, then dashed to the ovens and turned on every ventilation fan I could find. Within minutes, the smoke had abated and the alarm had mercifully quieted.

Sukie stopped crying, inspected her fingers, and wrapped a wet towel around her left hand. Arch continued to give me his I-*really*-need-to-talk-to-you look. I didn't know what to say. *Excuse me, Sukie, but may my son and I leave you, your burned hands, and your smoke-stinking kitchen so we can confer in your nondairy buttery?*

Arch tugged my sleeve. "Ah, I need to drop my stuff somewhere before I go to school. I need to do my hair, too, and finish getting ready. Okay? Please? And I do want Miss Kirovsky to take me to school, so you, Mom, can track down that lawyer and find out where Dad is."

"*Okay,*" I promised in a low voice. I pressed the power button on my cell phone. The tiny screen told me the phone was *Looking for service,* which is the telecommunications euphemism for *You're out of luck!* "Sukie, I'm desperate for a telephone. Is there one nearby?"

She said patiently, "It is just half past six."

"It's okay," I replied. *It's half past eight in New Jersey, and that's the only time that counts right now.* I said, "I really need to talk to my husband before he leaves for the airport." After that, I would fulfill my promise to Arch and leave a message for Pat Gerber, the assistant district attorney for Furman County. Clearly, the Department of Corrections was taking its sweet time getting around to informing us of its plans for the Jerk. Pat Gerber would give me the straight scoop—if I could find her.

"There is a phone on that wall—" Sukie began, but we were interrupted at that moment by the entrance of Eliot Hyde.

He banged open the heavy wooden door, glided into the kitchen, and surveyed his wife, his caterer, and his caterer's son. Then he sniffed the air suspiciously. The flickering chandelier turned errant strands of his hair to gold. This morning, Eliot's movie-star features and sad brown eyes seemed even more striking than before. He wore the ubiquitous silk scarf above a long, flowing bathrobe of royal blue velvet. *Tender Is the Nightgown.* Arch stared at Eliot Hyde with his mouth open.

"Cheerio!" Eliot called to us, as if we numbered in the hundreds, instead of just three. "Welcome to our castle!"

"Mom!" Arch was tugging on my sleeve again. "When can we—"

"Honey," I pleaded. "Stop! You're driving me nuts!"

Ignoring this, Eliot Hyde sniffed the air again and looked around. "Aw, honeykins, did you burn another one?"

To my dismay, before Sukie could reply, my son turned and bolted from the kitchen. After a stunned second, I scooted after him, paddling hard through an ocean of guilt.

Eliot called plaintively after us, "What did I *say?*"

CHAPTER 5

I caught up with Arch by the well. "Look, hon—"

"I want to leave. I want to see Dad. I want to know why our window was shot at. What if someone tried to shoot at *Dad*, too? Maybe that's why he hasn't gotten in touch with me. Did you ever think of that, Mom? Maybe somebody's trying to get us all."

Most of the time, Arch kept his feelings well in control. Now he was worried about his father, worried about the house, worried about me. Added up, this was too big a burden for a teenager.

"Arch, please," I told him, "the cops are working on the bullet through the window. Once, when I was little? Somebody threw a snowball packed with gravel through our picture window. Who ever heard of such a thing happening in a nice neighborhood of a small New Jersey town? The kid who threw it said it was a prank. So that's what I think. Whoever shot out our window was either drunk or playing a joke. Trust me, your father can take care of himself. Please, let's go back."

He mumbled, "If that's true, then it's a *stupid* joke," but grudgingly returned to the kitchen. Sukie had her hands in a bowl of ice water. Eliot had moved to the counter to make tea, and Arch squinted at the back of the royal blue robe, which we could now see was embroidered with the words *"His Highness."*

His water-heating mission complete, Eliot flowed back to the island and cocked an aristocratic eyebrow at Arch and me. The robe swirled around his ankles.

"I understand you two had a spot of trouble."

"We did," I replied. I did *not* want to discuss the window anymore. "Thank you so much for taking us in. Now if we could just—"

Eliot treated me to a dazzling grin. "You *are* ready to do the lunch today, aren't you? We should probably chat."

My mind swam. The lunch would start in five hours. I was earlier than I'd be for a wedding reception, which required much more labor-intensive preparation. But he was my employer. And my host, I reminded myself. "I am ready," I replied dutifully. "I brought the ingredients with me. You won't mind if I use your kitchen?"

"Certainly not," Eliot replied. "But...I never heard from the table people. Was the rental company supposed to call me when the tables arrived?"

My heart sank. The food might be ready, but if the notoriously unreliable folks at Party Rental had screwed up... "You don't know if they showed up? At the chapel, I mean?"

Eliot frowned. "I don't know. Oh, God! A glitch in our first event!"

"It's not a glitch—"I said weakly.

"*I* will call the table people," Sukie offered, "as soon as we get Goldy and her son up to their suites and I can bandage my hands."

Eliot crossed his arms and stared at the

ceiling, always the first sign that a client was going neurotic on me. He pleaded, "I *beg* you, Goldy, *tell* me you remembered to bring all your recipes and notes with you."

Crap and double crap. My recipes and notes. I'd brought my laptop, but not, I suddenly realized, the disk with all my Hyde Castle recipes and the research I'd done over the past two weeks on the history of English cuisine. "No. I'm sorry. I'll go home for them the minute we get settled." I added apologetically, "I mean, if that's all right, and the cops allow me in. And," I promised with a nod to Sukie, "I'll check on the tables at the same time."

Eliot circumnavigated the kitchen island, tapping his left hand pensively on the wood. I could almost see the wheels in his head turning. At the Hyde Chapel luncheon, Eliot intended to pitch the audience on his plans to transform the castle into a conference center. If that didn't go well, then the guests might think that he was just an academic who couldn't make the move to real business...that he was a failure in this, too....

"Let's move you two up to your suites," Sukie interjected, as she wiped her hands. "I have a *very* special room for you, Arch. Right next to your mom."

"We're not sure how long we'll be here," I murmured.

"We are practicing on you!" Sukie said cheerfully. "Our first guests in the refurbished rooms!"

Relieved to be out of Eliot's tranquilizer-needing presence, we followed Sukie down another marble hallway to carpeted steps leading to the castle's second floor.

The second story featured floors of darkly polished cherry wood. Matching English-club cherry paneling on the walls gave the place an elegantly homey look. Floor-to-ceiling leaded-glass windows lined the side of the hallway overlooking the courtyard. I peeked out at the garden. In the early-morning light, the iced pattern of plants had taken on a pearly cast.

We skirted a sawhorse and a splotch of dried beige paint on the floor. Sukie murmured something about *Eliot and one of his new messes.* Next we passed a closed door and rounded a corner, where Sukie opened another door. This, she announced as she switched on more electrified brass wall sconces, would be Arch's room. Awed, Arch walked into the palatial space, where a black-and-gray Aubusson rug set the decor for a mahogany four-poster bed and silver-tassled spread, black wing-back chairs, a long gray couch, and an ornately carved desk beside a fireplace. Pen-and-ink drawings of ships hung on walls that looked as if they'd been papered with silver silk. A subdued set of black-and-gray nautical-theme fabrics had been used for the floor-to-ceiling draperies.

Sukie led me through a set of wooden doors in the corner of the room, through another corner drum tower and another set of doors, then into the bedroom whose door we'd passed earlier. This place, equally spacious, was an homage to lime and coral.

"This will be your suite," she announced with a smile.

The lofty space reminded me of those magazine photos featuring Europe's most elegant hotels. The walls were covered with glowing pale green silk. A pink-tinted marble fireplace graced the wall facing the massive four-poster bed. Between the bed and the fireplace, Chardé had thoughtfully grouped a pair of rose-and-lime chintz-covered wing-back chairs. Against a wall with new windows looking out on the moat stood a long cherry-wood desk.

"Gorgeous, Sukie, really," I gushed, overwhelmed.

"You haven't seen your bathroom!" she exclaimed, eyes gleaming.

I demurred, recalling Eliot's anxiety over the day's event. I needed to get organized. And I really wanted to call Tom. "I'll check the bathroom out later, if that's okay."

Sukie motioned me back to Arch's room, through the same pair of wooden doors set at a diagonal in the southeast corner of the room. We again moved into the drum tower, which I had now figured out was at the southeast corner of the castle. As in the well tower, the air was icy, although here, glass had been put up on the inside of each of the two small windows that flanked a fireplace built into the far wall. Sukie led me to an opening in the tower wall, then pointed straight along a short, narrow passageway that ended abruptly in a wall with a seat. Wait: There *had* been one of these in the well tower; Arch had backed up beside it after his mini-meltdown.

"This is the garderobe where we found the letter," Sukie declared with a triumphant grin. She threw a rusty bolt on top of the toilet, lifted the lid, and pointed downward. I swallowed a sigh. Our hostess was determined to give me the tour, no matter what. I peered down the hole, *way* down, and listened, until I heard the slap of moat water against the shaft. I smiled, even though I was desperate to call Tom. "After six centuries," Sukie said, "even after the shaft was broken into pieces to be moved from England, *even* after they reassembled the shaft here, the place stank."

"I don't understand why they didn't clean up the shaft before they sent it over," I commented. I realized the little hallway smelled powerfully of disinfectant.

"They weren't Swiss," she replied matter-of-factly.

In his assigned room, Arch was running the bathroom fan full blast, a sure sign he was finishing his elaborate hairdressing routine, a regimen that started with mousse and ended with hairspray that acted like plaster of Paris. When he reappeared with his hair cemented into spikes, he was wearing khaki pants, a plaid shirt, and his white Elk Park Prep Fencing Team jacket.

"Those shafts aren't dangerous?" I murmured to Sukie as we made our way back to the kitchen.

She shook her head. "We're having them all covered with Plexiglas before we open the conference center. The bottom of each shaft has a grille, to keep out rodents and such. The only dangerous place in the castle is the moat pump room. But don't worry, it's all locked up."

I nodded as we came into the kitchen, where three of my boxes had appeared. Eliot was putting out a dish of crackers and a jar, the dark contents of which looked like homemade jelly.

"I'm not eating that," Arch whispered to me.

"Wow!" I exclaimed over his announcement. "Mr. Hyde, is this another one of your famous preserves? Like the strawberry jam we had with the scones?"

"This is chokecherry jelly," he said shyly, with a regal wave. "I also make fig preserves, blueberry jam, mint jelly, lemon curd—"

At that moment, Michaela Kirovsky clomped into the kitchen toting the last of my boxes. Abruptly, Eliot fell silent and bustled out the door.

Once again feeling responsible for someone else's rudeness, I thanked Michaela profusely for her help. She waggled her head and told me not to mention it. I looked closely at her. When I'd first met her at Elk Park Prep and talked about the banquet, I'd judged her to be about sixty. Now I saw that the prematurely white hair made her look older than she was, probably forty-five. She had that slightly pudgy, built-like-a-brick body often seen in high-school athletic coaches. Her wrinkled baby-face was exceptionally pale. Like Arch, she wore the school fencing jacket and khakis. When she heaved her load up on the trestle table next to my three other boxes, Eliot flowed back into the kitchen, clutching another jar.

"I'm sure today's luncheon will go beautifully. And we're very excited about the fencing banquet. Please remember, though, Goldy," he said as he placed the new offering—plum jam—on the table, "I want the Friday-night feast to conclude with a plum tart baked with jewels inside." He swept his hair back with his hand. I sighed: The fencing banquet was four days away, for crying out loud. "The jewels will be zirconia, of course, but the children don't need to know that. That's a typical Elizabethan treat," he informed us with a smile, "to bake treasures into something sweet. Only they used *real* jewels, of course. And sometimes they put in *other* surprises, such as, shall we say, four-and-twenty blackbirds? Goldy, how soon will you be able to get your recipes?"

"As soon as I pick up my disk," I replied. I fumbled inside the box containing my laptop to make sure I had my power cord, too. "I promise I won't take long getting it," I added firmly, before he could start fretting again.

"So you'll return when?" Eliot asked anxiously.

"I'll follow Michaela out," I replied. "Worst-case scenario puts me back here by eight."

"Eliot, darling," Sukie murmured as her husband opened his mouth to protest. "The recipes can wait. You are too enthusiastic, some-times. And—"

"That's all your boxes," Michaela interrupted.

"Thanks again," I said, and meant it.

She nodded, warmed her hands at the hearth, and grinned at Arch. "Ready to go, mister? Blastoff is in seven minutes."

Arch shouldered his pack, nodded a mature farewell to me, and told Michaela he'd meet her by the portcullis. He even managed to thank Sukie and Eliot before making his way out of the kitchen.

To me, Michaela said softly, "Eliot mentioned that someone took a shot at your house last night?"

"Yes," I said. "The police don't have any leads yet. But I took a call on my cell phone on the way over here. There's something I need to warn you about." All three faces became immediately curious. "My ex-husband, Dr. John Richard Korman, has just been granted an early release from serving a sentence for assault. If he shows up here, please do not let him in. I'm checking on the status of a restraining order," I added. "He'll have to see Arch at some point, but we haven't figured that out yet."

Their questions tumbled out as I put the chicken and other perishables into the refrigerator: Was John Richard the one who'd shot at our window? Did he know I was here at the castle? Did he know how to get here?

"We have no idea what the man looks like," Eliot mused, his voice concerned. "If we could have a photograph..."

"Yes, definitely, no problem," I replied. "I'll get one when I pick up the disk."

The snow had stopped as Michaela, Arch, and I drove off. My van followed Michaela's Elk Park Prep minibus down the slick, winding driveway. Her tires cut twin black tracks in the pristine trail of snowy pavement. Soon the minibus was out of sight.

When I came through the front gate and crossed the bridge onto the state highway, I remembered the rental tables that were supposed to be at Hyde Chapel. I pressed the accelerator, determined to see what was going on. Or *not* going on, as the case might be.

As I drove up the road, I punched the cell phone buttons for Tom's Atlantic City motel, on the remote chance he was still there. The man who answered said Tom had left several hours ago. I then tried the main number for Furman County government and entered the buttons for Pat Gerber's extension at the district attorney's office. Of course, since it was not quite seven, all I reached was her voice mail. I left a message: My ex-husband got an early release from prison, and a bullet shattered one of our windows at four this morning. With a temporary restraining order in place, what was our next step for visits with our son?

I disconnected as the chapel bridge across Cottonwood Creek came into sight. Beyond the bridge, the chapel's delicate gray spires and arched stained-glass windows looked ethereal in the soft morning light. After auctioning off the Henry VIII letter, Eliot had given the

Gothic chapel to the church, to offset his tax burden. In order to make Hyde Chapel a tourist attraction clients would associate with the castle conference center, Sukie had directed an extensive cleanup, and paid Chardé Lauderdale handsomely to decorate the place. The labyrinth had been the crowning centerpiece of the renovation. Saint Luke's had been thrilled.

This day's lunch event had been covered in a fluff piece in the *Mountain Journal* and in the Saint Luke's newsletter. Although the church had received lunch confirmations for twenty, the Episcopal Church Women had begged me to make enough food for up to ten more folks, for those donors untroubled by RSVP's. The ECW was handling the loan of church plates, silverware, and crystal for the lunch. I'd merely replied to the ECW that lunch for thirty or even thirty-five would be no problem.

I swung the van across the chapel bridge, intent on finding the tables. With the bad publicity generated by the Lauderdale incident impacting my business, it was imperative that the lunch event go without a hitch. If the tables had not been delivered, I would call Party Rental at nine and deliver a blistering harangue. In the catering biz, sometimes you had to get rough.

No spotlights illuminated the chapel. I pulled into the gravel parking lot and swung around to park facing the creek, as close to the building's carved front doors as I could get. Across the highway in Cottonwood Park, the sun lit the top of the thick cluster of pine trees.

As I sat with the van running, I tried to recollect the combination on the lockbox that held the chapel key. The chapel had been designed as a miniature of Chartres, and boasted some features of that enormous cathedral, including a rose window and, now, a labyrinth. I tapped the steering wheel and finally recalled that the letters on the lockbox combination were C, H, A, R, T, R, E, S.

There was a Gothic-lettered sign to my right, at the top of the creek bank. *Set your brake!* it warned. *Management cannot pull your car out of the creek!*

I smiled at the vision of Eliot and Sukie towing a vehicle out of the water. I pulled up on the brake, then leaned forward in my seat to check how far I was from the creek. Fifteen feet below, the narrow chute of black, gurgling water raced between the icy banks.

I squeezed my eyes shut, heart pounding. I hadn't just seen what I'd just seen. Or had I? Surely it had been an illusion, my sleep-deprived mind playing tricks with ice, water, stone, sunlight. You think you see something flesh-colored, something bobbing eerily in the water, and it turns out to be a rock.

I took a deep breath, jumped out of the van, and walked carefully to the edge of the creek bank. No, it wasn't quartz, granite, or even mountain marble. In the creek was a blackened hand. A hand attached to an arm clothed in plaid flannel. A blackened hand?

I stared into the water below. The rigid body of a young man lay half in the creek, as if he'd been tossed there.

I looked away, chilled. *He needs help,* my brain screamed. *Help him. Get him out of that water.*

I took a few tentative steps down the steep, boulder-strewn creek bank. Then I slid on a patch of ice.

Help him, get him out. But how could I get to him? I regained my balance and stared at the water. There were rocks in the creek itself, and a sheet of ice that might or might not hold my weight. Even if I got down there, was I strong enough to pull him out?

Now ten feet from the water, I caught sight of the young man's scalp. What I had thought was thick hair was a dark splotch of blood. I blinked and tried to make out his facial features.

Hold on.

His photo had appeared at least a dozen times in the *Mountain Journal.* I'd heard his voice once, on the phone.

But he wasn't supposed to be here. He was supposed to be hiding. In New Jersey. Where Tom was looking for him to question him about the FedEx hijacking. Not in Colorado. Not lying in Cottonwood Creek. Yet there was no doubt that Andy Balachek wasn't gambling at a casino table.

Andy Balachek was dead.

CHAPTER 6

It was hard to look at Andy Balachek. He was so young.

Had been.

Where was my phone? Wait: It was still plugged into the van outlet. Heedless of the ice, I scrambled back to my vehicle, and flung myself inside. With numb fingers, I punched in the numbers for the Furman County Sheriff's Department. My second call to them this morning, I thought morosely, as I glanced back at the creek and tried to find my voice. When the operator answered, I gave her the details of what I was looking at: a young man in lumberjack shirt and jeans, with no hat covering his frozen, blood-slickened hair. His skin was pale in some places, blue-black in others. It was Andy Balachek, I told her. At least, I was pretty sure...

The cell phone's call-waiting beeped. I told the operator that I'd had an emergency situation myself that morning and I had to take this other call. She snarled at me that I was *not* to hang up, and that I should quickly dump the other call while she waited. That's the thing about emergency operators: You're anxious to get off the phone and deal with your emergency, right? But the operators want you to keep talking and not do a thing. They get especially testy if what you're dealing with is not a natural gas emergency or a car wreck, but a crime.

"Goldy?"

"Tom! Where *are* you? I have so much—"

"On Interstate Seventy, just past Golden. Took an early flight out. I called the house—"

"Oh, Tom," I wailed. He listened in silence as I told him about the gunshot that had shattered our window, about John Richard's early release, about us having to take refuge at the castle. I told him my current location by Hyde Chapel, and about the young man in the icy water, a young man who was never going to move again.

"Oh, Tom—it's Andy Balachek."

"Miss G.—where are you exactly?" His voice was calm. "In the chapel parking lot?"

"Facing the creek and the highway. Across from Cottonwood Park. You know the chapel bridge? Andy's body is about fifty feet downstream from that. I'm above him, in a parking space, forty feet or so from the chapel doors."

Before he could confirm that he understood what I was saying, the call-waiting bleeped again. I'd completely forgotten about the emergency operator.

"Get yourself out of there, Miss G.," Tom ordered me. "Now. Drive back to town, this minute—"

"I...I can't!" Static invaded the cell phone and I stared at it. For some reason, I suddenly remembered Arch's Montessori teacher telling us parents that *I won't* means *I can't* and *I can't* means *I won't*. So...why was I telling Tom that I couldn't leave? Did it really mean that I *wouldn't* leave?

I glanced down at poor Andy Balachek and shuddered. If I left him, somebody might see his body and be compelled to stop and gawk, or maybe mess up the crime scene. They might even steal his body. Not only that, I reasoned blindly, but this could be related to whoever shot at our window. Tom had arrested Ray Wolff. Andy Balachek knew Ray Wolff. Tom was working on the case. Thanks to the newspaper article, virtually everyone in town knew that I, Tom's wife, would be catering at the chapel today.... I moaned.

More crackling assaulted my ear. Why had *I* discovered Andy? Most folks know a caterer is the first to show up at an event. Was I *meant* to find him?

No question, I was getting paranoid.

The static suddenly cleared and I heard Tom say my name.

"Dammit," I said fiercely, "Tom, I don't think I should just drive out of here."

The call-waiting beeped again. "Tom, I need to go, the emergency operator is holding. I've already called the department, I can't leave. Please understand."

"Don't worry about the operator," Tom said calmly, just as the beeping stopped. Had she given up? Had she decided my call was a prank? "I'll call the department," Tom went on. "They'll have a car up more quickly if I do it. I'll cut over from seventy, be coming from the direction of Denver. I should be there in less than ten minutes. Do you have a good view of traffic from the east?"

I glanced around. Cottonwood Park slanted steeply to the road all along the other side of the two-lane highway. "Pretty good."

"Do *not* go near that body, understand? You could fall into the water."

Oh-kay, I thought as Tom signed off. A chilly February wind rocked the van and pummeled the spruce trees across the road. A car swooshed past, then another. No one slowed to gawk. Andy Balachek's body must have been situated in such a way that it couldn't be seen from the road. No one gave me a second glance.

Do not go near that body.... What was Tom so worried about, besides my tumbling into the creek? The killer still being around? If you dumped a dead guy, you wouldn't wait to see who discovered him, would you?

I tried to warm up by snuggling closer to the dashboard heater. According to my watch, it was quarter after seven. Overhead, the charcoal sky was lightening to a velvety blue. Not far away, an engine growled. Less than a minute later, as promised, Tom's big Chrysler roared into view. It turned left to cross the creek, then roared into the lot and pulled up fifteen feet to the right of my van. Puzzled, I unbuckled and jumped from the van, then trotted toward him.

Tom was walking calmly in my direction. He passed Andy's body. Without glancing toward the creek, he motioned me back to the van.

A shot rang out.

Tom reeled back, clutching his left shoulder. I screamed. Without thinking, I raced toward him. When I reached him, his right hand grabbed my arm. Another shot fired and pinged off Tom's car. Then another shot hit one of my van doors.

"Move!" he hollered. Panting with pain, he wrenched me toward the boulders lining the far side of the parking lot. "Get behind those rocks and stay down! See if we can, see if we can..."

Running hard, my heart thudding, I thought he said, *See if we can dig a hole.* Dig a hole? I stumbled; Tom's hand wrenched me upright. I couldn't catch my breath. Those shots had not been like the explosion that rocked our house. They'd been higher-pitched, not as loud, more like a firecracker....

I let go of Tom's hand and leaped above the crevice between two boulders. When I slid down, Tom pushed himself next to me. Blood from his shoulder stained the rocks. I gasped. How badly was he hurt? Where was the shooter? Why was this happening?

"Stay down," Tom ordered me. His sleeve was wet with blood.

Oh, God, I prayed. *Help him, help us.* I couldn't tear my eyes from Tom's wound. Sometimes I think I learned too much in Med Wives 101. *The subclavian vein.* If that major artery had been hit, Tom could bleed to death in minutes. *Please, God. Not Tom.*

With his good hand, Tom pulled the radio off his belt. "Officer needs assistance. Shots fired." He bit the words, his face contorted with pain.

How could I compress the wound? *Think,* I ordered myself desperately as a voice answered Tom's call. "Unit calling?"

"X-ray six," Tom replied. "Location is south side of Cottonwood Creek, by Hyde Chapel, on Highway two-oh-three." Tom's involuntary groan sent my heart racing. If there were no broken bones, if the bullet had not nicked a lung, then perhaps I could compress it and stop some of the dangerous blood loss. "Am behind boulders by chapel parking lot," he went on. "Am now fifty yards from Cottonwood Creek, next to Highway two-oh-three. Do not know mile marker."

There was static on the other end of the radio, but I prayed the operator was telling him that units were responding. What have I done? Why didn't I get out of here when Tom told me to? Where had the shots come from? Was there someone on the other side of the road, up in the trees of Cottonwood Park?

"Believe assailant has a rifle, possibly AR-fifteen. My shoulder's hit...."

"Can you give location of assailant?" the operator's voice crackled.

"Believe he is on north side of road. Possibly fifty yards up in the trees, judging from sound of shots."

"Can we land a helicopter there, X-ray six?"

"Don't know—" The radio fell from Tom's hands. It was slick with blood. I picked it up and pushed what I hoped was the correct button.

"This is Tom's wife, Goldy Schulz," I yelled into the radio. "Send paramedics with your team!" Tom had slumped forward. Static spewed from the radio. I placed it on the ground and leaned in close to my husband. "Tom!" His eyelids fluttered. "I'm going to compress this wound," I told him. "You have to tell me if it feels like you've got a broken bone. You also have to tell me if pressure makes it harder to breathe. Do you understand?" His face paled as he nodded. I couldn't imagine his pain. If the collarbone was broken, any weight I put on the wound would cause him agony.

I steeled myself. He was losing *an awful lot of blood*. With shaking fingers, I pushed on the area where blood spurted through his once-white shirt. Tom moaned but did not tell me to stop. His eyes sought mine. Tears ran down my cheeks as I pressed on the hot, bloody slash in his left shoulder.

As I gently exerted pressure, I listened. Was the shooter planning to try again? All I heard was the gurgle of the creek.

The blood slowed to a trickle and fanned out into a delta of ripples, first on Tom's shirt, then on the snow-dusted rock. He blinked and grunted as he reached for the radio.

"Don't do that!" Hysteria threaded through my voice as my hands, slippery with blood, lost their grip on the wound.

He held the radio up with his right hand.

"Talk." His voice was thick. I composed myself and pushed in again on the wound. "Talk into the radio," Tom muttered. He groaned again, a deep guttural sound that didn't sound human.

"All right, all right," I promised hastily as I first stabilized my pressure on the wound, then scooted awkwardly to get closer to the radio. "Just don't move again. Please, Tom—"

"Goldy, I'm sorry..." His voice had descended to a hoarse whisper.

"Don't worry. Everything will be fine."

"No...Goldy...."

Fear spiked up my spine. Where was the shooter? My hands began to cramp on the wound. I willed them to relax.

Again Tom said, "I'm sorry...."

"*I'm* the one who's sorry. Somebody will be here soon. Ambulance, cops...they're on their way."

"I can feel my right arm, but not my left—"

"They're bound to be here any sec."

Tom's eyes rolled back in his head, then came forward again. "Goldy." He was struggling to speak. "I have to tell you." Each word heaved out, like an enormous, painful sigh. "I'm..." With great effort, he said, *"I don't love her."*

"Tom! Be *quiet*. You're delirious."

"I was just...trying to figure out...what was going on. So you'll understand...." His voice trailed off.

I stared at him.

"Listen," Tom said again, weakly. "I'm...so... sorry."

My voice made no sound as I concentrated on stopping the blood still leaking from the ugly wound in his shoulder. But my mind screamed, *"Sorry for what?"*

CHAPTER 7

How long had it been since Tom had been shot? Seconds. Hours. No, not hours. Minutes. Fractions of minutes. Tom floated in and out of consciousness, his face drained of color, his body slumped against the boulder. He looked like a dying bear. There was no further sound from the radio. I pressed against Tom's wound and begged for him to live.

Then something changed. At first I was not sure if the piercing noise was sirens or ringing in my ears. And perhaps the distant *wop wop wop* was the drumbeat of my heart, and not the helicopter I desperately wanted it to be.

Please, I prayed again.

Then: Men shouted. The sirens screamed closer. Not far away, a helicopter landed with a blast of air that hurt my ears and made my eyes water. The helo engine cut off and more men yelled. Overhead, I thought I could hear another copter.

"Here!" I yelled, without moving from Tom's side. "We're over here!"

After what seemed like a century, a policeman

in full SWAT gear leaped through the rock barrier ten yards from us. He was big, muscular, and limber, with dark skin and dark hair. Crouching expertly, he spoke into a radio as he scrambled across the distance to us.

A second later, he was crawling around Tom and me. He told me not to move my hands as he bent in to get a look at the wound. He felt for Tom's pulse, murmured into his own radio, then turned his full attention back to Tom.

"Schulz! Schulz! Can you hear me?" The SWAT guy's radio crackled. "Schulz!" he cried again. *"Are you in there?"*

"Of course," Tom said unexpectedly, and I almost laughed with relief.

The SWAT cop nodded to me. "Are you hurt?" he asked. I shook my head. "Can you talk?" I nodded. "Good. How many shots?"

"Three." My voice sounded weird. "One went into his shoulder. Another hit his car. The last one struck one of my van doors."

"Could you tell where the shots came from?"

"From across two-oh-three, it seemed. At the time, I thought someone was up on the hill in Cottonwood Park. In the trees."

"How far up the hill?" the cop demanded.

I didn't know. "Maybe a hundred feet, maybe fifty." Tom's eyes had closed again, and I leaned in close to him, murmuring his name.

The SWAT guy talked into his radio, then tried again to communicate with Tom until his radio crackled back. The cops must not have found the shooter, because the officer jumped up, waved over the boulder, and hollered for the medics.

Moments later, two medics—both young men with shaved scalps—clambered over the boulders. They instructed me to ease off the compression and move out of the way. I obeyed. One assessed Tom's wound while the other checked his vital signs. The second medic told the SWAT guy to get the police copter out of the meadow. They were bringing in Flight-for-Life. This meant the medics were skipping the ambulance. Again I wished I didn't know so much. They were skipping the ambulance because of the severity of Tom's wound. Time had become critical and an ambulance would take too long....

I felt dizzy and keeled backward. My body was shutting down, drained of its initial surge of adrenaline. One medic ordered me to lie on the ground. He told the SWAT officer to check me for shock.

Without realizing how I got there, I was suddenly lying on an uneven sheet of ice. A rock stuck into my left shoulder blade. My whole body turned very cold, very fast. *I have to call the Hydes*, I thought, as the blue sky whirled over my head. *There'll be no luncheon today.* The SWAT deputy was talking to me, telling me to keep my eyes open, to keep looking at him. He asked if my collar was tight. I didn't care about my damn collar. I couldn't see Tom. The deputy informed me that the situation on the other side of the rocks had stabilized. The shooter had fled. Captain Lambert of the Furman County Sheriff's Department had radioed to say I could follow the medical helo down to the hospital. If I wanted to. If I was well enough.

I said I was fine. I tried to sit up but my head swam and I sank back, helpless and frustrated. I wanted to be with my husband, my voice croaked. And could someone please call the Hydes, Eliot and Sukie, who owned the the castle on the hill above the chapel, and tell them what was happening? The SWAT man nodded and told me the police chopper was leaving now, so Flight-for-Life could land. When the medical helo left, the police chopper would come back to take me to the hospital. Did I understand? I nodded. Captain Lambert would meet me in Denver. A trauma team at the hospital was already getting prepared for Tom.

A trauma team. I was having trouble breathing. The SWAT deputy had not mentioned the body in the creek. When *officer needs assistance, shots fired* comes in, I knew, everything else gets dropped. My mind repeated the words. *A trauma team. Getting ready. For Tom.*

I couldn't hear the SWAT guy anymore.

I registered the deafening racket and harsh wind of one helo taking off and another landing. A uniformed man and woman—both flight nurses, I realized—threaded through the boulder wall. They stabilized Tom's head, tersely asked the SWAT deputy for a report, then bandaged Tom up and belted him into a stretcher. I craned to watch. My dear Tom, big in body and spirit, charismatic with his men, loving to Arch and me, was always on the move, without being hurried. Now he was unconscious, his face gray, his body drenched in blood. Working in sync, the two nurses expertly heaved the stretcher bearing Tom over the boulders. The SWAT man didn't stop me as I struggled to my feet. When I swayed and nearly fell, he gripped my elbow and walked me through the rocks.

The sheer number of cops assembled was astonishing. At least fifty police officers, their uniforms and cars emblazoned with the insignia of the Furman County and nearby Jefferson County sheriff's departments, as well as Littleton, Lakewood, and Morrison police departments, were crowded onto the road, talking into their radios, taking notes, investigating the scene, keeping tabs on more officers combing the trees. I wished that Tom could have seen it.

My mind backtracked to Tom's words about her. *Don't think about it,* I warned myself. He'd been shot. He was out of his head.

Still, as the medical helo whipped into the air, my brain again supplied Tom's shaky, apologetic tone. *I don't love her.* What could he have been thinking? That he was going to die, and that I would find something incriminating from before we'd met? Like what? Love notes? Hotel bills? Or was his concern more recent? Had he compromised himself with a hooker in Atlantic City? Had she threatened to give me a ring?

Stop. *Stop, stop, stop.*

I watched the medical helo recede into the sky.

Less than ten minutes later, the sheriff's department chopper took off with me in it. Below us, on the other side of the creek, police officers continued to swarm through the trees of Cottonwood Park. The corpse was still in the water; crime-scene techs were videotaping and combing the site. Half a mile east of the scene, where Fox Creek flowed down into the Cottonwood, cops had stopped traffic. On the south side of the road, on the hill far above Cottonwood Creek, rose the castle. Its moat glittered in the morning sun like a medieval vision. Had the police notified the Hydes of what had happened? Or were they still expecting me to be there to cater the lunch?

The helo swept eastward. The castle estate adjoined an enormous cattle ranch, and the noise of the copter drove dozens of steer below us into a brisk trot. To the south stretched acres and acres of pine trees.

I glanced back at Cottonwood Creek, where Andy Balachek's receding body was a bright spot in the dark water. In the county park, a cluster of uniformed officers had stopped at a dirt road that cut through the expanse of trees. They were studying something on the road. Shells from the bullets fired at us? Footprints in the snow? Tracks from a vehicle?

I turned and stared at Highway 203, now receding from sight. Had someone shot out our window, then somehow followed me to the castle? Had that same person murdered Andy Balachek and dumped his body in the creek, where I would be almost certain to discover it? Had that person then waited across the road, to try to shoot me? Or had Tom been his target all along?

I turned back, determined to focus on Tom. In the cockpit, the pilots' mouths worked as they spoke into headsets. Out the window, the endless spread of forest fell away beneath us. I closed my eyes and prayed for Tom.

But thoughts intruded. Either my mind was struggling to make sense out of all that had happened, or my soul was trying to generate hope. What had Tom told me about gunshot wounds? *It depends on the weapon.* If someone shot a high-powered rifle at your shoulder, good-bye shoulder. If it was a low-powered rifle, something might be salvaged if a bone hadn't been hit, or if a major blood vessel hadn't been opened up. If a bullet tore open the subclavian vein, you could bleed to death before you reached a hospital. Would they give blood in the medical helo? I didn't think a Flight-for-Life IV could contain anything besides glucose.

The helo pilot, who looked too young to be shaving, much less flying a helicopter, murmured into his radio, then swerved the aircraft to the right. Unless I was extremely disoriented, we were heading south-by-southeast. This was not the direction to the base for Flight-for-Life: Saint Anthony's Hospital in Denver.

89

"What's going on?" I yelled over the whir of the helicopter blades.

"Saint Anthony's is overloaded," the pilot hollered back. "They're on Divert. The medical helo is going to Southwest Hospital, so that's where we're heading. Southwest has a new trauma center that can handle this."

I bit my lip painfully, anxious to get Tom *somewhere*. I knew Southwest Hospital, across from Westside Mall in the southeast corner of Furman County. It was where Marla had been taken when she'd had her heart attack; afterwards, she'd donated money for a new coronary care wing. Southwest also belonged to the same chain of Denver hospitals in which John Richard had once worked.

I veered away from *that* thought as we swooped over one of the residential areas in the foothills, where houses sat higgledy-piggledy along a winding dirt road. Swing sets shuddered in the cold wind coming off the higher elevations. Week-old, wind-carved snowmen newly dusted with white indicated the presence of happy families.

In the not-so-happy family department, where was John Richard at this moment? I wished I knew. Could he possibly have shot Tom? Would he have? Yes, oh yes, no matter what Arch said about his father not being good with a gun. My head ached as I remembered an incident from when we were still married. The tale had come from a nurse at Cityside Hospital, one of the places where John Richard had done deliveries. Her voice trembling, she'd called me to confess she'd repeatedly rejected John Richard's advances. When she'd protested to Doctor that she was married, she told me, the Jerk had calmly replied, *How about if that troublesome husband of yours was out of the way?* I didn't know why the nurse had phoned *me* with this message. What did she think I was going to do? My advice had been that she put as many miles as she could between herself and Dr. Korman. Not long after, another nurse told me that the object of John Richard's affections had quit her job and moved to a hospital out of state.

I couldn't see the medical helo, but I knew it was in front of us. More knowledge I'd gleaned in Med Wives 101 came up like a fresh computer screen. The human body is mostly water. Even a bullet that only goes through soft tissue causes massive damage, beginning with the shock wave to the system known as the hydraulic effect.

Were the medics treating Tom for shock? Of course. Had I done enough to compress the wound? My teeth chattered. I grabbed a silver space blanket one of the pilots had put on the seat beside me. I was so cold. How to avoid shock? Stop *feeling* and start *thinking.*

But I couldn't. It was too painful. I saw Tom's body jerk back. Watched him bleed. Heard him say, *I don't love her.* I'd endured years of infidelity from the Jerk. But this was different.

Incredibly, I still had my cell phone. I drew it out and stared at it. Could I use it in the helo? Should I call Elk Park Prep? Should Arch be told? I looked down. We had left the mountains and were swooping over the Hogback, an ancient, jagged geological formation that rose between the mountains and plains. The Hogback had fascinated generations of elementary-school science students. But the rocks still screwed up any cellular communication you tried to make while crossing them. Plus, making a cell call was undoubtedly not allowed in the helo, as it wouldn't be in the hospital. So: Once I knew Tom was being taken care of, I'd find a pay phone, call Marla, call the Hydes, call the church. *All crises in due time,* my mind numbly supplied.

The helo was just starting over the flatlands that stretched toward Denver. We *whump-whump*ed over a development, row after row of gray-and-beige tract houses. Ahead, Westside Mall loomed. Beyond it, Southwest Hospital and its crammed parking lot shimmered in the sun.

The police helicopter hovered near the mall. From our vantage point, the hospital landing pad was in full view. It looked as if an emergency nurse and orderly were meeting the medical helo. I swallowed and watched the flight nurses unload Tom *hot,* that is, with the helo blades still going. Then I saw Tom, still on the backboard, being transferred onto a gurney and wheeled away.

First the trauma team, then a hot unload. You only unloaded hot when you thought you were going to lose somebody.

★ ★ ★

What felt like an eternity but probably was not more than twenty minutes later, after the police chopper had landed and the hospital security officer had escorted me to a bathroom to clean Tom's blood off my hands and arms, I arrived in the ER waiting room. I was told the ER doctor would come out to talk to me as soon as possible. A few moments later, Tom's new captain, Isaac Lambert, loomed next to me. Awkwardly, I got to my feet.

"Goldy," he murmured. He hugged me, but knew better than to ask some clichéd question about how I was doing. "They have a good team here."

"Okay."

Gray-haired, hawk-faced Captain Lambert was a tall, heavy man whose bones creaked when he sat in a plastic chair. The row of brown buttons on his tan uniform stretched to capacity across his Buddha-like belly. He smelled of Old Spice and gave the impression of a benevolent giant trying hard to be comforting. I sat down next to him, grateful to have someone with me.

"Where's Tom now?" I asked. "Have you seen him?"

"No, but I know the procedure." His voice was kindly and reassuring. "The flight team gives their report to the ER doc. Tom's age, how many shots fired, how much blood loss, that kind of thing. The ER doc assesses and then acts."

We said nothing for a few minutes. I looked around. Sitting in the waiting room felt like floating near the bottom of a deep well. Sunlight filtered through blue-tinted frosted glass and illuminated pale blue walls, dark turquoise chairs, navy blue couches opposite a wall of windows looking out on a busy hospital hallway. For the first time, I noticed that the room appeared to be full of women: women staring, women sobbing quietly, women listening with frozen faces to jammy-clad doctors giving them the news.

"They unloaded him hot," I told Lambert, just to be talking. "That means—" My throat shut.

The captain's expression and tone did not change. "They gave him blood while they were assessing him."

I could just imagine the ER team swarming around my husband: putting in IV's that contained blood and glucose, taking blood pressure and pulse, hooking up the heart monitor, checking for respiration and mentation, that is, assessing how cogent the patient is.

How cogently was Tom thinking when he told me he didn't love her?

"They do X-rays," the captain continued in that maddeningly soothing voice. "Once they know what they're dealing with and have their surgical team together, they'll put him right in—"

The doctor appeared, a short, slender man with gray hair, pale eyes, and a greenish tint to his skin that might have been the effect of the neon lights. He introduced himself as Dr. Larry Saslow and asked if I was Mrs. Schulz.

"Your husband's wound," the doctor began, "is not as bad as it could have been. The bullet missed bone, but nicked a major blood vessel. The subclavian, heard of it?" When I nodded mutely, he went on: "A vascular surgeon is working on him now. He should be out of surgery in a couple of hours."

I wanted to hold on to this man. *I want reassurances!* But I could do nothing but nod.

"Thanks. Good. Very good," replied Captain Lambert before the doctor walked away. When I continued to say nothing, Captain Lambert mumbled he'd be back in a minute. Moments later, he lumbered back with two plastic cups of coffee that looked like recycled motor oil.

"It's better than nothing," he said apologetically.

Mechanically, I took a sip and instantly burned my tongue. "It's great, thanks." My voice sounded faraway.

"This is good news, Goldy. What the doc said. They'll keep Tom in ICU overnight. A couple of our deputies can stay to check on him every hour, if you need to go home—"

"I am *not* going home," I said fiercely. My hand trembled and coffee slopped onto my knee. I knew I needed to make calls, but I wasn't ready.

"Okay, okay. Stay here, then."

I was being unreasonable and shrill, and I

didn't want to respond to the graciousness of Captain Lambert this way. Still, I didn't know how to act. So I just sat, prayed, and drank bad coffee. Finally, I asked the captain if he knew about a phone I could use. He said the waiting-room phone was ten feet away. Did I want him to walk over there with me? No, thanks.

First I called Saint Luke's Episcopal Church in Aspen Meadow. Into the priest's voice mail I crisply stated our news, adding that I was at Southwest Hospital and would be for the next twenty-four hours. I asked that Tom's name go out immediately on the prayer chain. Then I called Marla's cell. *Please pick up Arch from Elk Park Prep and call me at the following number,* I said numbly into her messaging system. *Better yet, please bring Arch to South-west Hospital, as I need to be with both of you. Tom's been shot,* I explained, my voice quavering.

Then I called the Hydes. With them, I was relieved to get a machine. Briefly, I announced what had happened, and where I was. *We'll have to postpone the luncheon until later in the week, since the area is now a crime scene. I'm sure the donors will understand....*

Finally I went back to my plastic chair. I felt numb.

"Goldy?" Captain Lambert asked. "I've been wondering, I'm just curious...of course, you'll be talking to a detective later, but...what happened?"

And so I told my tale: how the window at our house had been shot out, how Sergeant Boyd had politely ordered my son and me to

96

get out until Tom returned. We'd schlepped to Hyde Castle, just above Cottonwood Creek and Hyde Chapel, where I was supposed to cater a luncheon today.... And then I'd found Andy Balachek's body in the creek, and Tom had been shot.... "And there's something else you should know." I told him about my ex-husband's early release from prison.

"We're trying to find Korman now," the captain replied. "We think he's at his old country club home in Aspen Meadow. At least, that's where he told his parole officer he was headed—"

"Wait," I interrupted him. My attention veered to the far side of the waiting room.

At the window that looked out on the hall, a woman's face—porcelain skin, fine features, ink-black hair—appeared, then vanished. Goose bumps chilled my skin.

What was Chardé Lauderdale doing at Southwest Hospital?

CHAPTER 8

I jumped up, raced to the waiting-room door, and checked the hall. It was a noisy place. The intercom blared litanies of names and messages; orderlies rattled past pushing patient-loaded gurneys; families, nurses, and doctors chattered and strode, fast and slow, along the squeaky linoleum.

And there was Chardé Lauderdale, walking quickly away. Her black hair was swept up in a French twist held with a gleaming barrette. Her red and black suit hugged her athletic figure as her high heels clickety-clicked into the distance. Maybe she was here to have her little daughter Patty examined again, to determine if there were any long-term effects from the shaking Buddy had given her. Chardé turned and glanced at me, then trotted around the corner.

I rubbed my dry, cracked hands together. Curse of the caterer: too many washings, too little lotion. I stared at the hallway, as if daring Chardé Lauderdale to reappear. Had Tom ever mentioned someone trying to intimidate him? Was someone trying to intimidate *me*? Could the Lauderdales and their thirst for revenge be behind all that was happening? I walked back inside the waiting room.

"Captain Lambert, I need to tell you about some people named Lauderdale." My mouth filled with bile even as I said their name. Briefly, I told Lambert of the New Year's Eve party and its aftermath.

"I read the article," Captain Lambert mused. "Read the report, too. We're following up on the Lauderdales. And on your ex-husband. And on the hijackers Tom's investigating. At this point, the suspects in the shooting of Tom are the same ones we're considering for shooting at your house. First thing, we have to look at Balachek."

"What exactly *was* going on with Andy Balachek?" I asked. "Tom only told me a few details."

The captain pursed his lips. "Tom didn't tell you we used to call Ray Wolff the Stinky Beef Boy?"

My mind swam. "He never mentioned bad-smelling meat. I would have remembered that."

"A while back, Wolff stole a truckload of what he thought was prime-grade steaks. Turned out it was beef *rectums*." Lambert chuckled. "The rectums were unsalable to restaurants, naturally. So he abandoned the truck. Smelled up six city blocks before Denver P.D. figured out what it was. Witnesses gave a physical description of Wolff, whom law enforcement already knew about."

"So then Wolff got a couple of partners, one of whom was Andy Balachek?"

Lambert cocked an eyebrow. "You're not going to go chasing after them, are you?"

My reputation for poking around in unsolved crimes again reared its busybody head. I reddened. "Of course not." Lambert's look was skeptical. No doubt the captain knew all about my sleuthing.

"All right," Lambert continued after a moment. "The three-million-dollar stamp heist. The Stamp Fox is an unusual place. It's high-class and very specialized. This country doesn't have many fancy stamp stores, not the way they do in London or Zurich. George Renard, the owner, tried to get publicity for his store by getting articles in the local papers about Tucson's big philatelic show. Renard wanted the world to know the value of the stamps he'd be exhibiting, and wouldn't his boutique be a cool place to shop?" Lambert rubbed his large forehead, sighing over the store owner's stupidity. "Problem was, the article also said Renard was flying to Tucson and shipping the collection. So your smart thief will watch the store. How many days to the stamp show? What courier does the store use? How often does the courier come? That's how he figures out that when a FedEx truck shows up three days before the show opens, he can hit it and cash in."

"How many valuable stamps were taken?"

"Three of them were from Mauritius. Each of those was valued at half a million *pounds*, which is about eight hundred thousand dollars per stamp, at today's exchange rates. Know anything about old stamps from Mauritius? Do you even know where Mauritius is? I had to look it up."

My laugh sounded hollow, somehow. Every amateur stamp-collector quickly learns the location of small countries that produce important stamps. "Mauritius is an island country off the coast of Africa. East of Madagascar. Their old stamps are extremely rare," I said. "First issue was in...ah...1850, or thereabouts? Has a picture of Queen Victoria?"

"Very good. 1847." Lambert sounded impressed.

I thought for a minute. "But...aren't those stamps going to be hard to fence?"

"Maybe in this country, where using pawn-shops would be stupid. But if you've got contacts in the Far East, according to Renard, you can fence anything. Before you know it, the stolen stamps, now with huge price tags, show up in European shows. Watch it, though, Goldy. We haven't published any pictures of the stolen stamps, or even a list of the inventory. Got it? That's a key to our investigation. No one must know."

"Right, okay, thanks for telling me." The keys to a case were secret, and closely guarded by the authorities. Without willing it, I mentally placed The Stamp Fox in Furman East Shopping Center. The luxury strip mall was a mile from Lauderdale Luxury Imports. It was also, as I recalled, not far from The Huntsman, the euphemistically named gun shop for which the Jerk's new girlfriend, Viv Martini, worked as a sales rep. The Huntsman was a free-standing store, since mall developers didn't favor firearm retailers.

I felt dazed. "Where does shooting Tom come in?"

He shook his head. "We figure the thieves haven't fenced the stamps yet. But we also believe Balachek was getting antsy. The FedEx driver was killed in the robbery, and Balachek could face murder or complicity charges. Plus, he had stolen his father's truck last year, sold it for gambling money he lost, and then never paid him back. Now his dad's in coronary care. Andy wanted his share of the robbery money so he could make things right with his dad before he died. At least, that's what he told Tom. At first, Andy strung Tom along as to the location of the stamps. Andy told Tom when Wolff would be at Furman County Storage and Tom arrested Wolff there. It was a great collar. But our team found no stamps on Ray Wolff. Our theory is that Andy knew the location of the stamps, but wanted to trade that knowledge for a better plea deal. It's very tentative, but we're figuring Wolff's gang killed Andy to keep his mouth shut. And maybe they're after Tom because they figure Andy *did* tell him where the loot was." He gave me an apologetic look. "It's all really speculative," he repeated.

"And the other people in the gang?"

"We just have Wolff and Balachek as suspects at this point. But witnesses to the hijacking are very clear about seeing three people. Balachek refused to tell Tom the name of the other hijacker, or if there were more people involved. That kid was *scared*."

I nodded numbly. I was thankful the captain had shared his theory with me. He'd also given me more information than cops usually gave civilians. But he knew Tom talked to me about his cases. He also knew that I'd proved helpful—if a tad meddlesome—in the past. I didn't feel particularly helpful now, though. All I could think of was Tom slumping against a boulder as his blood ran down the granite.

I asked, "The other hijacker, could it be a woman?"

Cops have a way of hearing questions. The

captain's tone became guarded. "We don't know the exact number of people involved in the heist, or their gender. Why?"

I shrugged. Why? *I don't love her.* Had she pointed a loaded gun at our window in the wee hours, then shot Tom this morning, as he walked toward me? Was she, like the Jerk, the jealous type? Is there any way my husband would have become emotionally involved with a member of a theft ring?

Lambert shrugged, as if he'd made a decision. "Until recently, Ray Wolff had a girlfriend. Possibly she hooked up with Andy Balachek, too." The captain added carefully, "But...I would have thought you'd know about her. Tom ever mention Viv Martini?"

I choked. "Viv Martini? She's involved with these crooks?" Why had Tom not told me this? "Viv is my *ex*-husband's girlfriend."

"Yeah, so we heard. The woman gets around. Our most recent information was that Martini was involved with Ray Wolff. Last month, we thought we spotted her at a Denver hotel, either alone or with Andy Balachek. Then we heard she was interested in John Richard Korman."

She gets around? That seemed an understatement. To my way of thinking, the Furman County Jail sounded postively incestuous. I remembered Arch's words: *Dad stole the girlfriend of one of the convicts. The guy was pretty pissed off and yelled at Dad that he'd get back at him. But Dad and Viv are doing okay. Viv told me she's happier with someone finishing a prison stint than with someone who's just getting started on one. She likes it that Dad has money. He told her he was buying her something nice, a Mercedes or maybe a trip to Rio.*

I felt as if I were inside the washing machine with all the Jerk's dirty laundry, past and future. Let's see: The Jerk stole the hijacker's girlfriend. This past Friday, the Department of Corrections released the Jerk. Very early today, Monday morning, someone blasted out our front window. Two hours ago, Tom, who arrested the hijacker, was shot, right next to where the corpse of the hijacker's murdered young partner, the man Tom had been seeking in Atlantic City, had been dumped.

Even a paranoid has real enemies.

The captain's pager beeped. "I've gotta go make this call from my car," Lambert informed me, and left.

I used the waiting-room desk phone to call Marla again. My watch said half past nine. While I was waiting to be switched to my friend's voice mail, I ate one of the two emergency chocolate truffles I keep in my purse, then tore into a cellophane-wrapped package of crackers left for waiting-room families. Feeling slightly better, I told Marla's messaging that Tom was now in with a vascular surgeon.

"Please call the hospital's main number and see if they'll page me," I added. "I'm still hoping you can bring Arch to the hospital so we can decide what to do. I'll be spending the night here. Oh, and I'm desperate for some clean clothes, if you can scrounge anything up. Thanks, friend."

Captain Lambert trundled back into the waiting room. "Okay," he began without preamble, "our guys on the hill just called in a preliminary report. What they think are the shooter's footprints start by a picnic table in Cottonwood Park, then go down to a spot across from the creek, then back up to the table. At the point across the creek, a tech found a spent shell. There are some tire tracks by the picnic table. So someone was watching from above, then came back down to do the shooting, then went back up to his vehicle. Was the person waiting for *Tom?* Was the shooter waiting for the person who found Balachek's body? But that was you, right? Would the perp have waited all day to shoot at a cop? We can't tell yet."

Waiting for Tom? Waiting for any cop? My thoughts whirled. If you'd murdered Andy Balachek, why not just leave? *Why stay?*

The captain continued, "The investigative team has begun detection around the body. Rigor's already set in, so he'd been dead for a while. Which makes even less sense. How long had the perp been waiting up in the pines? Hours? Oh, and by the way, all this is for your ears only, Goldy," he warned.

"Yeah," I said. "Okay." As if I was going to ask some stranger how to make sense out of all this.

"Okay, regarding your house," the captain

105

said, switching back to his reassuring tone. "Since your security system's down from the shooting, your neighbor Trudy volunteered to watch your house. Another thing you should be aware of: I've assigned two of Tom's men to investigate this case. Officers Boyd and Armstrong. Boyd will be lead investigator."

I felt relief. The captain also had a long message from Marla, who had called the sheriff's department. She'd pulled Arch from school, Lambert reported. She and Arch were going to Boulder to find someone named Julian. Then the three of them were coming here to the hospital. Lambert talked on about how the policemen's wives had wanted to organize meals to be sent to the castle, where he assumed Arch and I would want to stay, but they weren't sure if I'd want them, with me being a caterer and all. I smiled involuntarily at the image of historic-food buff Eliot Hyde peering into a tuna noodle casserole. I thanked the captain and assured him meals would not be necessary.

While Lambert sat patiently, I paced for another hour. Finally a young, grim-faced doctor in surgical clothes came into the room. "Mrs. Schulz?" He nodded at Lambert. A pins-and-needles anxiety swept over me.

Dr. Dan Spier, vascular surgeon, was concise. His small fingers indicated on his own chest the bullet's point of entry. It had indeed gone through soft tissue only. He talked about the surgery his team had undertaken, and told me that Tom's shoulder would have to be immobilized for about a month, although he could start moving around as soon as he felt up to it. Tom was lucky, Spier continued dryly, that no bone had been hit, lucky that the weapon had not been an automatic, lucky that there had been only one bullet. And he was particularly lucky, Spier added with a pinched smile, that I'd had the presence of mind to compress the wound.

Lucky. I turned the word over in my mind.

Spier concluded by saying I would receive discharge instructions on changing the bandage and on bringing Tom back in to be examined. As long as all went well during a night in ICU, Tom could go home in the morning.

"That seems early," I protested. How could we go home, until the cops had a better sense of who the shooter was? And if we didn't go home, how would the Hydes take to having a wounded cop recuperating at their place?

Spier shook his head. "It's not really early. All you have to do is keep an eye on the wound and get the patient to rest." I thanked Spier. He nodded impassively and left.

Finally, finally, I was allowed to see Tom. His skin was yellow. With an IV in his arm and oxygen tubes up his nose, he appeared utterly helpless. The bedsheet rose and fell as he slept. I closed his hand in mine. His eyelids flickered but did not open. *I love you,* I told him silently. *I love you now and forever and ever. No matter what.*

A Furman County deputy was stationed

outside the ICU. An older nurse with a flat mid-western accent told me I could see Tom ten minutes each hour, the usual drill. I should not try to wake him.

"It's going to be a rough twenty-four hours for you, Mrs. Schulz," she warned, her voice laced with sympathy. "You might want to get some family here with you. Get yourself something to eat."

"Rough," I repeated numbly.

But we're lucky, oh so lucky. Tom is alive.

I told the nurse I would be back in an hour. When she turned to talk to a family whose daughter had just come out of surgery, I walked unsteadily to the ICU waiting room.

CHAPTER 9

Tom opened his eyes once, on my second visit to the ICU. When he turned his head a fraction, I jumped to his side and carefully took the hand not connected to an IV. I asked him how he felt. He groaned but said nothing before the medicated fog reclaimed him. With grim determination, I continued my hourly visits through the afternoon.

At six o'clock, Marla burst into the ICU waiting room with Arch and Julian Teller in tow. To their worried barrage of questions about Tom's condition, I replied that he'd had surgery and was on the mend. Arch, fighting back tears, gave me a brief squeeze before with-drawing behind Julian and Marla. Julian stepped forward and hugged me hard. His handsome face now boasted a college-grown mustache and goatee. Not tall, he possessed a lean, muscular, swimmer's body, barely visible as he shoved his hands into pockets of a khaki outfit that resembled an oversize uniform of the French Foreign Legion. When he pulled away, he ran his hand through his tobacco-brown hair, now a mown thatch, and mumbled that he felt terrible, that he couldn't believe someone had shot at us, that he wished he could have been at the hospital earlier.

"Julian." I pulled him in for another embrace. For almost three years, Julian Teller had been a much-loved member of our extended family. Not only was he dedicated to becoming a vegetarian chef, he was a great kid to boot. So I wasn't going to listen to him apologize about *anything*. "You say you're sorry again, we'll have Steak Tartare for breakfast."

Julian's mouth twisted into a shy smile. "I left messages for my professors." His body tensed with energy as he tried to make his shrug appear offhand. "Told them I was taking a few days off for a family emergency. I mean, I was already set to help you with that banquet Friday night. I can stay a few weeks if you need it. And if the people at the castle wouldn't mind having me," he added, his eyes pleading. I started to say that he need not leave school indefinitely, but stopped when I glimpsed

Arch's worried face. It would be good for him to have Julian around for a while. Julian was an excellent student and would manage. Whether the Hydes would welcome yet another live-in guest was another matter.

"Let me check with the castle owners," I murmured.

Marla, her face set in forced jollity, bustled forward in one of her "February is for Valentine's Day" outfits: a long-sleeved scarlet knit dress patterned with white hearts the size of fried eggs. Her voice was matter-of-fact. "We're *all* taking a few days or weeks off or whatever Tom needs. Who do these criminals think they are, anyway?" The dish-size hearts trembled as Marla handed me a shopping bag and leaned forward for her hug. "Sweat suit from the Brown Palace Gift Shop. I'm *so* sorry this is happening," she whispered in my ear. "If I had a husband I loved the way you love Tom, I'd be hysterical. You don't think El Jerko did this, do you?"

"Not sure," I murmured, then, in a louder voice, thanked her for the clothes and for bringing the boys. I turned my attention back to Arch. His static-filled brown hair, thick glasses, and pinched expression gave him the look of a young professor whose experiments had all failed. He waited until the others had hugged and spoken to me before giving me another hug.

"Mom." He kept his voice low. "Did they try to shoot you, too?"

"No," I said lightly, trying to be matter-of-fact. Arch still suffered from the occasional nightmare, and I needed to reassure him.

"I'm sorry I lost my cool this morning."

"It's okay."

It was not a bad apology, as apologies went. Obviously, he was afraid to ask about Tom yet. I answered the rest of their questions by giving the barest details of what had happened. Tom was almost certainly coming back to the castle the next morning, I said. The Hydes would just have to understand. After all, where else could we go?

We took turns seeing Tom. With his slack, jaundiced face, IV streaming under the bandage on his arm, and his heavy snoring, he looked and sounded terrible. At eight forty-five the priest from St. Luke's showed up. He saw Tom alone, and then the five of us prayed together briefly in the waiting room.

At nine-thirty, a yawning Marla announced that the boys should come back with her to the Brown Palace. Arch protested that he couldn't, that all his bags, clothes, and "stuff" were at Hyde Castle, and by the time they drove to Aspen Meadow, picked up his paraphernalia, and schlepped back to Denver, it would be morning and he'd have to leave for school. Julian jumped in to say he had a sleeping bag in his Range Rover and could drive Arch back to the castle. And, he added, he could find the castle at night with no problem. He was willing to sleep on a couch or even on the floor of Arch's room, if the Hydes would allow it. Then he could take Arch to and from school and help

111

with the historical cooking. "I'll stay for as long as you want," he concluded in a tone that brooked no argument.

"Thanks for the offer," I told him. "But it's up to the Hydes."

Marla left to call Eliot and Sukie about Julian's request to be housed at the castle. When she returned, she said she'd talked to Eliot, who couldn't have been nicer.

" 'Yes,' he gushed," Marla said, imitating Eliot's sonorous voice, " 'bring the injured policeman, bring the college student, we'll have a grand household here just as they did in medieval times.' He was *slightly* freaked out that you'd found the body of Andy Balachek," she added. "Apparently, Andy used to come to the castle quite a bit when he was little, because his father, Peter—the excavator, do you know him?—rebuilt the Hydes' dam after Fox Creek flooded. Eliot didn't know 'poor little Andy' might be involved in illegal activity. So he's spooked."

"Great," I muttered.

"Oh-kay," Marla went on, "Eliot also asked if you would be able to cater the labyrinth-donor lunch in three days, on Thursday. The police should be finished with the crime scene by then, he figures. Oh, and the St. Luke's staff is going to call all the donors, to notify them of the change." She raised her eyebrows at me. "Eliot was also worried that doing both the lunch and the fencing banquet on Friday might be too much for you." She grinned mischievously. "I knew you didn't have any

112

catering events until Saturday night's Valentine's Day dance. So I told him Thursday would be fine. Hope that's okay. I also offered Julian's services both days. The king of the castle," Marla said with a toss of her head, "was able to retire in peace."

"Wearing his nightcap, no doubt."

"Are you kidding? Wearing a *crown*." She frowned. "So you're all right with that catering schedule?"

"Absolutely, thanks. Tom needs to rest. Julian and I can do big-time cooking. It'll be good for us."

"Really," added Julian.

"Come on, guys," Arch pleaded wearily, "I've got a *ton* of English homework, and I've got to use the binoculars to see what phase Venus is in. The teachers don't excuse missed assignments unless you *yourself* are in the hospital. Maybe not even then," he added glumly. Poor Arch!

We made sketchy plans. Elk Park Prep had a late start the next day, so if the hospital released Tom early enough, we might return to the castle before Arch and Julian left for school. After Tom was settled in our castle suite, I'd finally go home for the disk that had my recipes and notes on historic English food, plus information on how castles were run, and background on labyrinths—all areas Eliot had asked me to research. I'd also find a photograph of the Jerk, I added silently, for the benefit of castle security. Then Julian and I would plunge into finishing the planning and doing the cooking for the luncheon and dinner. Before the three of them left, we gave each other one last reassuring hug.

When they'd gone, however, I felt a flood of loneliness, as if the events of the day were just now catching up with me. I changed into the gift-shop sweat suit. But dozing on the waiting-room couch did not seem to be in the cards. The bright overhead lights, intercom announcements, and shuffling and buzzing of folks in the hall, not to mention my own awareness of each upcoming ten-minute visit, all conspired against it. Chardé Lauderdale, I found out from a nurse who was an old friend, had indeed been in with baby Patty for a visit to the neurologist. To my relief, Chardé did not appear again.

Finally, near dawn, slumber overwhelmed me. Bad dreams brought visions of Andy's body in the creek, the crack of a gunshot, Tom falling toward me, his arms outstretched. The expression on his face... I unintentionally shouted myself awake, only to look up into the eyes of Captain Lambert.

He'd brought me a still-hot, four-shot latté, bless him, made just the way Tom had once told him I liked it. Chilled and stiff from my restless night, throat sore, eyes gummed from crying, I gratefully sipped the rich drink. The captain waved my thanks away and pointed to a brown paper bag.

"I brought a department sweat suit Tom's size. And we had your van towed up to the castle. Workmen's comp is paying for everything, including an ambulance to take Tom back to the castle with you, unless you want to go someplace else. We've had lots of offers from his friends. Tom has lots of friends," he reminded me gently.

"Thanks, but all my cooking equipment is at the castle, and I'm doing two events for the Hydes this week. If Tom's up to it, I'd love to get out of here ASAP."

Lambert obligingly pulled strings. I received my instructions about caring for him once he was released. Tom was discharged ten minutes later. That's the great thing about cops. Even doctors are afraid of them, almost as much as they are of lawyers.

An orderly piloted Tom to the discharge doors and then into the waiting ambulance. Captain Lambert strode along next to the wheelchair and told me Boyd and Armstrong would be up to the castle that afternoon to talk to me. Once Tom was strapped into the back of the ambulance and the wheelchair was folded and stored beside him, I climbed in. A moment later we were bumping out of the parking lot.

"I'm sorry to put you through this," were Tom's first words. Nonplussed, I blurted out my own apology. How wrong I'd been not to leave that area by the creek when he'd told me to. How I shouldn't have run to welcome him.

He shook his head. "I should have waited till backup arrived." His voice was hoarse, his breathing labored. "Then you never would have jumped out. No...blame." When he stopped talking, I knew better than to reply. "Andy," he added fiercely.

I squeezed Tom's hand. "Don't think about him. In fact, Tom? Don't talk at all."

"I want to get on with this." He spoke slowly, insistently. "I need to get back to—"

"Tom, *please.* You've got to heal."

"Working heals me."

"Tom—"

"Where was I?" He squinted at the beige ceiling of the ambulance interior. "Oh, yeah.... Andy just makes me so damn mad. *Made* me mad. And now he's got himself dead."

I didn't care about Andy Balachek; I cared only about Tom. Clearly, he wasn't going to follow doctor's orders and stay quiet. He didn't want that. He *wanted* to talk about the corpse in the creek. "Okay," I said. "Balachek's death was avoidable. Why?"

"That kid was the king of communication. Loved e-mail. Sent me a letter with no return address telling me to set up thus-and-such new e-mail address, operated only out of my home. So I did, with the D.A.'s blessing. Balachek said he'd tell me who killed the truck driver if I could get him off." Tom's eyes closed. I clasped his hand in mine.

The ambulance began the winding, westward ascent up Highway 203. When we'd left the hospital, shimmering white clouds had been hovering over the forests blanketing the foothills. Peering through the ambulance's windshield, I could see that the cloud cover had now turned the color of ash. A freezing fog misted the pine tops. More snow was on the way.

"Andy wouldn't tell me who his other partners were," Tom announced abruptly, startling me. "I mean, besides Ray Wolff. Andy wouldn't divulge information about the stamps. The home address linked with his e-mail was his father's, who'd kicked him out when Andy stole his excavation truck. And you know we thought Andy was in Atlantic City when he called last Friday."

I nodded. Andy, frantic, had called our house from a cell phone in Central City, Colorado, where gambling was legal. He was calling from a bathroom, because he'd stolen somebody's cell phone and wanted to talk to Tom. I'd said Tom was in Atlantic City, looking for *him*. Andy had bitterly replied that he guessed he'd have to go to New Jersey to see Tom, because his partner threw his computer into the lake. Then he hung up. With no leads materializing in New Jersey, Tom had decided to come home. And now he was determined to talk about the case. I sighed.

"Did you ever figure out who the partner was?" I asked. "Are there more than three people in the gang?" I paused. "Ray Wolff is in prison. Whoever the third person is, he or she or whoever couldn't have known Andy was talking to *you* over the Internet, or Andy would have been killed right then. I mean, if we're talking about the same person who *did* kill him in the end."

"I'm willing to bet," Tom said with great effort, "that the 'other partner' is the third hijacker witnesses saw. Maybe there *are* more people in the gang, but you usually don't use the word 'partner' unless you've only got a couple of them."

"So somebody got wind of Andy's e-mails?"

Tom grimaced. "Don't know."

Talking had exhausted him. He closed his eyes as the ambulance passed the sign indicating that Aspen Meadow was only ten miles away. I was glad he was finally asleep. Every time he opened his mouth, I was afraid he was going to confess to some terrible sin that I couldn't bear to hear.

Andy wouldn't divulge information about the stamps. I felt a pang of envy. Would I ever get to see those Victorian wonders? Like every other eleven-year-old on my block, I'd been a voracious stamp collector. My mother had gotten tired of all the philatelic packets pouring in "on approval," which meant stamp clubs sent stamps every month and I had to send them back by a certain date, or pay. Unfortunately, I never had the heart to return the beauties, and I'd ended up baby-sitting around the clock to fund my hobby. When my grades fell and I slept through a baby's sobbing, my mother canceled all my stamp club subscriptions. Heartless! And that, unfortunately, had rung the death-knell for my stamp-collecting hobby.

We rounded a sharp corner and Tom's stretcher shook. He groaned but did not awaken. *Andy sent e-mails. Andy called. Andy got himself dead.*

Maybe Tom did not blame himself for what had gone wrong in the hijacking investigation. Maybe he didn't love some other woman. No matter what, it sounded as if he'd gotten himself emotionally connected with hapless, "gotta-talk-to-you" Andy Balachek. And if there's one thing they teach you in cop school, it's that you shouldn't let a criminal live rent-free in your brain.

CHAPTER 10

The ambulance made a slow, wide turn onto the castle drive, then moved through the open gates. I checked my watch: eight-ten. We thumped over the causeway across the moat and stopped in front of the gatehouse, where the medics swung open the back doors. With a glance at Tom, I scrambled out. Michaela Kirovsky, her white cloud of hair and pale face the picture of concern, stood by the portcullis. She disarmed the castle security system and helped the medics set up a portable ramp for all the stairs inside the castle. After much grunting, heaving, and clicking of ramp parts, Michaela and one of the medics managed to get Tom inside the castle. An eternity later, they pushed Tom's wheelchair toward our assigned suite.

Following them, I felt light-headed with fatigue and hunger. I was thankful we had not run into the Hydes. Still, goose bumps raced down my skin. Why did I feel we were being watched? I glanced around for closed-circuit cameras, but saw nothing except stones, windows, and fading tapestries. Once I thought I caught movement out of the corner of my eye, but whatever it was disappeared before I actually saw anything. Just the day before, though, I'd decided I'd imagined a noise only seconds before our picture window was blown to fragments. I hadn't believed I'd seen something in the creek, and it had turned out to be poor Andy Balachek. So if I was persuaded I'd seen something out of the corner of my eye, then perhaps I *had*. I stopped and looked all around again: Nothing. Maybe I was just tired.

Michaela told me that Eliot and Sukie were out having breakfast, even though Julian had offered to make them his vegetarian Eggs Benedict. She brightened, and added that Julian was making breakfast, anyway, and had promised to go grocery shopping after he left Arch off at Elk Park Prep.

"I'll tell you," Michaela said with a wide grin, as I finished straightening the covers over Tom. "I love having that kid around. He works. You stay here much longer, I'm going to get lazy."

I smiled. Yes, Julian was a blessing. But hale-and-hearty Michaela drifting into laziness was impossible to imagine.

After Michaela and the medic left, Tom murmured, "I feel helpless."

"You're not helpless, you just need rest," I replied. My hands traced circles on the green-and-pink coverlet. I prayed that Tom wouldn't start up again on the subject of Andy Balachek.

"I've been here before, you know," he said mildly. "The castle."

"Investigating a case?" I asked, surprised.

"Not exactly." He chuckled. "Checking to see if the owner was a loony bird." He raised his jaunty, sand-colored eyebrows at me.

"What do you mean?" I demanded.

"It's a long story. I'll tell you later." He tried to shift his weight. "You stayed in a client's home once before," Tom reminded me. "Didn't turn out too well, as I recall."

"That was a family thing," I replied. Arch's and my brief stay with Marla's sister had indeed not turned out well. "This is business—"

My protest was silenced by twin thudding knocks at the door: Arch and Julian. They tumbled into the room, clustered around Tom, and demanded to know how he was feeling.

"Need chocolate?" asked Julian. "I was thinking of making cookies or cake after I get back from the grocery store. Plus I just put a frittata and some rolls into the oven. They'll be done in about ten minutes."

"Maybe later." Tom's smile was thin. My heart squeezed in sympathy. "Arch." He tilted his head at my son. "I need to laugh. I need to hear some jokes. It'll make me feel better."

"I just had to write a poem for my *Shakespeare and His Times* class," Arch piped up, straightening his glasses. "I could read that to you, if you want."

"I do," Tom said, with a small grin.

Arch pulled a sheet of paper out of his backpack. He warned, "It's, you know, *aa, bb, cc, dd,* like that." He poised himself at the foot of the carved four-poster bed. He cleared his throat twice, then read:

Two enemies met in a foreign field,
Each pointed his spear; each clasped his
bright shield.
I watched from afar, to see the pair fight,
Chivalry would bind them! Each was a
knight.
Their horses raced forward; a cold wind
blew;
One knight was gored; the spear went
right through!
Bloodied, he fell; the terrain was rocky.
"Wow!" I thought. "This is worse than
hockey!"

It was nice to have a laugh; it was great to be together. After a moment, Tom said he needed rest. Julian and Arch raced off for the kitchen, while I sat at Tom's side. By the time Julian poked his head back into the suite to invite me down for rolls, frittata, fresh fruit, Cheshire cheese, and tea, Tom was asleep. The Elizabethans hadn't eaten frittata, I was pretty sure. Nor, I'd been surprised to learn in my research, had they drunk tea. But having substituted packaged crackers for regular meals for the past twenty hours, I was ravenous. The heck with food history. Besides, I couldn't remember what the Elizabethans had for breakfast. That's what I was going back to our house for, right? To get the disk with all my research. I promised Julian I'd be right down.

When I entered the enormous kitchen moments later, Julian, Arch, and Michaela were already sitting at the oak trestle table. A cozy fire crackled in one of the kitchen hearths. Soon, I was slathering one of Julian's hot rolls with soft butter and homemade plum jam that Michaela had retrieved from Eliot's backup stash in the dining room. Heaven. The creamy, custardlike texture of the frittata provided a tangy complement to the sharp cheese. Relishing the delicious breakfast, I recalled that, indeed, Queen Elizabeth herself *had* indulged in enormous breakfasts—before she went hunting. I told Arch, Michaela, and Julian as much as I could remember of one menu: cold sausages and powdered neat's tongue. Arch asked what a neat was, and I replied that "neat" was an archaic term for cow or ox. Michaela grinned and served us steaming cups of strong English Breakfast tea. I asked Arch how the fencing was going.

"Pretty well," he answered cautiously, wary of appearing boastful in front of his coach.

"He's done brilliantly," Michaela declared as she split her third roll and piled the center with cheese slices. "I'm going to have him be part of our demonstration Friday night."

Arch blushed. Julian slyly added, "That's not because your former girlfriend is on the team? Maybe Lettie—"

"Stop!" warned Arch. His face had turned scarlet. I decided to say nothing. Arch had kept me in the dark about his post-Christmas breakup with Lettie, also fourteen. When he'd told me after the fact, he said that he wasn't going to tell me the reasons, because then I would try to argue with them. Oh-kay, I'd said. Now I wondered idly if the breakup had been so bad that Lettie might have shot at our window.

I took another sip of tea and told myself not to be ridiculous.

"Couple of messages for you," said Michaela as she gathered up the dishes. "One, your tables were delivered yesterday morning to the chapel. Or rather, they weren't delivered. The police turned the delivery guys away. Eliot asked them to come back early on Thursday."

I sighed. If I hadn't had so much on my plate, I would have called Party Rental and told them what was going on. "Thanks."

"No problem. The police have given me the go-ahead to set up the chapel tomorrow. I'll be unpacking our space heaters, opening our own serving tables and folding chairs, and setting up our screen for Eliot's slides." She paused. "Eliot wants to review the menu with you this afternoon. If you're up to it."

I nodded. "No problem. And the second message?"

"Two detectives want you to call them." She handed me a note with the names of Boyd and Armstrong, as well as their office and cell phone numbers. Then she loaded the rest of the dishes into the wood-paneled dishwasher, one of the kitchen's numerous disguised amenities. I thanked Michaela again for helping. She looked at the floor and said it was the least she could do, after what we'd been through.

After the boys had been assured that Tom and I would be *fine, just fine,* they gathered up Arch's gear and Julian's grocery list—he insisted he was making dinner tonight for everybody—and hustled down to Julian's Rover. From one of the narrow windows in the well tower, I watched them roar away.

Back in our room, Tom was still sleeping. I knew I had to go back to our house. I needed to check on the animals, too, and so I used the phone—a portable device placed in our magisterial bathroom, which I hadn't seen when we'd first arrived—to call Trudy. She reported that Jake the bloodhound and Scout the cat were in good shape. She'd collected today's mail and would continue to do so until we were home again. The police had come by early this morning, she said, and told her that deputies were working hard on the Balachek murder and the window shooting.

"Everybody on the street's watching the place till then," Trudy added. "We're even keeping track of unfamiliar license plates."

I murmured that that wasn't necessary. But Trudy interrupted me, her voice insistent. "There's a strange car out there right now. It looks as if the driver is keeping a close eye on your place."

"Is it someone from the sheriff's department?"

"I don't think an unmarked car would be covered with rust, Goldy. Plus, a cop would be more obvious. This guy is being *very* surreptitious. Actually, it's a woman."

My skin turned to ice. "Trudy, are you sure she's watching *our* house—"

"Goldy, she's been sitting in her car for two hours now. She's hiding behind a newspaper. I know she's not reading it because when I took out my binoculars, I could see her eyes peering over the top of the paper. I'm telling you, she's just *staring* at your broken window."

CHAPTER 11

"Did you c-call the sheriff's department?" I asked, cursing the choke in my voice.

"Not yet. The woman hasn't actually *done* anything. I took Jake out there on a leash, though, so I could talk to her. I said we'd just had a shooting on our street and that there were cops all over."

"What did she say?"

"She asked if anyone had been hurt. I said no and very obviously looked inside her car for a weapon. She didn't have one, or at least, not one that I could see. She said she was waiting for someone. When I asked who, she just drove away. Then a while ago, she came back."

It was as if I'd been punched in the solar plexus. Could it be Viv? If the Jerk's new girlfriend was haunting our street, I would sic Jake on her myself. "Is she skinny, with white-blond hair, big boobs, and a sort of rock-star face? Late twenties?"

"Nah, she's older," Trudy replied promptly. "Probably fifty. Dark hair. Pretty face, but weathered. Looks like she might be tall and slender. Maybe she's an ex-model who wants Tom to do some investigating for her. Anyway, she doesn't look like one of John Richard's bimbos, if that's what you're worried about."

I thanked Trudy and told her I'd be home soon. Then I replaced the receiver, filled a glass of water for Tom, and went back into our room. Holding the glass, I stared out the leaded-glass windows lining the wall of the suite. A snow flurry sent swirls of thick flakes into the moat. *She didn't look like one of John Richard's bimbos....*

"I'm awake," Tom said from the bed. Was that a suspicious note in his voice, or was I being paranoid again? "Miss G.? Want to tell me what's going on?"

"I need to get my computer disk with the research for this week's food prep," I replied lightly. I didn't mention the woman lurking on our street. Why worry Tom when he was immobilized? On the other hand, I was *not* going back to our place without giving the cops—that is, the cops who could do something—advance warning. I needed to call Sergeants Boyd and Armstrong. I went on, "I also have to get a picture of the Jerk, so that the Hydes can know not to let him in." *And I have to check out that woman,* I added silently. Not to mention that my curiosity was demanding a trip down to the creek. If the sheriff's department was no longer processing the crime scene, I wanted to have a look at the place myself.

"I don't think it's a good idea for you to go home alone," Tom replied. "And did you talk to A.D.A. Gerber about visitations for Arch?" So he was worried about John Richard Korman, too. Good old Tom.

"Not yet. On my way over, I'll call Boyd and Armstrong on the cellular. Not to worry. I'll be fine at the house. Plus, Trudy will be right next door. How are you doing?"

"I'm bored. I want to get up and call my office. I want to get cracking on this case."

I kissed his cheek, which smelled of rubbing alcohol. "I shouldn't be gone more than an hour," I promised, as I handed him the water glass and a long straw. "Unless by some miracle the window repair guy shows up. Then I'll stay and supervise."

"I'll be fine," Tom assured me, stubbornly placing the glass on the end table. "Just find me a portable phone, would you?"

I brought him the phone from the bathroom, then left. As I drove down the castle driveway, I put in a cell call to Sergeant Boyd's voice mail: I was headed to our house, I reported, since I had to pick up a few things, and hoped to meet him there. Oh, and a neighbor had reported a strange woman hanging out in a car across the street. Could the sheriff's department check it out?

The snow flurry ended. In its wake, winds in the upper atmosphere had left feathery traces of cirrus clouds. I crossed Cottonwood Creek and waited for the traffic to clear. Below, the narrow stream furrowing through ice banks winked in the winter sunlight. As I passed the bridge that led to the chapel, two uniformed sheriff's deputies stood outside the yellow crime-scene ribbons, conferring with Eliot and Sukie.

Next to the Hydes' matching silver Jaguars was another, newer Jag. To my horror, I recognized the car and its driver. Leaning against her sleek black vehicle, her arms crossed, was Chardé Lauderdale. She lifted her eyes and glanced at the road as I drove by. Recognizing me, she immediately turned back to the Hydes.

Clearly, I would have to return at a later time.

I stepped on the accelerator and the tires spun in the snow-frosted road. I needed to see what was going on at our house.

She was alone, sitting up very straight in the driver's seat of a beat-up, rust-spotted station wagon that had once been white. The car was parked directly across the street from our house. I drove by slowly and looked at the woman. She had shoulder-length black hair dramatically shot with gray, and Trudy was right: her unmade-up, slender face was quite beautiful.

Hmm.

She wasn't so much staring at our house as gazing at the framed crag that had been our living-room window. To keep out snow and deter looters, the cops had put up plywood behind what was left of the glass. If the woman was a crook or even the shooter, she wasn't acting very smart. A criminal simply didn't sit out here in the open in a small-town neighborhood, waiting to have her license plate recorded by an armed Neighborhood Watch.

Further up the street, I pulled into a driveway. I was about to reverse when I heard an engine revving, then groaning, like a sports car being downshifted. I felt a familiar unease. Glancing in the rearview mirror, I saw a shiny gold Mercedes descending our street. A laughing Viv Martini, her luminescent hair rippling in the frigid breeze from her open window, sat in the passenger seat. The driver was the Jerk.

I hunched over the steering wheel until they'd passed our house. They continued down to Main Street, then turned left, in the direction of the Grizzly Saloon. I waited five minutes and tried to catch my breath. What in heaven's name were *they* doing *here*? Even if the Jerk was looking for Arch, he had to know he was in school. Or had he heard about Tom's shooting and hoped to find a hearse in our driveway? Maybe Viv would get the flu from exposure to the elements.

I turned and piloted my van back toward our house. I eased into Trudy's driveway, hopped out, and headed toward the station wagon.

The woman in the wagon looked about fifty or fifty-five. She was even more lovely than I'd first thought, with high cheekbones, wide-set eyes, a full, sensuous mouth, and delicate chin. Now she tore her gaze from our front door to give me a perplexed glance. She didn't *look* like a crook, she *looked* like Jackie Kennedy. She certainly didn't seem like someone who knew her way around a gun. My legs wobbled the last few steps to the car, but I was *not* going to be scared off my own street.

"I'm Goldy Schulz," I announced with a courage I was far from feeling. "Are you from the window repair shop?"

The woman's mouth fell slightly open, and the gorgeous face darkened. I peered boldly into the station wagon. She wore a green sweatshirt with jeans, and no discernible jewelry. A newspaper and thermos were perched on the tattered seats. No tools, no plate glass. No weapon. No camera, either, trademark of the tourists who flood our rustic mountain town in the summer. And of course, this was winter.

So what was she doing here?

"I'm just waiting," the woman replied, as if she'd read my mind. Her voice sounded as rusty as the exterior of the wagon, and she spoke

131

in a half-whisper, as if English were her second language.

Shouting my name, Trudy launched out her front door with our howling bloodhound in tow. Red-haired and pear-shaped, Trudy has the kind of complexion that turns crimson when she is upset. The mystery woman turned the key in her ignition as Jake, bellowing mightily, tugged Trudy in our direction. Before I could think of another thing to say, such as *Do you need directions to Main Street?*, the station wagon had roared off.

"What was *that* about?" Trudy demanded. "What did she say?"

"Nothing." I took Jake's leash from her and ordered him to be quiet. He ignored me.

"A piece about that Balachek boy's body in the creek was on TV this morning. All the Denver channels. Did you see it?" When I shook my head, Trudy continued, "They also showed the front of your house and that window. They had a bit about Tom, too. Was Tom investigating Andy Balachek? The reason I ask is that a couple of nosy media people have called *me* wanting to know if it was a case of vengeance run amuck. Andy shoots out a cop's window, the cops gun down Andy."

"That is ridiculous!" I said fiercely.

"That's what I told them." Trudy nodded, as if to confirm the absurdity of such a notion. She squinted in the direction the old station wagon had taken. "Anyway, after all the fuss in the news, I guess you have to figure you're going to get some gawkers."

Maybe so. But that gal hadn't looked like a gawker. I couldn't concentrate to wonder further about the mysterious woman in the wagon, though, because Jake chose that moment to put his paws on my chest and slobber on my face.

I pulled out of the way to avoid being drowned. "Take Jake back to your place for a bit, would you?" I begged Trudy. "I need something from the house, and I don't want him stepping on glass and cutting his paws."

Jake howled mournfully as he was led away. I wanted to comfort him, but was distracted by a pickup now chugging up our street. Large rectangles wrapped in brown paper sat propped in the truck's rear. Were the rectangles large enough to be picture-window panes? Or would that be too good to be true?

The grizzled man driving the truck introduced himself as Morris Hart from Furman County Glass. Morris was amazingly bowlegged, with a voice like sand and a wide, deeply wrinkled face. I thought I smelled booze on him, but couldn't be sure. He asked if I was Goldy Schulz, and could I give him the okay to get started. The job should take an hour or two, he added optimistically. Despite the slight stench of whiskey—it *could* be on his clothes, I thought hopefully—I replied that he should begin as soon as possible, that I could stay until he was done, if he wanted. Then I zipped up to the door and let myself in.

The front room was dark because of the plywood. I turned on a light. The sudden sparkle of glass shards gave the place a desolate, abandoned air.

In the kitchen I retrieved my recipes-and-research disk. Outside, Morris Hart's ladder creaked open. I touched the blinking button on the message machine. Maybe Boyd had called to say he was on his way. Once our window and security system were fixed, would he think it was safe for us to move back in? Or would he want us to wait until the department figured out who had fired the gun at our house?

The first message on my tape dropped my spirits back to the nether zone.

"Goldy Schulz?" Chardé Lauderdale began, her Marilyn Monroe voice high and breathless. "How *dare* you tell the police that we shot at your house! After all you've put my husband and me through, don't you think it's time for you to *stop* your *hate* campaign against us? You discuss our conflict with anyone, and you can just add a little *defamation* suit from *us* to your list of woes. And by the way, we understand you will be doing some cooking for a group of donors to which we belong. This makes us *very* unhappy. We are demanding that the hosts find someone else to do that job *immediately*."

What was Chardé reading from? A text supplied by her lawyer? Or her child-abusing husband? Hard to believe that the former Miss Teen Lubbock could be so articulately bitchy. When I called the cops after her husband had shaken their tiny daughter to unconsciousness, all she'd managed to screech was, "Who the *hell* do you think you are?"

On our tape, Chardé went on stiffly: "If you persist in trying to harm us, we *will* retaliate. And not just in court," she concluded breathily, in what sounded like an afterthought.

Hmm. How 'bout I save this message, I thought, to play for the cops? Ever hear that making *a threat of bodily harm* is a *crime,* babe?

I put in another call to Boyd and was again connected to his voice mail. It was half past nine, I said, and I could wait for him at our house, meet with Armstrong and him in town, or see them later at the castle. His choice. The window repairman was here, I added, and I was grateful to the department for getting the repairs started so soon. Any chance the cleaning team could come in this week?

Hanging up, I suddenly felt that I had to get back to the castle. Tom might be in pain. But something was holding me back, and it wasn't just the window repair, which Trudy could supervise, if necessary. *That kid was the king of communication. Loved e-mail,* Tom had said. Andy Balachek had ended up dead in Cottonwood Creek...and somebody had taken a shot at Tom.

I don't love her. Don't love *whom?*

My eyes traveled to the kitchen's south wall. After dinner most nights during January, Tom had walked dutifully through that door to the basement. In the cellar, he had his own computer to type up reports, write notes on cases, send e-mails....

How much investigating of the Andy Bal-achek case would Tom be able to do from the castle? Probably not much. Unless, of course, I helped him by downloading his files.

This is not because I'm nosy, I thought as I headed down the basement steps. I mean, Tom was the one who kept saying he needed to work, that he wanted to get back to the case, right? And there might be files on this computer that he would need. Maybe he even kept an e-mail address book with Andy Balachek's screen names. This was all data he would need, data I could bring him. To be helpful.

Uh-huh.

Tom's computer sat on a massive, scuffed, department-discard desk that was piled neatly with files and papers. Morris Hart, the window guy, banged and clattered above as I booted Tom's computer. While the machine hummed, I scanned Tom's desk for other files he might need. Or, perhaps, that *I* might want to have a look at.

What am I doing?

Before this trickle of self-doubt could become a deluge, I stared at the demand for a password, then blithely typed in *chocolate,* the password Tom and I had laughed at when former clients had used it for their security gate. To my astonishment, the hard drive opened instantly. I slipped in my food-research disk and began to copy Tom's files. I wouldn't *look* at them— not without his permission. Not yet, anyway, I added to myself. I did, however, read the titles of the subfiles: *Balachek e-correspondence. Criminalistics course. Current cases. History.*

"Mrs. Schulz?" Morris Hart cried from above.

Startled, I composed myself and called that I was in the basement and would be up in a few minutes. But Hart schlepped across the kitchen floor, following my voice, then traipsed down the basement stairs. I clicked madly to finish my copying.

When he was two steps from the basement floor, I made my face impatient to hide my guilt. "I'm just going to be a minute or two longer."

"Sorry to bother you, but I have a high-powered vacuum to get up those glass shards. It has a tendency to blow fuses in older houses. Just wanted to warn you."

"Okay, okay," I said, resigned. "Just go ahead and start it." I worried briefly about our walk-in refrigerator. But with its surge protector and backup power source, it should be okay.

He grunted and tramped back up. *Copy, copy, copy,* the computer repeated as my disk filled up. *I won't read this material,* I kept telling myself. *I'm just being helpful here.*

I couldn't help it: I glanced back at the names of Tom's files. What did the file named *History* cover? Tom really wouldn't mind if I took a quick peek, surely?

I clicked on the file, which contained subfiles with dates. "S.B., January 1." And "S.B., January 3." "Follow-up, January 4." Then,

"Conv. W/State Dept., January 5." The State Department? U.S. or Colorado? And who was S.B.? I opened the file from the first of January, when I'd been dealing with the aftermath of the Lauderdales' party. The file contained an e-mail with the following text:

Do you remember me? You said you'd love me forever.
Your S.B.

My throat was suddenly dry. I should not be doing this, I thought. Curiosity can kill a cat...or a marriage. Still, I had to know. Without reading more, I copied all the rest of the e-mails onto the disk. My mission complete, my heart aching, I quit the program, ejected the disk, and slipped it into my jeans pocket.

I was shutting down the computer when there was an explosion behind me. Or was it *on* me? A cold, dark pain filled my head. I realized that someone had hit me, was hitting me, again and again and again. My skullbones reverberated in agony.

My sight clouded, then went black. I screamed for help and tried to cover my head, turn around, anything. I couldn't catch my breath. I'd been listening to the roar of the vac upstairs, reading Tom's personal correspondence—

My attacker hit me again and my chin slammed into Tom's desk. My knees crumpled and I was sliding, helplessly, whimpering, trying to cover my head, my body afire with pain. *This isn't fair.* Was I saying it or thinking it? *Damn, damn,* my inner voice supplied. My knees and then my body banged onto the basement's cold floor.

John Richard had never said he'd love me always. But Tom had. The day of our wedding. *I'll love you forever, Miss G. Forever and ever.*

As unconsciousness claimed me, I remembered Tom's handsome face that happy day, and the sound of his warm promise.

I'll love you forever.

CHAPTER 12

Getting banged up is bad. Gaining consciousness is worse. From my years with the Jerk, I was acquainted with sledgehammer-wedged-in-the-skull pain. The worst part is that you suspect that if you'd used the brain *inside* your head in the first place, this might not have happened to you. I'd been told that *an independent janitorial service* was going to clean up the glass. Not some guy masquerading as a window fixer. *Damn again,* I thought. *You idiot.*

Yeah, yeah, Tom had said something about not blaming yourself when you screwed up. So: Wracked with pain, lying sprawled on our basement floor, drowning in self-recrimination, I tried to talk myself into getting up on my feet again and calling for help. After agonizing minutes of thinking about moving, then searching for the least painful way to stand, I fought off nausea, trembling, and visual black clouds to get to my feet. Once upright, I gingerly touched my head until I found the beginnings of a lump. Agh! I sighed and looked around. Tom's desk was clean, as in, nothing on it anymore. No papers. No files.

No computer.

I blinked and swayed dizzily. My watch said ten-thirty. I walked—slowly, taking steadying breaths—up the stairs, into my kitchen. I called and looked all around; no attacker in sight. Did we have any painkillers in the house? My brain offered no answer. In fact, my thinking was extremely fuzzy, even as to the location of the Cognac I used to make Cherries Jubilee. Everything in the kitchen seemed turned around...or different.

Wretchedly, I realized that things seemed unfamiliar because the smashed monitor of my kitchen computer lay on the floor beside the keyboard. The kitchen computer itself was *also* missing.

I started to cry. Then I yelled and cursed. Of course, there was no question that folks on the street might hear me. But I didn't care what the neighbors thought. My own shouted curses miraculously seemed to clear my brain, at least until I could pour myself a glass of Cognac from the dining-room cabinet. Of course, I'd learned in Med Wives 101 that you didn't treat a head injury with alcohol, but my brain was screaming for reprieve from the pain. I had just taken a first naughty swallow when the front doorbell bonged, making my head spin. Great, I thought, things couldn't get much worse.

I peered through the peephole at the smiling faces of Sergeants Boyd and Armstrong. Not exactly in the nick of time, were they?

"Somebody broke in," I announced bluntly as Boyd, his barrel-shaped body somewhat rounder than the last time I'd seen him, came through the door.

"Here? Just now?" asked Boyd, eyeing me, my trembling hand, and my glass of brandy.

When I replied in the affirmative, Armstrong, whose towering frame and fierce face contraindicated what I knew to be his gentle demeanor, said, "You look as if you're in pain." Since I'd seen him last, he'd lost a few more of the sparse brown hairs he combed so diligently over his bald spot.

I said, "I am. Got knocked over the head. But...come on out to the dining room. I know the two of you won't have a glass of booze while you're on duty. Before lunch, no less. But I'm treating a nasty bump."

Boyd and Armstrong told me to wait. In the front hallway, they insisted on separately assessing my noggin, which involved painful pressing on my head, then unblinking assessment of my eyes. Both decreed I should see a doctor that day.

"I can't. I have to go back to Tom. He's resting at Hyde Castle."

"You need to get attention," Boyd insisted.

"Look, thanks, but I'm aware of the symptoms of severe head injury," I replied. "Blurred vision, slurred speech, nausea, loss of memory, fainting, and sleeping too much. If I show any of those signs, I'll call for help. Scout's honor."

Armstrong's scowl deepened. "Show us where this happened."

"I was sitting there," I said after I'd led them to the bottom of the cellar steps. I indicated Tom's swivel chair. "I was whacked from behind." I felt inside my jeans pocket and repressed a sigh of relief. The disk was still there. I knew I should mention to Boyd and Armstrong that I'd downloaded Tom's files. But I couldn't. Not yet, anyway. I couldn't even think. In fact, I did feel a bit dizzy. But I'd be damned if I was going to any damn doctor on this damned day. Was *rage* a symptom of brain injury?

"Can we go back upstairs?" I asked them. "I need to sit down. You might want to look in the kitchen, because whoever it was stole *that* computer, too."

"You pass out on me, I'm gonna get fired," Boyd announced glumly as we headed up the stairs. In the kitchen, Boyd called for help on his radio while I tossed out the rest of the brandy and made myself an espresso. The computer thief wouldn't have left prints on my coffee machine, would he?

"To process a crime scene," Boyd concluded to the dispatcher.

To process a crime scene at the Schulzes' house, again.

142

"Can we sit in the dining room?" Armstrong asked me. "We need to get through some questions."

In the dining room, Boyd opened what looked like the same smudged notebook he'd carried for years. I wondered if he ever bought new ones.

"So what were you doing in the basement?" he began gently. "I mean, what were you doing when you were sitting at Tom's desk? Working on his computer?"

His black eyes bored into me. I swallowed. "No, not on the computer. I was...looking on Tom's shelves, for our photo albums. I need a picture of John Richard Korman. You know, my ex. He was released last Friday. The Hydes want a photograph of him, since they need to know what he looks like in case he tries to get into the castle."

"There were photo albums on the desk down there?" Armstrong looked skeptical.

"I'm not sure..." I lied. But I could *not* tell Boyd and Armstrong that I was seeking the identity of *her*. Moreover, I was not ready to admit I thought *a)* that my husband might be having an affair and *b)* that I was snooping around in his stuff to get the answer to *a)*.

"I need that picture," I repeated firmly. "And the photo albums are down there somewhere. I think," I added. I was trying to sound confused in the aftermath of the attack. I knew full well that our albums were in an upstairs closet.

"If they're in the basement, we can't get them

now. We'll taint the crime scene," Armstrong murmured. "Do you have any ideas who might have hit you?"

I told them about the bowlegged man who'd showed up claiming he was sent to fix the window. I also told them about the woman in the car. Trudy would be eager to talk about the mysterious beauty in the station wagon, I said, and she had her license plate number, too. Armstrong checked to see if either the glass truck or the car was still outside. Neither was.

"Could you *please* tell me about Andy Balachek?" I asked when he returned.

Boyd sighed. "They finished the autopsy last night. Did it extra fast because Tom was shot at the scene. But Goldy," he added hastily, "we need to run through what happened with the window shooting first. Who you think might have done it and why. It may be connected to this attack on you. Then we'll talk about Balachek."

And so, for the third time, I told my story. I played Chardé's message for them. They asked for the tape and I gave it to them.

"There's something else," I added. "I saw Chardé Lauderdale at the hospital while I was waiting to see how Tom was."

Boyd stopped scribbling and looked up, frowning. "What was she doing?"

"Nothing. Standing at the waiting-room window."

Boyd and Armstrong exchanged a look. Then Boyd took a deep breath. "Mrs. Laud-

144

erdale has already complained to Captain Lambert about being questioned over your window shooting. She gave him an earful, especially since she and her husband keep getting calls about the child-abuse case. I guess the newspaper article didn't help."

I shuddered when I thought back to the sensationalist *Mountain Journal* headline: "Caterer in Hot Water Over Attempt to Save Child." I said, "I'm supposed to see the Lauderdales Thursday at a lunch I'm catering. Chardé'll probably behave herself there. And if she shows up here or at the castle, I'll call you right away."

"All right," said Boyd, nodding. "Now we need to know about what happened yesterday morning after you left here, up to the point where Tom was shot."

I recited the events of the previous morning. I added that I hadn't heard back from Pat Gerber, and they mumbled something about the A.D.A. being the hardest person in the county to reach. I told them Eliot and Sukie Hyde had been extraordinarily nice and welcoming.

Boyd said, "Tell us about finding Balachek."

I hesitated. Boyd and Armstrong worked well together. They dug for the right data and usually shed light on a case. Before, when I'd wanted information on an investigation that involved someone I knew, I'd had to wheedle it out of them. Now I needed their theory on who had murdered Andy Balachek and why.

It was highly probable, I reasoned, that Andy's killer either shot Tom or knew who had. But looking at their impassive, suspicious-cop faces, I was reminded of oysters that no pliers were ever going to open.

"I had to check the chapel to see if the portable dining tables had been delivered for the luncheon. When I parked and looked down at the creek, Andy was in it." Boyd and Armstrong waited for me to go on. I asked, "So what was the cause of death?"

When they resolutely said nothing, I thought back. Andy had been wearing a lumberjack plaid shirt and jeans. I didn't remember seeing a jacket on him, much less blood staining his clothes. What he had had was...wait.

"His hands were black," I exclaimed. "Was he tortured before he died? Then someone shot him and threw his body there?" The oyster faces looked mildly surprised. I was right. "Now are you going to tell me what your theory is?"

Boyd shook his head. "We don't know who dumped Balachek in the creek." He stabbed a stubby finger at me. "And you, Sherlock, can't divulge anything about the color of his hands."

"Was he shocked electrically?" I asked. They groaned. I pressed on. "Seems as if I remember somebody else dying of electrocution. The former spouse of someone at the castle, yes? Ring any bells?"

Again, the two cops looked at one another. Boyd sighed. "Carl Rourke, Sukie Hyde's first husband, died in a freak electrical accident while working on a roof."

146

"Do you think there's any correlation between the two deaths?" I asked.

"Not yet," Armstrong said. "I repeat, Goldy, you can *not* talk about Balachek's burned hands, or the possibility of electric shock, with *anyone*. It's a key."

Uh-huh. Before I could protest or reply, our doorbell rang again. Three men from the sheriff's department had arrived to process the basement. I showed them in, then murmured to Boyd and Armstrong that if they weren't going to share their theories on what had happened to Balachek, I really needed to get back to my injured husband.

"We'll be calling Tom," Boyd told me. "We've got copies of all of Andy's e-mails. Last one was ten days ago. Then he called you, wanting Tom. Said he was in Central City, but might go to Jersey after that. We're wondering if Balachek tried to communicate after that phone call. Like by another e-mail, phone call, whatever."

Maybe he sent Tom something by FedEx, I almost joked, but, for once, refrained. Had Tom mentioned anything else, they wanted to know?

Well, there's some woman. "No," I replied without looking at them. "He didn't. At least, not that I know of."

They said that was all for now, but they were staying at our house for a while, if that was all right. The doorbell bonged again and I went to get it. Thinking it was more cops, I pulled the door open without checking the peephole.

It was the Jerk, with Viv Martini at his side. He looked thin and pale, and his face seemed hard, a tad less confident. The effect of several months in prison, no doubt. He wore charcoal pants, a yellow pullover, and what looked like a new reversible down jacket, black on one side, bright blue on the other, visible at the open neck. His still good-looking face, though, revealed a dark mood. Viv, with her thin face and body, spiked blond hair, black-heeled boots, tight black pants, and fashionably poufed black nylon jacket, looked as if she were on her way to a stint with a punk rock band. When she unzipped the jacket, a tight V-neck revealing her significant cleavage sprang into view.

"Get out here," ordered John Richard, his command rigid with anger.

Without saying a word, I slammed the door and dashed back to the dining room. I told Boyd and Armstrong what was going on and asked them to accompany me back to the porch. Just in case, I added.

Oh, my, how I delighted in the look of dismayed surprise that clouded the Jerk's face when the conspicuously armed Boyd and Armstrong stepped onto the porch behind me. When we were all outside—John Richard and Viv to one side, me with my cop buddies beside the porch swing—Sharks and Jets—I asked the Jerk what he wanted.

"I want my son." His voice was thick with the attempt to be simultaneously mean and conciliatory. "How dare you slap a restraining order

148

on me? It's a good thing it's temporary, because I am going to stomp you so bad in two weeks, you're going to wish you'd moved to Florida. I already got the story on what happened to you here, by the way."

"You're in violation of a restraining order, and you're out on probation, buster," said Boyd. "So watch your mouth. And if you move even an inch closer to your ex-wife, I'm going to arrest you."

"I wasn't talking to you," the Jerk retorted. Viv sidled closer to John Richard, slipped her hands around his waist, then slid her fingers inside his belt. John Richard stiffened and actually blushed.

"Move back, ma'am," Boyd ordered. This Viv did, but with a reluctant pout. John Richard gulped. His time in jail must have made him awfully horny. Apparently, he'd found just the right gal to meet his needs.

Boyd walked up to John Richard. He folded his arms, lifted his chin, and waited. John Richard took a step backward, right onto Viv's toes, and she squawked. I wondered if she was having the tiniest flicker of doubt about her new boyfriend's power. After a moment's hesitation, she took another precarious step back from John Richard. I felt... well... *triumphant.*

"I'll make arrangements for you to see Arch," I told John Richard. "Call your lawyer."

John Richard's voice was cold. His eyes stayed on Boyd. "We want to see him *today.* We're going to take him back to my place, not some stranger's castle, where *you* have to stay because somebody else *you* pissed off is taking potshots at windows in *your* house."

I looked at Viv, who widened her black-lined eyes at me. In a deep, sexy voice, she said, "Windows don't turn me on, Goldy."

I raised an eyebrow at her. "Mac user?"

"Knock it off," John Richard snarled.

"I'll call your lawyer," I repeated to him. "Now, leave. Please."

"You have not heard the last of this," John Richard said softly.

"Ooh," Viv murmured. She leaned toward the Jerk's ear and purred, "I love it when you threaten the rough stuff." As I shook my head, John Richard took Viv's hand and descended the porch steps.

"You haven't heard even the *beginning* of the last of this," John Richard shot over his shoulder.

How very unfortunate, I thought as he climbed into the driver's seat of the gold Mercedes. How very unfortunate, indeed.

CHAPTER 13

Head pounding, body aching, I trod upstairs, tossed a slew of outfits and odds and ends for Tom, Arch, and me into a large suitcase, and retrieved the canvas sack Tom had filled with our photo albums. There were bound to be several photos of the Jerk in one of the old books...enough for the Hydes and Michaela to get a good image of the guy who needed to be kept out of the castle.

And then the suspicious side of me, that voice I wished would be quiet, insisted I had one more thing I needed to do. I called to Boyd and Armstrong that I would be right down.

Rifling through Tom's bureau made me wish that Episcopalians were as big on confession as Catholics. Yes, "reconciliation of a penitent" was a sacrament available to us. But it wasn't so common among the Chosen Frozen that the thought of cleansing away my sin—in this case, deliberately invading my husband's privacy—made committing the sin any easier. So I felt like a heel. Still, if there were love letters, charge receipts, anything, I wanted to find them, because I needed to know *what was going on.* After five minutes of frantic searching, I came up with nothing. Of course not, I thought, as I carried the suitcase and heavy sack of albums down the steps. I didn't really think he'd cheat on me, did I?

The suspicious voice admitted that I wasn't sure.

Boyd heaved the suitcase and sack into my van, then turned to me. "I don't want you and Tom moving back in here until we catch these guys, understand? We're putting a twenty-four-hour guard on the house, starting now."

I sighed, but nodded. Boyd told me to call anytime if I needed help. I promised I would. I thanked him for helping with Dr. Korman

151

and for pulling together a team to watch our place. He nodded impassively. When he walked back to the house, I saw Trudy and Jake watching him from her window. Jake's morose face about broke my heart.

I sat in my van and tried to think. My head throbbed. I couldn't face another historic-food discussion with Eliot Hyde just then. John Richard knew Arch was in school. His appearance at our house must have been meant to intimidate me. For a moment, I savored the memory of that astonished look on his face when confronted with two armed cops.

But what about the mystery woman who'd been sitting in the rusty station wagon? Did she know we were staying at the castle? Had she followed me there after shooting out the window?

Was she the one who'd shot Tom? Was she the one Tom didn't love?

I glanced around at the sack of photo albums on the floor. That suspicious voice again wormed its way into my brain…maybe *this* was where he'd stashed his credit card receipts for flowers, motel visits, jewelry. On the other hand, perhaps being whacked on the head and sustaining a visit from a violent narcissist unleashed more industrial-strength paranoia in the cerebral cortex.

I dug reluctantly into the bag of albums. As it turned out, Tom had purchased another photo album since our wedding. He hadn't mounted anything in it, but he'd tidily rubber-banded the photos from the last year and

152

stuck them inside. Guilt juiced through my veins when I saw Tom's pictures of me barbecuing for our little family's first picnic, of Julian standing by the fountain at the University of Colorado student union. I scooped up the photos and slapped them back inside the new album. Then, unable to help myself, I finished my nefarious snooping task, shaking each of our old albums to see if any incriminating papers fell out.

An old envelope dropped to the van floor. I bent and retrieved it. Inside was a snapshot of John Richard in his white doctor coat. His blond hair tousled, his hands in his pockets, he was smiling with all the charm that had hypnotized so many women—me included. I didn't remember saving the picture, but perhaps I had and just didn't recall. Or maybe Arch, ever the idealist when it came to his father, had tucked it away. I slipped the picture back into the envelope and dropped it into my purse.

Finally I reached Tom's own ancient album. When I shook it, newspaper articles and stray photos cascaded into my lap. "Army Veteran Graduates First," screamed a proud headline of the Furman County Sheriff's Department newsletter, detailing Tom's triumphant graduation at the top of his class from police academy. "Top Cop Honored" was another one, for the time Tom had received an award for finding a group of paintings stolen from a Denver art dealer and stashed in an Aspen Meadow garage. Then there was a much older

153

photograph: Tom in his Cub Scout uniform, curly sandy-brown hair, chubby cheeks, crooked smile.

It was too much. I cracked open the yellowed pages of the old album and admired each photo of my dear Tom. As I worked my way through the book, I tried to replace each item I'd shaken loose in its original order.

Page after page showed Tom with school friends, in his army uniform, with cop buddies. My suspicion turned to pride, then to bitter humiliation for doubting him. He had been delirious after he'd been wounded yesterday, that was all there was to it. I had replaced nearly every article and photo when, suddenly, I was brought up short.

"Local Nurse Reported Killed in Mekong Delta Helo Crash" was the headline from a 1975 article. I stared down at it and recalled what I knew: that Tom had been engaged to a woman named Sara who'd been a few years ahead of him in high school. Sara had gone to nursing school and then been assigned to a Mobile Army Surgical Hospital, a MASH, in Vietnam. As soon as he turned eighteen, Tom had enlisted and followed her over. That was all that he'd told me, except that they'd never actually seen each other in that war-ravaged country before she was killed. But hadn't she died in an artillery shelling, not a helicopter crash?

There was a graduation photo of her in her white nurse's cap and uniform. Sara Beth O'Malley had been a pretty young woman with wavy dark hair and a face glowing with youth, enthusiasm, and pride. I swallowed. On the photo, she'd written: *Love you forever, S.B.*

I sat there for a long time. I'd seen her, of course. Her face was now thinner, the youthful glow long gone. But the years had not rendered her unrecognizable. I'd announced I was Goldy Schulz. *I'm just waiting,* she'd said, when I'd stared into the battered station wagon. She'd started the car and pulled away. I'd been so eager to suspect her that I hadn't registered—much less understood—her expression as she whipped the wagon away from the curb.

Her lips had trembled; her eyes had been filled with pain.

A cold wind rocked the van as I started down our street. Questions tumbled through my mind: *Is she really Sara? What was she doing here?* I remembered the title of one of Tom's e-mails. *Call to State Department.* Even worse, I wondered how in the world I was going to broach all this to Tom. *Hey, honey? Any old flames still burning?* I did wonder how someone who'd been reported dead in Vietnam could disappear for all these years. If the woman in the station wagon was Sara Beth O'Malley, where had she been for the last couple of decades?

And in the question department, I had a few more: Why had our computers been stolen? Could Sara Beth O'Malley have doubled back to pick them up? No...it had to have been "Morris Hart," whoever he was. Besides the e-mails from Sara Beth, there had been all those communications from Andy to Tom. Was Morris Hart connected somehow with the stamp thieves? Was he Ray Wolff's missing partner?

To the west, swirls of fog scudded in front of a thin cloud cover the hue of gray flannel. My stomach growled. It was already eleven forty-five of a morning that felt far too long and threatened snow. My body was not going to allow me another crisis-laden day without regular meals.

Nevertheless, there was a place I wanted to visit before returning to Hyde Castle. Some injuries you take very personally. Your husband being shot, for example. I did not know if the Hydes and Chardé would still be at the chapel, where I definitely wanted to look around. But another site I wanted to check was the one staked out by the shooter. No doubt, the Furman County Sheriff's Department would do a good job investigating. But an attempt on Tom's life was too traumatic for me to just go back to the day-to-day life of catering without making *sure* the department was doing a *thorough* job. I envisioned Tom rolling his eyes.

I turned left on Homestead Drive, wound past the Homestead Museum, then gunned the van through an old neighborhood dotted with rustic log cabins. The road changed from dirt to pavement, and I ascended through an upscale subdivision filled with gray and beige mansionettes sporting tile roofs and landscaped lawns that looked desolate under their dustings of snow. I hooked the van right onto a dirt road that quickly deteriorated to a rutted trail. The van had a compass display, which indicated I was heading east, paralleling Cottonwood Creek. I tried to picture what I'd seen from the police chopper, then decided I was heading toward the right spot.

Finally, I entered Cottonwood Park, a county-maintained facility where folks could hike, picnic, even camp overnight. I turned right onto another dirt road that looked as if it snaked down to the creek. I bumped past empty, snow-crusted picnic tables, forlorn-looking free-standing grills, and carved wooden signs indicating trailheads. At length I came to a stand of pines cordoned off with bright yellow police ribbons.

I parked behind a pair of sheriff's department vehicles and made my way down one edge of the yellow tape, where two uniformed officers yelled that I should stop. I identified myself and asked to come in to talk. They considered this for a minute, then signaled me to enter.

I scooted under the plastic ribbon. My boots slipped on the thick carpeting of snow-slick pine needles. The two cops asked for ID, which I showed them.

"I want to see where the guy was standing when my husband was shot. Please," I added politely.

"That area's been thoroughly checked for evidence," one officer informed me, his tone

157

simultaneously defensive and weary. When I said nothing, he softened a bit. "All right, the crime-scene guys are done. You can look, but just for a minute." He told me to follow him.

We made our way through the snow and rocks to a picnic table about fifteen feet from a promontory overlooking the creek. It seemed an odd place for a table, since the ground fell away steeply to the narrow state highway. If you or your kids tumbled down the rocks and onto the pavement, could you sue the county park system?

"We figure the shooter was about here," my guide told me as we stepped gingerly to the edge of the promontory. "Hidden from the road by the rocks, so no one would notice him."

The view revealed only the top of one of Hyde Castle's towers. Below the castle's driveway and dense evergreens, the trickle through Cottonwood Creek was alternately black and still or white with suds, in sharp contrast to the steep creek banks covered with ice and rocks. Hyde Chapel's lofty spires and dark stone made it look as if it had been transported from an Arthurian-legend board game. In the parking lot, where Tom and I had been moving toward each other when he was shot, a police car and the crime-lab van were the only vehicles. I could see the line of boulders where we'd sought cover. Andy Balachek's body, of course, was gone.

The chapel, the bridge, the parking lot, Andy's corpse: I stared down and tried to make sense of what I was looking at. Maybe the shooter was aiming for whatever cop found the body. But if a law-enforcement person discovered Andy, wouldn't the shooter be putting himself in the line of fire? Then again, Tom was a cop, and he'd been helpless against a concealed sharpshooter.

Maybe someone wasn't just looking for whoever found Andy. Perhaps he was aiming specifically for Tom. Or maybe he'd been aiming for me, and hadn't obtained a good enough angle the first time I'd hopped out of the van to look at the creek. Or possibly there was some other motive that I did not know. Maybe someone had followed Tom, wanting to shoot him. Maybe someone had followed me and shot Tom instead. The answer to *why* remained elusive.

Discouraged, head throbbing, thoughts roiling, I drove back to the castle. It was almost one o'clock. On the way up the winding driveway, I pulled to the side so that two painting-company vans could roar past. After parking, I lugged the suitcase and bag of photo albums to the entry and tapped in the gatehouse security code. Walking through the elegant stables-turned-living-room, I noticed a blotch of beige paint over the cream of the walls. Next to it was taped another *Wet Paint* sign. What was this, more rethinking of the paint scheme by Chardé the decorator? Just how close to the Hydes was she? Close enough for her husband, herself, and her painters to have the gatehouse keypad code?

In the huge kitchen, Marla and Sukie were downing sizzling, Julian-made cheese croquettes, along with the creamy Dijon and tart cranberry sauces I'd brought. Oh, well. I was going to have to make a new hors d'oeuvre for Thursday's labyrinth lunch anyway, and I didn't begrudge anyone any goodies. Sukie and Eliot were hosting our family *and* enduring the disruption a crime brings. And Marla *was* my best friend.

Eliot was off somewhere, Sukie informed me, studying Elizabethan games the kids could play Friday night. "He does not think bear-baiting would be enjoyed by the parents," she added with a soft giggle as she ran her hand through her flyaway blond hair. "He does want to talk to you," she added as she ladled more ruby-hued cranberry sauce onto a croquette.

"I want to apologize again for all the confusion yesterday," I told her. "We're very thankful you've taken us in."

She waved this away. "You must not worry! This is a good way for us to test having people stay here! It is practice for our future conferences."

I felt a sudden chill and looked around the kitchen. One of the old windows had come loose and swung open. As I hastened across to close it, I asked if anyone had checked on Tom recently.

Julian had been up to our room just ten minutes before. "He's asleep, Goldy," he said, without sounding reassuring. Julian's face was drawn. He seemed preoccupied, despite the coos of admiration from Marla and Sukie over his lovely lunch. Worried about Tom? Arch? Me?

Marla studied my face as I walked back to the table. "You look awful, Goldy, almost as bad as Julian. Are you okay? Where have you been? What took so long?"

I gestured to the suitcase and bag of albums and mumbled that I'd been getting them from the house. I handed the photo of John Richard to Sukie. "Here's the guy we need to bar from entry. I don't want to keep him from Arch, but he's very volatile, and an ex-con to boot. So when he does see Arch, it's going to have to be in a place with a lot of people." I omitted the part about the attack from the computer thief, because I didn't want to upset Sukie.

But Sukie's blue eyes were full of worry as she handed me back the photo. "You did miss a call, Goldy, from the assistant district attorney. Her name is Pat Gerber? She wants you to call her." She showed me the phone, tucked between the refrigerator and the glass-fronted kitchen cupboard of Eliot's meticulously labeled Elizabethan conserves. I peered in at rows of chokecherry and redcurrant jellies, strawberry conserve with Champagne, and plum jam. "This is just half of his insomniac production from this summer," she said airily. "I was beginning to think we should not have destroyed the stillroom."

As I dialed the district attorney's office, I wondered how toasted brioche would taste with the plum jam, or whether I could make a good Cumberland sauce with the currant jelly. I was put on hold and amused myself with the image of a latter-day Jay Gatsby fretting over a bubbling vat of conserve. When I was finally connected with Pat, she said that since I hadn't specified parental visitation for John Richard in the restraining order, he was squawking to anyone who would listen. If I could work it out with the lawyers, the best thing to do—since everything had become so acrimonious, Pat added—would be to take Arch to a neutral site for the hand-off. I suggested an Aspen Meadow counseling center that included such a service. Good idea, Pat agreed. I told her I'd call my lawyer about letting John Richard have Arch overnight.

"Sounds workable," she said. I should be prepared for a battle royal in two weeks, she went on, when the temporary order expired and we had to go before a judge and argue about permanent visitation orders. "John Richard's got a prison record, which should make some difference, but it may not, since he's got money and position in the community. And by the way, if he does make any threats against you, write them down," Pat advised sternly. "If you can, have witnesses."

What do you know, I thought, *that's already happened.* After we hung up, I scribbled down what had transpired at our house, put in a call to my lawyer, and outlined the overnight suggestion. He said he'd deal with the Jerk's lawyer, who had already left three messages for him. Unless I heard to the contrary, I

162

should drop Arch off at the counseling center today after fencing practice, around five-fifteen, with his overnight bag. Then I should pick up my son after school tomorrow. My heart sank as I hung up. Was this what I was looking forward to—a constant shuffling of poor Arch to and from his ex-con father?

Julian slid me a plate arranged with two hot croquettes and two small bowls of dipping sauces. The croquettes were crisp and crunchy on the outside, tasty with a homemade roux-binder and hot melted cheese on the inside. I made *mm-mm* noises and dunked the second one into both the spicy Dijon mustard and tart cranberry sauces. I virtuously declined more, saying I had to go check on Tom.

I wanted to see Tom, that was true. It was so much better than brooding about the Jerk. But in reality, I mused guiltily as I trod up the carpeted stairs to our suite, I wanted to boot up my laptop—assuming Tom was still asleep— and read all the contents of that disk with its revealing electronic mail.

But he was not asleep. He was talking on the portable telephone, which he carefully put on his end table when I entered the suite. I wondered with whom he'd been talking, wondered if I had the guts to confront him about his communication with Sara Beth O'Malley. Had his state of blood loss, pain, and shock meant he'd forgotten what he'd said to me by the creek?

Was I going to live the rest of my married life like this?

"Sheriff's department," he said matter-of-factly, gesturing at the phone. Then he eyed me suspiciously. "What happened to you? You're so late!"

"Oh, I got knocked out. Boyd will tell you all about it. Somebody stole our computers. How are you feeling?"

"*What? Who* knocked you out? Where? Miss G., I want you to tell me about it."

"I was at the house." I told him about being hit, the theft, the threatening visit of John Richard and Viv, and my trip to the shooter's perch. "So we won't be going home anytime soon." I omitted any mention of the mysterious appearance of Sara Beth O'Malley, because I just couldn't face talking about that. Yet.

Tom stared at me in stunned disbelief. "You put your life in danger for some pictures and a disk on *food*? Why didn't you just get a police shot of Korman and go to the *library* for cookbooks?"

"Because I typed up very specific stuff for Eliot Hyde."

"This is all my fault," Tom said angrily. He shifted in the bed, obviously in pain, obviously peevish. "Damn this case."

"Forget the case and just get better."

He groaned and thumped his pillow, unable to get comfortable on the big bed. "I'll get *better* if I can just figure out how Andy Balachek got himself killed, and who's beating up on my wife." He paused, then looked back at me. "The whole thing's strange...."

"I...saw Andy's blackened hands. Tom, was he electrocuted?"

"If I tell you, will you promise me not to go back into our house?" When I nodded, Tom said, "He was, but he didn't die of the shock. That's what's so weird. You get a huge electric shock, you figure you can't go far. Right?"

"Did Andy go *any*where?"

Tom's eyes were grim. "It looks as if he was electrocuted, then shot. Then the killer put him in the creek, and either hightailed it out of there, or sat and waited for me to show up."

CHAPTER 14

Marla slipped into the room without knocking. "Goldy!" she whispered. Her eyes glowed. "I have news!" Then she was instantly apologetic. "Sorry, Tom! I didn't knock because I thought you'd be asleep." She tossed her head of brown curls and lifted an eyebrow at me. "Come out into the hall if you want gossip about you-know-who and his you-know-what."

"Ah," I said, understanding Marla-speak for the Jerk and his sex life, the Jerk and his money, or both.

"I don't know about you girls," Tom teased. His mischievous smile vanished, however, when he moved his shoulder.

"Need a painkiller?" I asked, immediately concerned.

"No." Typical male response. "I just want some quiet. Go visit with Marla."

To Marla, I said, "Let's hear it."

She giggled and scurried out the door. I kissed Tom's forehead and told him I'd be back soon to check on him.

Animosity manifests itself in a number of ways, I thought as I avoided another *Wet Paint* sign in the hall. I possessed a *passive* defensiveness toward the Jerk. I never knew when he might attack, but I had learned not to let down my guard. *Active* animosity, on the other hand, was Marla's specialty. She fed her obsessive hatred for the Jerk with information. She paid her lawyer a separate monthly fee to employ investigators to keep tabs on our mutual ex-husband's shenanigans, sexual adventures, and—her favorite—his financial woes. From the triumphant tone in her voice, I suspected her latest news fell in the last category.

"You're not going to *believe* what he's up to now," she began eagerly, once we were standing beside one of the tall windows that overlooked the courtyard.

"Try me."

"Well," she reported, her face set in mock disapproval, "it's a shady financial deal."

"Begin at the beginning."

"My lawyer just called." She ran a bejeweled hand through her hair. "Okay, you remember when he had to sell the Keystone condo?" I nodded. To offset monetary setbacks the previous year, John Richard had been forced to auction off his ski resort condominium. According to Marla, the condo had been the setting of much debauchery. "Okay, then he had to go through the inconvenience of being incarcerated, so he had to sell his practice. He realized about six hundred thou from that, after taxes and whatnot. His legal fees have reduced *that* by about half. So he's back in his country-club house after...what? Serving less than five months of his sentence. Payments on the house are six thou a month and have never stopped. Add to that, paying you child support. On the plus side, his new salary at ACHMO is, don't puke, eight hundred thou a year."

"Eight hundred thousand dollars a year?"

"Uh, yeah. His lawyer landed him a job with the same HMO where his last girlfriend— the one he assaulted, let us not forget—once worked. Now John Richard is tightening up ACHMO's formularies for prescription drugs. So when you ask, *Who at my HMO sets up the rules to deny me prescriptions?* here's your answer: *The Jerk.*"

"He's ratcheted up his stinginess to a grand scale."

"No kidding." Marla went on: "Okay, you've got an idea of his income, assets, and liabilities. Plus he's got a prison record now, and getting a *new* mortgage is a tad difficult. So: How do you figure he's buying a three-million-dollar town house in Beaver Creek?"

"Three *million?*" I gasped. "You have got to be— Wait, maybe he got a signing bonus with ACHMO."

She shook her head. "Nope. Lawyer's investigator says ACHMO took a hammering when they gave their new CEO a monster signing bonus. The news made it into the *Post;* the stockholders went ballistic at the annual meeting. ACHMO doesn't give signing bonuses anymore. But you haven't heard it all."

I thought I detected the sound of distant yelling, coming from across the courtyard. "What was that?"

Marla glanced carelessly through one of the windows, then back at me. "Who knows? Now listen, the down payment on this place in Beaver Creek was three hundred thousand. My sources have their ways with the mortgage company, and report that he got a loan for a hundred fifty thou, equity from his place in the country club. His partner in the sale put up the other hundred fifty. Down payment done. Payments are interest only for the first six months, then a big balloon payment. And guess whose names are on the deed?"

"I can't."

"John Richard Korman and his new sidekick, Viv Martini."

"But...he *never* goes for joint ownership. It was one of my problems when we were doing the divorce settlement."

She waggled a finger at me. "Don't you think I know that? The sources inside the mortgage company—oh, don't give me that look, anyone can be bought. Anyway, my investigator says John Richard was making noises that *he* would be making the interest payments for six months. Viv has a modest income from gun sales. But when it came to that five-hundred-thousand-dollar balloon payment? *Viv* was the one asking about when the half-mil would be due, *exactly*, and if the mortgage company would take a check from *John Richard*'s account. My theory is that the balloon payment is *her* responsibility. Otherwise he wouldn't do the deal, don't you think? I'm also thinking they're planning on selling the place for a huge profit, after they make the balloon payment. And they both go away happy. Or at least filthy rich."

Filthy, indeed. "But if Viv Martini had a hundred fifty thou to blow, why latch onto the Jerk? Why would you do that kind of deal with someone you'd just started going out with?"

When Marla shrugged, her diamond dangle earrings sparkled. "He's cute. He's a doctor. What the hell, Goldy, why did *we* hook up with him?"

Because I loved him, I answered silently. Because he'd promised he loved me, too. *Duh.*

"Wait a minute." I tried to think. "Arch told me John Richard was going to give Viv something when he got out of prison. A Mercedes, he said. Or a trip to Rio. Or maybe a Mercedes and a town house, huh?" I shook my head. "But even if you set aside the hundred fifty thou, where does the half-mil for the balloon come from?"

Marla's smile broadened. "I figure it's a drug deal. Prescription meds, sold on the black market at a huge profit."

While Marla chattered about how she was going to have this or that friend of hers in Beaver Creek keep a lookout on everything John Richard and Viv did up there, I resolved to talk to Sergeant Boyd on the subject of Viv Martini. Boyd would be willing to tell me what the department knew, wouldn't he? Well...he might if I threatened to follow Viv until I found out what she was doing. *That* wouldn't only be time-consuming, it would be dangerous. On the other hand, I didn't reckon it would be as perilous as going into a financial partnership with the Jerk. Viv was either one tough babe, or she was dangerously smitten with Dr. John Richard Korman.

Marla said, "And you know those leather duds Viv wears, well, there's only one leather specialty shop in Beaver Creek, and the owner is a good friend of mine—"

I nodded, paying little attention. Last month, Furman County had been the scene of the murder of a FedEx driver and the theft of his three-million-dollar cargo. Yesterday, the body of one of the suspected hijackers had been found. *Now,* if I wasn't making too much of a leap, a former girlfriend of Ray Wolff, the guy accused of masterminding the robbery, was doing a big real estate deal with a doctor whose assault conviction might not be known in ultrachic Beaver Creek. Was John Richard scamming the HMO? Was it possible that Viv Martini was laundering money through real estate? How probable was it that John Richard was being taken for a ride by his new girlfriend? Maybe John Richard would have to go back to jail. A shiver of delight wriggled down my spine.

"What do you suppose is the attraction between those two?" Marla demanded, then answered her own question by launching into a monologue on the subjects of sex and money. I thought of something else: If Viv was *not* doing a drug or other underhanded deal *with* the Jerk, did *he* know how she was getting her money? He had to trust that she'd come up with the cash. Then again, maybe all she had to do was wrap herself around his torso and ask for the rough stuff.

"Listen," Marla went on breathlessly, "I've found out something else about John Richard that might interest you. Has to do with your current employer."

I gave her a skeptical look.

"According to Christine Busby, Sukie's great pal on the labyrinth committee? Sukie's a cancer survivor."

"So? Lots of people are, Marla."

She opened her eyes wide. "Cervical cancer. Detected by John Richard, who did Sukie's hysterectomy. She's been cancer-free for five years and can't say enough to Christine about how wonderful El Jerko is."

"But she didn't act as if she knew him when I mentioned his name. Or when I showed her his picture—"

171

"Hmm. She didn't confide in me about her illness, either. Maybe she doesn't want to spill her secrets to her beloved ex-doctor's ex-wives."

"Marla, I need to tell Tom—"

Before I could finish articulating that thought, two people appeared on the far side of the courtyard. Both in hooded winter coats, they seemed to be arguing beneath the ground-level arcade that enclosed the courtyard. Their voices carried but the words were unrecognizable. The altercation rose a notch when the two tried to make their points by thrusting pointed fingers in each other's faces. I shuddered. Unless my own experience was wrong, it wouldn't be long before the conflict went physical.

Marla, ever willing to be diverted from gossiping about one situation to shoving her way into another, stared down avidly at the squabble. What looked like a tall man and a shorter, stockier one were now slapping each other's hands away. The short man put his hands on the chest of the tall one and pushed him back. The tall man stumbled, fell, rolled, and then jumped back to his feet. His hood fell off.

"Wow!" Marla exclaimed. "The lord of the manor just went ass-over-teakettle. And Sir Eliot is quarreling with..."

But neither of us could make out the other person until both of Eliot's hands flew up as if to choke the short man. Startled, the man pulled back and his hood flopped down...and revealed the disheveled white hair of Michaela Kirovsky, who was flailing as Eliot's hands closed on her throat.

"Good God," breathed Marla. "It's that caretaker woman. Goldy—call nine-one-one."

But there was no need, for at that instant, Michaela wrenched violently away from Eliot and pulled a gleaming rapier off one of the covered arch supports. While Marla and I looked on in horror, Michaela slashed downward with the sword and struck Eliot's left arm. I gasped. It was a move I'd seen Arch perform in fencing practice.

"I've got to tell Tom," I said. "Get someone on the phone—"

"Hey!" yelled Marla, as she banged on the leaded glass. "Stop that!"

Startled, Eliot and Michaela glanced up. I whispered a curse and pulled back from the window. Marla, undaunted, waved both hands over her head and bellowed, "No fighting! Stop that or I'll call the cops!"

Could they hear her through the glass? Did I care? I just wanted to be someplace else. So, apparently, did Michaela and Eliot, for when I peeked back out the window, both had disappeared through an unseen doorway.

"What in the hell do you suppose that was about?" demanded Marla. "I mean, they didn't even give us a second look. And anyway! Even if you disagree with someone who works for you, you don't try to choke 'em. I mean, not unless you coach college basketball."

"I can't deal with this now," I said abruptly,

173

realizing that if Michaela was not at fencing practice, it must have been canceled. "I've got to run." While Marla waited, I darted into our room—Tom was sleeping—and snagged my purse and jacket.

"Run where?" she whispered when I returned.

"I need to pick up Arch." I zipped to Arch's room, grabbed his overnight bag, and trotted back toward Marla. "I've got to drop him off for the Jerk, then come back and take care of Tom. And I want to get out of here before Eliot realizes I saw him. Should we report him to the domestic-abuse people, though?"

"Better wait on that," said Marla, "because I think we might have just saved *him* from being stabbed, gored, and left for dead." She walked purposefully down the hall. "Think I should tell Sukie? She's Swiss, she's used to being neutral, right?"

"Don't," I advised as I tried to hurry along behind her. Marla, heavier than I by about fifty pounds, had become devoted to a minimal but effective exercise routine since having a heart attack the previous summer. Still, I was surprised when she quickstepped down the carpeted stairs beside me. Following her, my head throbbed. I said, "Snooping around is hard on your health."

"Uh-huh," she replied. "I noticed what it's doing for yours." We pulled up in front of the kitchen door. "I just want to know why those two were arguing," she said, the very picture of innocence. She pushed into the kitchen and merrily asked Julian where Sukie had gotten to. Julian, chopping vegetables, called to Sukie, who peeked out, startled, from where she was crouching inside the hearth. We'd interrupted her scrubbing of the fireplace's interior walls, and she was not happy. Despite the twice-weekly visits of a cleaning company, Sukie felt compelled to check obsessively for spots they might have missed. Well, I'd probably be critical of any caterer I had to hire, so who was I to judge?

As I pulled out of the garage and accelerated across the causeway, a new question occurred to me: *Did Sukie's cleaning jobs include straightening out messes made by her husband?*

At quarter after three, Arch raced out the school gym entrance. "They're refinishing the floor of the school fencing loft," he announced as he heaved his bookbag into the rear of the van, "so Michaela gave us an assignment. She told us to run up and down five hundred stairs." His tone was weary. "Fifty times ten stairs. Or whatever. But I'm too hungry to do that right now."

"Why run up and down stairs?" I asked as I headed toward the Aspen Meadow Pastry Shop.

"Strengthens the legs." He glanced over the seat. "My overnight bag? Are we moving again?"

"Your dad and I have worked out a visitation policy for the next couple of weeks," I began, as if John Richard and I had actually peacefully cooperated on a new arrangement.

I explained to Arch that I'd be leaving him at the counseling center by the library. His bag held clean clothes and toiletries, and his dad would take him to school the next day. I pulled into a parking space on Main Street. After practice, I concluded, I would pick him up. Without responding, Arch jumped out of the van and shot into the pastry shop.

"Well, I'm glad to see Dad," he said finally, after he'd ordered two pieces of Linzertorte and a soft drink. "But Michaela promised that tonight Eliot would show me exactly where the young duke died. Would you tell her where I am? Ask her if I can see it tomorrow after practice?"

"Sure," I said, with some hesitance, as Arch wolfed down his first piece of torte. I guessed medieval history could be pretty cool if you focused on death and ghosts. Still, I wasn't certain I wanted Eliot and Michaela showing Arch *anything*. "Ah, honey? I don't want you poking around where someone died. Any chance I could go with you?"

He sighed and put down his second piece of torte. "First you want me to get along with these people, then you tell me you need to chaperone me around the place. Which is it?"

"The castle...is big, very big, and parts of it are closed off. I just... I'm not entirely sure the whole *place* is safe, that's all." The memory of Eliot lunging for Michaela's throat made my stomach knot. "Also, I don't want you going anywhere with Michaela and Eliot without me along."

"Okay, Mom," he said as he tossed his paper plate and cup, "just *forget* that I was trying to get along with the Hydes. I'll tell them I can't do anything or go anywhere without my *mommy* there to take care of me."

Why was mothering so hard? I exhaled, unable to think of a reply. Arch said he was going to find some steps to start running up and down. I sat in the van with the motor running and tried to think. Arch was due to turn fifteen in April, a fact he reminded me of whenever he accused me of babying him. But that was two months away. What I needed to concentrate on was where I should move our family next, before Eliot and Michaela killed one another, and while figuring out what John Richard and Viv Martini were up to. Not to mention *who'd shot Tom.* But immediate answers eluded me.

When Arch returned, gasping, he said, "I think I'm going to puke."

On that happy note, we drove to the counseling center in silence. When we pulled into the library parking lot and got out of the van, I glanced around. One could never be sure that the Jerk would actually show up at any particular prearranged time, I thought, as I chewed the inside of my cheek.

"Here you are," announced a throaty female voice behind me.

I whirled and the hair on the back of my neck stood on end. It was Viv Martini herself, dressed in skin-hugging chocolate brown leather pants and jacket. Once again, her jacket was zipped down to reveal cleavage. Would it be too prudish for me to put my hand over Arch's eyes?

"Hi, Viv," Arch said matter-of-factly. "Want me to put my stuff in the car?"

"Your dad's not here yet—" Viv began.

"Arch," I interrupted her, "would you run into the library and see if the new Jacques Pépin has come in for me? I requested it a month ago."

He sighed, rolled his eyes, and dropped his bag on the pavement.

"Please be nice to him," I told Viv, as soon as Arch had disappeared into the library. "He's really struggling with his dad getting out of jail."

"I *am* nice to him," Viv protested. "I got John Richard to buy a treadmill and free weights so we could both work out with Arch. Arch likes me."

I paused, but only for a moment. John Richard could be along any moment. "Look," I said, a tad desperately, "my husband is a policeman who's been shot—"

"So we saw on the news." To my surprise, Viv's eyes were sympathetic. "How *awful!* Do they have any idea who did it?"

"Not yet. But my ex said you knew Ray Wolff, who was arrested by my husband." I watched her closely, but saw nothing on her face except concern. "Do you have any idea if Wolff was involved in the shooting?"

"I don't give a damn about Ray Wolff!" she snapped. "There's no telling what *he's* up to. That's why I left him."

178

I managed a smile. Did I believe her? "A rumor in town also has you seen with Andy Balachek, whose body I found."

"Forget it," she said immediately. "I didn't touch Andy. He wasn't my type. He was a sweet kid. Ray seduced him into that theft, the way he does everybody. Ray's a son-of-a-bitch snake who will promise you anything to get what he wants."

Arch came out of the library and called to us. I said quickly, "So, Viv? You wouldn't have any idea who killed Andy, would you?"

She signaled to Arch. "Some buddy of Ray's, probably. Once they do what he says, they're like those bugs that crawl back under rocks, never to see the light of day."

Without warning, the gold Mercedes screamed into the lot. John Richard hopped out, crossed his arms, and glared at us. I squinted at the dealer's paper tags on the Mercedes. *Lauderdale Luxury Imports.* Was the Mercedes John Richard's car or Viv's? Arch announced that there were fifty holds on the Pépin, and I wouldn't get it for a while. Then he shyly looked up to Viv, who sauntered away with her arm slung over my son's shoulder. The sight made *me* want to puke.

Once they'd pulled away, I headed back to the castle. Dusk in the Rocky Mountain winter is a sudden, cold affair, arriving early and bringing with it a lengthy atmospheric gloom. I felt my mood drop with the temperature and the darkness.

In the kitchen of the castle, Eliot, wearing

an old-fashioned double-breasted gray suit and gray Ascot tie, was giving Julian instructions on the general outlines for a Tudor dinner. I looked closely at his left arm, the one Michaela had struck with the sword. Was that a slight bandage-bulge, or was I imagining it? In his right hand, Eliot held a crystal glass of sherry that he gestured with to make his points. "It was not a *supper,* although what the Elizabethans called *dinner,* we'll be serving at *suppertime* on Friday evening for the fencing team." The sherry slopped over the side of the glass.

Sukie, standing on the other side of the room in a full-length black velvet coat, groaned, undoubtedly thinking of her just-scrubbed floor. I put on an enthusiastic face. Whatever Eliot wanted in the food department, no matter how arcane, he was going to get. *I* didn't intend to get throttled.

"Now, as Goldy may have told you," Eliot said, jutting his chin in Julian's direction, "during the Renaissance, your typical late-sixteenth-century courtier would be served neither dinner nor supper in the Great Hall. Hollywood notwithstanding, of course," he added with a chuckle and sip of his drink. He continued: "The *large* change from medieval to Renaissance food service was that the king and queen—or lord and lady, as you will—withdrew to private chambers for meals. On very special occasions, such as Christmas, they would eat in the hall with a full complement of courtiers. The lord and lady and their intimates would be served on the dais, so all could see and admire them."

Julian's handsome face was set in a raised-eyebrow, pressed-lip expression of *I'm-trying-not-to-laugh*. Without warning, I felt suddenly cold again, and glanced around. Was I the only one noticing that the same window kept sliding open? While Eliot lectured, I sidled over to the window, shut it, and then hustled back to the kitchen table, where Julian had laid out trays of beautifully arranged vegetarian fare.

One platter contained a magazine-perfect stack of diamond-cut, grill-striped golden polenta, another a stunning array of steamed pale green artichokes, golden ears of corn, bright orange and green baby carrots, and broccoli florets. A third tray contained a bowl of arugula and romaine lettuces beside a heated crock of what looked and smelled like the recipe I'd shown him for a hot port wine and chèvre dressing. I looked closer. The creamy vinaigrette was studded with poached figs. So it *was* the recipe I'd shown him. I'd felt triumphant putting it together, for figs had been brought to Britain by the Romans. My mouth watered.

"But we'll have more time to talk tomorrow," Eliot concluded with a toothy grin and last delicate slurp from his glass. "Sukie and I are going out for the evening. Enjoy the...veggies. Goldy can tell you a Tudor courtier typically consumed two pounds of *meat* a day. Venison, rabbit, mackerel, goose, pheasant, peacock, *et cetera*." He nodded at the spread. "No cornbread, no carrots. The occasional potato."

181

Figgy Salad

4 ounces small Mission figs (13 to 15
  "figlets")
½ cup ruby port
½ teaspoon sugar
1 ounce (about 2 tablespoons) filberts (also called hazelnuts)
2 tablespoons balsamic vinegar
1 large shallot, minced by hand or in
  a small food processor
2 ounces chèvre, softened and sliced
¼ cup olive oil
¼ teaspoon salt
freshly ground black pepper to taste
8 cups field greens ("baby" variety, if
  possible), rinsed, drained, patted
  dry, wrapped in paper towels, and
  chilled

Cut the stems off the figs, rinse them,
and pat dry. Place them in a small
saucepan with the port and sugar and
bring to a simmer over medium heat.
Cover the pan, lower the heat to the
lowest setting, and simmer gently for
about 10 minutes, or until the figs are
soft. Drain the figs, reserving the

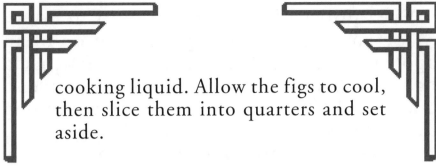

cooking liquid. Allow the figs to cool, then slice them into quarters and set aside.

Using a wide frying pan, toast the filberts over medium heat, stirring frequently, until they emit a nutty smell, about 5 to 10 minutes. Remove them from the heat, and when they are cool, coarsely chop them.

Reheat the cooking liquid over low heat and stir in the vinegar, shallot, chèvre, oil, and seasonings. Add the figs and raise the heat to medium-low. Stir the dressing until the cheese is completely melted.

Toss the field greens with the warm dressing and sprinkle the nuts on top. Serve immediately.

Makes 6 servings

Ever polite, Julian smiled and nodded. Sukie gave us her best approximation of an apologetic look and announced that Michaela had a small kitchenette in her castle apartment, and usually did not join them for the evening meal. Then she and Eliot swept away.

I was left wondering. Had Eliot's family treated the Kirovskys like family for so many years that it was impossible to fire her, even if she stabbed him with a sword? If Sartre was right, and *hell was other people*, what was *other people you don't get along with living forever at close quarters?* A lower circle of hell?

I put these questions aside as Julian and I shouldered the trays and trucked them up to Tom's and my room. Julian had already set three places at a card table next to Tom's side of the bed. Not a dais in the Great Hall, but absolutely perfect for a cozy family meal. We said grace. In addition to thanks, I prayed for safety and guidance, and for my son.

"Are we all sure we want to stay here?" Julian asked delicately, as he passed the salad. "That Eliot guy is *weird*."

"*I'm* comfortable," Tom offered. "We wouldn't have as good security in a hotel, I can tell you that, unless Lambert pulled some extra guys off the force to keep watch over us. So...unless the person who shot me can find a way into a heavily fortified castle, I'd say we're in pretty good shape."

"Chardé Lauderdale might be able to find her way in," I ventured.

"I think I could deal with that skinny decorator," Tom insisted with a chuckle.

I started piling goodies onto Tom's plate and my own. "Before you turn down a hotel, you should know I saw Eliot having a nasty fight this afternoon with his caretaker, Michaela Kirovsky. Marla broke it up."

"Yeah," Tom replied. "Marla called while you were running Arch around. She said none of her sources know if Eliot and Michaela fight all the time, or if what you saw this afternoon was a one-time thing." Tom laughed and shook his head. "I'd say Eliot Hyde is more than weird, maybe even certifiable. When we're done eating, I'll tell you all about his pranks."

"Oh, tell us now," I coaxed with a giggle, infinitely glad that Tom felt well enough to gossip. I finished heaping his plate with polenta and vegetables and set it in front of him.

Tom took a few bites, and complimented Julian. Then he said, "Eliot told the sheriff's department, and townsfolk who would listen, that any castle-property trespasser would be attacked by a ghost."

"I'll bet that brought in the gawkers," Julian said with a wry smile.

Tom laughed again. "You don't know the half of it."

CHAPTER 15

Iknew better than to interrupt Tom when he began a Tale of Law Enforcement. I took a first luscious bite of Julian's beautifully prepared salad. The warm, bittersweet dressing had melted the creamy chunks of chèvre and made a silky coating for the sweet, moist figs and bitter greens. It was a heavenly mélange. Was this really my recipe, or had Julian transformed it into something otherworldly? Maybe what made it delicious was someone else fixing it.

I felt myself relax. And I was thankful: That my husband was alive, that Julian was with us once again, that Arch and I had survived our first encounter with the Jerk-as-ex-con. As I munched the sumptuous grilled polenta, I ordered myself to set aside worries about Tom's wound, the other woman he claimed not to love, and Andy Balachek's corpse in Cottonwood Creek.

"Eliot had moved back from the East Coast and lived in this castle for almost, oh, five years," Tom continued, "when he realized his tours were a flop and his inheritance was going to drain away soon. So. About four years ago, he took out a loan against the equity in the castle itself and used it to refurbish the chapel by the creek. Vandals had broken some windows and spray-painted the walls and floor. Eliot spent fifty thou on folding wooden chairs, heaters, an antique organ, a handmade gold cross, spotlights, repairs to the stained-glass windows, and installation of electricity. The first wedding went off well. Unfortunately, Eliot hadn't thought of *security*, and vandals broke in after the celebration and stole the gold cross."

"Wow," said Julian, as he piled jewel-colored baby vegetables on our plates. "How much bad luck would *that* bring?"

Tom nodded. "Eliot's next strategy, in addition to installing a lockbox, was to arrange an interview with the *Mountain Journal*. He claimed the dead duke, the rich young nephew from Tudor times, still haunted the place and roamed the grounds. Eliot called his own estate 'Poltergeist Palace.' He warned that anyone breaking into Hyde Chapel or the castle could be attacked by the ghost."

"So he's the one who came up with the name," I muttered.

"A second couple tying the knot in Hyde Chapel didn't even finish their ceremony. The bride was spooked to begin with, because the groom had lost his first wife in a car accident. Before they got to 'I do,' a screaming started up in the chapel. Or near the chapel; the witnesses couldn't agree. Nobody could find the screamer. So the bride got hysterical and started hollering herself, claiming it was the ghost of her husband's first wife."

"How come none of this was publicized at Saint Luke's when Eliot gave them Hyde Chapel?" I asked, fascinated.

"Because Episcopalians have the *Holy* Ghost," Julian interjected.

"That's the Holy *Spirit* to you," I shot back.

Tom grinned. "You guys want me to finish this story?" When we both nodded, he went on: "The bride in the second ceremony refused to go on with the service. The groom demanded his money back. Eliot said no. The groom gave Eliot a fist to the jaw, and knocked him out. One of the guests called us. By the time we got there, the guests had all dispersed, and the bride and groom had skedaddled to a justice of the peace. Somebody had given Eliot Hyde smelling salts. We found him in the chapel storage area, where he was rewinding a tape of screaming sounds, probably broadcast through speakers in the chapel. He said he'd set up the tape to go off if the chapel was broken into, but somehow the recorder had gotten tripped by the wedding party. We told him to get rid of the tape, or next time we'd arrest him for creating a public nuisance."

"Poor Eliot," I said.

Julian rolled his muscled swimmer's shoulders as he polished off his plate of veggies. "Way I heard it, when I was at Elk Park Prep? Someone actually *did* die here. A child. And not four centuries ago, either."

"What?" Tom and I demanded.

Julian shrugged. "The story at school was that a couple came up here to have an illegitimate baby, and it was a stillbirth. They threw the baby's corpse down the well. As I said, this isn't an ancient ghost rumor, either. It was something in the last ten years."

"No one reported it to the sheriff's department," Tom replied, "or I would have heard about it."

"Search warrant!" I cried.

"Forget it," said Tom.

"Here's my opinion," Julian said, picking up our plates. "Eliot may have acted weird by scaring folks off. But if you ask me, Sukie's the nutcase." He frowned. "There is such a thing as *too* clean, you know. I finish with a bowl, she washes it. She wipes down the walls, then cleans the windows. Done with that? She sweeps the floor, gets on her hands and knees, and scrubs it. Why would a rich person with a hired cleaning service be so anal?"

"Julian!" Tom and I cried.

He went on: "I've only been here one day. Sukie seemed to like the lunch, right? But then I began thinking she was just keeping an eye on me, to make sure I didn't steal anything. When she grabbed away a sauté pan I was still using, I told her she didn't need to worry, I was *bonded*. She apologized. She says she cleans because she's Swiss. Next week, she's hiring a specialist to wax all the wood floors. She told me that while she was at a church meeting Sunday night, Chardé came in and she and Eliot splashed paint samples all over the place. Sukie went absolutely nuts. Then the paint guys came back today with more paint samples. Eliot told her not to worry, brighter colors would make the castle more attractive as a conference center." He motioned with the tray he had now filled with plates. "Anyway, if I don't put these in the dishwasher before

I go to bed, she'll come around in the middle of the night looking for them."

I didn't like the idea of Julian wandering around the castle alone at night, but tried to keep my voice serene. "Listen, Julian, do me a favor, okay? When you finish in the kitchen and come back up, just knock gently on our door. One knock. So we can be sure you're all right."

"So you know the ghost didn't snag me?" Julian said with a wink. He heaved up the tray. "Okay, Ma and Pa. I'll knock." We thanked him again for the marvelous meal. He grinned, delighted with our praise, and backed out the door.

When Tom and I were alone at last, I washed my hands and began the task of removing his bandage, cleaning the wound, then taping it back up. Lord knows, I longed to ask him about Sara Beth O'Malley. But I couldn't. The newly bloodied bandage, the ugly bruising around the wound, the black stitches on his swollen flesh, made me resolve to say nothing.

Even if I suspected Tom's old girlfriend had shot him for being disloyal to her and marrying me, what good would it do to confront *Tom?* I gently laid new gauze in place. What I really wanted to know, I decided, was if he still cared about her, and if he'd acted on that by...whatever. *Stop,* I ordered myself, as I gently pressed down the last bit of tape. The Jerk had betrayed me for years, years when I'd stuck my head in the proverbial sandbox so much I might as well have been living at the beach. By the end of our marriage I'd turned into a suspicious harpy who thought *everything* John Richard told me was a lie. If I got back into mistrustful thinking, I was going to make myself miserable.

"Something wrong, Goldy?" Tom gave me the full benefit of those all-knowing green eyes.

"I'm worried about you."

"Don't, I'll be fine." He paused. "Is Arch on your mind?"

"Yes, that's it." My voice cracked.

"The kid'll be all right. Korman won't try anything while he's on parole. Why don't you come to bed?"

And so I did. I wanted to ask Tom if he still loved me, but I couldn't. It had been a long day, a *very* long day. Still, once I was between the crisp cotton sheets and down comforter that were worthy of the most luxurious hotel, sleep eluded me. I switched from fretting about Tom, to wondering if I could safely boot my laptop and read his e-mails, to worrying about Arch. Where was my son at that moment? Did he miss me? I turned over and sighed.

"Goldy, what is it?"

"I'm just thinking about when Arch was a newborn. I'd lie in bed and fret about whether he was breathing, even though he was just down the hall. I found that if I lay very still and listened, I could hear him. It was like your eyes adjusting to the dark. My ears took in all the sounds of the night, and finally made out his tiny infant breath. In and out. It was comforting. Does that sound nuts?"

"He's breathing now, Miss G., in his bed at Korman's house. He's all right. If he wasn't, we would have heard about it."

At that moment a muffled knock on the door indicated Julian was retiring to his room. A few moments later, Tom snored softly beside me.

My eyes remained wide open, my body tense. Finally, I eased from beneath the comforter. Despite the heat pouring from the baseboards, the air in the big room was chilly. I sat down on the velvety wool rug.

Tom wasn't in a deep enough sleep for me to start tapping away on a keyboard. Besides, if I read the e-mails tonight, I'd feel too guilty to sleep. Especially if he caught me.

I hugged myself against the cold and thought about Arch. Yes, he was with John Richard, and no, I couldn't phone at midnight to check that he'd brushed his teeth and been tucked in. (Question: How do you tuck in an almost-fifteen-year-old, anyway? Answer: You don't.) And what if Viv decided to tell Arch a bedtime story about automatic weapons?

Don't think about it.

Very quietly, I slipped into my heavy coat, boots, and mittens. There *was* something I could do, a ritual that had always helped with worry about Arch's safety when he was spending the night at a friend's, or camping with the Cub

Scouts in the wildlife preserve. I'd face in the direction of my son's location and send him good vibes. This was not a spiritual exercise sanctioned in your neighborhood Episcopal church. But I'd always found it reassuring, and believed that God would understand.

I quietly maneuvered through the set of double doors to the southeast tower. My boots scraped the floor. The sharp air was dense with ice crystals. The dim light illuminating the tower cast long shadows on the dark stone.

John Richard's house lay southwest of the castle, in the Aspen Meadow Country Club area. I shivered, oriented myself, then stood by the window that faced southwest. I closed my eyes. Then I brought up the vision of Arch sleeping. I willed myself to be very still.

After a few moments, I could have sworn I heard breathing. It was not my own breath, but the rapid, shallow inhale-exhale of a child. Fear rippled through my veins. I opened my eyes and glanced around quickly: nothing. When I tipped forward to check out the window, there was only the barely lit black water of the moat below, and across the moat, a small neon light by the castle Dumpster. Ghosts didn't usually breathe, did they? Being dead and all? *I'm losing it,* I decided, as I tiptoed back to our room, shed my outerwear, and slipped into bed. *I need sleep.*

But I lay awake for a long time, thinking about what to do next.

★　　　★　　　★

Dawn brought frigid air and charcoal clouds hemmed with a bright blue sliver of sky. To my chagrin, my neck had stiffened from my nasty encounter with the computer thief. What sleep I'd managed to get had brought some clarity, however. Boyd and Armstrong had promised to touch base today. I would call them first, with some questions of my own. And I had to talk with Eliot about the new arrangements for the next day's labyrinth lunch. With Tom still asleep, I rolled quietly out of bed, emptied my mind, and began a slow yoga routine. Breathe, stretch, breathe, hold. Before long, I felt better.

As I started to get dressed, I remembered the disk and Sara Beth O'Malley. I frowned, remembering Tom's story. Talk about a *ghost*.

Tom's snoring was deep and sonorous. With my laptop tucked under my arm, I tiptoed into the bathroom. I didn't give myself time to think, much less feel guilty. I plugged in the computer and booted it up, covered the toilet seat with warm towels, and sat down to break into my husband's e-mail.

There were seven messages: three from "The Gambler," as Andy apparently called himself, three from "S.B.," and one from the State Department. I had already opened the first of S.B.'s messages: *Do you remember me? You said you'd love me forever.* Now I went straight to the second.

194

I need to prove myself to you? I smiled. Good old Tom. Figure out if she is who she says she is. *I'm putting myself in danger just writing to you. Nobody knows I'm here. Remember our secret engagement ring? We didn't want people to criticize us for being too young to know what we were doing. So you picked out a tiny ruby, my birthstone, set in platinum. In answer to your other question, I've been in a little village. After my so-called death, I went from being a nurse to being a doctor. —S.B.*

At least she wasn't calling herself "Your S.B." anymore. I battled guilt as I opened the third and final communication from her, dated three weeks ago.

Tom, I saw your wife and son today. I read in the paper that she's a caterer. I don't want to upset your life. I just would like to see you. Why am I here, you asked. An anonymous donor is giving us medical supplies. I'm picking them up. I also have a dental abscess and need a root canal. They don't have neighborhood endodontists in my country, although they can manage fake passports and counterfeit checks. I'm taking the risk to tell you all this for a reason. I have an appointment at High Country Dental on February 13 at 9 A.M. I'd like to see you before my appointment, if possible. S.B.

Wait a minute. *My country?*

The next communication, the one from the State Department, was unemotional and to the point.

Officer Schulz: As you were notified by the DOD in 1975, Major Sara Beth O'Malley, R.N., was listed as missing, presumed dead. Her Mobile

195

Army Surgical Hospital unit was destroyed during an attack three months before American forces withdrew from Saigon. Her body was not recovered, and the DOD has not had reason to change its assessment.

From time to time, we get unsubstantiated reports of war-era Americans still living in Vietnam. Neither we nor the Defense Department has any way of investigating these claims.

We urge all persons who have eyewitness reports of missing veterans to fill out a Form 626–3A, available on-line at the above address.

This happy epistle was signed by a minor dignitary of the Department.

So: Sara Beth O'Malley had somehow survived the war, unbeknownst to Washington bureaucrats. She'd also become a doctor for a village whose plumbing facilities undoubtedly wouldn't appeal to Sukie. The part I couldn't fathom was why she'd risk coming back to Colorado after twenty-five years to pick up supplies and have her teeth fixed, and oh, by the way, to check on her old fiancé, who had long believed her dead.

I don't love her. Tom had probably been afraid that if he died from the shot, I'd find the e-mails. Which I had anyway. She thought Arch was his son. If she read in the paper that I was a caterer, she knew I did local events, *like the one at Hyde Chapel.* Had she been waiting for me to show up for the labyrinth lunch, and shot Tom by accident, instead of me? I wondered if the army or her villagers had taught her to shoot, after all.

I stared at the blinking cursor. Was Sara Beth O'Malley telling the truth? Where was she staying? If she wasn't in Aspen Meadow, where was she?

Suddenly I remembered what Captain Lambert had quoted from the owner of The Stamp Fox: *If you have contacts in the Far East...you can fence anything.*

Maybe this was too far-fetched. Could Sara Beth O'Malley possibly be hooked up with Ray Wolff and his thieving gang? And, most importantly for my psyche and marriage: *In the last month, has Tom seen her?*

I sighed, rode a wave of caffeine-craving, and opened the first of the e-mails from "The Gambler," Andy Balachek himself. Whoever had shot Tom *must* have known about Andy's body right there in the creek. If I was going to figure out who the shooter was, it might help to know what had been going on with Andy before he died.

Hey, Officer Schultz, he wrote on January 20, *I really appreciate you letting me write to you. Look, all I want is to get enough money to pay my dad back for his truck. I don't want him to die with my stealing hanging over my head. And I don't want to go to prison. I didn't want anybody to die. I didn't kill the FedEx driver. So you can tell the D.A. that, too. Ray whacked him.*

Where's Ray Wolff? Where are the stamps? You don't want much, do you? Day after tomorrow, Ray will be casing places to store the stamps. When you think Storage *in Furman County, what do you think of?*

His next communication was equally defensive, written in the same flip, bravado tone. *Tom, man, are you trying to get me into more trouble? You got Ray Wolff, you got THE GUY who whacked the driver, why can't I come in now and collect the reward? My dad's not going to live much longer. Now you're telling me I can't get out of the theft and complicity charges without rolling over on my partner and telling you where the loot is? Come on, Tom, give me a break.*

The third and final letter was his farewell. *Tom, I've got a stake, and a chance to make big money to pay my dad back. Why do you keep asking me the same questions? No, I can't turn in our other partner. No, I can't tell you where the stuff is, or how we're going to sell it. It's getting hard writing you, I'm being watched all the time. I think my partner suspects I turned Ray in. But I had my reasons. I'll call you from Atlantic City. If I can.*

Well, there was one question answered, at least for me: our other partner. One person. Probably our shooter.

And as to Andy's movements? He had called me from Central City, not Atlantic City. Then he'd disappeared, and turned up dead in Aspen Meadow. Unless Pete Balachek was incoherent from his illness, the police would have questioned him about his son and his associates. I didn't have a clue as to who the "partner" was. Nor did I have the slightest idea where the stolen stamps were. So what was my next move?

One thing was sure: I wanted to visit with

Sara Beth O'Malley. She might or might not be expecting Tom to meet her at the dentist's the day after tomorrow. But I had a very easy way of finding out if she was telling the truth on that score. I knew where the endodontist's office was. Oh, the glories of living in a small town.

CHAPTER 16

While my disk coughed up recipes and menus for Tudor feasts, my mind traveled back to the fight between Michaela and Eliot. The figures on the screen swam. *At a Saint John's Day feast five years before the death of Henry VIII, the offerings included venison pies....*

Was I overreacting, or had that courtyard conflict struck a bit too close for comfort? If Eliot was physically explosive with his female staff, did I even want to *consider* a long-term job for him? I frowned and tried to think. My screen dimmed. I wanted to report their skirmish to the cops. But Tom had told me to stay out of it, and that's what I would do. For now.

I tapped a button; the screen brightened. In addition to consuming venison pies, the folks at Hampton Court had enjoyed a Saint John's Day first course of beef in vinegar sauce, carp baked with wine and prunes, bread, butter, and eggs. For the second course, the courtiers had dug into boiled mutton, swan, peacocks, roast boar with pudding, wafers, and marzipan. Ah yes: The high-protein, high-fat, high-sugar diet. No wonder their teeth had fallen out.

I browsed forward to 1588, when an Elizabethan feast had included *joints of venison roasted in rye, sides of beef, boars' heads; bacon, calves' feet, game pies with cinnamon; peacock, herons, blackbirds, larks; salmon, eels, turbot, whiting, sprats, oysters; sweetmeats, syrups, jellies, candied roses and violets, grapes, oranges, almonds, hazelnuts; cakes and syrup-soaked confections.*

Well. Eliot and I had already agreed that calves' feet and spicy elk pie wouldn't go over big with the youthful fencing team. Not to mention that any plan to serve herons and larks would ensure wrathful demonstrations from every environmental group in Aspen Meadow.

So we'd come up with compromises. "Sides of beef" had metamorphosed into veal roasts, already ordered from my supplier. Current seafood prices precluded offering oysters, salmon, or turbot, and I'd told Eliot the kids wouldn't touch eels. I'd been delighted to tell him, though, that a recipe from Roman Britain had included *prawns.* There was the Roman Empire, and then there was the British Empire, which had included India. So we had decided on a shrimp curry. That had left only dessert. In the end, we'd agreed the fencers would enjoy a real Elizabethan plum tart. And then Eliot had decided on tucking in the zirconia. Sara Beth might not be the only client for the dentist.

All this had left one uncharted territory: Side Dishes. Americans would not eat a meal composed only of meat and sugar. I clicked on a file marked *Potatoes, Corn, and Tomatoes*, all exotic European imports in Elizabeth's time. Sir Walter Raleigh, according to one source, had brought back potatoes from Virginia, and raised them on his estate in Ireland. Eliot had told me to be creative, so I would test-drive a potato concoction that night. If everyone liked it, I would serve it to the fencers and their families.

I closed down the computer, dressed, and knocked softly on Julian's door. After squinting at the carved wood, I extracted a note wedged between the frame and the brass doorknob. *Am doing 50 laps of crawl in the indoor pool. Meet you in the kitchen at 8.*

My shoulders hurt just thinking about fifty laps of anything.

It was quarter to eight. I snagged an extra cardigan in case someone had left the kitchen window open again, quietly closed our door, and reminded myself to act grateful toward our hosts, regardless of the argument I'd witnessed. I would find out what was going on between Eliot and Michaela one way or another. Meanwhile, we had a meal to fix. My banged-up body ached with each step down to the kitchen. So I focused resolutely on the breakfast Julian and I could whip up. Ricotta-stuffed pancakes. Poached eggs smothered in steamed baby vegetables. One of the joys of the first meal of the day is that it can melt away most pain.

When I banged into the kitchen, I saw Sukie first. Bent over the double sink, she was wearing rubber gloves and viciously scrubbing a suds-filled coffeepot. Behind her, the errant window was closed. Michaela and Eliot sat at the kitchen table, sullenly eyeing a plate of frosty prepackaged strudel. Beside the pastry lay a dozen boxes overflowing with fabric swatches and paint chips.

Uh-oh, I thought, *too late.*

Standing by the hearth with her arms crossed, Chardé Lauderdale gasped when she spotted me. She wore a dark green pantsuit with a fur collar that set off her pretty features. Two red spots flamed on her cheeks. Clearly, she wasn't expecting to see me. Or was she? I held my chin high and gave her an even look.

Buddy Lauderdale, standing by one of the windows overlooking the moat, turned slowly to face me. He touched the lapels of his camel's-hair coat, narrowed his glassy eyes, then straightened his swarthy face into a passive, self-consciously blank expression. Next to his father, sixteen-year-old Howie Lauderdale shifted his feet. Howie wore de rigueur shabby-chic khaki shirt and pants, along with his fencing jacket. He was short for his age, with a chubby, angelic face, dark curly hair, and a smile I had always found endearing, especially when he encouraged Arch with his fencing. How such a great kid could have been produced by Buddy Lauderdale was beyond me. Then again, I hadn't known the ex-wife Buddy had dumped to marry the lovely Chardé. Probably she'd been a great mother.

"Hi, Goldy," said Howie in a low voice. He colored when his father touched his arm.

"I am *very* sorry to hear you've moved yourself in here," Chardé spat in my direction.

"Now, Chardé," Eliot began soothingly. Today he wore tweed pants and a smoking jacket. Did the man even own a pair of jeans? He said, "You and Buddy and Goldy have merely had an unfortunate misunderstanding. Howie, chap, come on over here and help me figure out how to defrost this thing in the microwave."

Chardé snorted; Buddy crossed his arms and didn't budge. Michaela set her lips in a scowl. Howie and Eliot busied themselves with the microwave while Sukie ran the faucet full blast to rinse out the coffeepot. When the microwave beeped and Eliot pulled out the strudel, poor Howie looked from one adult to another, probably hoping someone would somehow break the tension.

"Uh," Howie said to me, his face crimson, "Arch is doing real well with the foil. The whole team is amazed at how he's come along."

"I'm glad," I said. Since no one had told me what they were doing in the kitchen at this hour, I ventured, "Do you all have an early practice today?"

"No, no," Howie replied, as Eliot handed him a piece of pastry that looked like iced cardboard. "I was just working with Michaela in her loft. My dad and Chardé wanted to watch. We're going to school as soon as Chardé leaves her stuff...and then I guess we'll see you, uh—"

Sukie finished drying the coffeepot and wiped her hands on her apron. "Buddy, Chardé, Howie," she murmured. "Goldy and her family and her friend are staying with us *through* the fencing banquet."

"That's a mistake," Chardé announced. I turned away and searched in the Hydes' refrigerator for unsalted butter and eggs. When I headed for the mixer, Chardé cocked her head at Eliot. "I hope she's paying you *rent*, Eliot."

Michaela interrupted to say it was time for her to leave. After she clomped out, Eliot slumped at the kitchen table, looking as chilled as the strudel. I pulled a loaf pan out of a cupboard and glanced at Buddy, who was stroking his dimpled chin and frowning. Should I ask him where little Patty was? *With a nanny? Better off with a baby-sitter than with her parents, right?* I rummaged in the cupboards and pulled out two types of dried fruit: pineapple and sour cherries. I found a cutting board and a knife, and placed everything on the kitchen table across from Eliot. *Just concentrate on the cooking.*

Buddy Lauderdale sauntered forward and pulled a fat catalog out from under the mountain of paint chips. With annoying deliberateness, he laid it on top of the cutting board. Then he asked in that oily voice I knew only too well, "Ever heard of *Marvin*, Goldy? They make *windows*."

Taken aback, I stared at the catalog jacket for Marvin Windows, casements and bays floating against a background of blue sky.

"Are you trying to tell me something, Mr. Lauderdale?" I managed to say. "Or would you rather tell my husband, upstairs?"

"Oh, yeah," said Buddy, as he tapped his cheek in mock thoughtfulness, "how *is* your husband?"

I turned to Sukie, who was standing in front of the microwave cabinet. "I need to make a call. Someplace private."

"Don't you *dare* call the police again," Chardé Lauderdale shrieked at me as she began gathering up her swatches and chips. She stopped only long enough to stab a scarlet-painted nail in my direction. "I am a good person. I don't want you to get in my way *anymore*. I don't want to run into you at Elk Park Prep, I don't want to run into you here, I don't want to see you at the luncheon tomorrow. You stay out of our lives, do you understand?"

"*Please*, people—" Eliot faltered. He had a pained expression on his face, like a king whose courtiers' conflicts were giving him a headache.

"I'm going to Elk Park Prep today, I'm staying here, and I'll be catering the lunch tomorrow," I informed Chardé, getting angry myself. "So if you don't want to run into me, you'd better stay *home*. Oh, and that includes the banquet Friday night, too."

Sukie hustled over to Buddy, Howie, and Chardé, helped scoop up the paint chips and catalogs, and murmured about coming another time to work on the new color schemes. Howie muttered that he needed to get to school, and Eliot announced that Buddy should take a look at his car. When they all left, I didn't offer any good-byes.

Instead, I returned to the sweet bread I intended to make for breakfast. The combination of dried pineapple and cherries would make a not-too-sweet-or-too-tart, gloriously colorful loaf. I closed my eyes and imagined holding a bread slice up to the light.

Don't think about the Lauderdales, just cook.

I chopped the fragrant dried fruits, set them to soak, and revved up the mixer. The beaters whipped through the butter and sugar until it resembled spun gold. By the time I was adding flour, leavening, and orange juice, I had a name for the concoction: *Stained-Glass Sweet Bread.*

"Dear Goldy, I am *so* sorry about the Lauderdales," Eliot announced in his kingly, regretful voice, as he swung through the door from the dining room. "*Everything* to them is a drama, and I *do* get tired of being their audience. We were at their New Year's Eve party, but did not see the conflict that so upset everyone." I stifled a response: *No one*

Stained-Glass Sweet Bread

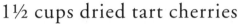

1½ cups dried tart cherries
½ cup chopped dried pineapple
4 tablespoons (½ stick) unsalted
   butter, softened
1½ cups sugar
2 eggs
4 cups all-purpose flour (High altitude: add 2 tablespoons)
4 teaspoons baking powder (High
   altitude: 1 tablespoon)
½ teaspoon baking soda
2 teaspoons salt
1½ cups orange juice

Place the cherries and chopped pineapple in a large bowl and cover with boiling water. Let stand 15 minutes, then drain and pat dry with paper towels. Set aside.

Butter and flour two 8½ x 4½-inch loaf pans. Set aside.

Cream the butter with the sugar until well blended. (Mixture will look like wet sand.) Add the eggs and beat well. Sift the dry ingredients together twice. Add the flour mixture alternately to the creamed mixture with the orange juice, beginning and ending with the dry ingredients. Stir in the fruits, blending well. Divide evenly between the pans. Allow to stand for 20 minutes.

While the mixture is standing, preheat the oven to 350°F.

Bake the breads for 45 to 55 minutes, until toothpicks inserted in the loaves come out clean. Cool in the pans 10 minutes, then allow to cool completely on racks.

Makes 2 loaves

saw it except for me. That's the problem. Meanwhile, Eliot turned his attention to the mixer bowl. "Let's chat about something more pleasant. Historic menus."

I nodded an assent, finished scooping the thick batter into the prepared pan, and decided to let it rise a while to lighten the texture.

"May I use the phone first?" I asked him. "I need to make a couple of important calls. I'd like to do it where I won't be interrupted."

He wrinkled his brow, a sure sign of mental wheels whizzing. *Is my caterer spreading more bad publicity for my castle?* "Yes, yes, of course," he said, with effort. "My office is more private."

I set the timer, glanced at my watch, grabbed my extra sweater, and followed him out. We ran into Julian in the hallway. His brown hair was wet from his postswim shower, and he looked dapper in black chef pants and a white shirt. I begged him to preheat the oven, and put in the bread. He said he'd love to, then whistled cheerfully as he banged into the kitchen.

"Damn!" he yelled as the door swung closed. "It's cold in here! Who opened that window again?"

"Eliot?" I asked as he held open a door that led through the courtyard. "If you've got a loose catch on a window, why don't you have it fixed?"

Eliot's voice was rueful. "It's original glass."

Outside, a bitter wind smacked our faces. I pulled on my sweater and reflected that if *I'd* made millions selling some old letter, I'd get a new kitchen window, no matter what anyone told me about preservation. I gasped at the cold and caught the word "shortcut," as a cloud of steam issued from Eliot's mouth. I struggled to match his long strides as we trotted along an ice-edged brick pathway through the Tudor garden. Overhead, a Red-tailed hawk teetered on the wind. Below, the snow-dusted, dun-colored plant stalks rattled and swayed.

"Even with all the money we made from the sale of our famous letter," Eliot called back to me, as if reading my mind, "we did not have sufficient funds to redo the entire castle. You see the north half of the east range?" I hugged myself, turned, and looked back obediently. "We did the first floor where the dining room and kitchen are. Above that, it's all closed off." He pointed to the window that Marla had banged on when she'd yelled at him. "That's the *south* side of the east range," Eliot continued. My eyes swept over the rapiers on the arch supports. "There, where you're staying in the guest suites, we redid the upper story. On the south range—" He pointed to his right, to the wall with the postern gate "—we did restore both stories."

Okay, okay, my mind screamed. *I don't need background on the refurbishing effort when I'm freezing to death!*

"The Great Hall on the east side of the south range is on the second floor," Eliot blithely persisted, "while four conference rooms are below it. On the west side of the

210

postern gate," his hand arched to the right, "there are the swimming pool and locker rooms on the lower level, and conference rooms above. My study is in the west range"—he gestured farther to the right, directly across the courtyard from the kitchen— "where we've only redone half of the lower story. Further down the hall from my study is Sukie's and my room."

"And Michaela?" I couldn't help asking. "Where does she live?"

He gave me a sharp look, then pointed back to the gatehouse. "She occupies the western section of the north range, including the gatehouse. According to my grandfather's will, Vladimir Kirovsky's descendants may stay there as long as their family remain the castle caretakers. Sukie and I intend to hire a whole staff of caretakers, of course, as soon as the conversion to a conference center is complete." He exhaled without saying where all those worker-bees were slated to reside. "And you've already seen our lovely living room, decorated by Chardé, who does have talent, even if she's a tad rough around the edges."

Not merely rough around the edges, my mind supplied, *but sharp and dangerous.*

We entered the arcade on the west side of the courtyard. Eliot tapped numbers on a security keypad beside a massive wooden door. "Of course," he added, "Chardé *does* disrupt us sometimes, coming in unannounced to try new paints and toss swatches all over the place. I bumped into her one night when I was coming over to work on my jams. I didn't even realize Sukie had given her the security code, but Sukie said Chardé insisted, that it would make the decorating effort easier for everyone."

Doggone it, I thought as I moved through the wooden doorway into a hallway lit by new windows on the arcade side. The last thing I could tolerate in the middle of the night was crashing into Chardé Lauderdale. Eliot touched a switch, and electrified torches on the far wall illuminated tapestries of battle scenes.

"Mr. Hyde," I began, as I hugged myself to warm up. "We're very thankful you could have us here. But if Chardé and Buddy Lauderdale can't be kept out of the castle, then my husband and I need to take Arch and Julian somewhere else. The Lauderdales and I...are in conflict, as you know, from that New Year's party. They might have shot at our house. They might even be the ones who shot Tom."

Eliot's brown eyes shone with indulgence. "They would *never* do such things. In any case, dear Goldy, you, your husband, your child, your dear young friend—you are all perfectly safe. Each suite has a security pad outside the room, did Sukie not show you? You determine your own code. Once you set it inside your room, no one can come through your door. The instructions are in your night tables." He waved at a tapestry of a unicorn. "When Chardé figures out the colors for the last paint jobs, we'll change the gatehouse codes and she won't be back."

I asked hesitantly, "How much do you really know about the Lauderdales?"

"We've been friends...well, since all the hoopla about the letter, and I bought our first Jaguar. I'll tell you what I know: The Lauderdales are so concerned about looking rich, they're lavishing money they don't have on charity. For example, we're happy Buddy helped pay for the refurbishment of the labyrinth. But when I tried to convince him to have a salesman recognition dinner here, he said entertaining his employees was not something he really did. My take on it was that a salesmen's dinner doesn't pack as much prestigious punch as a lavish gift to the church, and therefore isn't worth more debt."

"Do you know I saw him shake his baby until she passed out? That he was arrested?"

"Of course," Eliot replied, with more regal regret. "And I know his reputation has suffered. But I can't believe that he would go out shooting windows and people."

I shook my head. How did you get through to someone who believed the only problem with being caught half killing a child was what it did to your *reputation*? Without further discussion, Eliot ushered me into his study, a large, mahogany-paneled room. Outside, the clouds had softened to luminescent puffs, and light streamed through a leaded-glass bay window. In the room itself, the illuminated bookcases and massive desk were decorated with models of ships and castles, brass flasks and horns, and other British-male accoutrements. Royal-blue carpeting, blue-and-gold draperies, brass fixtures, and oxblood leather chairs all screamed *English Club*—no doubt exactly what Eliot had told Chardé he wanted.

"Lovely," I breathed.

"Thank you." He seated himself at his gargantuan desk and launched into an explanation of what we needed to do. "The lunch menu for the labyrinth donors we have all set, with two minor changes. The priest from Saint Luke's is allowing me to give a pitch about the conference center after the lunch." Eliot sniffed. "Awfully big of him, seeing as how Saint Luke's now possesses a genuine medieval chapel. Anyway, Sukie would like to simplify things and offer caviar with toast points, onion toasts, and English cheese puffs for hors d'oeuvres." He waved his hand. "We already have these from mail order. But we still need a first course, which should be English-y."

English-y. I nodded.

"Do you have a recipe on your disk for an Elizabethan-style soup?" he asked, worried. "A soup not running and not standing, as they say?"

"I do," I said, thankful I had picked up the disk, even if I'd gotten banged up in the process. "How about a hot cream of chicken soup made with rosemary and thyme, both herbs mentioned by Shakespeare?"

"Wonderful," Eliot replied with a sigh. "Now, for Friday's plum tart." He opened a drawer, drew out a small brass box, then dumped the sparkling contents onto a leather-edged blue blotter. "Zirconia," he said proudly, "to be tucked into the plums."

I nodded, not having a clue how I would conceal the stones so that guests wouldn't accidentally ingest them. "Okey-doke."

"Now," Eliot continued, as he fingered a miniature brass cannon, "for the banquet. We can't just have food; the fencing team must have entertainment and games. You don't suppose the boys and girls would be interested in English country dances, do you?"

"Uh...no."

"It's too bad we don't have a small troupe of players to *act* for us." He tapped a long finger on the leather blotter. "Or better, musicians."

"Sukie said you were researching games?" I ventured. "I seem to remember the Elizabethans loved to make wagers. Right?"

He looked as if I'd said *excrement*. "Wagers? Ah, yes, I suppose I *do* know they were gamblers. But I can't allow the castle to be the scene of—"

"I'm not talking Las Vegas. You should steer clear of financial wagers, because the parents won't be happy if the kids beg for dough. But how about some small ball games, in addition to the fencing demonstration?"

"Brilliant!" he exclaimed, slapping the desk. "Penny prick! Shuttlecock! We'll use half of the Great Hall for the games! Can you give the food some game-playing names?"

"We can have the veal roast with..." I frowned, then inspiration struck. "Penny-

215

Prick Potato Casserole. Raisin Rice with...Shut-tlecock Shrimp Curry. I don't know if you can give molded strawberry salads, steamed broc-coli, or chutney and curry side dishes Tudor names. But after the meal, we'll play games and have the plum tart."

"Perfect!" he cried. "I am so delighted I employed you!"

He beamed, I beamed, the sun beamed in on us. Then he announced he had to go figure out how to arrange the Great Hall. He man-aged another regal wave, this time in the direction of the telephone, and told me to feel free to make my calls. *Mi palacio es su palacio*, he announced grandly, then departed.

The Furman County Sheriff's Department was first on my list. Once through, I pressed the numbers for Sergeant Boyd's extension.

"Listen," I said after he'd asked about Tom and I'd assured him Tom was on the mend, "you know those intelligence files you keep on people?"

"For crying out loud, Goldy, you know I can't give you a file."

"I just want to know what you've got in *one*. Viv Martini."

"Your ex's new girlfriend? How do you think that's going to look, somebody hears I'm giving you that information?"

"Sergeant Boyd, Captain Lambert already told me she slept with Ray Wolff and possibly Andy Balachek. But now she's doing a com-plicated real estate deal with John Richard Korman. To be specific, she plunked down a hundred fifty thousand dollars to go in on a condo sale with him in Beaver Creek. He *never* agrees to joint ownership, so something's going on."

"Where'd she get a hundred fifty thousand bucks?" Boyd's voice was distant. He was riffling papers.

"You tell me."

"We watched her bank account after those stamps were stolen. Nothing happened."

"Well," I said, "did you all check any stores besides pawnshops after the stamp heist?"

"I don't know. Our guys are supposed to, but sometimes they don't have time to get to specialty places." He sighed. "Okay, here's the file. You breathe a word of this, I'm fired. Viv's been hooked up with Wolff since she got out of high school. But, let's see...it says here a snitch in Golden put Viv Martini back...okay, seven years ago, she was shacked up with your good buddy there at the castle, Eliot Hyde."

"*What?*" I glanced around the room. Any listening devices? Where had Eliot gone?

"That's what it says."

I gulped. "So Andy Balachek and Tom were shot right near Eliot's property, and Viv Martini, who's been involved with Andy, possibly, and definitely Andy's accomplice, Ray, who was arrested by Tom, this same Viv has an old relationship with Eliot Hyde? Did you guys question Eliot after Tom was shot?"

"Of course we did! He claims not to have seen Viv in years."

217

I shook my head, puzzled. "What possible attraction could there have been between Eliot Hyde and Viv Martini?"

"For crying out loud, Goldy! She's good-looking, he's not bad, he wanted a cute girlfriend and she figured he was loaded. Our snitch says she wanted him to start an illegal casino there. This was just when gambling was legalized, but only for Central City and Blackhawk. The snitch says Viv wanted to accommodate the home-town gamblers at the castle. They could use all those halls and rooms to hide people, in case of a cop raid."

Remembering how Eliot had blanched at my mention of wagers, I still felt skeptical. "Was this casino-castle her idea? Or Ray Wolff's?"

"Who knows? All I know is Eliot nixed it, said it would make him look bad if he was caught, and he couldn't afford that." Boyd paused, and I thought of Eliot's sensitivity regarding *reputation*. Boyd asked, "How'd you find out about the condo?"

"I have my snitches, too, Sergeant." When he sighed again, I asked, "What about those specialty stores, then? Any stamps show up there?"

"Why, you got something I need to know?" When I said I didn't, he went on: "The insurer for The Stamp Fox is hiring a private investigator, and has promised to share anything he gets. We're concentrating on the investigations into the deaths of the driver and Balachek."

"You must have investigated Viv Martini."

218

"Of course. She was sleeping with your ex-husband all night Sunday night. And they weren't getting much sleep, according to your ex. Please *don't* interrogate either one of them."

"Whatever you say," I replied, then pretended to ponder a bit. "Listen," I said, trying to sound thoughtful, "do Buddy and Chardé Lauderdale have alibis for the time Tom was shot? A little while ago, they were both here at Hyde Castle, giving me a hard time."

"What kind of hard time?"

I told him about the incident in the Hydes' kitchen, to which Boyd replied, "Their alibi is each other. Oh, and we checked on Sukie Hyde's first husband. One of his guys was on the roof with him when he stepped on a stray wire from a bathroom fan. Nobody seemed to think it was suspicious." He paused. "But here's something related to the stamp heist. Our friend Buddy Lauderdale was in The Stamp Fox a month before the theft, asking about values. He said he wanted to invest in stamps, but never did." When I made a *hmm*-ing noise, Boyd warned me to be careful, that Buddy Lauderdale was reputedly one of the best shots in the county. I promised him I would be, and signed off.

One thing was certain. There was no way I was waiting for some faraway insurance company to get around to hiring an investigator. Eliot's lowest desk drawer yielded a Yellow Pages, and under "Stamps—Collectors," I found four shops in the Denver area. I blithely let my fingers do the walking while presenting myself as Francesca Chastain, collector of any stamp with a picture of royalty. Price, I said, was no object. Even over the phone, you could hear those store owners' hearts speed up.

The first three, general dealers in stamps and coins, said they hadn't seen a cover with Queen Victoria on it anywhere but at stamp shows. But the fourth philatelic dealer, an estate auction agent named Troy McIntire operating out of his home in Golden, gave me an evasive reply.

"What *exactly* are you looking for?" McIntire demanded.

"I collect anything with kings or queens on the stamps. What I'm especially looking for is covers with Queen Victoria on them."

"I might be able to help you," McIntire said, with a forced reluctance that sounded cagey. "If price really is no object, and the price is paid in cash."

I eagerly made an appointment for that afternoon, then leafed through the phone book for Southwest Hospital. I talked to three nurses before I located the flight nurse who had helped Tom. Her name was Norma Randall. She was on duty on the third floor, and said she could talk for five minutes.

"The cop," Norma Randall said, remembering. "Day before yesterday? Tom? Couldn't forget *him*. Or you, either. He's doing okay?"

"Yes," I replied. "Thanks to you all. You... seemed to be...more experienced than most flight nurses." Once you passed thirty, I'd observed, being *experienced* was the euphemism for being *older*.

She laughed. "I've been doing it a long time. Too long, I think sometimes." She paused. "Weren't you married to Dr. John Richard Korman?" When I replied that I was, she went on: "I worked with him one time, after we brought in an Aspen Meadow woman with a retained placenta."

I made a noncommittal *mm-mm* noise.

"Don't worry, he did a fine job," she said, reading my mind. "What can I do for you now?"

"I don't want to keep you, Norma, but I'm... trying to locate a cousin who's a flight nurse. Where did you do your nursing training?"

"Nebraska."

"Well," I said boldly, "do you know anyone at the hospital who would have gone to The Front Range School of Nursing in the late sixties? I'm particularly interested in *women* who would have had flight nurse training."

She said she didn't know anyone off the top of her head, but her relief had just come in, and she could ask a few people, if I wanted. I thanked her and said I didn't mind being put on hold.

"I found one of the older ER techs," she informed me triumphantly on her return. "He told me there was a flight nurse named Connie Oliver who graduated from Front Range at about the time you're talking about. He thinks she may have switched to being a school nurse. Denver or Furman County."

I thanked Nurse Randall and signed off, then decided to bypass Denver and hope for luck with Furman County Schools' central office. I was listening to the choices of an automated phone-answering system when rapping at the study door nearly made me drop the phone.

Julian cried, "Breakfast! And it came from across the North Pole, via the castle garden!" Flourishing a large silver tray, he pushed through the heavy door. Michaela Kirovsky followed him, holding a coffeepot. Julian's energy filled the study as he bounced forward. "Hey, boss?" he asked me with a grin. "Don't give me that look like you can't eat." When I hastily hung up, he cried, "Hey! Wha'd you swallow, a canary?"

CHAPTER 17

Y ou're going to love this," Julian announced as he set the tray laden with golden-glazed miniature Bundt cakes on Eliot's desk. It was actually two trays, one on top of the other.

"Got multiple orders for room service?" I asked mildly. "When in doubt, Bundt?"

"I'm putting half of this on the other tray for Tom. He's still asleep, I just checked. Michaela's helping because she forgot some equipment and had to come back to the castle." In addition to the cakes sparkling with orange zest and sugar, there were two plastic-wrapped crystal bowls. Julian pulled off the plastic and revealed snowy yogurt artfully topped with slices of kiwi, strawberry, banana, apple, and plum. "Oh," he said, "I'm saving that sweet bread you made for later, since it was too hot to cut. I made these orange cakes last night while the dinner was cooking." He glanced around the study and wrinkled his nose. "Man! What decade is it?"

"Any decade you want, for a price," Michaela supplied with a wicked smile.

"Do I detect animosity toward the decorator?" I asked mildly.

Michaela snorted. "Chardé keeps asking when she gets to do my place. I keep telling Eliot: Never."

When she didn't elaborate, I said, "Thanks for bringing the goodies over, guys. I thought if I didn't have caffeine soon, I was going to pass out."

Michaela nodded wordlessly as Julian relieved her of the coffeepot and poured me a steaming cup. I thanked him, took a sip—*Zowie!* good stuff—and glanced at Michaela. Her pale skin glowed in the daylight. But her eyes remained clouded. She pressed her lips together, and I wondered if she thought she'd said too much about Chardé. But there was something else there…. What? Did she know something she wasn't sharing?

"Michaela, I need to ask you a question." When I put down my cup, it clattered in the china saucer. "As you know, my husband was shot next to Hyde Chapel. By Cottonwood Creek, near where poor Andy Balachek's body was found. You live in the gatehouse, with a view of the front of the castle. Did you see anything at all late Sunday night? Or early Monday morning? People moving? Cars parked?"

She flushed deeply. "No. Sorry. The police already asked me about that, when they came over to talk to Eliot and Sukie. I don't have a view of the creek. I didn't see anything."

She's not telling the truth, my mind insisted. *Why?* "How about Andy Balachek? Did you keep up with him after his father fixed the dam?"

More blushing. "Yes," she replied, "I knew Andy. His mother died when he was little. We used to have a small...club, I guess you'd call it, for locals of Russian and eastern European descent. In my father's time, we gathered here at the castle, for the holidays. We'd visit and make our favorite foods. Peter and Roberta Balachek always brought baby Andy." She cleared her throat uneasily. "And then Roberta got cancer and died, and little Andy grew up and became big Andy. We got gambling in the state, and Andy—well, his addiction just about killed poor Peter." She looked at her hands, struggling visibly to compose herself. "I know Andy was found near where your husband was shot. You want to know all you can about him. There just isn't much." She inhaled. "My free period's almost over. I need to get back to school...."

"You seem very sensitive to boys. Andy Balachek. My Arch. It's a gift."

She hesitated at the study door. "I didn't do Andy much good, though, did I?"

"*Whoa,*" observed Julian when she'd left. He refilled my cup. "What was *that* about?"

"I don't know. What was she like at Elk Park Prep?"

A frown wrinkled Julian's handsome face. "Quiet. Really hard-working. Lonely, it seemed to me, but I didn't fence, so I didn't know her very well. One time when we had a senior tour here, we asked her about the baby who'd supposedly been thrown down the well. She said that story was borscht, a mix-up from the ghost story about the duke. She isn't the most charismatic coach at Elk Park Prep, but she's, you know, a *stalwart.* Like Tom. Everybody likes her. Everybody likes Tom. What's the matter?"

My ears were ringing. *Everybody likes Tom.* At this point, I couldn't talk to Tom, Arch, or gossip-hungry Marla. But I had to talk to *somebody* I trusted, or the secret was going to explode inside of me. "Julian." I looked him straight in the eyes. "I'm afraid Tom is having an affair—"

"Bull!"

"Or maybe he *was* having an affair and broke it off." I choked. "I think he might have been shot by this other woman, who could be his ex-fiancée. Then again, unless she was somehow involved with Andy Balachek, she couldn't have guessed he would show up at the chapel, right?"

"Tom's ex-*fiancée?* What are you talking about?"

"Her name is Sara Beth O'Malley. She was a nurse who supposedly died at the end of the Vietnam war."

"*What?*"

"She reportedly died in a helo crash on the Mekong Delta, but she didn't. I'm telling you, she's not dead. She sent him e-mails." I gulped. "And she was watching our house, too."

"Watching the house? When? Did you tell the police?"

I tore my gaze away from his face: His concern and love tugged at my heart. Outside, the moat reflected the sky. "I told the investigators a woman was there, not who she was."

He plopped into one of Eliot's leather armchairs and softened his tone. "When did you first think this woman wasn't dead?"

"After Tom was shot, he said, 'I don't love her.' Then he passed out. Since he got out of surgery, he hasn't talked about who he meant. I'm not even sure he remembers saying anything." I felt blood seep into my cheeks.

"And you saw this same woman outside the house?"

"Trudy next door saw her first, the morning after our window was shattered. This woman parked outside our house and kept staring at it. I tried to talk to her, but she refused to talk to me. She just took off. From old photographs, I thought she looked just like an older version of the woman Tom was once engaged to. She's very pretty.... And her name's Sara Beth O'Malley. Those old photographs? Signed just like the recent e-mails: 'S.B.' "

226

"So she *didn't* die over there. Incredible. And now she's back. But why?"

"According to her e-mail, she's here to get supplies. To get her teeth fixed. To hook up with her old flame. All of the above, or none. Besides e-mails from her, there was one from the State Department. Tom had written them to see if there'd been any old or new reports of Sara Beth O'Malley surviving the attack that supposedly killed her. State said no."

Julian was pensive. "Goldy...do you want me to ask Tom about it?"

"No!" My hands clenched. "I just don't know what to do."

Julian stood, picked up the top tray, then moved a silver place setting and the coffeepot to the bottom tray. Using tongs, he transferred one of the miniature Bundt cakes to a small plate, then set out a place mat and silverware on the desk.

He hefted up the tray and studied me a moment. "Boss, you've got a sleep debt the size of a jumbo mortgage. You need to rest, have something to eat, wait until you can think again. There's too much going on to keep it all straight. Why don't you just concentrate on Tom, Arch, and our catering jobs this week? We'll get Tom better, then we'll ask him." When I said nothing, he headed for the door. "Look," he said over his shoulder, "how 'bout I tell Tom about one of my old high-school girl-friends who showed up at C.U. We broke up and she got cancer, supposedly. Then it turns out she got better and decided to go to college, where she looked me up." He balanced the tray and opened the door. "See what he says."

"An old girlfriend of yours? With cancer? Is that true?"

He flashed a smile back at me. "I wouldn't tell *you,* Miss Nosy, if it was."

"Thanks, Julian."

"Don't mention it."

I swigged the rich coffee, spooned up the yogurt, downed half of the succulent cake, licked my fingers, and redialed the Furman County Schools' central office. After maneuvering through the options network, I was finally connected to an administrator in charge of student medical care.

"I'm from Aspen Meadow, and I'm looking for a school nurse named Connie Oliver," I began pleasantly. "I need to check on an outbreak of strep."

When I was put on hold, I scanned Eliot's elegant office. To the right of the glowing bay window, Chardé had placed an Oriental-style silk screen. On the other, I noticed, was a molding-framed opening. With sudden recognition, I realized it was one of those wall indentations that indicated a garderobe. Sheesh! Those medieval folks must have had to go to the bathroom a *lot*—

"What strep outbreak?" I was rudely asked. I'd almost forgotten I was on the phone.

"It was reported in January at our middle school," I shot back. I knew about the strep outbreak from the *Mountain Journal.* After several more long minutes of holding, the administrator returned.

"We can't search the medical files over the phone."

"That's all right. If I could just speak to Nurse Oliver, we could clear up the question of my son's medication. She treated him."

"Without the files, Ms. Oliver cannot be expected—"

"Don't worry, I'll take the responsibility!" I replied, trying to sound chipper. "I just want to chat for a sec, if she's available. Do you know which schools she'll be visiting today?"

A sigh. "Ms. Oliver will be overseeing vision tests at Fox Meadows Elementary from ten-thirty to noon," the woman informed me tartly. "Please identify yourself at the school office before seeking her out." She hung up before I could thank her.

Bureaucrats!

I finished the last of the luscious cake and considered what to do next. It was quarter to nine. I needed to work out the prep for the next day's lunch and then check on Tom. And of course we all had to eat tonight, so there was also dinner for six to consider. But not yet. First, I had to think.

The drawers to Eliot's desk were not locked. With only a slight pang of guilt—*if he didn't want folks going through his drawers, he'd lock them, right?*—I rummaged for a clean sheet of paper. One drawer yielded pamphlets from conference centers across the country. Under that lay a legal pad filled with painstaking notes comparing prices, accommodations, and length of stay. Apparently, Eliot had no truck with computers, which could have produced such a spreadsheet in seconds. There was no blank paper. The next drawer held worn, slightly dusty pamphlets: *Medieval Castles and Their Secrets. Have Your Wedding at Hyde Chapel!* And *A Brief Tour of Hyde Castle.* There were also several copies of the audiotape Eliot had been urging me to listen to: *The History of the Labyrinth.* I slipped one of the audiotapes in my sweater pocket, then rifled through the pamphlets: There were between six and ten banded copies of each one, so I helped myself to one of each—the better to know the place where I was doing my job, I rationalized—then stuck them in my pocket, too. Finally, I went back to the first drawer and ripped a clean sheet of paper from the back of the legal pad.

CHRONOLOGY, I wrote at the top of the page.

1. *January 1.* The Lauderdales, in financial trouble, have New Year's party. Buddy shakes baby. I call cops. The Lauderdales swear revenge.
2. *January 15.* Valuable stamps—easily fenced in the Far East—are stolen from FedEx truck. The driver is killed. Witnesses say there were three robbers. Peter Balachek has a heart attack.
3. *January 20.* Frightened, worried that

his father will die, Andy Balachek identifies himself to Tom as one of the truck-hijacking gang. Andy tries to make a plea deal. Tells Tom where Ray Wolff will be.

4. *January 22.* Tom arrests Ray Wolff on Andy's tip. In another e-mail, Andy refuses to give location of valuable stamps.

5. *January 24.* Andy sends a third e-mail to Tom, saying he has a stake and is going to Atlantic City to gamble. Tom takes off for New Jersey.

6. *February 6.* Andy calls me from Central City, desperate to talk to Tom. John Richard Korman gets out of jail early. He immediately hooks up with his new girlfriend, Ray Wolff's old lover, who is also Eliot Hyde's old lover, Viv Martini. He has told Arch he's going to buy an expensive present for Viv.

7. *February 9.* Our window is shot out.

8. *February 9.* I find Andy's dead body in the creek, near Hyde Chapel, where I'm supposed to cater later in the day. Andy had an electric shock, then was shot and killed. Tom is shot.

9. *February 10.* Our computers are stolen. I discover that Tom's long-lost fiancée, Sara Beth O'Malley, has reappeared after many years of "death." Supposedly, she is living under an assumed identity in Vietnam, and works as a vil-

lage doctor. The Jerk is driving a new gold Mercedes from Lauderdale Imports. He and Viv Martini have entered into an unusual real estate venture.

10. *February 11.* Michaela Kirovsky says she knew Andy Balachek when he visited the castle, but acts as if she's covering something up.

How were these people—Andy, Viv, John Richard, Eliot, Sukie, Chardé and Buddy, Sara Beth, and Michaela—linked? Or were they? Had Tom been the target of the shooter, or had I? And what event would disrupt our lives next? I did not know.

I *did* know one thing, contrary to Michaela's assertion: *Andy was the key*. Andy who stole, Andy who gambled, Andy who talked, Andy who ended up dead in Cottonwood Creek. And I wasn't going to learn any more about him sitting in Eliot Hyde's fit-for-a-prime-minister office.

I tucked the packet of zirconia into my pocket with the pamphlets and tape, then scooped up the tray. I maneuvered my load into the hall and decided that before checking on Tom, I would see if Michaela was still in the castle. If I could convince her that whoever had shot Tom had to be connected to Andy's death, maybe she'd come up with some information about the dead young man.

To my left, double glass doors opened onto the hallway that led to the north range and the

232

gatehouse, where Michaela resided. I hesitated when I read a hand-lettered sign spanning the glass doors: UNDER CONSTRUCTION—NO ADMITTANCE! I listened for the bang and clatter of construction workers, but heard nothing. Was this northern side of the west range where Chardé was doing intensive new decorating work, I wondered? Did she insist on being left alone? Did I care?

I wondered what kind of construction could be taking place. The castle already had a pool, a Great Hall, and a fencing loft. Maybe a movie theater was next. Surely they didn't mean *I* couldn't be admitted, I reasoned, as I pushed through the door. If I ran into Chardé, I could use the tray as a shield.

The hall looked almost identical to the one next to Eliot's office. Pale green Oriental runners bisected the dark hardwood floor. Medieval-looking tapestries lined the walls. There were two doors. The first one, Eliot had told me, led to his and Sukie's bedroom. Past the door at the far end, another glass entryway led, presumably, into the northwest drum tower. I walked down the hall with great care, just in case I encountered a hole in the floor or an unfriendly decorator.

The construction, such as it was, was used-to-be-fresh paint by the far door—more of the same paint that was elsewhere in the castle—with another *Wet Paint* sign by the door. Here, it looked as if someone had spilled or thrown a can of the viscous beige stuff on the wall, on the floor, and on the lower half of the wooden door. The door itself had no security pad, but had some holes in it at regular intervals. Above the doorknob was a formidable, new-looking brass padlock.

I stared at the spilled paint. The hardened, abstract pool of beige looked worse than in the living room or up in the hall by our room. It was so unsightly and random that I wondered if this was what the argument between Eliot and Michaela had been about. *Chardé keeps asking when she gets to do my place.* Maybe Michaela had spilled the paint, when she was just supposed to dab it around artistically. Had Eliot suspected Michaela of making the mess, and accused her, or caught her? And they'd fought? That seemed pretty silly.

Hold on. I put down the tray and peered intently at the padlock. Only half of it was completely screwed into place; the other hung limply from a single screw, as if the package containing the lock had not yielded enough of the little suckers that you needed to attach it to whatever you were trying to lock.

And I thought buying a not-enough-nails package only happened to me.

I knocked on the door. No reply. Quickly, before I could think about it, I applied the same principle to this door that I had to Eliot's unsecured desk drawers. *If you don't want me checking on things, better make sure they're locked up.* I pushed through the door.

"What the heck—" I said aloud, as I stared at stained white walls, arched windows filled with plain, not leaded, glass, and a jumble of bookshelves bursting with toys, worn picture books, wooden blocks, and boxed games. Ranged at the edges of a stained, odd-size pink rug, was battered furniture in shades of green, blue, and pink. What was *this* room used for? Was Eliot so eccentric that he kept a playroom for the dead duke, in case Ghost-Boy got tired of haunting the castle and wanted a quick game of Chutes and Ladders? Or was this a nursery where Eliot and Michaela had played as children—a place that would be turned into a baby-sitting room for the conference center?

I thought I heard footsteps coming from the direction of the study. When I peeked around the doorjamb, however, the hall was empty. I scurried out, carefully closing the door behind me, and picked up my tray. Then I continued away from the study, soldiering on down toward the drum tower.

It must have been some kind of baby-sitter's room, I decided as I scurried along. I shoved through the second set of glass doors—also marked with NO ADMITTANCE signs—and again encountered the chill of a corner tower. Was the door to the sitter's room getting a padlock because the Hydes didn't want Chardé to give it a decorating overhaul? Had visitors in Eliot's father's time come to the castle for a tour, and brought the children because there was free baby-sitting? Later, I'd have to check my snitched pamphlets for a Hyde Castle floor plan.

I pushed into the last hallway, which was

identical to the one by Eliot's office. These two doors, however, were marked with small brass plates that read *Private Residence.* Hoping to find Michaela, I knocked on each one, but received no reply.

Finally I walked out onto the ground floor of the gatehouse, where Arch and I had entered upon our arrival. The front portcullis and the massive wooden gates were closed; the alarm was set. Good, I thought. No way for the Jerk to push his way in.

When I arrived in the empty kitchen minutes later, the air was once again frigid from the open window. I banged my tray down, looked out the window—a forty-foot drop to the moat, with no way for the Jerk or the Lauderdales to climb up—and slammed the errant window shut. I was thankful that the kitchen held only a tiny reminder that the Lauderdales had even been there: Chardé had left a pile of decorating magazines and folders by the hearth.

Once my dishes were stowed in the dishwasher, I scanned the menu for the following day's lunch. The boxes of frozen homemade chicken stock I'd brought would form the base for the luncheon's cream of chicken soup and the banquet's shrimp curry. I chewed the inside of my cheek and used the kitchen phone to reconfirm with Alicia, my supplier. She had been scheduled to bring all the ingredients for the banquet—veal roasts, frozen jumbo shrimp, fresh strawberries and bananas for the molded salad, and bunches of broccoli—

to our house on Friday morning. I left a message asking that the foodstuffs, plus a lamb roast and a couple of extra bags of *haricots verts* and Yukon Gold potatoes, be brought to Hyde Castle today, if possible. I provided the phone number and a warning that she'd have to alert the residents to the time of her arrival, so they could open the portcullis. Knowing Alicia, she'd think portcullis was a drink, and want some.

While giving my message to Alicia's voice mail, I'd found a second, larger microwave oven cleverly hidden inside what looked like a bread box. After some experimentation with programming, I started the chicken stock defrosting, then minced a mountain of shallots, carrots, and celery. Soon the hearty scent of vegetables simmering in a pool of melted butter filled the kitchen. I tried to recall what I'd read that morning from my research disk on English food. After some thought, I sketched out a simple plan for the evening meal: lamb roast with pan gravy and mint jelly, baked potatoes, steamed *haricots verts*, a large tossed salad with grated fresh Parmesan cheese, and homemade bread. I'd brought the potatoes, beans, bread, and greens from home. If Alicia couldn't make it today, Julian could go out and pick up the lamb roast.

For dessert, it would probably be good to make a dish with some historic significance. But the Elizabethans had favored marzipan, and I wasn't up to doing marzipan *anything*.

My eyes fell on the Stained-Glass Sweet Bread I'd made earlier that morning, but decided it would be better for tea. I chewed the inside of my cheek some more.

The Hydes' freezer yielded a gallon of premium ice cream: Swiss Chocolate, no surprise. With ice cream, I'd learned long ago, it's better to serve at least two different kinds of cookies. One should be crunchy and redolent of a spice, such as ginger, or a flavoring, like vanilla or almond. The other should be soft and rich, smeared with a creamy icing, if possible. After some deliberation, I decided on a shortbread for the former, which I'd name after Queen Elizabeth's rival to the north, Mary, Queen of Scots. The other, a chocolate cookie whose dark, fudgy essence and brownie-like texture I could already savor, I would call 911 Cookies—for chocolate emergencies. I was in an extended one right now.

I beat confectioners' sugar into butter, added a hint of vanilla, and mixed in two kinds of flour sifted with a tad of leavening. I patted the shortbread dough into round cake pans, scored each into wedges, and fluted the rims. Once I'd started the buttery shortbreads on their slow bake to divine flakiness, I melted dark bittersweet chocolate with butter and sifted dry ingredients for the 911's. Like the sweet bread, these, too, would benefit from a brief mellowing, only in the refrigerator. Once I'd mixed the dough, I covered the bowl with plastic wrap, set it to chill, and slipped up to see Tom.

"He said he wants to rest," Julian whispered to me as he precariously balanced the tray while closing the door. "I changed the bandage after he ate. He only had a few bites, but we did have a good visit. He didn't say anything about getting any on the side."

"Julian!" I scolded, "I need to set our security system," I said, feeling guilty that I hadn't come up earlier.

"I did that, too. I found the directions in the bedside drawer of the room Arch and I are in." Gripping Tom's tray, he looked all around before whispering, "Both of 'em are set to Arch's birthday."

"Thanks, Julian." Arch had been born on April the fifteenth, a happy respite from thoughts of the Internal Revenue Service. At least, that was the way I had always viewed it: *Joy and Taxes*. Julian showed me the red light on our armed door, and the green-lit keypad beside it.

"One more thing," Julian warned as we started back down the hall. "Tom wants to start cooking again."

"You're kidding."

"Nope. He has an idea for a hearty breakfast dish."

"Good Lord."

"Well, at least that means his mind is getting hungry, even if his body hasn't caught up. He says he's going to start tomorrow. He wants to get on with his life."

I rolled my eyes. "Did you tell him your girlfriend story?"

911 Chocolate Emergency Cookies

6 ounces semisweet chocolate chips
6 ounces bittersweet chocolate, broken into large pieces (recommended brands: Lindt Bittersweet, Godiva Dark)
8 tablespoons (1 stick) unsalted butter, softened and divided
1½ cups all-purpose flour
⅓ cup unsweetened Dutch-style cocoa (recommended brand: Hershey's European-style)
1½ teaspoons baking powder
½ teaspoon salt
¾ cup dark brown sugar, firmly packed
¾ cup granulated sugar
3 large eggs
1½ teaspoons vanilla extract
Vanilla Icing (recipe follows)

In the top of a double boiler, melt the chips, chopped chocolate, and 4 tablespoons (½ stick) of the butter. When melted, set aside to cool briefly.

Sift together the flour, cocoa, baking powder, and salt. Set aside.

In a large mixing bowl, beat the remaining 4 tablespoons of butter with the sugars. When the mixture is the consistency of wet sand, add the eggs and vanilla. Mix in the slightly cooled chocolate mixture, beating only until combined. Stir in the flour mixture, mixing only until completely combined and no traces of flour appear.

Cover the bowl with plastic wrap and refrigerate for 25 minutes, until the mixture can be easily spooned up with an ice-cream scoop.

Preheat the oven to 350°F. Butter two cookie sheets.

Using a 4-teaspoon ice-cream scoop, measure out a dozen cookies per sheet. Bake one sheet at a time for about 9 to 11 minutes, just until the cookies have puffed and flattened. Do not overbake; the cookies will firm up upon cooling. Allow the cookies to cool 2 minutes on

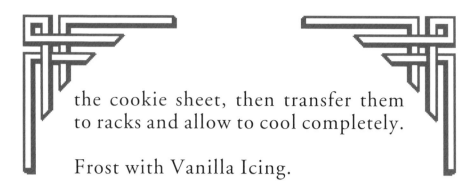

the cookie sheet, then transfer them to racks and allow to cool completely.

Frost with Vanilla Icing.

Makes 4 dozen cookies

Vanilla Icing:

4 tablespoons (½ stick) unsalted
   butter, softened
⅓ cup whipping cream
¾ teaspoon vanilla extract
2¾-cups confectioners' sugar, or
   more if needed

Beat the butter until very creamy. Gradually add the cream, vanilla, and confectioners' sugar and beat well. If necessary, add more confectioners' sugar to the icing. It should be fairly stiff, not soupy. Spread a thick layer of icing on each cookie.

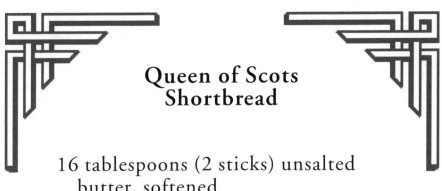

Queen of Scots
Shortbread

16 tablespoons (2 sticks) unsalted
   butter, softened
½ cup confectioners' sugar
¾ teaspoon vanilla extract
1½ cups all-purpose flour
½ cup rice flour (available at health
   food stores) or all-purpose flour
¼ teaspoon baking powder
¼ teaspoon salt

Preheat the oven to 350°F.

In the large bowl of an electric mixer,
beat the butter until it is very creamy.
Add the confectioners' sugar and beat
well, about 5 minutes. Beat in the
vanilla. Sift the flours with the baking
powder and salt, then add them to the
butter mixture, beating only until well
combined.

With floured fingers, gently pat the
dough into two ungreased 8-inch round
cake pans. Using the floured tines of a
fork, score the shortbreads into eighths.

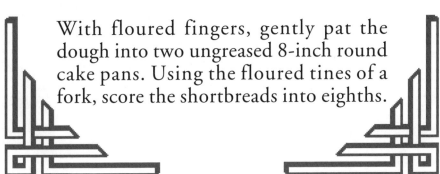

Press the tines around the edges of each shortbread to resemble fluting, and prick the shortbread with a decorative design, if desired.

Bake for 20 to 25 minutes, or until the edge of the shortbread is just beginning to brown. Allow to cool 10 minutes on a rack. While the shortbread is still warm, gently cut through the marked-off wedges. Using a pointed metal spatula or pie server, carefully lever out the shortbread wedges and allow them to cool completely on a rack.

Makes 16 wedge-shaped cookies

"Nah. Didn't seem right—trying to get the truth out of a cop who's confined to bed because he's been shot."

After a few moments, we banged back into the kitchen, where—miraculously—the window had stayed closed. I showed Julian the beginnings of the soup and the shortbreads, and told him about the now-thickened fudgy chocolate cookie dough. When I pulled out the shortbreads, Julian dug into Sukie's perfectly organized kitchen-equipment drawer, extracted an ice-cream scoop, and offered to make the chocolate cookies.

I thanked him and mentioned I should be going. "Taste the chocolate cookies," I added, "to see if they need icing. We'll be serving everybody chocolate ice cream, too. Oh, and if Alicia doesn't show, do you think you could pick up a lamb roast?" I recited the evening meal menu; he said that would be no problem. I told him all the places I'd be that day, if he got a hankering for cell-phone communication.

"I'll keep an eye on Tom, too," he offered. "And take him snacks, to jump-start his energy supply."

"You're great," I said, and meant it. My eyes fell back to the pile of folders and magazines Chardé had left on the kitchen hearth. I picked them up. On the bottom was Chardé's portfolio, a slick two-page folder with photographs of some of her decorating assignments. On the back of the folder was a photo: a family portrait of Buddy, Chardé, their teenage son, Howie, and their baby girl, Patty. As an afterthought, I snagged one of the framed newspaper photos from the kitchen wall. This one featured a picture of Eliot and Sukie caught in an enthusiastic kiss, with a caption about the auction of Henry's letter being complete.

Figuring they could come in handy, I tucked the portfolio and picture into my oversize canvas tote bag. I could show the pictures to the stamp agent in Golden...which, in turn, might lead me closer to finding out who had shot Tom. Impulsively, I climbed up to Arch's room and grabbed his high-powered binoculars. Constellations at night, bad guys during the day: Not a stellar combination.

CHAPTER 18

I blinked at the sunshine that suffused the sky. Fair days in the Colorado winter feature a low-hanging sun glazing snow-covered fields and hills. The glare can become so intensely bright that to drive without sunglasses is to invite disaster.

I adjusted my shades, set my jaw, and headed east toward The Stamp Fox. Tom had repeatedly told me that the most profitable time to catch a crook was the first forty-eight hours after the commission of a crime. I had just passed that landmark forty-eighth hour, with zero results. I lowered the driver-side visor against the dazzle, and accelerated down the mountain.

I slowed when I spotted Lauderdale's Luxury Imports on the north side of the highway. Not too many businesses are situated at the base of the foothills above Denver, as the sloping sites provide monumental construction challenges. But Buddy Lauderdale had found a plateau for his sprawling enterprise, and acres of Jaguars, Mercedeses, BMWs, and Audis glittered enticingly in the sun. I exited the highway, wended along a northbound frontage road, then parked across from the showroom and a lot crammed with late-model Jaguars. Jumping out, I focused the binocs on the eastward view from the offices that flanked the showroom.

Not surprisingly, the Furman East Shopping Center sprang instantly into view. Designed like a rustic Mexican town, with dark pink stucco and orange-brown roof tiles, the cluster of shops boasted a fake bell tower sandwiched between an upscale women's clothing store and a glass-fronted independent bookstore. The Stamp Fox was a bit harder to spot, but eventually I nailed it, flanked by an Italian ice cream store and a florist.

Out front stood a FedEx box.

So you could see everything from here, if you knew what to look for. Hmm. I jumped back in the van and hightailed it to the mall.

The Stamp Fox was a tiny, gold-wallpapered shop that resembled a fifties-era jewelry store. Electrified candles from an oversize fixture reflected in the brass-lined glass cases. Inside each case, handwritten envelopes with gloriously colored stamps—*covers* with *frankings,* to the connoisseurs—begged to be studied. Maybe stamp-collecting was like riding a bike; you never forgot how. I sighed, and wondered what had happened to my painstakingly collected box of glassine-enveloped stamps. I'd left it behind at home when I'd gone off to boarding school. Probably been eaten by mice in the attic.

The shop owner was out, according to his overweight, pale assistant, whose name tag informed me he was *Steve Byron, Philatelist.* This Byron, whose only romantic inclination had to do with postal history, had a round face to match his round body. He was about twenty-two, and had neatly waved short brown hair and small, colorless eyes behind glasses as thick as bottle-bottoms. *The Michelin Man as Stamp Guy.* Byron finished locking a glass case, parted his thick lips in a hopeful smile, and waddled toward me.

"Collector?" he asked cheerfully. "Looking for something in particular? We've got a brand-new estate sale just in. You're the first. Top-flight stuff."

I blurted out, "I'm Francesca Chastain, and I'm a thematic collector," before I had a chance to think. I was careful not to touch my purse, as I'd heard that showed a subconscious desire not to spend money. Instead, I put a voracious gleam in my eye and tried to think of a nonexistent theme for my obsolete hobby. "I'm the *first* to see a new set of covers?" I asked greedily. "Do you take Visa?"

Steve Byron gurgled with happiness. "Oh, *yes*. Your collecting theme is...?"

I gulped. I was looking for news of the Mauritius Queen Victoria stamp theft, and some indication that Sara Beth O'Malley had come back from Vietnam with an agenda that included more than fixing her teeth. Still, I did not want to appear to be the snoop I actually was. I swallowed and tried to think how to mask my intentions while weaseling information out of Byron.

"A picture of any place or person beginning with the letter *V*." To Byron's look of puzzlement, I waved a hand in the air, à la Eliot. "Uh...Vatican City. Venezuela. Venice. Frankings with pictures of...Queen Victoria." Steve Byron's fleshy mouth fell open. "And don't ask me if I have a Penny Black. I don't. I'll buy one from you, though." Almost as an afterthought, I added, "Stamps from *Vietnam*."

"I didn't catch your name," stammered Byron.

"Francesca Chastain. Do you have any pieces to show me?"

He licked his lips. "We don't have anything with Victoria. We did, but they're gone." He hesitated. "I do have a couple of covers showing Venice, from a time when there was an international effort to save the city from sinking. And I've got one from Vietnam. I'll show them to you."

The first case he led me to displayed a

cover from Tunisia depicting a mosaic from Venice's Saint Mark's Cathedral. I pretended to show interest. The second cover, though, stunned me. The label indicated that it was from 1973. It depicted a stylized lion, symbol of Saint Mark and, by extension, Venice. The printed words on the stamp were in French: *Pour Venise UNESCO*. This cover was not from France, however, much less Italy. It was from Cambodia, or, as stated below the lion: *République Khmère*.

"Where'd you get this one?" I demanded, too sharply.

He was taken aback. "From the same collector who sold us the one from Vietnam. An American serviceman was stationed over there in the seventies and collected stamps. He came home, became an alcoholic, and was in pretty bad shape when he stumbled into our showroom last fall. He sold his collection to help pay his deductible for thirty days of treatment at a facility." Byron moved to another case. "The Vietnam stamp he sold us is here. It's from '72, from what was then still called South Vietnam. Shows reconstruction after the Tet Offensive. Would you like to see either one of them?"

"Could I talk to the veteran who sold you these covers?" It was a long shot, but maybe he knew something about a local woman who'd turned up dead...if indeed the "veteran" story was true.

Byron shook his head. "He died. He got out of treatment, got plastered, and drove his car the wrong way on I-seventy. A tractor-trailer obliterated him."

"What was his name?"

"Trier. Marcus Trier. His family went to our church, but they moved to Florida. Why do you ask? Did you know Marcus?"

"Just...wondering if we have a mutual friend." I cursed silently and tried to think what to do next. I was still set to visit the stamp agent in Golden, to check out the long possibility that the stolen Queen Victoria stamps had been fenced there. For that expedition, though, I needed something in particular. "Do you have a current catalog of your items for sale? With prices and pictures?"

"Not quite current, but I'll get you what we have." Byron trundled off. After a moment, he returned with a pamphlet-size catalog. "Only some of our inventory is pictured. The reproductions are in color, though." He flipped through the pages. "Prices are from three months ago. Only a few would have changed. Oops, here's some of the Victoria stuff." He picked up a black marker. "I'll just cross it out, since we don't have it any-more."

"No!" I shouted. Startled, the poor boy almost dropped his pen. "I want prices for *every-thing*." To his look of surprise, I gushed apolo-getically, "I'm really a *passionate* collector."

"Guess so." He handed me the catalog, unhappy not to be making a sale. "We can take your Visa over the phone, once you decide what you want."

251

I thanked him and backed out of the store. I had ninety minutes before I was due at the auction agent's house in Golden, and in that interval I had to pick up a few things, find Fox Meadows Elementary, and try to get some information out of Connie Oliver. Worse yet, my stomach was growling on a day that held no lunchbreak. The last emergency truffle in my purse was *not* going to do the trick.

On the other hand, just ten steps away was that Italian ice cream store....

Ten minutes later, I was clutching a bag with newly bought school paste, scissors, and blank paper, and diving into a sugar cone with a triple scoop of dark chocolate gelato. Fox Meadows Elementary, the gelato-scooper had informed me, was a mere fifteen minutes away. The creamy chocolate melted in my mouth as I balanced the cone in my left hand and piloted the van with my right—no easy task. I finally came to the turnoff of a new, winding road that led to the elementary school. I crammed the rest of the cone into my mouth—ecstasy!—and hopped out of the van.

Connie Oliver had just finished testing the vision of the fourth-graders. At least, that was what she said when I introduced myself as Francesca Chastain, my *nom de jour*. Nurse Oliver was of medium height, with makeup covering remnants of freckles in a plain face. I judged her to be about fifty. She greeted me and then self-consciously touched her stiff, frosted-to-cover-the-gray hair. I said I was doing a newspaper piece on how Vietnam had affected graduating classes from high schools, colleges, and nursing schools.

"I wouldn't know," she said flatly, as she led the way out of the stuffy, cabbage-smelling cafeteria to a bench overlooking the playground. The air was cold, but our seat in the sun was warm enough. The children, happy to be out of their classrooms, shrieked and chased each other through the swings. Connie Oliver put on her sunglasses and fixed her eyes on the playground. "We've never had a reunion," she said finally. "It would be too sad. Our class was small, fifteen in all. Right after graduation, two died on a helicopter mission into the foothills, freak snowstorm kind of thing. Later that year, another died in a car crash, and one more died in Vietnam. The rest of us didn't want to get together. It would have been too sad."

"Who died in Vietnam?"

"Aren't you going to take notes?"

"If I need to remember something."

Connie shrugged. She kept her mouth closed for a long time, and I feared she'd changed her mind about talking to me. Finally she said, "Her name was Sara Beth O'Malley. She was with a MASH unit in a valley. It was right before the end of the war. Her unit was overrun and she died...."

I said, "I'm sorry."

Connie looked at me, then returned her gaze to the playground. I knew I hadn't sounded sincere, so I waited a few moments before continuing.

"Did you all get together for...the funeral

service when they shipped Miss O'Malley's body back? To commemorate her belonging to your class?"

Connie Oliver tugged her coat tightly around her and shook her head. "The Army wasn't able to retrieve her body. We didn't have a memorial service."

I *mm-mm*ed sympathetically, and again waited. "Is there anyone who *would* know whether there was a ceremony for Sara Beth O'Malley? Family in the area, something like that?" *Somebody who might be hiding her now?* I added mentally.

"Nah. Sara Beth didn't have a lot of family. Her parents were fairly old when she studied to become a nurse, so they must have passed away by now." Connie Oliver wrinkled her forehead, remembering something. "She was engaged, though. The guy was younger. I think he might still have been in high school when she finished nursing school." I held my breath. She squinted at me. "His name was Tom. Schwartz or Shoemaker or something like that. He adored her. Much later, I heard through the Fox Meadows D.A.R.E. officer that Sara Beth's fiancé had become a cop. I guess you could see if you could find him through the sheriff's department."

"Okay, thanks." I paused, almost overwhelmed by so many words from her strung together at once. I had to ask another question. "Did you ever hear anything about Sara Beth coming back from Vietnam? Like she wasn't really dead after all?"

"No!" She paused, shaking her head, clearly annoyed. "The things you journalists come up with, I swear." A bell rang and she stood up. "I have to go in. You want to know more about Sara Beth, you need to go talk to Tom Schlosser or whoever he was."

"Okay. Thanks. You don't happen to know any more about him?"

She gestured to a boy who was limping toward her. "What is it, George?"

"Mike kicked me. I'm *crippled*. I think I'm going to have to go home."

Connie's voice turned indulgent. "Let me have a look."

As George scooted onto the bench, I said, "I *promise* I'll get out of your hair if you can just finish what you were telling me about Sara Beth's fiancé. Did he grieve over her death?"

"That I don't know," Connie said as she carefully folded down George's sock. I winced at the swelling bruise. No question about it, life on the playground was still pretty darn rough. Connie's voice was quick and dismissive. "All I remember, Miss Chastain, is that even though Tom was younger than Sara Beth, he was terribly protective of her, always calling to see how she was holding up during exams, seeing if she wanted to go out to eat. That kind of thing. He was crazy about her. Some girls have all the luck."

"Thanks again," I repeated forlornly, before sneaking George my last emergency truffle. He gave me a wide smile. I winked at him and left.

On my way to Golden, I called the castle. To my astonishment, Tom answered.

"Hello, husband," I said, hoping he wouldn't hear the tremor in my voice. "I'm just phoning to check in. How are you feeling?"

"Great, for a one-armed guy. Where the heck are you?"

"Doing errands." It was sort of the truth. "I'll be home in no time."

"Julian keeps stuffing everyone around here with food. Nobody's going to be hungry until midnight."

"Incorrect!" Julian yelled from the background.

"Okay," Tom said, laughing. "Alicia hasn't arrived yet. But the Hydes talked to Julian about tonight's dinner. They have a leg of lamb and won't let him go get one. It's thawing now. They're excited you all are fixing dinner, and want to have it in the Great Hall."

I told him that would be no problem, signed off, and parked on the steeply sloping street that boasted the residence of Troy McIntire, auction agent. It was a mixed area of run-down houses, I noticed, as I cut and pasted from The Stamp Fox catalog. Some older dwellings were made of stone, while others were cheaply faced with vinyl siding or false brick. My assembling mission complete, I walked up to a one-story brick house with peeling white trim.

"I'm Francesca Chastain," I told the short, stooped, sandy-haired man who opened the door. I judged him to be in his mid-sixties. "We have an appoint—"

"Yeah, yeah. McIntire," he snapped brusquely as he offered a gnarled hand and closed the door behind him. "What exactly are you looking for?"

So, we were going to stand on his porch to conduct business? Oh-kay. I remembered Lambert's words that the types of stamps stolen had never been reported in the newspaper. I handed McIntire the cut-and-pasted page I'd made from The Stamp Fox catalog. On it I'd slapped five pictures of the most valuable Queen Victoria stamps. Troy McIntire held the sheet up to his face and perused it, then quirked a thin eyebrow.

"Okay, yeah, I have one of these." A crooked finger pointed to a picture on my sheet. "A man was going through his great-grandmother's stuff and found it. There might be more, but he has to go through a ton of stuff. You wanna buy it?"

"How much?"

He squinted at me, rheumy bloodshot eyes in a pale face. "It's in mint condition. Two hundred twenty-five thousand."

"Actually," I said tartly, "I'm an investigator working with the police."

"Go away." He dropped the sheet and turned toward his door.

"I'm going to need to see that stamp," I said, my voice firm.

"The heck you say."

"Please turn around and look at me."

He slowly turned back and shot me a baleful look. "You're not coming in without a warrant. And let's see some ID."

"It's in the car."

"You ain't no investigator!"

I sighed. "You're right. I'm a collector. Part of my collection was stolen when I gave a party. It's driving me nuts."

"You ain't the first to have stamps stolen."

"I know. I've already been over to that place at the mall."

McIntire snorted contemptuously. "That guy's a piker."

"Could you please help me? Could you just tell me who sold you those stamps?"

"It was just some *guy*. I don't remember his name." He quickly whirled, pulled on the knob, and slid through his door.

"Please wait." I planted my elbow on the door. McIntire groaned. With my legs braced and my right elbow forcing his door open, I used my right hand to grasp my wallet and my free left hand to rummage around for my wad of photographs. I thrust the packet across the threshold. "Recognize any of these people?"

He looked down at the first one: the cuddle of saccharine-smiling Chardé and Buddy and family. "These are the people who were at your party?"

"Have you seen either one of them?"

"Nope." He shuffled past snapshots of Sukie and Eliot and one of Arch in his fencing

258

gear, being corrected by Michaela on his lunge. Then he stopped dead.

"What is it?" I demanded.

"Nothing." He tried to hand me back the photos, but they fell on the ground. Avoiding my eyes, he swiftly wrenched the door away and slammed it shut.

"Can't you tell me anything?" I pleaded. "Did you recognize anybody?"

"Scram!"

"Thanks for nothing!" I snarled, suddenly deeply exhausted, frustrated, and extremely angry. I dropped to my knees and started to scoop up the fallen photos.

Chardé and Buddy. Sukie and Eliot. Michaela and Arch.

I gasped and my blood ran to ice. The final photo was the one I'd shown Sukie and Eliot. The Jerk. In his scrubs.

"Hey! Was your mystery seller a slender, good-looking guy?" I hollered at the closed door. "Blond hair, drives a gold Mercedes? Real pale, like he'd just gotten out of prison?"

Inside, all was silence.

CHAPTER 19

I hopped into the van, revved it, and made a hasty U-turn. I glanced back at the house, knowing McIntire was watching my departure through a crack in the curtains. But maybe I was imagining it, the way I was everything else. I punched in Sergeant Boyd's number on the cellular and told him of my interview with the auction agent. After I described the interchange about the stamps and McIntire's reaction to my photos, I took a deep breath. Then I said:

"I suspect that the person who sold McIntire the stamp was my ex-con ex-husband, John Richard Korman."

"Goldy, that is *such* a long shot."

"Listen, Sergeant Boyd. John Richard knew Ray Wolff in jail, and now he's deeply involved with Viv Martini, Wolff's ex-girlfriend. John Richard just bought a car from Buddy Lauderdale that he can't possibly afford, not to mention a condo he can't even *begin* to afford. He *must* be getting that money from somewhere. Maybe he cut a deal with Buddy. Not only that, but John Richard treated Sukie Hyde for cancer, and she never mentioned it to me—"

"Take it easy, Goldy," Boyd interrupted, obviously determined to put an end to my speculations. "First, we have to question McIntire. Then if we *strongly* suspect the man received stolen goods connected to a robbery, we'll try to get a search warrant for his house. *If* we can arrest him and he agrees to identify Korman from a lineup, we'll have something to go on. But, all this stuff about Buddy Lauderdale?" He hesitated. "I don't know, Goldy. It's beginning to look like you've got something against the guy."

"Maybe *he* sold the stamp to McIntire," I said

quickly. "It's so obvious. You can see The Stamp Fox from his showroom, I was just there—"

"Goldy, stop."

"I want to know who shot Tom."

"So do we all. But you're reaching. For example, do you really think Sukie Hyde would give *you* the details of her cancer treatment? Especially since it was your ex-husband who treated her? Come on."

I exhaled. "You think I'm losing it."

"I think you're reading bizarre stuff into the way some people act. And I think you need to be cautious."

"A driver's been killed. A robber's been killed and dumped in a creek. My husband's been shot. Our house has been vandalized and burgled. And you're saying my problem is I can't deal with *some people,* and I need to be cautious?"

"Just trying to help out," Boyd replied. "We think we might have a line on your computers, by the way. An older guy matching the description you gave offered to sell a couple that sounded like yours to an undercover cop this morning."

"Where?"

"In a bar."

"Morris Hart brought our computers to a bar? And tried to sell them there? And one of your guys just happened to be tying one on, first thing in the morning?"

"Hey, our undercover guys go to bars when they open. It's their job. Where do you think crooks go in the morning? To the office?"

"Can you visit McIntire soon? Please?"

261

Okay, I was wheedling, but I really needed his help. He agreed and signed off.

It was three o'clock. Either Julian or I needed to pick up Arch from fencing practice at five. At the castle, I had a lot of cooking to do and labyrinth research to review. I shook my head and pressed the accelerator.

Approaching the Hogback, a sudden cold wind rolled out of the foothills and rocked the van. Was I deluded? Or did I truly believe that Buddy or Chardé or Viv—all of whom either did have or might have the security codes for the castle—or Eliot, or Sukie, or even Michaela, who also had access to everything and seemed awfully angry about something, was guilty of grand-scale theft? Could any one of them commit murder? Or was the killer some compatriot of Ray Wolff's, such as the man who stole our computers?

Fast-moving dark clouds raced from north to south as I headed west, up into the canyon that led to Aspen Meadow. It was true that Andy had been found in the creek, not far from the place where Tom was later shot...and both spots were within spitting distance of the fence surrounding the Hyde Castle estate. Somebody was up to *something,* but whether it was John Richard, Viv Martini, Chardé Lauderdale, or her smarmy sharpshooting husband Buddy Lauderdale, I did not know. What worried me more was having Arch, Tom, and Julian in such close proximity to the Hydes and their friends. Yes, we could arm our doors at night, but what about during the day? If someone brandished a gun like the one that killed Andy Balachek, a butcher knife wasn't going to be much defense.

Boyd's warning had been, *You need to be cautious.* I even imagined what he would say to me, if I presented him with my worry about susceptibility. Boyd would insist that our family had already been at the castle one night, enough for a determined killer to have a go at us. *So if the killer was in the castle, why hadn't he or she made a move?*

Tom will know what to do, I thought as I swung through the castle gates. Snowflakes swirled down. I slowed the van, as the icy patches of the long drive were treacherous in the white blur. Concentrating on not slipping, I reflected that being completely honest with Tom was not something I'd been very good at lately. Covert ops and frustration had intruded—in the form of Sara Beth O'Malley. My mind spun back to the question tormenting me for the last two days: *What secret is Tom keeping from me?* For my part, I was definitely shielding my investigation of Nurse O'Malley from *him.*

He was crazy about her, Connie Oliver had said of Tom and Sara Beth. *He was terribly protective of her.* Maybe he didn't love her anymore, as he'd claimed to me. But could he be protecting her? From what? How would I find out without asking him? As I strode into the castle, I realized that while I had many questions, I didn't have a single answer. It was time to bite the bullet.

I was surprised to see Tom in the kitchen, groping through one of the glass-fronted cabinets. With his right shoulder bandaged and his arm immobilized by the sling, he was moving with a slowness that made me cringe. In contrast, Julian bounced back and forth from the counter—where an enticing array of miniature finger-shaped sandwiches was arranged—and the kitchen table. Tom shuffled to a stop and gave me a baleful look.

"Miss G." His voice was an attempt at joviality, but his eyes betrayed his physical pain. "I've been worried about you."

"Tom," I scolded, "you shouldn't be up."

"Please. I couldn't lie there another minute. Looking at all that old English furniture gave me the heebie-jeebies. So I thought Julian and I could make tea—"

Julian interjected, "Make that he *tells* me what he wants for a Brit-style tea, and I make all the sandwiches and cakes. Hungry?"

The Italian ice cream was a distant memory. I grinned and nodded. Tom loved to cook and to direct cooking. Before relaxing, though, I had to check the dinner ingredients. On the counter beside the refrigerator, the Hydes' lamb roast was happily defrosting. I washed my hands and stuck the meat with a thermometer probe so that room temperature for the interior wouldn't be a matter of guesswork. Now all I had to find was some mint jelly to go with the lamb. If you were going to be English, you had to go all the way, right?

"Well, boss," Julian remarked, "In one

264

department, our tea won't be authentic." His smile was impish. "No smoked salmon. So I made cucumber sandwiches. And I'm about to spread cream cheese on that sweet bread you made. Eat your heart out, Weight Watchers."

Tom awkwardly stretched his free hand to unlock a high cabinet. "If this isn't where Sukie stores her tea, strainer, and teapot, I'm going to have words with that woman." He fumbled about on the shelf and ultimately drew out a box of English Breakfast tea leaves, a silver strainer, and Eliot's ceramic teapot shaped like an English butler. Tom pulled the key from the cupboard. "And before you ask, Goldy, Sukie gave me the keys and told me to get out anything we needed. The trick is just to find which key goes with which hole." He surveyed the kitchen table. "What else do we need?"

"Scones!" Julian and I said in unison.

Julian offered to put together butter, jams, and thick whipped cream if I would bake the treats. I was happy for scone duty, since I had a recipe that I'd been tinkering with back in Ye Olde Home Kitchen, the same one I'd tried—unsuccessfully—to make for the cops. Eliot had mentioned that he eventually wanted to serve Victorian-style tea to conference clients, and I was eager to offer irresistible samples of my wares. My laptop booted while I rummaged through my boxes for a package of currants. I inserted the disk with British-fare recipes. Eventually the scone recipe flashed on the screen.

I preheated the oven and poured boiling water over the currants. While the currants were plumping up, I measured dry ingredients into the Hydes' food processor. Chunks of cold unsalted butter went in next, followed by a quick binding with egg, milk, and cream. I patted out and cut the resulting rich dough, then slid scone triangles into the oven. While Tom merrily squabbled with Julian over the taste merits of meat-based over vegetarian chili, Julian searched through the kitchen jam cabinet for lemon marmalade.

"See if you can nab some mint jelly," I begged him. After a few minutes of clattering, Julian brought out small crystal jars of blackberry jelly, orange and lemon marmalades, and raspberry jam.

"No mint jelly," he said, discouraged. After a moment, he brightened. "Hold on, I think I remember seeing some mint jelly in Eliot's other jam cabinet." He grabbed the keys, disappeared into the buttery/dining room, and cursed colorfully. Then more sounds of clanking glass reached the kitchen. After a moment, Julian marched back into the kitchen, clutching jars of mint and sherry jelly.

While the baking scones filled the kitchen with a homey scent, we sipped Tom's dark, hot, perfectly brewed English Breakfast tea and ate the delectable cucumber and cream cheese sandwiches. Julian remembered that Michaela had called to say she was bringing Arch home. When I expressed guilt that we weren't including our hosts, Julian said the Hydes would be out until the evening meal. Eliot, Julian went on, had signed up to attend a late-afternoon seminar on running a home-based business. Sukie, vowing that she was the only Hyde who had any business running *anything*, had insisted on accompanying him. Julian had packed them a snack of gourmet vegetarian wraps. They'd said they'd be back at seven for dinner in the Great Hall, where Eliot had already set up the Elizabethan games he wanted us to try. Great, I thought. Cook, eat, and play a rousing game or two of indoor badminton and horseshoes. Excuse me—*shuttlecock* and *penny prick*. Why did Elizabethan games sound like naughty sex? Would the Elk Park parents call after Friday's banquet and complain?

I put these worries out of my head when the steaming scones emerged from the oven. We cooed and chattered and spread layers of whipped cream and jams on each split half. *Yum,* my brain cried, when I bit into flaky, moist layers slathered with cream and melting sherry jelly. I noticed Tom was still not eating much. Nevertheless, his spirits seemed to have perked up in the presence of family and food. I glanced at the clock: quarter to four. If we were going to have our heart-to-heart, the time was approaching.

"Goldy?" asked Julian. "I forgot to tell you your supplier finally arrived. She brought another lamb roast, plus all the extra foodstuffs for tomorrow and Friday. When we finish here, do you want me to keep working on the labyrinth lunch? I finished the soup. Eliot said before he left that he wanted us to check that the tables would arrive *early* tomorrow morning."

"Let's wait on that," I replied. "And thanks for helping Alicia, and for getting started here. I want to work on tonight's dinner, but not quite yet." Even though the bedroom would have been a better setting for my tête-à-tête with Tom, the time was ripe. I gave Julian a meaningful glance.

"Okay!" Julian exclaimed. "I guess I'll go set the six of us up in the Great Hall." In a wink, he was gone.

"Tom," I plunged in, "we need to talk. Something's been bothering me...." I faltered.

He furrowed his brow, but his face was blank. "Go on."

"Right after you were shot, you said something strange to me. You said, 'I don't love her.' "

His shoulders slumped and he looked away. "Oh, God. So it's true. I didn't imagine it."

"Didn't imagine what? That Sara Beth O'Malley is alive?"

Tom's eyes, when he turned back to me, were the lucid green of sunlit seawater. "Goldy, I love you. I'm married to you. When I woke up in that hospital, I didn't know whether I'd dreamed that she'd come back or not. They warned me that the pain medication might be hallucinogenic, so I put it down to that. Then I woke up here, and I thought I saw somebody run out of our room."

No wonder he'd been looking so full of

pain. My heart ached. "A man or a woman was running out of our room? Didn't you have your door armed?"

"The door was *armed*." There was more than a hint of irritation in his voice. "It didn't look like a man or a woman. It looked like a kid in a suit of armor, like that ghost story last night. It looked like a hallucination, except the armor clanked pretty loudly."

"But Sara Beth O'Malley isn't a hallucination, right?"

He shook his head. "No, I think she's alive. All these years of silence, then she starts sending me e-mails. I was trying to figure out what was going on when I was shot."

He looked so forlorn that I took his big hands into mine. "Since it's full-disclosure time," I said hesitantly, "I want to tell you that I downloaded her e-mails, plus the one you received from the State Department. I also downloaded Andy's e-mails, because I thought it might help figure out who shot the two of you. I put all the e-mails on a disk before our computers were stolen."

He lifted a sandy eyebrow. "Let me get this straight. You not only read my personal, private e-mails from Andy Balachek, you also read my personal, private electronic correspondence from and about Sara Beth?"

"I'm sorry. It's just that when you told me that you didn't love some woman, I was sure she was the one who'd shot at our house *and* shot you. I was trying to figure out who it was, too."

269

"But I'd already told you I didn't love her."

"So, you haven't actually seen her yet?"

"No."

"Well, I have to tell you, I have."

"What?" Tom's face furrowed. "Are you sure? You saw her? Talked to her?"

"Both. But not for more than a minute. The day after you were shot, she staked out our house. I looked at an old photograph of her from your album. She looked like the same woman, only older."

"Uh-*huh*."

I tried to control my trembling voice. "I'm wondering if she shot out our window, and then she shot *you*, because she's the jealous type." I forced myself to stop talking.

"My, my."

I paused, then went on: "Look, Tom, I'm terribly sorry about prying into the Sara Beth thing. Can you just please tell me what's going on?"

He lifted his left shoulder. "She didn't die. Or else, I figured, someone was doing a great hoax job. But if you saw her and talked to her, I don't know. I do think I should try to meet her. She said in her e-mail she has a dentist's appointment Friday morning...."

I swallowed. Did I trust him meeting with that lovely, enigmatic woman? What were my choices? I could hear the reluctance in my voice when I said, "I won't do anything else about her if you don't want me to. But here's one more thing I've been wondering about... although it's a bit far-fetched."

270

"Don't worry, Miss G." His voice was grim. "I'm used to far-fetched these days."

"The owner of The Stamp Fox insists any stolen philatelic material can be easily fenced in the Far East. Do you think there's a possibility Sara Beth could be part of the stamp robbery?"

He considered the crumbs on our plates, then shook his head. "It's not like her. Or at least, not the way she used to be. Obviously, I didn't know her as well as I thought I did."

"As long as this is truth time, you should know I've been doing some poking around on a related matter." Tom groaned and I continued hastily, "I'm not sure it's safe for us to stay here. Sukie was treated by John Richard for cancer, and didn't tell me—"

"That makes her dangerous?"

"The Lauderdales hate me, and Chardé is the castle decorator. She can get into the castle anytime she wants."

"Now *there's* an indication of guilt."

"And Eliot Hyde had an affair with Viv Martini, who is John Richard's new girlfriend and was Ray Wolff's—"

"You *have* been busy. Listen, I want to go home, too. And we will, soon. Meanwhile, I think it's *fine* for us to be here. Eliot Hyde is so afraid of looking bad in the public eye he wouldn't dare try anything, and Sukie knows where her bread gets buttered."

"I'm not so sure—"

"You'll have to trust my judgment. Of course, you haven't been doing too well in the trust department lately."

271

"I'm sorry," I said, and meant it. Still, my brain buzzed with unanswered questions. The minutes ticked by. I had lied to Tom by not immediately 'fessing up to my e-mail snooping; he had lied to me by covering up the whole resurrection-of-Sara-Beth problem. We sat in silence, not sure how to react to one another. The room shadows lengthened. Finally Tom said he was going to rest a while, and would meet us in the Great Hall at seven.

I preheated the oven and washed the tea dishes. Then I rubbed the thawed lamb roast with garlic, put it into the oven, and started the potatoes boiling. When I was washing the green beans, Boyd called.

"There was no sign of Troy McIntire when we got to his house," he began matter-of-factly. "Neighbors say, about half an hour after you left? Old Troy came out of his house lugging several big suitcases. We're hoping for a search warrant, but I'm sure that even if we get one, we wouldn't find anything incriminating. As for your ex-husband, he's not at home. I should know more about your computers tonight."

"Thanks for trying," I told him, then returned to my culinary duties. After the exchange with Tom, my mood had dropped. With no good news from Boyd, it plunged to a new low. To distract myself from the worries that seemed to beset us on every side, I decided to make the plum tarts for Friday's banquet dessert.

The thought of laboriously wrapping the zirconia stones in foil with no accompaniment besides my own thoughts—the Hydes either didn't have a stereo or I just couldn't find it—was abhorrent. In one of our hastily packed boxes, I remembered seeing Arch's Walkman, so I poked around until I found it.

I inserted the labyrinth-background tape from Eliot's desk, washed my hands, and assembled the ingredients for the tart crusts. Eliot had wanted me to bone up on labyrinths so that I could field questions during the next day's lunch. What he didn't realize was that except for the dieters, no one ever asks the caterer much. The dieters have two questions: "What's in this?" and "Is it low-fat?" They can be tiresome clients.

The labyrinth was a very ancient form, the tape began. It differed from a maze, a laid-out puzzle where you had choices as to which way to go. A labyrinth led only one way, but unless you paid attention to every twist and turn, you wouldn't make it to the center. The oldest surviving labyrinth formed a stepping-stone path laid into the floor of the nave of Chartres Cathedral. The distance to its center from the front door was used as a mystical measurement, and mirrored the distance from the door to the center of the rose window. *At the center you will find God*, the tape informed me. Pilgrims now walked the labyrinth only once a year, but in medieval times it might have been walked often. These days, chairs covered the Chartres labyrinth.

As I sliced the dark plums into juicy slices,

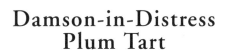

Damson-in-Distress
Plum Tart

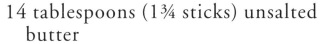

14 tablespoons (1¾ sticks) unsalted
  butter
2¼ cups all-purpose flour, plus an
  additional 3 tablespoons for the
  filling
3½ tablespoons sour cream, plus an
  additonal ½ cup for the filling
¾ teaspoon salt
9 Damson or other plums (If using
  small Italian plums, you may need
  as many as 24.)
2 eggs
1½ cups sugar

Preheat the oven to 325°F. Butter the
bottom and sides of a 9 x 13-inch glass
pan.

For the crust, first fit a food processor
with the steel blade. Cut the butter
into chunks. Place it into the bowl of
the food processor along with the 2¼
cups flour, 3½ tablespoons sour cream,
and salt. Process until the dough pulls
into a ball. Gently pat the dough into

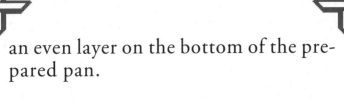

an even layer on the bottom of the prepared pan.

For the filling, pit and slice the plums into quarters. Cover the prepared crust with rows of sliced plums to completely cover the crust. Beat the eggs with the sugar, 3 tablespoons flour, and ½ cup sour cream until well blended. Pour this beaten mixture carefully over the rows of plums.

Bake the tart for 45 to 60 minutes, or until the top is golden brown and the custard is set in the middle. (I use a spoon to check the middle of the tart. The custard should be congealed, not soupy.)

Allow the tart to cool completely on a rack. Cut into rectangles and serve with best-quality vanilla ice cream. Refrigerate any unserved portion.

Makes 16 servings

the taped voice launched into a discussion of labyrinth symbolism, which, in fact, *was* similar to that of the maze. Theseus had wound into the maze of the Minotaur, slain him in its center, then found his way back out to safety with the help of thread, thoughtfully provided by Ariadne. Christians walking to the center of the labyrinth could only get lost if they weren't paying attention. By treading the path of the labyrinth, Christians took a spiritual journey to the death of Christ, and his temporary descent to hell. By symbolically descending and then ascending again, a pilgrim retraced the messianic journey, found God, and, hopefully, figured out all his or her life problems along the way. The idea of a walking meditation was appealing, but I wondered what happened if you got stuck in the center. Who helped you out of a temporary descent to hell, if you failed to find God? The tape, as it whirred to its close, provided no answer.

I put the Walkman away and proceeded to wrap the zirconia in bits of foil and place them on top of the plum slices. I wanted them to be in full view because, unlike Eliot, I thought tucking stone-hard trinkets into food was a very bad idea. The Elizabethans had eaten far too much sugar and crunched on far too many baubles, and all before the advent of false teeth.

I mixed a rich, creamy custard and sloshed it over the plum slices. As I was slipping the tarts into the oven, Arch blasted into the kitchen. He was wearing his fencing outfit, and looked very dashing.

"Dad's wasn't very much fun," he blurted out. "His lawyer sold some of his old furniture and he needs to buy more. He had to go to Vail today for his new job." *No*, I wanted to say, *he went to check on his three million-dollar town house*. "He's coming Friday night. To the banquet. With Viv."

"Not if I can help it, he isn't."

My sometimes-sage son Arch changed the subject. "Is our window at home fixed yet? Is Tom awake? Is Julian around?"

"The window's not fixed. I don't know if Tom's awake. Julian's setting up for dinner in the Great Hall."

"Michaela says she and I are doing a fencing demonstration after dinner. She told me to keep my uniform on, and not to get any food on it." He gave me a soulful look from behind his tortoiseshell glasses. "It's good to get back here. I had to sleep on the floor at Dad's. I'm...sorry I was so upset the first day."

"You already apologized, honey."

"I know, but I wrote a note to the Hydes, too. I slid it under their door. I...like it here. It's not as good as our regular home, but it's okay."

"It's good to have you back," I said, and hugged him. Fourteen-year-old boys do not like motherly embraces. But if you don't mind putting your arms around a kid-dying-to-get-away-from-you, you can let him know you care.

277

"I'm starving," he announced, peeking into the oven. "And I've got a ton of astronomy homework. How long to dinner?"

I told him it would be a few hours and he should wash up for a snack. While he soaped his hands, I fixed him scones, cheddar slices, and a soft drink. When he finished, I told him, he could help Julian set up in the Great Hall, then ask for homework help.

"Michaela's idea is *so* cool," Arch enthused, his mouth crammed with scone. "We're going to show everybody how to fence, then we're going to reconstruct a duel where some guy insulted another guy. The insulting guy got stabbed and bled to death."

I shuddered, remembering the Lauderdales and their threats. "I think anyone who resorts to weapons to resolve conflicts has already lost."

"Yeah, well, I think that's why we always yelled that saying on the playground. Y'know, 'Sticks and stones may break my bones, but names can never hurt me.' Michaela says that when duels started, they used swords. Then they switched to pistols. You got in a duel with both guys packing guns, *somebody* was going to get whacked." He sounded ecstatic.

I remembered Buddy Lauderdale's face as he was led away in handcuffs on New Year's Eve. By the time I commented, "Now *there's* a happy thought," Arch had already whisked away.

CHAPTER 20

At quarter past six, Arch returned to the kitchen to pick up the hot-water baths for the chafers. He reported that he'd done all of his schoolwork, except for astronomy. For that, he had to wait until the stars rose. *Might be up late,* he added with mock ruefulness, but I let it go.

Julian, meanwhile, fretted that the night's menu had no gourmet vegetarian dishes. So he scurried about to prepare two of his bistro specialties: a colorful lentil-tomato-scallion salad, and a bowl of baby spinach leaves tossed with a balsamic vinaigrette and topped with slices of goat cheese and tiny dollops of a red onion marmalade he grabbed from the dining-room jam cabinet.

"I might want to get this recipe from Eliot," I commented, when I tasted the spicy relish. Julian nodded.

Arch, careful to protect his white fencing outfit, put together a heaping basket of warm rolls and butter. As we were loading the lamb roast and fixings onto trays, Eliot appeared. He was wearing a double-breasted black suit that gave him a vaguely military air— probably a captain-of-the-castle look he was going after. With great ceremony, he announced that the seminar had been a success. While we picked up the gravy boat, extra candles, and matches, Eliot shuffled and banged in the dining room. Eventually he emerged with an elaborate corkscrew and two bottles of red wine. The only thing he and Sukie had disagreed on, he went on, was the number of people the castle could feed on a daily basis.

"This castle held a hundred people in the Middle Ages," he told us, as he eyed his marmalade on top of Julian's salad, "with complete self-sufficiency. And besides, we've done fine with you four," he added over his shoulder. He sashayed ahead of us through the heavy wooden hallway doors that led to the stairs.

"And we're thankful," I gushed. I didn't point out that Eliot had done no cooking, cleaning, or conference-running, not to mention battle-preparation, during our stay. Not only that, but medieval kitchen staffs usually numbered over fifty. I didn't point *this* out, either. If a caterer wants to keep her job, she does *not* correct the client.

I had never been in the Great Hall at night. Chandeliers and candles illuminated the cavernous space. The walls, paneled with dark, elaborately carved wooden squares, were hung with rich tapestries depicting battle scenes. Rows of arched leaded-glass windows bisected the walls. On the second story at the far end of the hall, a large balcony I had not noticed before projected out over the room. That area, Eliot said as I directed the food into the chafers, had been the minstrels' gallery. Below the gallery, the wood-paneled wall also jutted into the hall—another medieval toilet, Sukie told me, pragmatic as ever. The corner also held an arched doorway that led to the postern gate. Eliot went on to inform us that in the Middle Ages, only the courtiers dined in this hall. The servants had been relegated to their own dining hall on the castle's south range.

Eliot, his chin held high, led us to the far end of the hall, where he'd set up a badminton net and marked out a court with tape. The penny-prick game looked straightforward enough: players stood behind a boundary and threw knives at an empty bottle, trying to knock a penny off the bottle's lip, without overturning the bottle itself. Although the game historically was played with real knives, Eliot, ever wary of folks hurting themselves at the castle and the story getting into the paper, had bought a dozen of the rubber variety.

Tom appeared as I finished organizing the buffet. He walked over slowly and gave me a one-armed hug. Tears stung my eyes. I squeezed him back and prayed for all of Sara Beth O'Malley's teeth to fall out of her mouth before Friday.

Sukie, Eliot, Michaela, Tom, Arch, and I dug into the tender lamb roast, the garlicky potatoes, the crunchy beans, the rich, hot gravy, and the cool mint jelly. Julian fixed himself a heaping plate of vegetables and salads, while Eliot waxed eloquent on the fact that the ceremonial procession of the courses from the kitchen to the Great Hall—which we'd unconsciously imitated when we'd lugged the food up the stairs—had been extraordinarily important in medieval and Renaissance times. The lord of the castle wanted to put on a big show, to prove to everybody how rich he was.

Julian surreptitiously rolled his eyes, then offered to clear the table and return with dessert and coffee. I nodded and thanked him. Eliot tapped Michaela to play the first game of shuttlecock as teammate to Arch, with Eliot and Sukie for opponents. Tom kept score, and I straightened up the table while cheering for both teams.

When the score was nine to nine, a cold sweat rolled over me. Had I really detected movement in the shadows of the postern-gate corner? Without warning, a shift in the flickering light revealed—what was it? A miniature knight, dressed in plate armor? Watching the game?

"Agh!" I yelled, pointing at the corner. "What the *hell* is that?"

The badminton game ceased. Eliot, Sukie, Michaela, and Arch gaped at me. I looked at them, then squinted at the corner, now suddenly empty. I sprinted over to where the two walls met, only to find no statue, no movement, no miniature knight. I tore open the door that led to the postern gate. The tower was icy cold and deserted. Disappointed, I slammed back inside.

"Miss G.?" Tom's voice was full of concern.

"Sorry, everybody. I thought I saw something...." I felt acutely embarrassed. I really did seem to be losing my mind. Except Tom had had a similar vision/hallucination/whatever. What was going on?

Sukie shot Eliot a stern look and murmured that sometimes it was better *not* to share the legends of the castle with guests. Eliot tossed his hair off his forehead and replied that he hadn't told me *any* ghost stories. But I noticed that his eyes had become anxious. Tom tilted his head at me: *Did my Tale of Law Enforcement scare you?* I shook my head, as in, *It's okay.*

"Let's do the fencing demonstration," Michaela interjected, and I was thankful for the change in subject. The last thing a caterer wants to make is a gaffe, especially when the guests then proceed to discuss it for the rest of the evening.

Michaela and Arch took swords and masks from a bag stored under the buffet table. While Arch rolled out a mat, I kept an eye on the dark corner. So, I noticed, did Sukie. Tom, meanwhile, engaged Eliot in a spirited discussion of the escalating prices of antique furniture. But I couldn't help noticing that Eliot's gaze also kept straying to the shadows through which I'd seen the armored figure glide.

"This is an épée," Michaela announced in her gravelly voice, commanding our immediate attention. "With the foil, which Arch and I usually use in practice, one may score a point by a touch on the upper torso. With the épée, touches *anywhere* on the body count. Arch, come here, please." My son dutifully hopped up from the mat and strode over.

"The first thing we teach," Michaela said, pointing to Arch's feet, "is how to advance and retreat. Okay, Arch." My son obliged by stepping deftly forward and back. Michaela continued: "The front arm and hand holding the weapon are parallel to the ground."

At this she handed Arch an épée, which he brandished in showmanlike fashion. Tom grinned.

"The back arm," Michaela went on, "is crooked up at the elbow, hand facing the sky, for balance, until someone attacks, and lunges. Go ahead."

Arch lunged. As he straightened his back leg and arm, he thrust the sword forward. It gleamed dangerously in the light from the chandelier. My son, the swashbuckler.

Michaela picked up a weapon. "The final skill we teach newcomers is parry, riposte. Your opponent attacks. You slap his sword aside, then counterattack." She lowered the mask over her face. "*En garde,* Arch."

Michaela and Arch touched their swords to their masks in formal greeting. And then they went at it, back and forth across the mat, moving with remarkable swiftness and an impressive snapping of swords. *Clink, clink, swoosh, clink.* I found myself growing more nervous with every flourish. I didn't know if Michaela was letting Arch win, or making a good show. Arch scored a hit. Both took off their masks, bowed deeply to each other, then to us.

We all clapped enthusiastically. All of us, that is, except Eliot, who appeared increasingly anxious. As if on cue, Julian entered with a tray. He had shortbread cookies, ice cream, and frosting-slathered Chocolate Emergency Cookies, plus an insulated coffeepot and cream and sugar containers.

"And now," Michaela said, "we will—"

Somewhat rudely, I thought, Eliot interrupted her with, "Great! Come on everybody, time for our sweets!" Tom and Sukie attempted half-hearted applause for the fencers.

Downcast, clutching his weapon, Arch raised his eyes to me for a cue. I gave a tiny shrug. Michaela murmured to him that the demo was over, and would he please roll up the mat.

With exclamations of pleasure, Eliot and Sukie received demitasse cups of coffee and crystal bowls of ice cream, with cookies perched on the scoops. Ignoring Michaela and Arch, Eliot resumed his somewhat shrill monologue on the exorbitant prices of antiques. Julian, his intuition alerting him that something had run amuck, appeared at my side.

"What's going on?" he murmured.

"I thought I saw a ghost, and now Eliot's acting a little uptight," I said under my breath.

"Oh, is that all?"

"Julian, I saw *something*. So did Tom, when he woke up today. So either there *is* a ghost here, my husband and I are both having hallucinations, or a kid or midget or something is romping through the castle, wearing knight's armor."

"If it's a girl in her late teens, tell her I'm available."

"Julian!"

"Early twenties would be okay." He scanned the Great Hall. Eliot and Sukie called their thanks to us and waved good night. Standing not far from us, Arch looked crestfallen.

"Jeez, Goldy, Arch looks like a friend just died," Julian commented, concerned.

"He was enjoying being the center of attention for once—"

"Mom!" Arch appeared by my elbow and I yelped. It was his silent disappearing-reappearing act, learned in his eleventh and twelfth years, otherwise known as his magic-trick phase. I didn't like it any more now than I had then.

"Michaela wants you and Tom and me to come over and see the fencing loft," my son said eagerly. "And Julian, too, if he'd like to. We can finish our demonstration over there, if everybody still wants..."

"Oh, no, thanks," Tom said. His face was haggard, and I knew the evening had worn him out more than he was willing to admit. "I'm going to turn in, if that's all right."

"Mom?" asked Arch, his face pleading.

"I have to do the dishes," I said, with a pang. "Sorry."

"Forget the dishes," Julian told me firmly. "Go watch the demonstration. And, hey! I'm getting good at cleaning up. Makes me feel helpful."

Arch's expectant look, Julian's offer, Michaela's generosity, and, of course, my admonition to Arch not to go anywhere in the castle alone, made me say yes, I'd love to watch the demonstration. But not for long, I told Arch hastily: I still had prep to do on the labyrinth lunch, and he had astronomy homework. Not to mention, I added silently, if there was going to be a ghost-knight flitting around the castle, I wanted to be at my son's side when the specter made his next appearance.

Toting armloads of fencing equipment, we wended our way through the cold, dimly lit postern gate tower, then down a drab hall to a set of steps leading to the first floor.

"How come part of the inhabited section of the castle is downstairs," I asked Michaela, "and part is up?"

"In Eliot's grandfather's time," she replied, "two of the castle's original four stories were what their family and our family lived in and used. Then when the flood of '82 came, Eliot had to make some decisions. The wall of water blasted down Fox Creek, broke the dam, and flooded the basement and first-floor rooms on the west range. Eliot wanted the study redone, because of the beautiful old fireplace in there, and his and Sukie's bedroom. Chardé has worked hard on the place." She shook her head. "But, whoa, did we all get tired of her, begging to refurbish the rest of the flood-damaged rooms, telling Eliot that he'd look cheap if he didn't spend more money getting everything redecorated. That woman's a money-grubber if I ever saw one."

Don't hold back on your feelings, I thought as we tramped past the entry to the indoor pool, the door to Eliot's study, and then through the glass doors marked UNDER CONSTRUCTION—NO ADMITTANCE. The Wet Paint sign was gone. The splattered paint, however, was still all over the place, and the new padlock was securely fastened.

"Was Chardé working over here?" I asked casually, trying to disguise my interest. I couldn't exactly admit to breaking into a playroom.

"I hope not," said Michaela. "We try to keep that woman as contained as possible. Or at least, I do," she added with a sourness that was impossible to miss.

I stopped in front of the playroom and tilted my head at the door. "What's in here?"

"It used to be old living quarters," said Michaela with a smile. "But we're having them fixed up. Without Chardé, hopefully. Let's go."

To my surprise, Michaela did not live on the ground floor of the north range—the castle front—but through a door and up another set of stairs to the second story. At the top of the steps, she slipped a brass key from under a plastic welcome mat. Interesting to note that while the Hydes were extremely security-conscious, Michaela was not....

"In the flood of '82?" she explained as she fiddled with the lock. "The west side of the north range's first story was also completely flooded. This side of the gatehouse has been our living quarters since my grandfather's time." She sighed and pushed open the door.

"We lost boxes of books and letters that I had stored in closets. Our family used to have the two stories, but now my whole operation is upstairs. Downstairs is more storage area."

Inside her door, Michaela flipped on lights that illuminated a golden-oak floor, a narrow, white-painted room lined with racks of swords, and a higgledy-piggledy arrangement of mats and open folding chairs. At first I thought we were in a gym of some kind, but I realized belatedly that this was the Kirovsky fencing loft, where Eliot's father and grandfather had learned the Royal Sport from Michaela's forebears.

"This is *so* cool," said Arch, entranced.

"This is where I've been coaching Howie Lauderdale and a few other juniors and seniors before the state meet. Elk Park Prep doesn't want us in the gym late at night or early in the morning, so we sometimes have to meet here. When you're a member of the varsity, Arch, this is where I'll coach you, too."

"Great," said my son, trying in vain to suppress a smile. *When you're a member of the varsity.* To my son, those were magical words.

"Come into the rest of the apartment," Michaela told us. "It's set up like railroad cars, one room after the other. Loft, living room, kitchenette. The loft takes up so much space that we didn't have much left for family quarters, upstairs. But it's enough for me. Come on, I want you to see my collection."

The living room, a spare, austere arrangement of old—not antique—furniture, consisted of a couch and one chair. A threadbare green rug lay on the floor. There was no coffee table, only two mismatched end tables. But brightly colored crocheted afghans and an assortment of garage-sale pillows gave the room a comfortable feel.

The walls immediately captured my attention. I slid beside the fraying couch and stared at row after row of cheaply framed photos, hundreds of them, all cut from magazines. Every one seemed to be of armor, castles, and the crowned heads of Europe. A magazine copy of a portrait of Queen Elizabeth I, her red hair swept up above her wide, white ruff, was hung next to a photograph of a youthful Prince Charles. There were dozens of photographs of stodgy-looking Queen Victoria, sometimes alone, sometimes with Prince Albert. Nicholas and Alexandra had a row all to themselves. This wasn't really a collection: It was more like the room of a passionate Royal-watcher.

"What started all this?" I asked.

"Family tradition," Michaela answered. "We were living in a castle, so when I was a kid I wondered about the people who lived in castles."

"Did you take all this over to Furman County Elementary?" Arch demanded. "I mean, for Show and Tell, when you were little?"

Michaela laughed and shook her head. "I was home-schooled before it was fashionable, Arch. Then went to community college as a commuter student. But the kings and queens have always remained my friends, and the collection has grown over the years. I have a passion for *any* royal portrait."

Ah, God, I thought. *On stamps, too?* No, I decided in the same moment. No way. Michaela had no connection to Ray Wolff and Andy Balachek, except that she'd known Andy when he was little. She'd loved him, and truly deplored his descent into the gambling lifestyle. Plus, a woman who'd never ventured farther than the nearby community college, and had always and only known caretaking at the castle, wouldn't take a flyer on a risky hijacking venture, would she?

"Got any more?" Arch asked eagerly.

A wall devoted to French royalty, Michaela announced, was actually the bottom of her Murphy bed. When she folded it down, there wasn't much room in the place, she added, so she'd spare us the sight. Each night, she announced with a hint of naughtiness, it helped her to know she was sleeping on Louis XIV.

"Okay, enough of my nutty hobby. I make great hot chocolate," she said to Arch. "Or tea or instant coffee or even instant hot spiced cider, if you're interested," she told me.

I said that hot spiced cider sounded terrific, and followed her into the tiny kitchenette. The cramped space had a stone floor, a small set of cupboards, and a narrow counter crowded with a hot plate, an ancient electric vat coffeepot—the same kind I used for catered events—and a cookie jar in the shape of the Kremlin. Inside the jar were Russian tea cakes. Michaela pulled the vat lever for hot water that made Arch's cocoa and my cider, along with some tea for herself. I burned my tongue sipping the steaming cider, but it cleared my head.

Soon we were seated in the royal-photos living room, munching rich, buttery tea cakes while savoring our hot drinks. That's the thing about a big dinner; you eat it and then half an hour later you're wishing for a snack. I tried not to notice the grandmotherly eyes of Queen Victoria, or how that plump countenance seemed to watch my every bite. Arch and Michaela chatted happily. She really was wonderful with kids. Why, though, given her apparent animosity for Eliot and this crummy apartment, would she stay in the castle? Did Elk Park Prep pay their coaches so badly that she couldn't afford a place of her own? Or did she stay because of the gorgeous fencing loft?

"How about that dueling demonstration?" I suggested.

Arch and Michaela grinned, set aside their plates, and stood. While Arch donned his mask, Michaela explained, "In 1547, two French noblemen fought the first private duel of honor. François de Vivonne, *seigneur* de La Châtaigneraie, insulted Guy Chabot, Baron de Jarnac, by publicly accusing de Jarnac of having sex with his own mother-in-law. De Jarnac immediately challenged Châtaigneraie to a duel, which was viewed by the French king, Henry the Second, and hundreds of courtiers." She stopped to put on her mask. *"En garde,* Arch."

Again the two of them went back and forth, grunting, thrusting, parrying, and offering aggressive ripostes. They seemed entirely focused on their match. When Arch scored a hit just below Michaela's shoulder, she laughed out loud and asked him to stop for a moment. Removing her mask, she told me, "De Jarnac and Châtaigneraie did not solve their conflict so easily. Slowly, now, Arch, lunge and I will parry and riposte. Then stop."

My son lunged. Michaela's parry deftly flicked Arch's sword aside. Then she did a slow-motion riposte onto Arch's calf. He froze, as instructed.

"De Jarnac," Michaela said, "instead of going for the heart, cut the major artery in Châtaigneraie's leg. Then de Jarnac slashed his opponent's *other* leg, and demanded that Châtaigneraie withdraw his insult. Châtaigneraie refused and bled to death in front of the king. That was the end of court-sanctioned dueling in France. The leg-attack became known as the 'Coup de Jarnac.' "

"But you're not allowed to hit in the leg," Arch protested as he tugged off his mask. "Except in épée, I guess."

Michaela laughed, pleased. "You're right. End of demonstration." I clapped and thanked them both. She said, "For tomorrow night, Arch, we'll have Josh and Howie demonstrate épée. Then, if Kirsten's over her mono, you and she can do foil. She has long arms, which is an advantage. Then we'll have Chad and Scott do saber—"

The telephone rang. I hadn't even noticed it in the sea of photos, probably because it was on a lower shelf of one of the end tables. Michaela drew it out and stared at it before answering. It took me a moment to realize she had been puzzling over a tiny screen with caller ID.

"Sheriff's department?" she asked. "Sergeant Boyd?"

"It's for me." Without thinking, I launched myself across the couch, sloshing cider onto the rug. As I gabbled apologies, Michaela relieved me of my cup. Then she dropped some paper napkins on the rug and handed me the receiver, all in one smooth motion. If I ever did learn to fence, did that mean I'd become coordinated?

"This is Goldy," I said.

"Boyd here. Where's Tom?"

I murmured that he was in bed.

"And how's he doing?"

"On the mend. He wants to start working again."

Boyd *mm-hmm*ed. It was past ten o'clock. He'd had all day to check on Tom. So what did he really want?

"Goldy, I'm afraid I have some bad news for you."

My heart lurched. Arch, Tom, and Julian were all here at the castle. Oh, God—*Marla*.

"This is about your computers. And the guy who stole them."

294

"Okay." Puzzled at how this would warrant a late-night call, I waited.

"We went to visit Mr. Morris Hart, whose real name, it turns out, is Mo Hartfield. Hangs out in bars, does odd jobs for crooks, stays in the pipeline. When we got to his place this evening, somebody had already broken in. We found your computers trashed. A keyboard was in the toilet." Boyd paused.

"Was he there?" But even as I asked it, I knew the answer.

"Yeah," Boyd said tersely. "Shot dead."

CHAPTER 21

No." The window guy killed? With our trashed computers all around? "Do you have any idea who—"

"Nope, nothing yet. We found him in his bathtub. I just wanted you to know, especially with what's been going on. Tell Tom about it, okay? The ballistics guys should be back to us ASAP, since this case includes the shooting of a cop. And Tom needs to be careful. He shouldn't go out without one of us along. Whoever's doing this is killing mad about something. Have Tom give me a ring tomorrow, would you? If he's up to it?"

"Sure. Thanks," I murmured numbly, and signed off. *Somebody was so angry they'd kill a small-time thief? Angry about what?* That Andy

Balachek had sent e-mails that landed Ray Wolff in jail? That I'd turned in a wealthy couple for child abuse? That Tom had married someone else?

"Bad news?" asked Michaela softly.

"No." I paused. *Never divulge anything about a case,* Tom had warned me on many occasions. "Thanks for asking, though. And it was very nice of you to have us over. Come on, Arch, time to rock."

He groaned, but scrambled to his feet and thanked Michaela. We walked across the second floor of the gatehouse itself, looked down at the empty entryway through the *meurtriers,* then descended the darkly paneled spiral staircase into the living room. When we entered the hush of the living room, it was bathed in shadows.

Arch said, "I need to check on Orion and those other constellations. Do you have my high-powered binoculars? They're not in with my stuff."

I promised to get them from our room. We entered the frigid drum tower, passed the well and the garderobe, then moved into the silent hall by the dining room and kitchen. The castle was a spooky place at night. Although I'd planned to do some night-time cooking for the next day's luncheon, there was no way that was going to happen. As we passed the kitchen, icy shivers ran down my neck. I was glad Arch had his foil with him.

Finally upstairs, I disarmed our door, tip-toed into our room, retrieved the binoculars, and tiptoed back out. In the hallway, Arch whispered a request for assistance. This was the first time in three weeks that he'd asked for my help with the astronomy. Then again, I wouldn't want to be up later than everyone else in the castle, working alone. It would be like reading *The Exorcist* on an overnight camp-out: not something you wanted to do.

I followed Arch into the room he was sharing with Julian. Arch shuffled around for his notebook. Inside his sleeping bag on Arch's couch, Julian's form rose and fell. I felt a pang of guilt that our dear family friend had done all the dishes *again*. Bless Julian Teller's wonderful heart.

From the tall window, Arch and I could make out Orion, complete with belt and sword, the Little Dipper, Cassiopeia, the lovely W that had been my favorite constellation since I was little, and even the Big Dipper, just above the horizon. Once Arch had noted the Big Dipper pointing to the North Star, he was done.

"Thanks, Mom." He closed his notebook. "You can leave now."

I didn't mind being summarily dismissed, as that was the way of almost-fifteen-year-olds. I thanked Arch again for the fencing demonstration, made him promise to arm his door, then did the same in our room. I set the tiny alarm for five A.M. and snuggled in next to Tom. Finally, I said a prayer for Mo Hartfield, even if he had hit me over the head.

As often happens on the day of a catered event, I awoke seconds before the buzzer went off. Outside, the sky was dark as tar. I turned on a small lamp on the far side of the room, moved through my yoga routine, showered, dressed, and congratulated myself on getting up early. I had over two hours before Arch had to be off for school, more than enough to get a good start on the labyrinth luncheon.

For some reason, I seemed to be making no noise. The castle, I reflected, had two moods: Either it creaked and moaned and you saw and heard things that weren't there, or your every sound and movement was absorbed by the palatial trappings and walls.

"I'm coming down to fix breakfast," Tom mumbled, deep in his pillow.

"With one arm? No way. You should sleep," I said softly.

He moaned and turned over.

Julian met me in the hall, his brown hair damp from showering. He wore his bistro work outfit: white T-shirt, paisley-printed balloon chef pants, and high-top sneakers. "I heard you running your shower," he murmured. So all my sounds had not been muffled, after all. "Didn't want you to have to work alone."

"Julian, please. You've done so much. Why don't you just sleep?"

"For-*get* it." His voice had that stubborn tone I'd come to know well.

In the kitchen, I made two cups of espresso. I drank mine black, but Julian doused his with two tablespoons each of cream and sugar. The kid had the metabolism of the speed of light.

Because we'd always worked so well before, we knew how to divide the chores and estimate the time required for prep. *Reservations for twenty, but expect thirty,* the church had said. We decided I'd make the steak pies, while Julian would do the Figgy Salad and green beans with artichoke hearts. We would cook until seven, then we would make breakfast for Arch and anyone else who showed up.

As we started our prep, we discussed the schedule. If Michaela was willing to take Arch to school again, then at eight, we could start setting up the food and drinks in Hyde Chapel. This was provided the police were gone, which they'd promised they would be, and the Party Rental tables had finally arrived. We'd take the same chafers and electrified hot platters that we'd used the previous evening, along with packaged, chilled salad ingredients. We'd bring the rest of the foodstuffs down at ten-thirty. At eleven, we would start serving the guests champagne, cheese puffs, onion toasts, and caviar.

Before all hell broke loose on Monday, I'd planned to bring my portable ovens to bake the pies. I often did this for catered events at kitchenless sites; I'd just forgotten to pack them after our window was shot out. Still, after the debacle with the computers, there was *no*

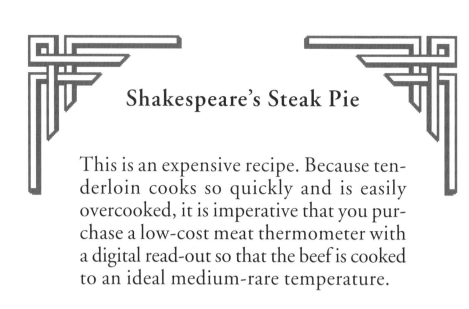

Shakespeare's Steak Pie

This is an expensive recipe. Because tenderloin cooks so quickly and is easily overcooked, it is imperative that you purchase a low-cost meat thermometer with a digital read-out so that the beef is cooked to an ideal medium-rare temperature.

2 tablespoons (¼ stick) unsalted
   butter
1 medium or ½ large onion, chopped
1 medium carrot, chopped
2 cloves garlic, pressed and minced
2 tablespoons minced fresh parsley
6 tablespoons all-purpose flour
½ teaspoon crumbled dried thyme
½ teaspoon crumbled dried oregano
½ teaspoon crumbled dried sage
1½ teaspoons salt
¼ teaspoon freshly ground black
   pepper
2½ pounds beef tenderloin,
   trimmed, cut into 1½-inch cubes
   (You should have 2 pounds of
   trimmed, cubed beef.)
¼ cup high-quality dry red wine
Upper Crust Pastry (recipe follows)

In a wide sauté pan, melt the butter over medium-low heat. Gently sauté the onion, carrot, garlic, and parsley for a moment, stirring until the vegetables are well mixed. Cover the pan and cook over medium to low heat, stirring occasionally, until the onion is limp and translucent and the carrot has lost some of its crunch, about 10 minutes. Uncover the pan and set aside to cool.

Place the flour, thyme, oregano, sage, salt, and pepper into a large, heavy-duty zip-type plastic bag and mix well. Add the beef to the bag, zip the top closed, and shake until all the cubes are evenly covered with the dry mixture.

Butter a 9 x 12-inch oval au gratin pan. Place the floured cubes into the pan along with the sautéed vegetables, mixing very lightly with your hands, just until the vegetables and meat are evenly distributed. Place the filled pan in the refrigerator while you prepare the crust. (Or you can cover the filled pan with plastic wrap, place it in the refrigerator, and chill until you are ready to prepare the crust and cook the pie. It is best not to prepare the crust in advance.)

Preheat the oven to 350°F. Remove the pan of meat and vegetables from the refrigerator and pour the wine into the pan. Gently fit the crust over the pan, fluting the edges and slashing the center in 3 places to vent and decorating the top as directed in the pastry recipe. Carefully insert the thermometer through a slash in the crust, making sure it spears a piece of beef.

Bake until the meat thermometer reads 125°F for medium rare, about 25 minutes. Serve immediately.

Makes 4 large servings

Upper-Crust Pastry:

1¼ cups all-purpose flour
½ teaspoon salt
6 tablespoons (¾ stick) chilled
    unsalted butter, cut into 6 pieces

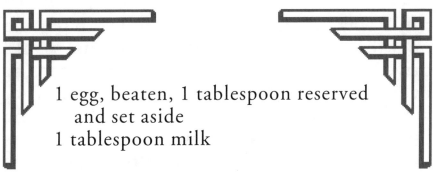

1 egg, beaten, 1 tablespoon reserved
    and set aside
1 tablespoon milk

In the bowl of a large food processor, combine the flour and salt and process for 5 seconds. With the motor running, drop in the butter, one piece at a time. Combine the egg and milk and pour into the food processor. Process for a few moments, just until the dough pulls into a ball. Gently flatten the dough and place it into a rectangular jumbo-size zip-type plastic bag. Using a rolling pin, roll the pastry to the edges of the bag, or until it will fit over your pan. Open the bag at the zipper, and using scissors, carefully cut down the sides of the bag. Remove one whole side of the bag and place the pastry side down on the pan. Gently peel off the top of the bag. Flute the edges of the pastry and make the slashes in the top as directed in the recipe. Using a pastry brush, paint the reserved tablespoon of beaten egg on top of the pastry.

way I was going back to our house to get the portable ovens. Instead, one of us would drive back to the castle to put the pies into the oven at eleven-fifteen. Meanwhile, the other would keep the appetizers and soup going until the hot pies came down around noon. As long as the tables had been delivered and the labyrinth cake arrived at ten as ordered, we'd be in great shape.

For the pies, I chopped carrots, onions, and parsley for what the French called a *mirepoix,* and started butter melting in a Dutch oven. Julian steamed the *haricots verts,* then moved on to preparing a complex sauce. With the *mirepoix* sizzling in the pool of butter, I sharpened my largest chef's knife before tackling the slabs of steak. Eliot had argued for steak-and-kidney pies, but I'd been adamantly opposed. The Olde English crowd may have loved 'em, but your modern American diner was going to think a kidney tasted like liver, and give it a pass.

"So what did the Elizabethan folks eat besides meat?" Julian asked as he swished balsamic vinegar into the fig salad dressing.

I finished cutting the steaks, floured and seasoned the pieces, and laid them over the sautéed vegetables. "Every meal offered the ever-present manchet bread," I replied. "It was actually a small loaf. I used Julia Child's hamburger-bun recipe last week and made a bunch of them, which I brought. Odd as it may seem, sixteenth-century folks also had sweet dishes with each course. At least, the rich ones did. Gingerbreads, tarts, marzipan, and cakes, plus conserves, preserves, and marmalades of every type. Served alongside the cooked sparrows."

"Now there's a healthful diet."

"The theory is that Henry the Eighth died of scurvy."

"Wha'd I tell you?"

I went hunting for the bottles of burgundy I'd brought in one of my boxes. Judicious amounts of red wine would be poured over the meat mixture, before it was covered with pie dough. With any luck, we'd have juicy, tender, flavorful pieces of steak topped with a golden flaky crust.

Yikes! I was making myself hungry. Tom must have received my telepathic message, for he chose that moment to amble into the kitchen.

"Enter the one-armed breakfast chef," he announced jovially. He wore dark chef pants—a gift from Julian—and a buttoned white Broncos shirt. "Please don't try to talk me out of anything. Just give me an apron. I'm not leaving. If either one of you protests, you'll only raise my stress level and make me ill."

Julian and I laughed while Tom rooted around in Alicia's delivered boxes of foodstuffs for chili ingredients. With a pang of guilt, I realized I'd mishandled the confrontation over Sara Beth. Besides, what had I promised myself in the hospital? That I didn't care if there was another woman; I would love Tom always. Now I just had to behave as if I didn't care about her.

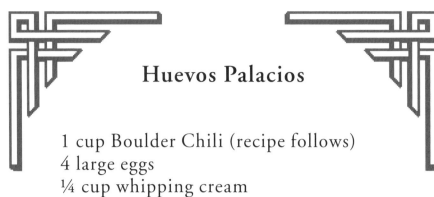

Huevos Palacios

1 cup Boulder Chili (recipe follows)
4 large eggs
¼ cup whipping cream
½ teaspoon salt
¼ teaspoon freshly ground black
  pepper
2 tablespoons (¼ stick) unsalted butter
½ cup sour cream
1 cup grated Cheddar cheese
1 medium tomato, peeled, seed pockets
  removed, and chopped
2 scallions, chopped

Make the chili and allow it to cool.

Lightly beat the eggs with the cream, salt, and pepper. Melt the butter over medium-low heat in a medium-sized, ovenproof nonstick frying pan. When the pan is hot, pour in the egg mixture. Cook over low heat until the edges begin to congeal. With a heatproof rubber spatula, gently push the edges of cooked egg into the center of the pan, using a minimum number of strokes. Tilt the pan so that the uncooked portion of egg flows out into the bottom

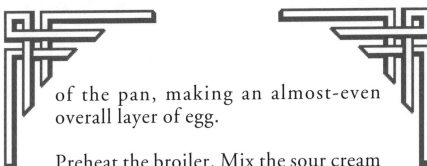

of the pan, making an almost-even overall layer of egg.

Preheat the broiler. Mix the sour cream with the grated Cheddar and set aside. When the eggs are about halfway done (i.e., when they are about half liquid and half solid), spoon on the chili in 3 spoke-like lines that bisect the eggs to make 6 equal sections. (The eggs will look like a pie.) Scatter the chopped tomato and scallions between the lines of chili. Carefully spoon the sour cream–cheese mixture on top of the chili spokes. Do not worry if some spreads off the chili.

Place the pan 6 inches from the hot broiler and broil, watching carefully, between 5 and 7 minutes, or until the eggs are done and the cheese has melted and puffed slightly. Serve immediately.

Makes 4 large servings

Boulder Chili:

1½ pounds lean ground beef
1 large onion, chopped

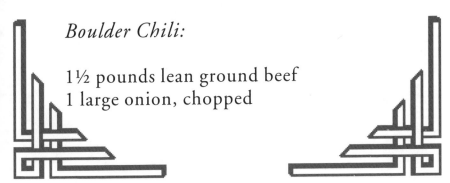

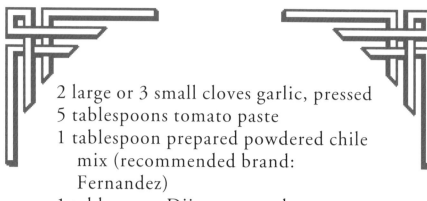

2 large or 3 small cloves garlic, pressed
5 tablespoons tomato paste
1 tablespoon prepared powdered chile mix (recommended brand: Fernandez)
1 tablespoon Dijon mustard
1½ teaspoons salt
1 cup plum tomatoes, chopped (about a 14 ½-ounce can)
1 tablespoon Italian herb seasoning
1 15-oz. can chili beans in chili gravy, undrained
2 to 4 tablespoons water
2 tablespoons red burgundy wine

Sauté the beef, onion, and garlic over medium heat until the beef is just browned and the onion and garlic are tender. Turn the heat down to low and add the tomato paste, chile mix, mustard, salt, tomatoes, herb seasoning, and beans. Pour 2 tablespoons water and the wine into the chili bean can and scrape down the sides, then pour into the beef mixture. If the mixture is too thick, add the extra water. Heat over medium-low heat, stirring occasionally, until bubbly.

I sighed and got back to work. Within thirty minutes, Julian and I had completed our preparation. Tom, meanwhile, worked assiduously on his breakfast concoction. The Hydes, wearing matching royal blue robes, floated into the kitchen and offered to prepare juices and hot drinks. Michaela, dressed for coach work, showed up a few minutes later, surveyed the goings-on, and announced she'd toast English muffins for all. I gladly acquiesced. I was ravenous.

Arch appeared just after seven, wearing an oversize olive shirt and large khaki pants. Did anyone at that school actually wear anything in the correct size? Sheepishly, he asked if I'd be willing to wash his fencing outfit today, so he could have it fresh for the banquet. To my surprise, Sukie volunteered to do it; she had state-of-the-art washing and drying machines, she explained, that no one else could understand.

Arch thanked her and peered into the wide frying pan on the stove. Tom was stirring his aromatic, bubbling Boulder Chili: sautéed ground chuck, onions, garlic, chili beans, and the most hearty collection of spices north of the Rio Grande. Arch frowned.

"I'm pretty sure the Elizabethans didn't have chili first thing in the morning."

"Oh, yeah?" said Tom. "Too bad. Huevos Palacios are coming up." His voice was still buoyant, but I could see lines of wear in his face and eyes. Maybe I shouldn't have let him do any cooking.

Summoning everyone to sit, Tom and I served up sauté pans hot from the oven. Each one brimmed with creamy frittata-style eggs topped with a sunburst of chili, grated Cheddar, and sour cream. Tom had even made one without chili for Julian. When I took a bite of the spicy concoction, I nearly swooned.

"Good *show*," mumbled Eliot Hyde, as he chewed. Julian, Sukie, Michaela, and Arch, too, murmured compliments as we wolfed the food down. When we finished, Sukie insisted she was cleaning the kitchen.

I pulled Tom outside the kitchen door. "Boyd phoned last night," I murmured. "The guy who stole our computers was shot to death. Boyd wants you to be careful. He doesn't want you going out without a police escort. And you're supposed to give him a ring today." Tom nodded once, instantly somber, and said he was going upstairs to make calls.

"You're coming with me, Arch?" Michaela asked when I reentered the kitchen. I nodded that it was fine. Michaela added that the police had not allowed her to start setting up early for the luncheon, after all. So we would have to attend to the space heaters and serving tables, in addition to everything else. I told her that was no problem.

Tom wouldn't have reached the upstairs phone yet, I knew, so I quickly called the sheriff's department from the kitchen, to check on the status of the crime scene by the chapel. A deputy informed me that the crime lab van had finished Tuesday, but they'd kept a guard these past three days and nights because investigators hadn't quite finished. He put me on hold, then came back and assured me the guard and police ribbons would be gone by eight.

Last, I put in a quick call to Party Rental to make sure the long-promised dining tables were indeed being delivered that morning. I was told they'd arrive no earlier than eight, no later than eight-fifteen. Sweetly, I asked: If the tables weren't there by eight-thirty, would they give me a refund, so I could call another company? The guy hung up on me.

It was going to be one of those days.

CHAPTER 22

As Julian and I packed up our equipment, the president of Saint Luke's Episcopal Church Women phoned. She said the church-owned plates, glasses, and silverware would be delivered to Hyde Chapel at nine-thirty, and would somebody besides the police be there to receive them? I assured her of our catering team's presence.

I sighed. The tables, the dinnerware, our equipment, the set-up, the food, the cops. Maybe the first thing I should do at Hyde Chapel was *pray*. *Dear God*, my mind supplied, *can You please get me through this lunch? Thanks.*

Outside, the ground boasted five inches of new snow, which formed a thick, sugary crust on the rocks surrounding the moat. Chickadees fluttered up and down ladders of pine branches and spilled showers of flakes. Everything was silent; the glittering blanket of snow seemed to muffle all sound. Instead of enjoying the winter splendor, though, I worried what the new white stuff would do to our lunch attendance.

Eliot, now dressed in Gatsby-esque tweeds, vest, and white satin scarf, insisted on driving ahead of us in his Jaguar. When we arrived ten minutes later in Hyde Chapel's parking lot, two sheriff's department cars were sending plumes of exhaust into the icy air. One of the deputies talked to Eliot for a few minutes, after which Eliot, his countenance subdued, trudged over and said he'd open up the chapel.

I'd been in Hyde Chapel for christenings and weddings. But I had not seen it since the money from Henry VIII's letter had allowed for a complete refurbishment. The stone walls had been cleaned to a sparkling silver. The multicolored slate floor tiles set off the flat marble stones of the labyrinth's winding path, which gave the floor an eerie, pure-white patterned centerpiece. Most spectacular were the stained-glass windows. When the just-risen sun shone through them, the effect was like being inside a lighted jewelry box. The ambience was serene, until honking erupted from the parking lot.

"Hey, boss?" asked Julian as he stuck his head outside the carved wooden doors. "The tables are here!" he called. "Where do you want 'em?"

"I'll show them, thanks."

While Eliot and I directed Party Rental, Julian placed champagne bottles in tubs he filled with ice, then ferried in wrapped trays of hors d'oeuvres. Things were going well until he brought out the electrified hot platters: Their cords refused to stretch to the outlets in the stone wall. Looking on, Eliot had become agitated at the prospect of the table people scratching his precious slate floors. Promising to oversee the last table setup, he pointed toward the left side of the chapel and told me there were more extension cords in the storage area.

I skirted the labyrinth and hustled to an unmarked door, which opened into an enormous storeroom that smelled of Sukie's favorite antiseptic cleaner. Flipping on the light revealed yet more evidence of *la Suisse* at work: Paint, glass cleaner, wood polish, tools, brushes, a ladder, and every other imaginable odd and end was laid out on shelves—alphabetically. The fancy folding wooden chairs Eliot had bought were stacked along one wall. I found *Extension Cords* after *Chair Cushions* and before *Fans*, then zipped back to the newly opened tables.

After seeing Party Rental off, Eliot had set up the space heaters and serving tables. Now he was busy with his slide machine and screen. He helped me unwind the cords to the outlets, at which point Julian and I plugged everything in. Mercifully, no fuses blew. We then taped down all the cords, a trick to keep even the most inebriated guest from tripping and doing a face-plant on the floor.

We were so busy we didn't hear two women banging on the wooden doors to be let in. They were emissaries from the Episcopal Church Women, there to set the tables. When they finished and I let them out, I was the one who reclosed the door. I was sure of this, just as I was sure Eliot had told me we had the only key to the chapel, retrieved from the lockbox outside. So…when Buddy and Chardé Lauderdale slithered unannounced and unadmitted into the chapel at ten after nine, I was more than a bit surprised.

"*What* are you two doing here?" I demanded.

Startled, Chardé dropped her lemon-colored Chanel purse, which matched a lemon-colored wool pantsuit and lemon beret set at a jaunty slant on her dark hair. *When life hands you a lemon…you get Chardé.* Buddy, ever the casual type, had his hands thrust into wool khaki pants beneath a black turtleneck shirt, an outfit meant to make him look attractive and powerful, and which succeeded in neither. "How did you get in?" I snapped.

"Eliot?" Chardé called sweetly, ignoring me.

Buddy, meanwhile, glanced nervously around the chapel, obviously ill at ease. I knew he and Chardé had donated five thou to the labyrinth, but that he only came to church at Christmas. He was breathing deeply, and

314

his face was pinched with the guilty expression of a holiday-only churchman. If he hyperventilated, I wondered, would I feel compelled to call 911?

"Chardé, darling!" crowed Eliot, striding forward. "Come to check that we're using your beautiful cushions on our chairs? Of course we are!"

They smooched like old pals and began to murmur. With an air of concentration, Buddy made a shuffling circuit of the chapel. *If I stay near the edge, I'm not really here.* Meanwhile, I arranged the cups and helped Julian bring the first stack of wooden chairs out of the storage room. We were about to go back for more when the door to the chapel opened again. In walked John Richard Korman, with Viv Martini in tow.

What was this—Open House? I cursed myself for being so surprised by the Lauderdales that I'd neglected to check the chapel doors.

John Richard and Viv, dressed head to toe in black, looked like a couple of undertakers. Then again, maybe they were aiming for that chic eighties rock-star look. Eliot, who was still engaged in intimate conversation with Chardé, glanced up abruptly. His face registered shock, then a deep blush. *Now that's a new look for the king,* I mused, intrigued.

"Well, *Eliot,*" said Viv in a mock-accusing tone. "Imagine seeing you here. And with a cute decorator, no less."

"It is, uh, my family's chapel," Eliot began, but Viv only tilted up her pointed little chin and blew him a kiss. His face went from a patchy scarlet to an even crimson. I actually felt sorry for him.

"And Buddy," Viv went on, still the charmer.

"Hey, Viv," Buddy replied, his voice low and sexy. Had Viv slept with *every* rich older guy in the county? Would John Richard mind being classified as a *rich older guy*? Ha.

Before I could ask my ex-husband if he remembered the restraining order, he strode across the space between us and wagged a finger in my face.

"I don't want to hear any crap from you, understand? Arch said you were going to be against it, so *I'm* warning you *now*." His blue eyes blazed in his handsome face. "Viv and I are coming to the fencing banquet. Whether you like it or not. Got it? So don't give me any of this restraining-order crap. It's for Arch, and you should recognize he wants me there."

"Cocky when the cops aren't around, eh?" I shot back. "Hey, Viv! You don't know what you're in for!"

Viv shook her pale hair, which stuck out at every possible angle. "I love what I'm in for!" she proclaimed, as she sashayed closer to the Jerk. Standing behind him, she opened her black leather jacket—*Is she carrying,* I wondered? *How do you slide a gun into pants that tight?* She cocked one elbow and used the other hand to pat John Richard's behind. Her clear voice crooned, "We're not going to cause any trouble, are we, honey? If my guy here gets out of line, I'll use force."

When John Richard blushed, I burst out laughing. "Promise?" I asked.

"Promise," she replied in a deep, throaty voice that sent shivers down my spine. Well, she was John Richard's choice. Or vice versa, if she was just using him as a rich-old-fart conquest. Wouldn't I love to see that? Maybe not, if this blond bombshell ended up taking money designated for Arch. Viv snaked an arm around John Richard's waist and tilted her head to murmur in his ear. *Ever done it in a chapel?* Or something like that, because John Richard let out a surprised grunt. I longed to ask my ex-husband if Viv was the type of gal recommended in your average male-menopause support group, but for once I kept mum. I had work to do.

"If there's nothing further—" I began.

"So do we understand each other?" the Jerk said to me. I think he wanted to shake his finger in my face again, but Viv had him entwined. Instead, I walked quietly toward him and pointed a finger less than an inch from his aristocratic nose.

"Split. *Now.* You understand? I *heard* you. Remember General Farquhar, who could kill people without making any noise? *I* make a *ton* of noise. Now, buzz off before the nice neighbors have to hear it."

"Now, now, Goldy," Viv said, her voice conciliatory. "Let's not make threats we can't back up." She gave me a knowing look. "I make a ton of noise, too, don't I, baby? Let's go."

John Richard pressed his lips together and swallowed. Come to think of it, he *did* look kind of tired, especially in his *noir* outfit. Buddy and Eliot stood aghast: *Were we actually hooked up with this woman? How'd we survive?* Chardé seized the opportunity of this dramatic tableau to stride toward me: *Lemon in Motion.*

"*We're* coming to the fencing banquet, too," she declared, her pert nose in the air. I prayed that the yellow beret would plop to the floor, but it didn't slip. "We eat *no* undercooked meat, *no* raw eggs, and *no* sugar in any form. And by the way, our son Howie is lactose-intolerant. You probably don't remember any of this from when you catered for us. You were too busy being *nosy,* isn't that right?"

"I—"

"Howie likes lime sorbet. No dairy. Got it?" Chardé said.

"Okay!" Julian bellowed, extending his arms. "That's *it!* Everybody *out! Out!* You, you, you, and you!" he snarled, pointing to the Jerk, Viv, Buddy, and Chardé. "We cannot work for our clients with *you* here. *Leave.*"

"*We* are your clients," chimed in Buddy Lauderdale, with that nasal arrogance I knew only too well.

"Then please come back at *lunchtime,*" Julian said firmly. No question, the kid had it all over yours truly in the assertiveness department.

Eliot made soft cooing noises that were meant to reassure his good chums, the Lauderdales. The Jerk and Viv banged out through the chapel door. When Eliot and the Lauderdales also departed, I slumped down in one of the wooden chairs. Julian made sure the doors were firmly shut and locked. He called to us that there was also an inside bolt, and he was throwing it until lunchtime.

"I'm not sure I can make it through this day," I moaned when he returned.

"Sure you can. There'll be new deep-pocket folks here who'll love your food. They will line up to book you for their next catered event."

He made me laugh. I was about to tell him how proud I was of him when thunderous pounding interrupted us yet again. This time, I unbolted the door and opened it myself. It was the baker's assistant, come to set up the labyrinth cake. It looked scrumptious, a huge fudge-frosted round cake with white-iced loops reflecting the intricate pattern on the chapel floor.

"I brought you something," Julian said, when I had firmly locked up behind the baker's assistant. He was holding an upscale shopping bag. "Chocolate Emergency cookies, remember? I figure we're in one now." He drew out a wrapped packet and a small hot-drink container. "I even brought you an espresso."

"You're a lifesaver, Julian." I bit into the cookie. Dark fudgy flavor exploded in my mouth and a burst of chocolate euphoria sparked up my spine. The cookies were chewy without being too sweet, with the smooth, buttery vanilla icing a perfect complement to the rich chocolate. A hearty swig of the espresso sent all worries about the Lauderdales, the Jerk, and Viv down Cottonwood Creek.

For the nonce, anyway.

Two hours later I was letting the mood fit the food by being upbeat while serving trays of mail-order English cheese puffs, onion toasts, and caviar with toast points. The big donors, a handful of vestry members, and a few Episcopal Church Women, along with our parish priest, were all chugging champagne while gushing that Eliot had been *so* generous to donate the chapel to Saint Luke's. The Lauderdales had snubbed me, of course, and recommended that others do so as well, Marla reported. Meanwhile, Marla announced that she didn't understand why she'd given so much money to the labyrinth, when walking it was going to be so confusing after all this champagne.

While Julian served the soup, I hustled up to the castle and put in the Shakespeare's Steak Pies. The Lauderdales were bad-mouthing me? Those *creeps*! "Anger's my meat," I whispered, congratulating myself on remembering something from *Coriolanus*. What was the rest of it? Oh, yes. *Anger's my meat: I sup upon myself/And so shall starve with feeding*. So there! One more word from the Lauderdales and they'd be supping on raw hamburger with manchet bread. New play from the Bard: *Mac*DEATH.

After we set out the pies, salad, and bread,

the guests happily moved through the buffet line. Julian bustled about, teased by his Aunt Marla and admired by the women. As far from the buffet tables as possible, the Lauderdales had seated themselves with Sukie, Eliot, and another couple from the church. Buddy and Chardé were working hard to appear deep in intellectual conversation. I, of course, was not fooled.

At length, Eliot dimmed the chandeliers and began his talk. He clicked on a slide of the Chartres labyrinth, and offered the same historical and architectural background I'd heard on the audiotape. While he was showing Before and After slides of the chapel restoration, Marla sneaked up to my side.

"No more on the Jerk's real estate deal, sorry to report," she whispered, with one eye on the cake table. "The lunch was scrumptious. The only historic food *I* have is in my refrigerator!"

"Thanks. And thanks for checking on the town-house deal. I still think John Richard's up to something."

"He's always up to something." Then she hustled off toward the untouched cake that the guests were going to have after the slide show.

"Please, sir," Marla whispered to Julian, "may I have some *more*? Or just a *nibble*, anyway?" Before I could protest, Julian had carved an enormous piece of cake, heaped it on a plate, and handed it to her.

"Call it reverse nepotism, Goldy," she stage-whispered, fingering up a dollop of icing. Heads turned and I sighed.

Eliot had moved on to Before and After shots of the renovation of his castle. He ended with effusive thanks to the donors, and an invitation to have cake and to book their conferences into the castle next year. Then he invited them to quiet their souls and walk the labyrinth to arrive at their spiritual truth.

If the clapping from twenty-six people wasn't thunderous, it was at least enthusiastic. Julian and I served cake and coffee, which I hoped would tame any aftereffects of champagne. When they finished their dessert, the guests began to process single-file through the labyrinth.

An eerie silence fell over the chapel as the silent parade went back and forth over the stones, all the way to the end. The few people who spoke as they were leaving did so in hushed tones. By two o'clock, the crowd had dispersed. Wow, I thought. Next time I felt uptight, I would give the labyrinth a try.

The churchwomen gathered up their plates, silver, and glasses, to trek them back to the Saint Luke's kitchen for washing. Eliot and Julian broke down the Hydes' serving tables and chairs, and hauled them back to the storage area. Then Julian and I folded up the rented dining tables and left them in the gravel parking lot under a tarpaulin. Party Rental would return before four to pick them up. Sukie and Eliot conveyed their video equipment back to the castle. I emphatically told Julian that he was going to take the rest of the afternoon off. He'd earned it, I insisted.

"Yeah, yeah, yeah," he said, scanning the chapel interior, which still contained remnants of the party. "And what are you going to do if the Lauderdales show up again?"

"I'll throw the bolt while I'm finishing up," I said diffidently. "And I'll park the van right next to the door."

"Tell you what, boss, I'll take the ice tubs, the chafers, and the last of the serving dishes. If you want, you can bring the platters and trash."

"I'll *be* okay." I strode to the door and pointed to the dead bolt. "Chardé and Buddy, even Viv, might all have keys. *My* mistake was in trusting Eliot's memory that we were the only ones who had one."

"That guy's nice," Julian commented, "but he's a birdbrain, for sure."

"I'll be fine."

Julian still looked unconvinced. "All right, listen. I'll take my load up while you finish here. You're not back at the castle in an hour and a half, I'm coming back."

I agreed. It would not take me more than twenty minutes to load the platters, then pack the trash and toss it into the castle Dumpster, located on the far side of the moat by a service road. Each time Julian overestimated how long I needed to do a chore, I accused him of treating me as if I were old and decrepit. He never denied it, drat him.

I bolted the door and reflected on what I had not told Julian: that I wanted to have a good look at the chapel myself, as it was awfully close to the crime scene created by Andy's body and Tom's being shot. First I applied myself to finishing the cleanup, which took seventeen minutes. I scrutinized the interior space to make sure we had not forgotten anything. The chapel looked spanking clean. Even with Marla's premature dive into the cake, the luncheon had been a success, and I was thankful.

At that moment I felt as if the shiny stones of the labyrinth were beckoning to me. Pink light from the rose window skipped across the marble, and my skin prickled. What had Eliot said? *You walk the labyrinth to arrive at your spiritual truth.* I hadn't been doing too well in the truth department lately, so why not try it before I snooped around?

My mind dredged up a bit of Scripture: *I still my soul and make it quiet,/like a child upon its mother's breast;/my soul is quieted within me.*

After a few moments, I moved forward, feeling strangely hesitant. As I walked, concentrating on the tortuous path seemed to clear my mind of the questions currently plaguing me—who'd killed Andy and why, who'd shot Tom and why, who'd shot at our window and why, and who'd killed Mo Hartfield after he'd inexplicably stolen our computers. As I put one foot in front of the other, I felt a calming presence. I was moving forward—either into or away from my life, I couldn't tell which.

Finally I arrived at the labyrinth's center. I could have sworn I heard my heart beating.

Gazing back at the swirls and turns of the flat marble stones, I felt serenity—for the first time in a week. Outside, the sun emerged from behind a cloud and splattered pink light over the path. Eliot's audiotape as well as his lecture had detailed the mystical significance of distances at Chartres. From the center of the labyrinth to the base of the portal was the same distance as from the base of the portal to the center of the rose window. I looked up at the rosy pattern of stained glass.

Now *there* was a surprise. Instead of Sukie-inspired cleanliness on the multicolored sections of glass, the center of the rose window looked as if someone had left a blotch of dirt....

At the center you will find God, the tape had said.

Maybe what was up there wasn't dirt. Maybe someone who knew the symbolism of the labyrinth had put something else there, something important. Or maybe my paranoia was kicking in again.

I checked my watch. I had thirty minutes before Julian would start to worry. Undoubtedly breaking all rules of labyrinth-walking, I sprinted across the tiles to the storage room and hauled out the ladder. It was one of those extension affairs that creak horribly and feel rickety as the devil. Nevertheless, after five minutes of struggling, I wrestled the thing open and laid the top just above the center of the rose window. I took a deep breath and started climbing.

Outside, the wind whipped around the chapel walls. As I ascended, I could hear the cold air whistling through tiny cracks in the glass. Finally I reached the fourth rung from the top. I peered into the center of the rose window, which was actually a pocket of pink glass soldered inside a metal circle. What I saw there didn't make sense. I was looking at—torn tape, paper, and plastic.

I reached in and gently tried to remove the paper and tape. It was not easy. The paper had become wedged underneath the soldering, and all my attempts to scoot it out were unsuccessful. At length, I had the bright idea to reach into the adjoining pocket of enclosed yellow glass and coax the paper the *other* way. Ten minutes of scraping and pushing later, the scrap of paper slipped free.

I examined it, hoping against hope that it wasn't just an invoice from Bill's Stained-Glass Repairs, left as a joke.

What I held in my hands was not a bill. It was the torn half of an envelope. I reached into the envelope and pulled out a small, plastic case. Inside the clear envelope was a stamp. I gasped and grabbed the rung to keep from toppling off the ladder.

The color: red-orange. The printing around the sides: *One Penny, Post Office, Postage, Mauritius.* And in the center, the profile of a woman: Chubby cheeks. Severe hair. Grandmotherly eyes.

Queen Victoria.

CHAPTER 23

I hastily tucked the paper envelope with the plastic case and its eight-hundred-thousand-dollar stamp deep in my apron pocket. After a few heart-stopping teeters on the ladder, I finally reached the bottom, rattled the ladder down, and scooted it back to the storeroom. Then I pulled out the envelope and dropped it into a clean brown paper bag—Tom had taught me a thing or two, such as, *try not to muck up evidence*—before serenely transporting it out to the van along with the trash.

No one was in the Hyde Chapel lot, but I tried to act normal anyway, just in case I was being watched from somewhere, anywhere. I relocked the chapel, deposited the key in the lockbox, and revved my van up the service road, to the edge of the moat, by the castle Dumpster. I heaved in the lunch trash, hopped back into the driver's seat, and called Sergeant Boyd on my cellular.

"Part of the loot, eh?" said Boyd, who sounded either amused or skeptical, I couldn't tell which. "In the middle of a stained-glass window, way up high? Uh-huh." Skeptical, definitely.

"Listen, would you?" I gulped down the impatience in my voice, trying to remember Boyd was just doing his job. "The Lauderdales and John Richard and Viv Martini all came into the chapel this morning right after you guys pulled off your detail. Maybe this is what they were looking for."

"That's an awkward place to check, without a bunch of witnesses noticing. You know—how do you disguise the fact you're pulling out a twenty-foot ladder?"

"Sergeant!"

"Yeah, yeah, okay. Stay where you are. I'll send somebody up to get the evidence from you."

"I'm not staying on this service road, thanks. I just finished a catering event and I've still got to prep for another one tomorrow. Tell your people to meet me at the Aspen Meadow Library in twenty minutes."

"Gee, Goldy, our homicide guys will gladly work around your catering timetable. Especially since we're dealing with evidence worth close to a million dollars and connected to three homicides and a cop-shooting."

"One more thing," I said, unfazed. "Did your guys find anything in Hyde Chapel, after you took Andy's body from the creek?"

"Nope, it was clean. In fact, that chapel brought a whole new meaning to the word *clean*." He sighed. "I thought you were in a hurry to get to the library."

I signed off, realized I'd neglected to close the lid on the Dumpster, rushed out and whacked it down, then raced to the library to meet the deputy. A uniformed young man with red hair and a red mustache unceremoniously plucked the bag from my hand and roared away.

I waved at Julian in the castle driveway. He was coming out as I was headed in. He rolled down his window and yelled that I was over my ninety-minute limit.

"I'm just an old lady caterer who can't move as fast as you young folks!" I hollered back.

"*As fast as us young folks?*" Julian yelled gleefully. "Check this out!" He clanked the Rover into reverse and *backed* up the icy driveway. As if that weren't enough, he then gunned the SUV backward across the causeway, over the moat. I watched from the far side, shaking my head. One error of steering, and Julian would be sleeping with the fishes.

When I caught up with him at the gatehouse, I said, "That's not a quick path home, Julian, that's a quick path to drowning."

He grinned and pressed the buttons for entry to the gatehouse. Once inside, I glanced overhead into the space above the murder holes. No one appeared to be in that empty room next to Michaela's kitchen. But in the remote event that my paranoia was translating into imagining hidden electronic eavesdropping devices, I decided not to tell Julian about the stamp.

In the kitchen, a note from the Hydes was propped up against the toaster. The luncheon had been fabulous, Sukie wrote, but utterly exhausting. She went on to say that she'd felt so sorry for me, she'd washed all the serving dishes. Now she and Eliot were eating dinner out, and we were to feel free to scrounge whatever we wanted.

"Ah, speaking of going out to dinner,

Goldy?" said Julian. "Arch asked me to take him to McDonald's, after his fencing practice. I know, I know, even the salads aren't up to your culinary standard. But I figured, what the heck, give the kid a break from the gourmet stuff for one night."

I smiled, paid Julian for his afternoon of work, and gave him some extra money to treat Arch and himself. Then I asked about Tom.

Julian shrugged. "I don't know. When I looked in on him, he said he was going to change his own bandage. I have to run to Boulder to get some books before I pick up Arch, so I'm taking off. Why don't you bring Tom some tea with fixin's?"

Julian quickstepped away. I looked at my watch: just after three. Tea, goodies, and puzzling over an eight-hundred-thousand-dollar stamp I'd found in Hyde Chapel...was Tom up to it?

Half an hour later, I had baked a fresh batch of steaming scones and set them on a tray next to a plate of dewy butter slices, a jar of Eliot's chokecherry jelly, and a pot of steeping English Breakfast tea. Making my way up to our room, I noticed that the courtyard looked magical under its fresh blanket of snow. If I lived here, I decided as I disarmed our door, I'd turn it into a school. A cooking school, where we ate our cookies and cakes out in the courtyard, while black-suited butlers served tea and sherry.

"I was just about to ring for all that," Tom commented as I sashayed in with the tray. He was sitting in one of the wing-back chairs doing leg-extension exercises. "I missed you today, Miss G."

I set the tray down and gave him a careful hug. "Poor Tom. Sorry I had to work. Want to hear about it?"

And so I ran through the whole thing for him, from the early intrusions of Buddy, Chardé, John Richard, and Viv, to discovering the stamp from Mauritius in the center of the window. He whistled.

"Tom," I said when I'd finished, "I think *all* the stamps might have been there. They were all *in the chapel*. Then they were moved. By someone in a hurry."

"Or by someone who didn't know he'd left one behind." He gazed into the cold fireplace. "The chapel has that big storeroom. If you were a crook trying to hide something in the chapel, why not put it in the storeroom? Especially since Ray Wolff was arrested while scoping out a storage area?"

"Because it's too obvious?" I replied. "There's *something* we're missing." I followed his line of sight to the hearth. "I keep thinking about Andy. Did he find the stamps after they were stolen and hidden away? He indicated to you that he knew where they were, so what's the deal? How was he electrocuted? If he was shot in the chapel, why couldn't the sheriff's department find any evidence there? The stamps were *in* the chapel, and he was dumped in the creek *by* the chapel. But the crime scene itself was clean." I paused, baffled. "I just don't get it."

331

"Here's one more thing," Tom commented. "The ballistics report came in on the bullet they took out of me. It came from the same gun that killed Andy and Mo Hartfield. The bullet that shattered our window came from a different gun. No match."

"Oh, for crying out loud." Would anything in this case ever add up?

Tom surveyed the tea detritus. "Know what? That just felt like an appetizer to me. Let's go see what we can find in that big kitchen."

Delighted to see that his appetite was back, I followed him down to the kitchen, where we feasted on leftover meat pie, reheated green beans, manchet bread, and labyrinth cake. Arch and Julian came home, as did Sukie and Eliot. My son joyfully announced that because tomorrow, Friday, was a half school-day, and this Saturday was Valentine's Day, the teachers were assigning no homework for tonight or the weekend.

"That calls for a toast," decreed Eliot. "To our successful donor lunch, and to no homework." He breezed out of the room and returned with a bottle of port.

"I think we have something special in the refrigerator, too," murmured Sukie. Sukie brought out a chilled bottle of bubbly nonalcoholic cranberry stuff. Arch rewarded her with a murmured thanks and one of his suppressed smiles.

While we were sipping our drinks and nibbling on cake, I guiltily remembered Michaela. Shouldn't we have invited her to join us?

But when I suggested it, Eliot waved this away. "Sometimes you see Michaela. Usually you don't."

Sukie added, "We don't try to force it."

I nodded and didn't pursue the question. I wondered if I'd ever figure out the dynamic between Eliot and Sukie on the one hand, and between Eliot, Sukie, and Michaela on the other. Was she sort of an employee, sort of a tenant, sort of a neighbor, sort of a pain in the behind, or all of the above?

I didn't know and was too tired to try to find out. We all loaded our dishes into the dishwasher, said good night, and headed our separate ways.

Before we went to bed, Tom told me we should be back in our own house by Sunday. "They put in the glass, finish the cleanup, fix our security system, and we go back."

"Uh-huh. And what about the person who shot it out?"

"They're still working on it," said Tom. His green eyes sought me out. "I'm not feeling up to seeing Sara Beth at the dentist tomorrow."

"Whatever feels right to you," I said stiffly, as I snuggled into bed. He told me he loved me and that he hoped I slept well. I guess he wasn't in the mood for one-armed lovemaking.

I lay there, staring at the dark ceiling, and made a decision. Sara Beth O'Malley may have been expecting Tom. But she was going to get me.

Friday the thirteenth dawned very cold and bright. I moved through my yoga routine while Tom slept. In the kitchen, Michaela and Arch were having miniature sugared doughnuts and tiny cans of a chemical concoction that claimed to be better than chocolate milk.

"Don't get upset, Mom," Arch begged as he stuffed a doughnut into his mouth. "Julian let me get these goodies last night. He was up late studying, and said you should wake him when you need help this morning. Otherwise his alarm is set for eleven. Julian is great, man. I can't *remember* the last time I had two junk-food meals in a row."

Michaela's indulgent smile stopped me from scolding. At least Arch was amusing someone.

When they left at a quarter to eight, I made a swift overview of the fencing-banquet preparation. I'd already baked the plum tarts. The veal had only to be rubbed with oil, garlic, and spices, then roasted just before the banquet. The potato casseroles I could easily put together in the afternoon. That left the molded salad, shrimp curry, and raisin rice. I looked over my recipes. If I moved ahead with the salad and curry sauce, the former could jell while the latter mellowed before the arrival of the shrimp. With any luck, I could finish those dishes and take off for the dentist ahead of schedule.

While the pineapple juice for the gelatin was heating, I sliced bananas and more fat, juicy strawberries—bless Alicia—and reflected on everything I knew about the events of the past week. There were those acts someone—or ones—had committed. *Shoot out our window. Kill Andy. Shoot Tom. Steal the computers. Murder the man who steals the computers. Somewhere in there, hide a multimillion-dollar stamp haul in the center of a rose window. Then move the loot. But accidentally leave one behind.* The *sequence* of those acts, I realized, had to be part of the solution to the puzzle.

I wondered about Sara Beth. If jealousy were the motive for all this activity, could you remove shooting out our window and shooting Tom as being related to the stamp theft? If so, then how could you account for those acts being done by two separate guns?

You have to think the way the thief does, Tom was fond of saying. In this case, you had to start with the facts you knew, try to extrapolate the thinking behind them, and from all that, deduce the identity of the thief.

Yeah, sure. My mind was as clear as...well... unmolded salad.

I mixed the gelatin into the boiling juice, added chilled juice, then folded in all the fruits. Unlike my mother's generation, I never waited before mixing ingredients into gelatin. No one ever seems to notice if the fruits sink or float, do they? Sinking or floating in real life, on the other hand, is another matter.

In an oversize Dutch oven, I gently sautéed

chopped apples and onions in melted butter, then stirred in curry powder, flour, and spices. I shelled, deveined, and cooked the shrimp, then dropped the shrimp tails into bubbling chicken stock. Finally I stirred the stock, vermouth, and heavy cream into the sauce. The mixture gave off a divinely pungent scent.

Once the salad molds and shrimp were chilling in the refrigerator, and the curry sauce was cooling, I powered up with a double espresso, two reheated scones, two thick pats of unsalted butter, and generous dollops of blueberry preserves. *Yum.* Why Arch preferred chalky, store-bought doughnuts to homemade baked goods was one of the mysteries of the ages.

At quarter to nine, I was seated in my van, sipping another double espresso, and eyeing the front of Aspen Meadow's endodontist office. What I was actually going to say to Sara Beth O'Malley I had not worked out yet. Of course then again, last time, outside my home, she hadn't allowed me to say much.

Well, what *was* I going to say? *Hey, Sara Beth! Why didn't you tell anybody you were alive? Why'd you come back to taunt your old fiancé and his family? Oh, and anonymously donated supplies notwithstanding, why didn't you go to a dentist closer to home? Was it because your "supplies" were from a big stamp deal going down here? So you decided to kill two birds with one stone? Or rather, two thieves with one gun?*

She came walking up the steps by the dentist's office as stealthily as a cat, and just as quietly. Had she acquired get-around-in-the-jungle skills? Her eyes scanned the upper lot for Tom. Her distinguished, Jackie Kennedy face and dark hair streaked with gray once again gave me a *frisson*.

I believed Tom when he said he hadn't met with Sara Beth—or done worse—in the last month. She was a woman from his past who'd just appeared out of nowhere. What I wasn't sure of was whether he still loved her. She was certainly one of the most striking women I'd ever seen, especially since in twenty-degree weather, she was dressed only in a clingy gray turtleneck and long gray pants. I look fat in gray, and never wear it. Sara Beth didn't look fat in anything. I sighed, and wondered. The ability to survive cold, the ability to move stealthily. Despite my first impression that she was a nonshooting type, had she also learned the jungle skill of killing a target?

Before I could chicken out, I assumed a friendly demeanor and walked up to her.

"Please don't run away," were the first words out of my mouth. "I'm Tom's wife. Won't you just talk to me? I'm not going to turn you in. For anything."

She lifted her chin. She wore no makeup, and looked younger and better for it. *Stop it*, I scolded myself. In her quiet, rusty-from-disuse English, Sara Beth said, "I am sorry I ever tried to contact Tom."

"You've got a few minutes, right? Please. Just come sit in my van and talk. I need to talk to you about Tom being shot," I added, studying her face.

She turned so pale I thought she might faint. Startled, she almost lost her balance. When she faltered, I tucked my arm in hers and led her to the van.

Once I'd coaxed her inside, I turned the heat on full blast. She rubbed her hands and shivered.

"I'm Goldy Schulz," I said.

She gave me a slight smile. "That's what you said last time. What happened to Tom?"

"Some bad guy shot him Monday morning. He was hit in the shoulder, but he's mobile and recovering."

"Was this before or after the window?"

"After. Do you know anything about either shooting?"

Her face darkened and she stared at the windshield. "No. I just came here to get supplies and have my teeth fixed."

"Here?" I asked calmly. I tried to make my voice soothing, the better to coax out information. "You've been away twenty-some years. Why'd you stay in Southeast Asia all that time? Why didn't you come home to your fiancé?"

"Look, I *attempted* to let him know I'd survived. Not right away, of course. It was too dangerous. I was afraid of trying to get back."

"So you became a village doctor?"

"I did it for survival," she replied. Her face was chiseled into seriousness, and I suddenly imagined interviewing her for some postwar documentary. Sheesh! "Stories came back about Saigon as a madhouse," she was saying.

"People were trying to get out before all hell broke loose. Many of them failed. I'd broken my back when the copter crashed. By the time I recovered, the Americans were long gone. The Vietcong weren't going to say, 'You forgot somebody! Come on back and pick her up!' The village people told me I'd never get out alive. So I stayed, and worked hard, so the villagers would want me there. So they would keep my secret. They adopted me," she added, "and I grew to love them. The American government did a terrible thing to that country."

"Uh, thanks. We figured that out, but only after thousands of our own soldiers died."

"I tried to communicate with Tom. I just never had any luck. For example, fifteen years ago—"

"Fifteen *years* ago?"

She ran her fingers through her streaked hair. Her voice had turned calm. She was finally reciting a story she'd prepared for a long time. "Fifteen years ago I gave a letter to Tom to a French agricultural worker who showed up in the village. But the Frenchman died when he stepped on a mine beside the railroad track. After that, I didn't try to communicate anymore, because I figured it would be too disruptive to Tom's life. And then I had to pick up some supplies and deal with this tooth problem. Another visitor to the village told us about e-mail, so I...changed my mind and tried *that* once I got to the States, through a friend's account." The face she turned to me seemed profoundly sad. "You always think, or hope, maybe, that people haven't changed. That somehow you can touch base with your old life. I'm sorry I did." She hesitated. "I'd still like to see Tom, if he isn't too badly hurt."

Not so fast, I thought. *I still have a couple of questions.* Again, I reminded myself to be sweet and polite. "Do you happen to know anything about stamps? As in, the valuable kind that are so easy to fence overseas? Especially in the Far East?"

"What are you talking about? I told you, I used e-mail." She gave me a wide-eyed *Tom-married-a-nut* look, then reached for the door handle. "I have to go. If Tom can manage, I'd like him to drive me to the airport at four o'clock this afternoon. The dental pain meds will be wearing off by then, and talking will be a challenge. But I'd like to see him before I go. I'm staying in the Idaho Springs Inn, under the name Sara Brand. If he's not there, I'll take the shuttle bus." She opened the door and swiveled one of her slender legs out of the van.

"Wait," I said. "Just...tell me, do you still love him? Are you here because you're trying to steal him back? I have to know."

She lowered her chin and gave me the full benefit of her intense brown eyes. "We had a good relationship, but it's been over for a long time. Enjoy what you have, Goldy. He's a good man."

Without saying good-bye, she trotted toward the dentist's office.

Great. Either she was telling the truth, or she was an incredibly good actress. Did I care? I wasn't sure.

The maxim *When you feel really low, focus on the food* had always proved useful. This time would be no exception. I torqued the van out of the lot and drove to the grocery store, where I bought not one but two quarts of nondairy lime sorbet for lactose-intolerant Howie Lauderdale. I knew he probably wouldn't eat all sixty-four ounces, even if he *was* a teenager. But a Caterer's Basic Rule of Dessert is that you must have plenty of backup food, even for a single special-request treat. Then if eight more folks communicate a sudden desire for lime sorbet, they won't feel cheated when you say you don't have any.

I hit the brakes hard halfway through the store parking lot. Behind me, a VW Bug beeped. What had I just said to myself? *If eight more folks communicate a desire...*

I pulled into a vacant parking space. What had Sara Beth said about my husband? *I tried to communicate with Tom. I just never had any luck.*

Who else ran out of luck communicating? How about Andy Balachek? First by a letter to Tom at the department, then by e-mail, and finally by telephone, that young man had been obsessed with *staying in touch*. The last time we'd heard from Andy had been via cell phone from Central City. Or had it?

You have to think the way the thief does.

Trudy Quincy had been taking in our mail

all week. Was it possible Andy had somehow tried to communicate, and we just *hadn't had any luck* receiving it?

Heart in mouth, I threw the gearshift into drive, stepped on the gas, and thankfully only skidded once while racing over the snow-packed streets back to our house. I avoided looking at our plywood-covered window, leapt from the van, and hopped through the new snow to the Quincys' house. *Please let my neighbor be home*, I prayed. *Please let her not think I've gone bananas.*

When Trudy opened her door, she was cuddling our cat on her left shoulder. Scout gave me that slit-eyed feline greeting: *Who the hell are you?* Then he snuggled in closer to Trudy.

"Goldy!" Trudy cried. "C'mon in! This kitty thinks he's my baby. I fried him up some trout Bill caught and froze last summer, and now I don't think he's ever going back to your place."

"Oh, well—" I began, but got no further before Jake bounded around a corner, leaped up on me, and started slathering my face. *No way I'm staying at the Quincys'! Leave that stupid cat here and let's go home!* I told him to get down, then patted him feverishly so Trudy and I could talk without further interruption.

"Do you have our mail?" I said casually. "I'm looking for something in particular. Something important."

"Sure." She frowned and glanced down at

Scout. "It's in a big pile on the dining-room table. We can walk in there, but not too fast. Kitty doesn't like to be hurried."

I sidled into the Quincys' dining room. Scout and Jake eyed each other, but I ignored them. I asked Trudy—who was no Sukie Hyde in the organizational department—if there happened to be any order to the mountain of letters. She said the new stuff was on top of the old stuff. I turned the heap over and started going through it.

From Monday there were two bills, seven ads, three catalogs, the sheriff's department newsletter, and a postcard for Arch.

From Tuesday, there were nine ads, six catalogs, a bill, notice of a cooking equipment sale, and a bulk-mail fundraising letter from Elk Park Prep.

And then.

His handwriting was uneven and loopy, the b's and l's tall and unevenly slanted, the i's dotted with tiny circles. The letter was addressed to Tom, with "Gambler" scrawled in the upper left-hand corner. Postmarked Monday. No return address. I snatched it, thanked Trudy, and sprinted out. Behind me, Jake wailed.

Over my shoulder I called, "I'll be back tomorrow, Jake!"

He raised his howl several decibels, unconvinced. Scout, a.k.a. Kitty, took no notice.

CHAPTER 24

R acing back to the castle, I could have
sworn that letter was burning a hole in my
purse. But I could *not* open it; I'd already
committed all the invasion-of-privacy sins I
cared to in this lifetime. Still: If Tom was
asleep, this was one time I was going to shake
him awake.

He was awake, sitting in one of the wing-
back chairs, talking on the telephone. From
the bits of conversation I snatched before
urgently waving the letter in his face, he was
discussing the ongoing investigation into the
whereabouts of Troy McIntire. Paying no
heed to my antics, Tom turned his head
toward the fireplace and continued talking. Troy
McIntire, philatelic agent, seemed to have
mailed himself somewhere without a known
address. Clutching Andy's letter, I scooted in
front of the fireplace and did a few jumping
jacks. Since Tom knows how much I hate to
do jumping jacks, he cocked an eyebrow and
signed off. I slapped the letter onto the coffee
table.

"What's this, Miss G., another stamp from
Mauritius?" he asked, without looking at the
missive. "You keep finding them, they're
going to think *you* stole 'em. I just learned that
stamp you found in the chapel was part of the
heist. No discernible fingerprints besides
yours."

I slipped into the chair across from him.

344

"Tom, this letter's from Andy Balachek. Mailed to you. Postmarked Monday. Which probably means he mailed it sometime Sunday. A day before he died. Or rather, a day before someone murdered him."

Tom, who is seldom surprised, leaned over the envelope and frowned.

"Is it Andy's handwriting?" I demanded, increasingly impatient. In addition to Tom's other skills, his ability to analyze handwriting means he is often called to testify in forgery cases. I held my breath.

"Maybe. All I've ever seen is his signature. It's a long, skinny 'A' that's a scripted 'A,' not a printed one. His 'A' looks like the back of a bald guy's head, tilted to one side." He picked up the envelope and examined it on both sides. "Trudy picked this up with the rest of our mail? What day?"

"My best guess is it came Tuesday."

Tom whistled. "Could you get my tweezers out of my suitcase? Then you could use them to open the letter without getting your fingerprints on it, and put it down here for us both to read."

"You trust me to open your mail?"

"No. But do it anyway."

And so I did. The struggle with the damned tweezers took an agonizing eight minutes.

Tom, the letter read. *I'm getting scared now because I need to pay my dad back for his truck. If I don't, he's going to die in the hospital. So I'm going to get the stamps tonight. If I don't make it, if you get this and I'm dead, then my gamble didn't work.*

You tried to help me, so I owe you. I'll tell you what my partner told me. Maybe it's a lie and that's what I'll find out. Anyway, the stamps are in the Hydes' chapel. If you get this and my dad has a new truck and I've gone to Monte Carlo, then you'll know I made it. If not—well, then it's up to you. A.

"Oh, crap!" I cried. "He told us where the stamps were, but didn't tell us who his partner was! We're not any closer than we were before!"

But Tom was thinking. "We know Andy believed the stamps were in the chapel, and they were, weren't they? Or at least *one* was. Still, how would Andy know the lockbox combination? Would his partner have been so naïve as to tell him *that*? When that chapel's locked, you can't tell me it's easy to get into, or it'd be the local site for every teenage beer bash."

"Let me assure you," I retorted, "our town doesn't possess a single building that's easier to get into than that chapel. Yesterday, Julian and I locked the door to keep out early lunch arrivals. But remember, I told you first Buddy and Chardé showed up, then the Jerk and Viv Martini. I'll accept that Buddy and Chardé might have a key, and might not have completely shut the door before the Jerk barged in. But

346

I don't think so. I think Eliot told his dear close friend Chardé the decorator, *and* his ex-girlfriend Viv, how to get into the chapel. Or gave them keys. Or else they're both splendid at picking locks."

Tom pondered this for a minute. "Maybe Andy's partner intercepted him, shot him, left his body in the creek by the chapel, put up a ladder and grabbed the stamps, but somehow missed one. And didn't realize it until he'd made off with the loot."

"Yeah, that's what I've been thinking. Except there's no blood at the crime scene. No sign of a struggle. No obvious way Andy was electrocuted."

"Right." He stared at the cold fireplace. "Let me call down to the department, have somebody come get this letter."

"Wait a minute!" We had to be close. I'd found a clue, and now Tom was just going to pass it off? "Let's speculate." I thought back to my visit to the shooter's site, on the north side of the state highway, up on a cliff in a county park. "Say Andy's partner uncovers Andy's double-cross, electrocutes Andy, shoots him, removes all but one of the hidden stamps from the chapel, then plants Andy's body in the creek. Okay, then he waits for *you* to show up."

"How does the partner know I'm coming back Monday?"

I shrugged. "Let's say he doesn't know what cop will show up when the body's discovered. He just suspects Andy's been communicating with the sheriff's department, because he caught Andy in the double-cross. Or *thought* he caught Andy in a double-cross."

"It's weak."

I closed my eyes, thinking back to that morning, running it through my mind in slow motion. *Tom gets out of his car, motions for me to move away from the edge of the creek. Then he walks— not toward Andy's body, but straight west, toward me, which is also the direction of the chapel....*

But if the thief-sniper thought he'd removed all the stolen stamps, why try to keep Tom, or any cop, away from the chapel? Because he was terrified Andy had confided in his good buddy, Tom Schulz? Confided not only regarding the whereabouts of the stamps, but also regarding the third partner's identity? If that was the case, why did he shoot at our window—with a different gun—before Andy's body was even discovered? It made no sense... unless the shooter was someone else altogether, not one of the three who heisted the stamps, someone with some agenda we hadn't yet figured out.

I leaned back in the chair. Fatigue and frustration rolled over me. And it wasn't even eleven in the morning.

When I glanced up, Tom gave me one of his soulful looks. I felt an overpowering desire to drag him into the four-poster bed for some Late Morning Delight—forget the gunshot wound, the bandage, and the sling. Forget the old fiancée, too. He smiled. "Don't you have cooking to do for the fencing banquet?"

My heart sank. Maybe Tom couldn't read my let's-make-love signals anymore. Was that because I wasn't sending out good signals? Or was his mind somewhere else...somewhere I didn't want to go?

"Yes, I do have kitchen work waiting. But there's one more thing I have to tell you." I took a steadying breath. "Tom, I confronted Sara Beth this morning. She denies having any... ill intent. She still wants to see you. Says she needs a ride to the airport at four o'clock this afternoon. She claims to be staying at the Idaho Springs Inn under the name of Sara Brand." I paused. "In case you *are* feeling up to it."

He took a deep breath. "Look, I should go. I'm not feeling too bad now. If I take her and we can talk about what's happened, then we'd all have closure—you, me, her, everybody."

"Uh-huh." I didn't ask how he was going to pilot a car with his one good hand. I didn't want to discuss his driving or his desire for closure with his ex-fiancée. Or whether he would take a gun.

He said quietly, "They towed my Chrysler to the department garage. May I borrow your van?"

I didn't trust my voice, so I just nodded.

Tom said, "Goldy? We've talked about this. You're my wife, and I love you. Don't you believe me?"

With my lips pressed together and an unseen force squeezing my heart, I nodded mutely and handed him the van keys. Then I picked up my laptop, walked quickly out of our big English-castle bedroom, and quietly shut the massive door. Trying not to think, I headed down to the castle kitchen.

When you feel really low, focus on the food.

While my laptop was booting on the trestle table, I took a bite of one of the strawberry salads—still half-liquid—and tasted the curry sauce, which was spicy-hot, creamy, and mellowing superbly. Then I inserted my disk to check the recipes for the potato casserole and raisin rice. I may have teased Julian about thinking of me as old. But the fact was that my memory for recipes was *not* butcher-knife sharp.

I reflected on that evening's schedule. Although adult-only banquets usually start at eight, the over-scheduled Elk Park Prep fencers had Saturday morning commitments to indoor soccer and club basketball. So we were starting at six with the fencing demonstration and Elizabethan games, accompanied by bowls of mixed nuts and soft drinks. Julian and I would serve dinner at seven, after which Michaela would lead a brief awards ceremony. Would Tom be back from his rendezvous with Sara Beth in time for that?

Don't think about it.

Instead, I began to peel the potatoes and thought about Michaela. What was the story on her?

Shuttlecock Shrimp Curry

3 tablespoons unsalted butter
2 cups unpeeled chopped Granny
    Smith apples
2 cups chopped yellow onions
3 large cloves garlic, pressed
4 teaspoons curry powder, or more
    to taste
3 tablespoons flour
½ teaspoon dry mustard
½ teaspoon salt, or more to taste
¼ teaspoon paprika
¼ teaspoon crumbled dried thyme
¼ teaspoon freshly ground black
    pepper, or more to taste
2 cups homemade chicken stock
1 pound (39 to 40) large peeled
    cooked shrimp (shrimp
    cocktail–style shrimp), deveined,
    tails removed and reserved
1 tablespoon catsup
¼ cup dry white vermouth
½ cup whipping cream

Side dishes: best-quality chutney, dry-
roasted peanuts, chopped hard-boiled

egg, sweet pickle relish, crushed pineapple, flaked coconut, mandarin oranges, chopped scallions, chopped crisp-cooked bacon, chopped olives, raisins, yogurt, and orange marmalade

Raisin Rice (recipe is in *Killer Pancake*)

In a wide frying pan, melt the butter over low heat. Add the apples, onions, and garlic, and cook gently over medium-low heat for a few minutes, until the onions start to become translucent. Add the curry powder, flour, mustard, salt, paprika, thyme, and pepper, and stir well. Keeping the heat low, cook and stir occasionally for a few more minutes, while you prepare the stock.

In a large saucepan, combine the stock and shrimp tails. Bring to a boil, then turn off the heat. Drain and reserve the stock. Discard the shells.

Keeping the heat low, add the shrimp-flavored stock to the apple mixture, stirring well. When all the stock has been

added, raise the heat to medium-high, stirring constantly, and add the catsup and vermouth. Stir and cook until the mixture is thickened. Lower the heat and add the cream, stirring well, until the mixture has heated through. Add the shrimp, and stir and cook until the shrimp are heated through but *not over-cooked.*

Serve with the side dishes and Raisin Rice. Beer is the traditional beverage.

Makes 4 servings

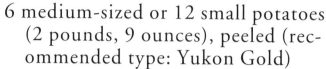

Penny-Prick Potato Casserole

6 medium-sized or 12 small potatoes (2 pounds, 9 ounces), peeled (recommended type: Yukon Gold)

1 small garlic bulb, or ½ large garlic bulb

1 tablespoon olive oil

2 tablespoons (¼ stick) unsalted butter

½ cup milk (approximately)

½ cup whipping cream

1 cup freshly shredded Fontina cheese

⅓ cup freshly shredded Parmesan cheese

½ teaspoon salt, or to taste

¼ teaspoon white pepper, or to taste

Preheat the oven to 350°F. Butter a 9 x 13-inch pan.

Bring a large quantity of salted water to a boil. Place the potatoes in the boiling water and cook until done, about 40 minutes.

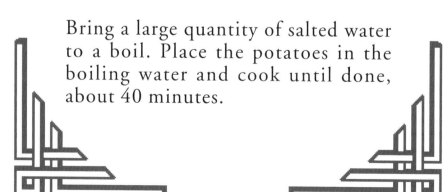

While the potatoes are cooking, cut a piece of foil into an 8-inch square. Quickly rinse the garlic bulb under cold running water and pat it dry. Place the bulb in the middle of the foil square and carefully pour the olive oil over it. Bring up the corners of the foil and twist to make a closed packet. Put the foil packet with the garlic inside into the oven and bake about 30 to 40 minutes, or until the cloves are soft but not brown. Carefully open the package, remove the garlic bulb with tongs so it can cool, and reserve the olive oil.

When the garlic cloves are cool, remove them from their skins. Using a small food processor, process the garlic until it is a paste.

Drain the potatoes and place them in the large bowl of an electric mixer. Add the garlic, reserved olive oil, butter, milk, cream, cheeses, salt, and pepper. Beat until creamy and well combined. If the mixture seems dry, add a little milk. Scrape the potato mixture into the prepared pan. (If you are not going to

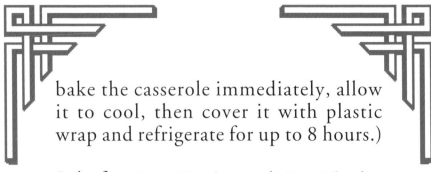

bake the casserole immediately, allow it to cool, then cover it with plastic wrap and refrigerate for up to 8 hours.)

Bake for 15 to 20 minutes (10 or 15 minutes longer if the casserole has been refrigerated). The casserole should be hot through and slightly browned. Test for doneness by scooping out a small spoonful from the middle of the casserole and tasting it.

Makes 4 servings

I placed the potatoes into two vats of boiling water. Maybe I *had* found Michaela's Royal-memento collection a tad unusual. But a number of my friends had oddball hobbies. Take Marla, for instance, who obsessively tracked the Jerk. Now *there* was an offbeat hobby—and not one for the squeamish.

And speaking of squeamish...tonight was another meal in the Great Hall. The last time I'd served food there, I'd glimpsed a long-dead duke-to-be. That ghostly fellow, dressed in what looked like a child-size suit of armor, had *been* there, I was certain of it. And in an instant, he'd vanished. Colorado was famous for ghost *towns,* not ghost *dukes.* Maybe I needed contact lenses.

I retrieved a huge bowl of prawns ready to be enrobed in the velvety curry sauce, and set them aside. For the potato casseroles, I slathered several whole bulbs of garlic with olive oil, wrapped them in foil, and popped them into the oven. In my mind, there is nothing better than roasted garlic to give mashed potatoes a rich, mellow bite. Not to mention that mashed potatoes in any form are good for the soul.

As I was grating mounds of Fontina and Parmesan, Julian called. He had picked up Arch, who had convinced him to go for a pizza snack. They were going to eat heaps of fancy food tonight anyway, Arch had claimed. Did I need help, Julian wanted to know? I said thanks, but reminded him that he had already done more than his share of catering work for

357

the last four days. Did I mind that they were eating pizza, he asked? I laughed and asked him to bring some back to the castle. He promised they'd return by four to help set up.

Eliot bustled into the kitchen wearing a twenties-style, Scottish-inspired golf outfit. I didn't know any other man who could wear (without deep embarrassment) tan wool bloomers—known in the golf world as plus-fours—forest-green knee socks, a tan-and-gray checked wool shirt, and a gray herringbone V-neck sport coat. Oh yes, and tan-and-white saddle shoes. To my credit, I didn't stare. Instead, I asked him how he was doing.

"Terribly. I haven't had a nibble of interest in the conference center." He looked around the kitchen. "Sukie is cleaning up the Great Hall—"

"It's *clean.*"

"Goldy, for six months I dated a woman who was an unrepentant slob. Dirty dishes, piled-up laundry, stacks of bills and papers, unmade beds, unrecognizable bathroom. Finally I couldn't take it anymore, and we broke up. Now look at the woman I married. Nothing— *nothing*—is *ever* clean enough for her." He shook his head, as if trying to remember what he had come down here for. "She's going to set the tables up there, too. She's using her own lace tablecloths and a set of silver plates she picked up at an estate sale. In Medieval and Renaissance England, diners went from consuming their food from bread trenchers, to eating on wood platters, until they graduated to pewter, and on from there to silver and ah, finally, to gold plates. But gold is so *damnably* expensive. Anyway, Sukie needs to know how many people are expected for dinner and if you need steak knives."

"We're expecting thirty-five. Fourteen kids, twenty-one adults, give or take. If she sets us up for forty, that should work." I thought of the veal roasts. "And sure, steak knives would be great. Plus a dozen serving spoons, and a couple of carving sets."

"All right," he said, scribbling on an index card he'd found in the pocket of his plus-fours. "Before Michaela gives out the awards, I'm going to pitch the castle again. I'm going back now to set up my pamphlets and information. Do you think the literature should go on the serving tables?"

"Better to have it at the door," I advised. "It'll be the first thing people see."

He nodded, a golfer attending his caddy. "Good thought. I'm going to set up the games, too, while Sukie's working. Oh—and the Lauderdales are sending flower arrangements with small swords in them. They really *are* good people, Goldy."

"Uh-huh." *I don't think so.*

He disappeared. I sautéed rice kernels in butter until they sizzled and gave off a nutty scent, then mixed in broth and raisins. While the rice simmered, I pulverized the roasted garlic. Finally, I mashed batch after batch of potatoes with butter, the roasted garlic mush, cream, cheeses, and spices, and managed to have only eight spoonfuls—using eight different spoons, of course—to make sure the seasoning was exactly right. I kept telling myself that I hadn't really had any lunch.

At three o'clock, Tom walked through the kitchen door. He'd retrieved some clothing from the suitcase he'd taken to New Jersey, and now looked businesslike and dashing in a black wool shirt and khaki pants, with a black down jacket over his good shoulder. I realized with a jolt that I'd been so busy cooking, I'd forgotten to take *him* lunch.

"I'm on my way to Idaho Springs, then the airport," he announced. "And I'm going to stay at the gate until Sara Beth's flight gets off. So I might not be back until after the banquet, especially if the flight's delayed." I said nothing. "Please understand," he said, then gave me a one-armed hug and headed off.

What kind of farewell, I thought forlornly, *was that?*

Don't dwell on it.

So I didn't. Cooking consumed the next hour. At half-past four, I scuttled to the gatehouse to let in the floral delivery man. He opened his van to reveal four miniature sword-bedecked, English-style arrangements of roses, lilies, daffodils, freesia, and ivy. I breathed in the perfumed scent of flowers, picked up two of the overflowing baskets, and led the florist up to the Great Hall, where Eliot and Sukie exclaimed over the generosity of the Lauderdales. *That's the problem with rich folks*, I concluded silently, as I placed the baskets on Sukie's flawlessly set, lace-and-silver-covered tables. *They think they can make up for large-scale bad deeds with a couple of superficially good ones.* In the catering biz, I'd seen the adulterer who builds a new Sunday School, the thieving bank president who sponsors a dozen soccer teams. Now we had a child-abuser sending flowers.

Ah well, who made me World Moral Cop? I trotted back to the kitchen, where I was greeted by a blast of cold air. Once again, the errant window was open. Michaela, Julian, and Arch were all out; Sukie and Eliot were up in the Great Hall. I marched over to the window, pushed it all the way open—the metal sash shrieked in protest—and looked down. There was no walkway, there were no metal rungs. The moat glimmered far below. Its surface riffled with a slight breeze, but no one was swimming across it. At the edge, the castle Dumpster shimmered in the sun. There was no sign of life anywhere. So how was the window being opened?

I examined the latch. It was not broken. I slammed the window shut again, then searched through the highly organized kitchen drawers until I found some mailing tape. Cursing under my breath, I assiduously pressed a double layer of sticky strips all the way around the window sash. I stepped away from my work and admired it.

"Take that," I muttered to the window.

Repair job complete, I hustled back to the Great Hall with bowls of mixed nuts. Eliot had once again laid out the penny-prick game. This time the boys would toss their plastic knives at a Susan B. Anthony coin set on the lip of a wine bottle. I didn't particularly like the antifeminist symbolism inherent in *that,* but I kept my mouth shut. Sensing my lack of enthusiasm, Eliot insisted the kids wouldn't play for less than a dollar prize.

I zipped back to the kitchen and was greeted by Arch, Julian, Michaela, a cold extra-cheese pizza, and a still-closed window. I wolfed down the pizza without reheating it. Hunger, as my fourth-grade teacher always said, makes the best sauce.

"I'm changing the schedule a little, Arch," Michaela was saying. "I'm going to have you and Howie Lauderdale demonstrate foil first. The Lauderdales called and specifically requested it."

My heart plummeted. "Forget it," I retorted. "They're up to something. The Lauderdales, I mean. Use the kids you already have scheduled. Howie's too old to be paired with Arch. Arch might get hurt."

Arch's lips thinned in disgust. His cheeks reddened with anger. "Howie will *not* hurt me."

"I said no!"

"Mom! Howie's the best fencer on the team!"

"I don't care!"

Michaela made her voice reassuring. "Goldy, I promise, I know Howie. He's a good kid. Arch is definitely up to fencing him."

Julian murmured, "C'mon, Goldy. Let him

362

do it. The kids wear masks. Everyone will be there. It's an honor for Arch to go first, to fence with Howie."

"*Yeah,* Mom," Arch cried. "Stop making me out to be a *wimp.*"

I gestured helplessly. With the three of them staring at me, I said, "Okay, I give up. Fence away. But it wouldn't surprise me if Buddy was paying his son to hurt you."

Arch snorted. Michaela silently shook her head. After a few moments of uncomfortable silence, she said she'd bring the ice and drink coolers up to the Great Hall. Arch offered to help, and they both left.

Julian and I now set to our work in earnest, putting in the veal for a slow roasting, timing the reheating of the curry, rice, and potatoes, and deciding on the flow of the buffet. Julian got the chafers going and set up the electrified serving platters. This was the third time this week we'd transported keep-stuff-hot equipment hither and yon. No wonder the medieval folks built their kitchen close to the Great Hall.

As my last culinary act before the guests arrived, I prepared the curry condiments. Americans rarely take more than a spoonful of chutney, raisins, or peanuts from that classic dozen side dishes known as a twelve-boy. But they feel gypped if they cannot at least *survey* lots of extra bowls containing chopped bacon, chopped hard-cooked egg yolks, chopped hard-cooked egg whites, shredded coconut, crushed pineapple, chopped green onion, sweet pickle relish, orange marmalade, and yogurt.

Just before six, Eliot and Sukie breezed into the kitchen. Eliot had changed from the golf outfit into another dapper double-breasted suit—this one charcoal gray—and a snowy white shirt. Sukie's blond hair was swept up in an elegant French twist, and she glowed in a long, bright-red wool dress. She retrieved a silver tray, glasses, and napkins, while Eliot clanked bottles around in the dining room and proudly emerged with two bottles of vintage dry sherry. They announced that they were on their way to the gatehouse to greet guests in the grand fashion. Murmuring that the kids needed to be welcomed in style, too, Julian snagged two twelve-packs of soft drinks and hustled after the Hydes.

I dashed up to the Great Hall with the covered curry side dishes and quickly checked the buffet, the tables, the makeshift bars, the ice, and the bottles of water and wine. Eliot had straightened the fencing mats and marked out the shuttlecock court with masking tape. Michaela had set up a small table for the trophies. Overhead, the chandeliers flickered. The gold trophies, silver plates, and crystal glasses reflected the glimmering light. Everything looked perfect.

Always a bad sign.

CHAPTER 25

Tom was still gone on his airport errand when John Richard and Viv Martini sashayed in, the first to arrive. Standing alone behind the makeshift bar, I was unnerved by their appearance. They glanced in my direction, then sniffed and looked away. John Richard looked handsome in an open-necked blue shirt, charcoal vest, and black pants. His twenty-nine-year-old girlfriend, slinking along in a clingy silver dress with matching spike heels, made my stomach turn over. Her dress was slit so far up the side, *she* should have been doing jumping jacks.

I, on the other hand, feared the worst, appearance-wise. Not only did I pale in comparison to Viv, I couldn't bear the thought of how Tom would assess my appearance vis-à-vis that of Sara Beth, with her aristocrat-in-the-Peace-Corps beauty and moral high ground. I glanced at myself in the reflection of a silver tray. Working in the hot castle kitchen had made my hair *very* curly. My makeup was long gone; my face shone with exertion. The cavernous Great Hall was cold, and I needed a sweater over my thin caterers' top, not to mention a new apron, as the one I had on was liberally dappled with curry sauce.

Julian took over the bar while I dashed back to our room, dragged a comb through my hair, dabbed on makeup and lipstick, and grabbed the only sweater I'd brought, the cardigan I'd worn to Eliot's office. As an afterthought, I seized my cell phone from its charger and dropped it into one of the sweater pockets. Reception in the castle was iffy, but carrying a phone somehow made me feel more secure.

In the kitchen, I tied on a clean apron, rechecked my list, made sure the roasts weren't cooking too quickly, started reheating the rice, and slid the potato casseroles into the oven. In forty-five minutes, Julian and I would bring forth all the food. I launched myself back up to the Great Hall. I didn't care if I looked like a plump little ex-wife who was also the caterer; I didn't care how I would stack up to the tall, gorgeous nurse from the jungle. I was *not* going to miss Arch's fifteen minutes of fencing fame.

"The attack in foil is like a charge," Michaela was saying to the assembled group of parents and students. Most were listening, but a few were milling about the shuttlecock court, where no one was playing, and the penny-prick game, where someone had already swiped the Susan B. Anthony dollar. Eliot, standing to one side of the group, looked depressed.

Arch and Howie, in fencing uniforms and masks, stood on the mat. Arch had his back to me; Howie, who looked frighteningly anonymous in his mask, faced me.

"We will have Arch," Michaela gestured in my son's direction, "and Howie," she nodded to the taller boy, "demonstrate attack, parry, riposte. Then one of them will charge. *En garde*, boys."

Arch and Howie moved smartly back and forth, their foils clanging, their feet slapping the mat. Howie attacked. Arch swiftly parried and riposted. The spectators tightened into a semicircle in front of the mat. Watching Arch, my heart swelled with pride and I didn't care if John Richard was only fifteen feet away. I wanted to holler, *That's my son!*

Without warning, Howie leaned forward, extended his sword, and *ran* toward Arch. I gasped so loudly half a dozen parents turned and glared. As Howie hurled himself toward Arch, my son froze, unsure what to do.

"*Stop!*" I shrieked, then wished I hadn't.

Arch tumbled backward just as Howie's sword whacked his chest, then his leg. Unable to keep his balance, Arch flailed off the mat. Howie, in full launch, could not stop. I watched helplessly as his right foot came down hard on Arch's left ankle. Arch screamed. Howie fell on top of him.

Michaela, John Richard, Julian, Buddy Lauderdale, and I all rushed forward. Howie seemed to be unable to extricate himself from the tangle of limbs. Buddy Lauderdale wrenched his son's arm and demanded to know if he was hurt. Howie muttered something I couldn't hear and clumsily righted himself. Leaning over Arch, Howie kept saying that he was sorry, very sorry, and why didn't Arch *parry*? I was so intensely angry that I had to restrain myself from shaking Howie Lauderdale. How could a supposedly "good kid" have taken advantage of a younger boy like this?

Tears slid out of Arch's eyes as Michaela and I removed his mask. His cheeks had purpled, but he made no noise to indicate he was crying. Instead, he croaked, "I think my foot's broken. Dad, is it broken? Dad?"

John Richard shoved past Buddy and Howie Lauderdale. He removed Arch's shoe, then probed with both hands along the foot and ankle. "Hard to tell." He looked up, not at Arch, but at Viv, who had sidled up to the action. John Richard said, "It should be x-rayed."

Viv said, *"Now?"*

"I'm taking him." It was Julian's voice. Our friend pushed forward to kneel beside Arch, who gave him an imploring look as tears continued to flow down his dark cheeks. "The father of my best friend at Elk Park is an orthopedist," Julian explained matter-of-factly. "Dr. Ling. He lives by the lake, five minutes from his office, where he does X-rays. He made me promise if I ever needed anything, I would give him a call."

"I know Ling," John Richard said.

You idiot Jerk, I raged internally, *take your son to the orthopedic surgeon yourself.* I turned my attention back to Arch.

He was trying not to writhe in pain. Tears still streamed down his cheeks. I knelt beside him and asked what I could do. Miserably, he shook his head. Michaela appeared with a plastic bag filled with ice. She gently laid it on the rapidly swelling ankle. I wondered if she was thinking of the *coup de Jarnac.*

I said, "Maybe he should go to the emergency room at Southwest—"

"Let me go with Julian," Arch said to me, his voice low. "Just let me, okay?"

"Dr. Ling is closer and better than Southwest," Julian insisted. "If the X-rays show Arch needs to go to the hospital, I can take him. Arch, can you sit up, put your arm around my shoulders?" When Arch nodded mutely, Julian deftly hauled him to a standing position. My son's left ankle dangled, and he winced.

"I'm going with you—"

"No way," Julian told me firmly. "Stay and handle the banquet. Have a couple of parents help you out. I'll call as soon as I know anything."

"Arch, honey, do you want me to come with you?" I asked.

"I'm okay, Mom."

"I'm really, really sorry," Howie Lauderdale gargled, increasingly distraught. "I was just trying to be aggressive, the way Dad—"

"Howie!" Buddy snapped.

To avoid strangling Howie, Buddy, or both of them, I accompanied Julian, who supported a hobbling Arch, to the hall's east door.

"Wait!" called Michaela in her commanding-coach voice. "We have something for Arch." She snatched a trophy from her table and strode over to us. She announced loudly, "For Ninth-Grade Fencer of the Year."

Arch's tear-streaked face instantly lit up. The parents and kids all clapped. I would have been elated, if I hadn't felt so miserable.

Easing Arch into the Rover proved difficult. Away from his peers, he squawked at every move that jiggled his injured foot. Around us, midwinter darkness pressed in. A high-pressure system must have moved across Colorado, though, because the air felt unusually warm—which probably meant it was forty degrees instead of five.

"Friday the thirteenth," commented Julian as he slid into the driver's seat. "Go figure."

"You all right, hon?" I asked Arch for the hundredth time.

"I'm *fine*, Mom. We'll call you."

I cursed myself all the way back up to the Great Hall. Buddy Lauderdale must have told his son to press hard in the attack. I'd heard enough tales of fathers sharpening football spikes and bribing sons to crash into hockey and soccer goalies not to be certain of *that*. But I never would have thought *Howie* would play along. Of course, I'd seen Howie fence, and beneath that cherubic face was an ambitious athlete. Once he was in a competitive situation, he might be unable to stop himself. No doubt that was what Buddy Lauderdale had been counting on, when he'd called Michaela and said he wanted the two boys to fence tonight.

Arch had frozen when Howie commenced

his attack. Why? Because I'd gasped, and ruined his concentration?

Was everything that went wrong with my child ultimately my fault? I didn't want to contemplate that one.

Lost in thought, I stared at one of the *Wet Paint* signs plastered in our bedroom hallway. Was it really my gasp that had distracted Arch? Or could it have been something else? Was it possible Arch had seen something under the minstrels' gallery? He'd been standing in virtually the same place where I'd been the previous night, when the boy-duke apparition had materialized. But if he had seen the ghost, why hadn't he mentioned it? Too afraid of looking like a wimp?

In the castle kitchen, two team moms had somehow found Eliot's key ring, unlocked the cupboards, and were poking around. Both expressed concern for Arch; I said he'd be fine. The women told me they were trying to help with the buffet. They'd lit the burners under the chafers and plugged in the hot platters. They'd had to be as quiet as possible, since Eliot was doing his castle-as-conference-center monologue. At least I wouldn't have to hear *that* again.

One of the moms said, "He was looking for clients. And tossing in a little history."

"Like croutons," the other one added, giggling.

I smiled, thanked them for helping, and checked my watch: quarter to seven. The women gushed over the scent of the roasted veal and the garlic-laden, cheesy potatoes. They were only too glad to carry trays with the molded salads upstairs. I gently stirred the pans of shrimp curry and rice. When my helpers returned, we turned the rest of the food into the serving dishes, then trooped back upstairs.

"Ah, our feast!" Eliot cried when we made our entrance. He turned to his audience. "You are probably not aware that in Henry the Eighth's time, one of the favorite meats was *peacock*, more for its glory than for its taste. So! In the kitchens of Hampton Court, a peacock would be skinned and roasted. The head, skin, and feathers would be set aside until the meat was cooked, and afterwards be replaced on the roast. The peacock's *beak* would then be gilded, and the roast bird in all its feathered glory would be carried forth to the Great Hall!"

Under the low sparkle of the chandeliers, it looked as if all the guests' stomachs had knotted and their faces turned chartreuse. By the time Eliot finished the peacock story, the students were mock-gagging. That would teach Eliot to discuss uncooked bird head, skin, and feathers. The exception was the Lauderdales, who were deep in a whispered conference. Howie Lauderdale, his head hung with guilt, would not meet my gaze. And then there was John Richard, who had refused to leave with his son, because his girlfriend had demanded they stay and eat the Hyde-subsidized dinner for which they'd paid. Now the Jerk sported his own plucked-peacock look, an expression of embarrassed surprise I had come to associate with Viv massaging one of his nether parts. Sure enough, her hands had disappeared under the table.

Eliot asked if there were any questions. The guests murmured. I didn't quite have the food set up, so I was desperate for someone to ask *something. Is it true chambermaids were sexpots?* Anything. *Does that woman with Dr. Korman count?* On second thought, maybe we could skip the questions.

A parent called out, "Was this castle ever under siege?"

"Ah," said Eliot, warming instantly to his topic. "Yes. But the siege ultimately failed. Now, when a siege *succeeded,* it was usually because there was a confederate within, or because the besieging army was able to bore underneath the castle foundations, or because the attackers had found another way to undermine the self-sufficiency of the castle, say, by poisoning their well."

"What about that high-priced letter from that king?" another parent called. "Found any more of those?"

Eliot's chuckle was indulgent. "Alas, no. The toilets, or garderobes, have all been thoroughly cleaned and restored, with no further finds. We got a royal flush the first time, what?"

Only a few people laughed. I grabbed a silver spoon, tapped a crystal glass, and announced that dinner was served. I asked the guests first to thank Eliot for his enlightening presentation. The parents and students clapped with much relief, then made a beeline toward the buffet table. I had the two team moms go first, demonstrating the way lines should go down each side of the buffet. Once that was under way, I hustled back to the kitchen for the plum tarts-with-zirconia, two cartons of vanilla ice cream, and the first quart of lime sorbet. As I sped back up to the Great Hall with my rich cargo, I wondered if any of those self-sufficient castles had ever had to deal with melting ice cream.

What? What did I just say to myself?

I pushed into the Great Hall and was thinking so hard I almost upended the Jerk, plate and all. He cursed under his breath. I sincerely hoped he'd served himself *lots* of molded salad. He was allergic to strawberries.

I sandwiched the ice cream cartons between the ice cubes in the cooler, then began to cut the plum tarts. *The castles were self-sufficient.* All of the needs of the courtiers and servants were met within the walls: food, water, entertainment, and, oh Lord, forgive me for not thinking of it before now: *worship.*

Every castle had a chapel, of course it did. But where was the chapel in *this* castle? I'd been so focused on the Gothic structure down the road, *Hyde Chapel,* I'd forgotten to ask the question. Andy had written to Tom, *The stamps are in the Hydes' chapel.* Could there be more than one? And which one had he been talking about?

Folks were already clustered back at the buffet

374

line for seconds. One of the team moms zipped to my side and gushed that she *had* to have my recipes for potato casserole and shrimp curry. I told her no problem. The buffet line did not need my attention. So, acting as if I had business there I strode over to the rack of pamphlets Eliot had set up by the east door.

The only two pamphlets on display both looked newly printed: *Hide Away at Hyde Castle!* and *A History of Hyde Castle*. I glanced quickly through both of them. The second had a current floor plan, but no indication of how the spaces of the castle had been used in the Middle Ages, when the building had been constructed. The living room, for example, was designated by Eliot as "The Grand Parlor," when Sukie herself had told me it once stabled the horses. The playroom I'd discovered was labeled "Moat Pump Room." Why would Eliot, with all his concern for casting out historical tidbits, not tell how the spaces were originally used?

And then I remembered the pamphlets in Eliot's study. I'd grabbed one entitled *Medieval Castles and Their Secrets*, as well as *Have Your Wedding at Hyde Chapel!* But hadn't I taken another old one, one on taking a tour of the historic castle? Where was that thing?

Out of habit, I patted my pockets. Nothing in my apron. I prayed and felt inside my sweater pockets. Ah: paper. I pulled out all three pamphlets that I'd picked up in Eliot's office. As the guests had no immediate food needs,

I quickly opened *A Tour of Hyde Castle* and pored over it.

It contained a historic floor plan.

I ran my finger across the space allotted to the stables, the old kitchen next to the Great Hall—now the bedroom suite where Julian and Arch were quartered—the duke's bedroom, now the new kitchen, and, in the area marked Moat Pump Room in the new floor plan, next to what was now Eliot's study on the west range: Chapel. But I hadn't seen a pump, broken or no. I'd seen games and toys and kiddie-style furniture. I'd also seen a new lock, a lot of spilled paint, and a *Wet Paint* sign.

Plus, I'd asked both Michaela and Eliot about the current uses of that room. They'd both either lied or been evasive.

So what did all this tell me? I wasn't sure. And I didn't have time to think about it, because at that moment the second mom who'd helped me came trundling up.

"Goldy? What are you doing? Several of the guests have asked what you were reading so intently. Mr. Hyde said it was an old map of the castle."

"What's the problem?"

"Well, the Lauderdales want the nondairy dessert for Howie now. They said they asked you to buy lime sorbet."

I stuffed the pamphlet back into my pocket. "I haven't started to serve dessert yet." My voice was stiff with anger. After what the Lauderdales had put Arch through, they had *some nerve* demanding early dessert service.

"I told Buddy that," the mom explained, "but he said he wants to get Howie home, in case he was hurt in the collision. *I'll* serve him his special dessert, if you want. Just tell me where it is. The Lauderdales are very anxious. Chardé says she wants to get her money's worth from the banquet, and neither she nor Buddy are having any of the plum tart."

Oh, man, would these people never stop? "All right. Howie's sorbet is resting on ice in the cooler. If they *must* have it now, you can serve it to them. Eliot wants to say a few words about the jewels in the plum tart, so I'm not going to start with the whole dessert service yet."

"Okay. Except here's the thing. I thought the sorbet was in the cooler, too," she explained. "At least, I thought I saw it there. But now it's gone."

Clearly, this evening was not going to rank among my Top Ten Easily Catered Affairs. I stopped arguing with Team Mom Number Two and strode over to the cooler.

My heart sank.

The sorbet *was* gone. No carton. No telltale drips. I counted the bowls. None missing. No missing spoons, either. So, someone had come along, swiped the sorbet, taken the box into a bathroom, then eaten the contents with their fingers?

I sighed. I missed having Julian to help. Among other things, we managed to keep a close eye on the food, because people *do* steal at catered events, and not just because they want to take something home to Fido.

Thank heaven I'd bought two containers of sorbet! I asked the team moms to signal Eliot to start his discourse on How English Nobility Loved Hidden Treasure in Dessert. The women enthusiastically agreed to serve up tart slices with scoops of vanilla ice cream. If anyone asked, I told them, I was going back for sorbet for a demanding guest, and would return soon. They smiled in sympathy.

I sailed out of the Great Hall door, intent on my dessert-retrieval mission. But in the hallway between the Great Hall and Arch and Julian's bedroom door, I came face-to-face with one of those ubiquitous *Wet Paint* signs. We'd been here four days. The mistress of the castle, Sukie Hyde, was the neatest neatnik I'd ever met. So how come these signs were still up?

Was any real painting going on?

If you were trying to conceal something with a *Wet Paint* sign, wouldn't you put up lots of *Wet Paint* signs, to confuse the issue?

My curiosity got the better of me. Eliot wouldn't have left all the alarms on, would he? Especially since he had promised to take the guests on a tour later? I raced down the stairs to the ground floor and crossed the courtyard. The door to the hall leading to the "Moat Pump Room" opened easily. I wanted another look at the entry to that room, which had actually been filled with toys, and which had formerly served as the castle's chapel.

CHAPTER 26

The hallway glowed from the same overhead crystal fixtures and flickering wall sconces that were everywhere in the castle. Eliot had left on all the lights, probably because of the promised post-dessert tour. After his lengthy discourses and Arch's accident, however, I thought it unlikely anyone would stick around to explore.

Unlikely for anyone except me, that is.

By the entrance to the old chapel, I removed the *Wet Paint* sign and scraped the wall with my fingernail. Underneath the new splotch of paint was a dark spot. What was I looking for? Blood? If I found it, what would I do? And would the police accuse me of destroying evidence?

All right, think, I ordered myself as I studied the empty hallway. What exactly *was* I looking for? When Andy Balachek had been getting antsy, I was willing to bet, his partner-in-crime had strung him along with the information that the precious stamps were in the Hydes' chapel. Andy's father Peter had worked on the west range after the flood of '82. According to Michaela, Andy had explored this side of the castle extensively as a child. So maybe Andy had figured *in the Hydes' chapel* meant *in the castle chapel.* Say he had broken into the castle looking for those stamps. What was the one thing that had most haunted Tom and me since the discovery of Andy Balachek?

How he'd been electrocuted.

Using my fingernails to scrape was going to be too slow. I unscrewed the thin brass base from the bottom of one of the wall sconces. With this brass disk, I began to scrape random spots on the splash-painted wall. At last I uncovered another dark spot. Following it from the base of the wall to the door of the chapel/playroom, I quickly scratched out a dark, smoked arch.

This was it. It had to be. This was the arc left by a high-voltage bolt of electricity. Had Andy Balachek's body been a part of the arc? Had the electrocution been delivered on purpose, or had Andy made a deadly mistake in trying to penetrate security? Why would *this* door have its own electric lock, anyway?

I was getting the creeps in that deserted hallway. I still had to replace the sorbet and finish the banquet. I sprinted across the courtyard toward the kitchen. Andy Balachek had sneaked into the castle because he'd thought the stamps were hidden in the *castle* chapel. I doubted very much that the stamps had ever been there; I'd found where they'd been stashed, in the chapel by the creek.

How had Andy gotten in here, anyway?

But even as I moved into the kitchen, I knew the answer to that question: Michaela and Sukie had given it to me. Michaela had mentioned that while Peter Balachek ran his excavation equipment to rebuild the moat dam, his little son Andy had been fascinated, and had followed the reconstruction each day. What would the boy have learned during all those hours of watching? What Sukie had told us that very first night: the same knowledge that attackers of Richard the Lionheart's castle on the Seine had cleverly employed to invade—that the way in and out of the castle was into the water...and up through the garderobes.

Instinctively, I glanced up at the taped kitchen window. Could someone have been coming up a garderobe and through the window into the kitchen? I couldn't imagine it, as there was no ledge on the outside wall. This *had* been a bedroom—that of the child-duke—and some of the garderobes were corbeled out from the living quarters, as in our suite. But Sukie had shown me the closest garderobe to the kitchen. It was down past the dining room, in the drum tower with the well.

Andy, on the other hand, had known *exactly* where the garderobe was that led to Eliot's study. Believing the stolen stamps were in the *castle* chapel, Andy had planned to cheat his partner by sneaking in through the moat—wearing a wetsuit, perhaps? The moat was aerated for the ducks, so it wouldn't freeze. Sukie herself had told me she'd had mesh grilles installed on the bottom of the garderobes to keep rodents from making their way into the castle. But grilles could be popped off, I knew, and loosely bolted tops could be crashed through with a hammer. In this way, a garderobe could open a way into the castle, a way unprotected by security.

I stared at the kitchen windows. Once in the castle, Andy had encountered some kind of electric force he hadn't expected—a lock? A light? A security guard box? What had *I* found when I'd burst into the former chapel, a space that clearly had been ruined by the flood and never remodeled? I'd discovered a cheaply furnished playroom, with a new bolt that was missing one screw. The arc of electricity leading to the door seemed to point to an armed security device that had blown out when someone had unwisely tried to disarm it. Sukie had told me the room with the moat's pump was the only dangerous place in the castle. But I'd discovered the moat pump room, with no pump. Had the pump been in a closet I just hadn't seen? I doubted it.

No, I was willing to bet several rare stamps that that arc of electricity I'd just discovered was at the very spot where poor Andy had received his fatal or near-fatal shock. He'd been trying to break into the playroom, and had failed, miserably. And then he'd been discovered by someone. And shot by someone. And moved to the creek.

I stared down at the trestle table, almost forgetting what I'd come for. Oh, yes, the sorbet! But I couldn't concentrate; my mind raced. In Hyde Chapel, down by the creek, where *had* the stamps been hidden? I'd found a solitary stamp, in the one place that represented the mystical treasure—the very heart of the rose window. Who would have hidden an eight-hundred-thousand-dollar stamp *there?*

My first thought was Eliot. Eliot was the one who was big on labyrinth symbolism. But he was also loaded with money, and didn't need proceeds from a theft. Still, he dearly wanted his precious conference center to be a success, and anyone, no matter how rich, could be greedy for more cash. On the other hand, even before he'd profited from Henry VIII's letter, he'd turned down Viv's gambling idea, which could have garnered *oodles* of cash. But that didn't account for the utmost importance of Eliot's *name* to him. Illegal gambling would have been very bad for his beloved reputation, if he'd been caught.

I tapped the freezer door. You had to conclude that whoever hid the stamps in the center of the rose window knew Eliot's passions. *You have to think the way the thief does.* If the stamps had been found by the authorities, who would have been blamed?

Why, Eliot, of course. He'd been my first suspect, and he'd surely be the cops', too.

I snatched the second carton of sorbet from the freezer, but felt no compulsion to go rushing back to the Great Hall. I was in a mental zone, the kind where you know the ideas will keep coming if you persist in asking the questions. I didn't intend to leave that zone until I'd explored every inch of it.

Okay: Say the person who hid the stolen stamps wanted Eliot to be blamed and arrested, and to take the fall, *if anything went wrong.* Something did go terribly wrong when Andy double-crossed his hijacking partners and tried to swipe the stamps himself. Then the killer shot Andy, and left him...near where the stamps *had* been. Somehow the killer must have figured out that Andy had broken into the *wrong* chapel in the process of trying to steal back the stamps. Since the killer couldn't be too sure that Andy hadn't told somebody "the stamps are in the chapel," he or she had had to *move* the stamps *again,* before they could be discovered. But where would the killer hide them this time?

I whacked the frozen sorbet carton onto the counter. Figure it out, I ordered myself. *Think*. If you're trying to think along the same lines as the murderer, aren't you going to once again put the booty somewhere relatively accessible...*but still somewhere that Eliot would be blamed if the booty were found?*

Where would Eliot hide something?

What had Eliot said to me? The Elizabethans hid surprises in their desserts. *Wait.* I struggled to recall his exact words. *A typical Elizabethan treat...to bake treasure into something sweet...* Giving me cooking directions in a rhymed couplet, no less. But what *something sweet* was Eliot's special preserve? What place would he be likely to hide something extremely valuable, where it probably wouldn't be found? But if the loot *were* discovered, what place would point directly to Eliot as the culprit—?

Wait a second. Eliot's special *preserve?*

My eyes traveled to the jam cabinet. It was in plain sight, but locked with a key that was available to anyone who had the slightest knowledge of the ways of the castle. Too obvious? Still, like the labyrinth, the still-room products were Eliot's pride and joy...was there any other place where he stored them?

My mind cast up a memory. *This is just half of his insomniac production,* Sukie had told us, referring to the jams in the kitchen. *Think.*

Last night when we'd had lamb, I'd requested mint jelly. Julian had searched in the kitchen jam cabinet, with no luck. Then he'd disappeared into the buttery/dining room...the same place he'd gone to get the equally recherché sherry jelly....

No, that's stupid, I corrected myself. *This castle is enormous. You could hide something in a million places.*

With trembling fingers, I shoved aside the rapidly softening sorbet and reached for the key ring where the team moms had left it, on the counter. Swiftly, I sorted through the keys, heart pounding, until I found the tiny skeleton key used for the kitchen preserves cupboard. Maybe...I thought. Tom was at the airport with his high-school sweetheart, thirty-some people were waiting for me to provide dessert upstairs, my son and Julian were racing to the doctor, and I intended to solve a major murder case by ransacking shelves of... jelly?

Tomorrow might bring better ideas, but for now, I moved in rows, holding each jam jar up to the light. *Currant. Blackberry. Cherry. Blueberry. Marionberry.* All these preserves were just what the labels said they were.

Orange, *Fig*, and *Grapefruit Marmalade*, ditto. Feeling increasingly foolish, I began lifting the last row of jars: *Strawberry Jam*. Nothing.

I hastened into the buttery/dining room. The antique wine cabinet, an elegant mahogany piece with diamond-shaped leaded glass, had a tiny keyhole. I thought back. Julian had come in here, probably with the keys in his pocket. He'd only taken a moment to locate the mint and sherry jellies. I tried the smallest key on the ring. After a minute of my jiggling it in the lock, the glass door popped open.

The light in the dining room was dimmer than in the kitchen. I stared hard at each jam jar as I held it up to the light. *Mint Jelly*, *Sherry Jelly*, *Pear Chutney*. I was beginning to feel stupid. I started on the last row of jars, *Lemon Curd*.

On the tenth jar, I inhaled sharply. Pay dirt? Instead of being filled with pale golden curd, this jar was lined with...paper. I unscrewed the top and peered inside.

Clear plastic envelopes. I pulled out one and detected the unmistakable homely profile of Queen Victoria.

Unfortunately, before I could shout "Eureka" or even "God save the Queen," the floor in the hallway creaked ominously. The hairs shot up on the back of my neck. As I pivoted toward the sound, Michaela burst into the kitchen, then ran into the dining room. She was clutching a saber.

"Where are they?" she demanded. She was

enraged. Her white hair, lit from behind, made her look like a banshee.

"Where are *who*?"

Michaela's wild eyes fastened on the jar in my hand. "What is *that*? What are you *doing*?"

"Trying to figure out why you put the stamps in here." I took a deep breath. "It's because you want Eliot to get caught, isn't it? I know you hate him. I saw you fighting—"

She burst into a humorless laugh that was more like a cackle. "You don't know anything! I don't hate Eliot! Quite the opposite!"

At that moment, the lights in the kitchen and dining room went out. In the hazy light cast by the hall sconces, I could see only the silhouette of another human form, holding a glinting sword aloft. I heard two people grunting, fighting, pushing furniture over, whacking each other, shouting whenever they were hit.

Time to scram, my brain screamed, and I obeyed. I shoved the precious jam jar in my sweater pocket, pushed blindly forward, fell onto the dining-room table, then scrambled upright, knocking over a chair. The combatants in the kitchen barged into something. The crash of exploding glass shattered the darkness.

Run, I ordered my frozen legs. I groped out in the darkness; my knuckles whacked the china cupboard. Where was the door to the dining room? *Run.* I stumbled forward.

Someone was in the dining room with me.

A sword slashed the air, with the sound of a cold wind. I screamed and reached out again. My hand closed around something—one of Eliot's wine bottles. Again the rapier hissed, this time closer. I whirled and parried hard with the bottle. It broke as it smashed on my attacker's shoulder. Whoever it was went reeling backward.

I had seconds to move. I stumbled. Found the edge of the dining-room door. Slipped through and ran for my life.

Down the hall, into the well tower, past the well and garderobe, into the spacious living room. *Run, Run, Run,* my mind screamed. The cell phone and jar of stamps bobbled around in my sweater pocket. I was still clutching the neck of the broken bottle. It would be little use against a sword. I had to get away from that slashing weapon, had to get out of the castle, had to *escape.*

Behind me, footsteps pounded. Whoever it was could move, I'd give 'em that. *Run,* I told myself. *Run faster.* I slammed through the glass doors to the gatehouse, punched the code into the security keypad, and waited for the portcullis to rise. Panting, I grabbed the front door.

Behind me, there were no more footsteps. Had whoever it was given up? Or had my attacker gone to get a confederate? I stared at the front door, wheezing. What next? It was cold outside, and I had no car keys. I had no *car.* What was I going to do—run all the way into town? Whoever was chasing me was in much better shape than I could ever hope to be.

I whirled and looked across the courtyard. Just a couple of hundred feet away were parents who could help. Should I chance it? Or should I run out into the night, over the causeway spanning the moat?

Indecision is the enemy of mortality. Overhead, there was a clunk. Without warning, a splash of boiling liquid bit into my skin. I screamed as pain flared from my shoulder to my elbow. I jumped out of the way of the steaming cascade.

"Help!" I yelled as I jumped aside. More boiling water poured implacably down. "Help!"

The water was coming through the arched ceiling, through the ancient murder holes. My elbow and left arm were alive with agony. From the floor above came a woman's scream. I looked up and saw blond hair, a pretty child's face. Then I heard a *thwack,* and another, followed by more struggling and crashing. I was shaking, trying to open the front gatehouse door. My skin was on fire. I couldn't turn the knob.

"Flee, cook!" a child's voice hollered over the din above me. *"Flee!"* There was the sound of whacking, followed by grunts. "We tried to warn you not to come!"

And so I ran, back the way I'd come, my arm on fire, my skin melting. *Dear God,* I prayed, *help me.*

And then, like a miracle, I had a vision of pulling Sukie to the sink when she'd burned her hands trying to rescue the scorched coffee cake. *Water. Cold water.*

I was slowing down. Could my attacker have made it back to the kitchen? I was going to faint. I was going to die from my burns. I'd never see Arch or Tom or Julian again.

I was sobbing now. My body was a current of liquid fear and pain. *Water.* The top of the well was sealed tight with canvas. *Water.* I was going to die if I didn't find it. I unbolted the seat to the garderobe, yanked it up, and scrambled up on the ledge. Then I dropped feet first, down, down, down the latrine shaft. My feet whacked a grille and it gave way.

The shock of the icy moat was such an instant relief that I shouted with joy—underwater. I was rewarded with a choking lungful of creek water. Heaving and gasping, I flailed my way to the surface. Just as I thought *Grab the cell phone and jar of stamps*, I felt them fall away from my sweater pocket and drop, along with my shoes, deep into the dark water.

My head bumped against something and I recoiled. A duck? A fish? A rat? What else was there in this damn moat? I blinked, moved my arms and legs, and shoved through the icy water. The spotlights from the castle revealed what I'd bumped into. The missing sorbet carton.

Huh?

Swim.

Suddenly I was so deathly cold I knew I was going to sink to the bottom. *Swim, paddle, kick, do some damn thing,* I commanded myself. And, miraculously, my body obeyed. A hundred feet away, I could see the edge of the moat. A swimming-pool length. No sweat. I lunged through the water. *Swim. Kick. Move your arms.*

My scalded arm was numb with pain. My feet felt bruised from crashing through the grille. When I reached the side, what was I going to do? Was someone still after me? Wet and chilled to the bone, how would I get through the dark woods that surrounded the castle? I didn't have a clue.

Swim, dammit.

I raised one arm, then the other. The burnt arm wouldn't obey my mind's commands, so with great effort, I turned on my side and started an awkward, slow sidestroke. I gasped for breath. Swimming had never been so hard.

Finally, my fingers touched the slimy moat rim. The slippery rock wall, covered with algae, gave me no footing. Wheezing, I grabbed an overhanging aspen branch, only to slide backward into the icy water, gasping. With a huge effort, I hauled myself up on the rocks. *One foot in front of the other. Get out of the water, get through the woods, go back to town. Call Boyd. Call the police. Get a grip.*

Flee.

I heaved myself over the rock wall and tumbled hard into a bank of snow and leaves. All around, unseen trees rattled and swayed. I couldn't feel my feet. But I was in snow, I knew that. My burning skin began to sweat and scream with pain.

I glanced back at the castle. The kitchen was

lit by an eerie glow that did not come from the sconces or chandeliers. I squinted: There was a figure, a small figure, beside the window, which was once again open. Who was it?

I'd heard a child yell, "Flee, cook!" It had sounded like a girl, and she'd been in Michaela's overhead rooms, by the murder holes. I peered at the figure, which stood motionless, framed by the open window. Was I dreaming, or was it a young boy wearing a ruff? None of the kids at the fencing banquet had been sporting one of those stiff Elizabethan collars.

Crap, I thought. Either I'm seeing a ghost or I'm losing my mind.

CHAPTER 27

I turned away from the castle and tried to get oriented. Close by, light from a solitary lamp shone through the pines. I sniffed a putrid smell. Coming from...what?

I steadied myself, knelt carefully, and whisked soothing snow up my left arm. I belatedly recalled hungry mountain cougars, who did their hunting at night. Was I soon to become a feline hors d'oeuvre? I laughed aloud. *Put that worry out of your head, dummy.* The human hunter who stalked me was far more dangerous than any four-footed ones who might prowl through these woods.

I staggered to my feet, almost overwhelmed

by the smell of...garbage. Suddenly I realized I stood about half a dozen yards from the castle Dumpster, and the light beside it. I needed to get to help, I knew that. But all my thinking of the evening had not brought resolution to the questions that kept cropping up. When I was very young, my mother's first act whenever she came home from shopping was to check the garbage. This was especially true if I looked guilty. Had I broken a glass? Burned a pan with popcorn? Eaten forbidden ice cream bars? All the evidence my mother ever needed was in the trash.

I stumbled through the snow and threw open the top to the trash bin. Inside were my tied bags of trash from the labyrinth lunch. I leaned in, snatched them, and tossed them aside. Beneath those bags were two more black garbage bags, tied with yellow plastic ribbons. I ripped into the first one and was rewarded with household trash: aluminum platters and sauce-splattered folding boxes from Chinese carry-out. I leaned out of the bin and took a couple of deep, cleansing breaths.

I heaved myself back up the side of the bin and savagely tore into the final bag. Paint cans. Brushes. And below them, a metal sign and what looked like metal attached to a bunch of wires. I grabbed both, pulled them up, and held them to the light.

The sign said: PUMP ROOM! HIGH VOLTAGE! DO NOT ENTER! DANGER—ELECTRIC SHOCK! The other was an electric lock, complete with dangling wires. One side was blackened.

"Andy!" I gasped. "You got yourself into a real mess, didn't you, kid?"

I dropped the lock and the chain back into the trash, and tried to figure out where to go. A small service road ran up to the Dumpster. It was slick with ice, but traveling along it would bring me back to the driveway. *Think,* I ordered myself.

But I couldn't think: my burned skin felt so hot I flung myself back into the snow. I felt dizzy, swimming against the movement of the earth.

After a few moments, I felt a bit better. I blinked. The blur in my vision had cleared. So what did I need to do? Pretend you're Dorothy and *follow the Yellow Brick Road.* Or in this case, the *Iced Service Road.* My own spontaneous, halfhearted chuckle surprised me. Humor in despair. I heaved myself to my feet and lurched forward. How far was I from the driveway? A quarter of a mile? Half a mile? Overhead, through the swaying branches, I could just make out the Big Dipper, pointing to the North Star, at the end of the Little Dipper. *You can do this. Flee,* I told myself.

And I did, clutching my pained left arm. My stockinged feet had turned numb in the snow. I was going to make it, I told myself. Half a mile at the most.

The pine boughs swayed and creaked. *Who had done this to me?* The answer remained tantalizingly elusive: someone in the Great Hall, someone who saw me read Eliot's pamphlet, perhaps, someone who had followed me to the chapel and watched from afar as I'd scraped the new paint off the incriminating arc, the arc of electricity made where a young man had been electrocuted. Had it been Michaela? And if so, who had attacked her and rescued me? What had really happened back there?

My mind spun: *Flee, cook! We tried to warn you not to come!* I'd looked up into a face, with blond hair.

Andy had broken into a playroom, a playroom guarded by an electrified lock.

I don't hate him, Michaela had said. *Quite the opposite...*

The electric-locked playroom had been cheaply furnished, and the toys had been old, but not covered with dust.

The only dangerous place in the castle is the moat pump room, Sukie had said. *But don't worry, it's all locked up.* Was the room without a pump truly dangerous? Or was it locked to keep Our Lady Swiss-Clean out?

Tonight, I'd seen the face of a child, a little girl, I was almost sure. I was almost sure I'd heard that girl attacking my attacker, up in Michaela's apartment.

There was a child—a living, nonghostly little girl—in Hyde Castle.

The rumor of the baby drowning in the well had been just that: a *rumor*, started in a deliberate attempt to ward off the curious. And what about the screaming in Hyde Chapel? There hadn't been any ghost of a dead wife, I realized. The real child had been crying; maybe she had been hiding in the chapel storeroom when the ill-fated wedding had started. Eliot could have put together his whole tape-and-player show to cover up for it.

So Eliot had to know. He had to know *something*. He had to know why and how Andy had been electrocuted. Did he also know who had murdered Andy? Or had Eliot murdered Andy?

I was nearing the driveway. I had to be. But I couldn't hear cars from the state highway, only the moaning of the trees. Of course Eliot knew. Poor Andy had broken into the chapel—not the chapel where the stamps were hidden, but the castle chapel where the *child* was hidden, in its playroom...behind an electric lock and a sign saying that it was a pump room, to keep Sukie out.

But whose child...?

Stories in town had him living like a hermit in one room of the castle. For how long had Eliot lived like that? From the time he lost his teaching position on the East Coast to the time he met Sukie, almost nine years had passed. He'd had at least one girlfriend during that time: Viv Martini. That relationship hadn't lasted long, according to Boyd.

The family of the original fencing-master, meanwhile, had been given permission to live in a section of the castle rent-free....

Uh-huh. Almost nine years in a desolate, falling-down castle was a long time. Before his relationship with Viv, I was willing to bet, Eliot had found solace in the arms of his caretaker.

I don't hate Eliot...quite the opposite.

396

I was also willing to bet Michaela had had a child she wouldn't give up, but whose existence had to be kept secret, if Eliot was going to realize his dreams for the castle, with his reputation intact. The child, I wagered, occasionally wandered away from her playroom and made sudden appearances around the castle, perhaps even wearing a miniature suit of armor. Perhaps it was one of those appearances that had somehow provoked the nasty falling-out between Eliot and Michaela I'd witnessed in the courtyard....

Not only that, but the news of Andy Balachek's murder had brought the hard glare of publicity to the castle, a glare that might very well reveal a desperate secret that would undo all the owner's ambitious plans.

The child. I'd heard her breathing...that night I'd stood in the drum tower by our room. I'd glimpsed her once, in the shadows of the Great Hall, wearing her little suit of armor, undoubtedly lured by the fencing demonstration my own son was putting on. Even Tom had seen her, but had put it down to hallucinogenic drugs. This curious child, I was willing to wager, could get around the castle through the unrenovated areas, climb up into the towers, and scare us with unexpected appearances....

Flee, cook! We tried to warn you!

I stumbled down the service road, my thoughts spinning. After what seemed like an eternity, my ears made out another sound, a roaring noise...the creek. I thanked God. And when had I heard another roaring noise? Not long ago.

We tried to warn you....

I lurched to the driveway, and saw the lights of a distant vehicle. Was it on the road? I tripped on the snow-covered ground and fell to my knees. A wave of nausea rolled over me.

What had Boyd said? *The bullet that hit your house was not from the gun that shot Andy, Tom, and "Morris Hart," the computer thief.... The bullet was a warning. Somebody had tried to warn not Tom, but me. Away from what? From catering at Hyde Chapel. From catering at Hyde Castle. Why? Because a murder had been committed in the castle, and the body had been dumped not fifty feet from the doors of Hyde Chapel.*

Who lived in that upstairs apartment where the child's voice had come from? Michaela. Michaela who loved children, Michaela who had her own child, I was almost sure. Michaela had tried to warn me away by shooting out our window. *Scare her,* she must have thought, *close down the catering business for a while, anything to keep the mother of one of my favorite fencers away from this place where Andy died....*

I walked forward. I stayed in the shadows, knowing the person who'd perpetrated these crimes, who'd struck at me with a sword and poured boiling water onto my arm, was probably still searching for me.

And who was that person? Who had access to both the castle and Hyde Chapel? Who knew about the Lauderdales' demand for sorbet for their son, and could ensure my return to the kitchen by tossing the first carton into the moat?

As soon as I started to dig through the pamphlets, and started to unravel the lethal web spun through the castle and its history, *somebody* had gotten very scared.

Who had access to Tom's return time from New Jersey? The only way to get that was to have access to our family's private doings... through Tom, through me...or through Arch.

Whom did Arch visit every week? His father. And who had latched onto John Richard of late, convinced him, I was willing to wager, to fence some stamps and use his doctor-status and real estate greed to buy an expensive town house? No doubt she'd also figured she'd be able to follow our every move while planning her disposal of millions of dollars' worth of stolen stamps.

The roar of an approaching van interrupted my thoughts. *My* van. Tom! I waved at him with my good arm. He braked, jumped out, and insisted on helping me into the passenger seat. Relief and love for him overwhelmed me.

"Miss G., look at you!" His face was wracked with worry. "You're all wet! How did you ever—"

"Listen, Tom," I interrupted him, shivering like a madwoman. "You need to arrest Viv Martini."

CHAPTER 28

M y only question," said Julian the next night, as he poured bubbling ginger ale into a punch bowl, "is what's going to happen to Eliot and the castle?"

We were in the Elk Park Prep gym, readying for the Valentine's Day Dance. My left arm, which had received second-degree burns, was bandaged. I was sitting in a chair beside the table, unable to help much beyond dispensing advice, which I did freely.

Tom was not there yet. I hoped he would come, believed he would come. After all, he'd been willing to accept my rapid explanation of what had transpired at the castle, before he'd found Viv Martini, barely conscious, on the floor beside the murder holes. He'd brought her to her feet, told her her rights, and cuffed her. When a parent had offered to drive me to the hospital emergency room, it had been my great pleasure to see a defeated Viv being guarded by Tom in my van, where they were waiting for police cars to show up.

My mind turned back to Julian's question: What was going to happen to Eliot? I didn't know. He'd had to tell first the cops, and then Sukie, who had been oblivious to his hidden life, the truth: that Andy Balachek had climbed through the west-side garderobe into the study. That Balachek had received a nearly lethal charge of electricity trying to break into the castle's former chapel. That the sudden loss of electricity had brought Michaela to the room, and that she had run to Eliot, working on jams in the kitchen, as was his wont in the wee hours. She had told him of Andy's comatose state.

Eliot, panicked and desperate, had called Viv Martini, the third partner in the stamp heist. Viv, Eliot claimed, had been blackmailing him, threatening to expose the secret of his bastard daughter, whom Viv had discovered when she and Eliot were having one of their trysts.

All these years after their affair, Viv had decided to use Hyde Chapel as a hiding place for the stolen stamps, after Ray was arrested. She had not told Eliot what she was doing. But when Andy, who'd been getting restless to sell the stamps, had misinterpreted what Viv had finally told him about the stamps' whereabouts, he'd been killed in his attempt to steal them. Everything had gone south, just at the very moment all Eliot's dreams for a well-financed Elizabethan conference center seemed to be coming to fruition.

Eliot and Michaela had told police—in exchange for immunity from charges of complicity—that Viv had driven Andy away from the castle. She had used her pickup truck—her other vehicle besides the Mercedes—the same truck she later loaned to Mo Hartfield. Eliot, meanwhile, hastily threw paint over the blood, the arc, and other random spots in the castle, hoping to hide the incriminating evidence of Andy's near-fatal accident.

The police were speculating that there was one thing Viv had been unsure of: What Andy had told Tom. She must have been certain that Andy had betrayed Ray Wolff to the police. She knew he'd tried to steal the stamps before she was ready to fence them. After he'd been electrocuted attempting the double-cross, she'd shot him and thrown his body in the creek. Then hastily, too hastily, she'd removed the stolen stamps from Hyde Chapel, leaving one behind. Unbeknownst to Eliot, Viv had sneaked back into the castle and hidden the remaining stolen stamps in the jam jar, again using her knowledge of his security system and his still-room hobby to conceal the valuables in a way that would point away from her, if they were discovered. After that, the theory went, she'd sat in Cottonwood Park and waited to see if Tom had an inkling of what was going on. If he started to walk toward the chapel, instead of toward Andy's body, she had to conclude he knew not only where the stamps were hidden, but her identity as well.

And when Tom headed toward me—toward the chapel—she decided he had to die.

And then there were all the other aspects of the story that we suspected, but could not prove: that at the instigation of her true boyfriend, Ray Wolff, Viv had wormed her way into the Jerk's affections. Ray knew John Richard's ex-wife was married to the cop who'd arrested him, because John Richard had *told* him so. John Richard, for once, had been the one who'd been used. As a source of data and a *sex object,* no less. If he wasn't in a male-menopause support group, he certainly was going to need one now. Not to mention the help he was soon going to need if it could be proven he'd fenced stolen stamps. Plus there was that three-million-dollar, highly leveraged Beaver Creek town house to unload. Marla was going to be in heaven.

After I was released from the hospital, the helpful parent had driven me back to the castle. The police were questioning Eliot in the Great Hall. I'd gone looking for Sukie. She was alone in the kitchen, not cleaning for once. She'd been crying. She said when she'd survived cancer and her first husband's death, then found the historic letter that had led her to a new husband, she'd thought God was finally helping her get her life back. Now she wasn't so sure. I'd hugged her and murmured that Eliot loved her and wanted to protect her. And so did God.

Now, a commotion at the gym door made me look up. Julian and Arch, hobbling on the crutches required for his ankle sprain, had moved to greet Michaela and her daughter, a beautiful, seven-year-old child. I stood to greet them, too.

The little girl had thick blond hair that wound into spiral curls, held back with twin gold barrettes. She wore a calf-length blue taffeta party dress that looked old-fashioned, a pair of white socks, and black patent leather Mary Janes.

"I'm the cook," I told her, as I extended my hand.

She took my hand and curtsied. "I know." Her voice was clear and lovely. She hesitated, unsure how to use social graces that she'd been taught. "My name is Mildred. Tonight is my debut into society."

I nodded, unable to find words. This little child had tripped Viv Martini with a sword after Viv, her sword broken, crashed into Michaela's apartment through the living-room staircase. Viv had been looking for another weapon when she'd been tripped. Unfortunately, Viv had regained her balance, grabbed Michaela's old electrified cauldron, and poured scalding water down on me through the murder holes. But then *this little girl* had whacked Viv Martini unconscious with Eliot's precious copy of *Burke's Peerage*. This darling little thing, whose delicate-featured face was so uncannily like that of Eliot Hyde, her father, had done all that. I didn't know whether to laugh or cry.

"Thank you, Goldy," Michaela said, her voice trembling. "I'm sorry I yelled at you last night. I knew Viv had caused all the problems, and I was afraid she'd gone after Eliot. I wanted to find them and, and..." She stopped, aware of her daughter's gaze.

Mildred looked back at me, let go of my hand, and curtsied again. In the past twenty-four hours, I had learned more about why Michaela had kept Mildred's existence secret all these years. Eliot had guiltily confessed the rest of the story: Michaela *did* love him; she also adored their child. Michaela was also reluctant to leave her own father, the old fencing-master, and the castle home she'd always known and loved. And Eliot had been afraid to kick out Michaela and their daughter: That would guarantee the publication of his paternity. So Eliot had promised to let Michaela and Mildred stay in the Kirovsky family home, and to pay for all the child's expenses, until Michaela could take early retirement from Elk Park Prep next year. Then, she'd promised, she would take Mildred to a new home, when the conference center opened. Eliot would finance Michaela and Mildred doing all this, he had sworn to his caretaker, as long as no one—especially Sukie, whom he genuinely loved—knew that he was Mildred's father. This was why Mildred's playroom had boasted its heavy-duty electric lock.

But secrets do have a way of getting out.

Mildred curtsied again and allowed Michaela to lead her to the punch table.

Arch was enthralled. "Oh, Mom! A hidden kid! That's even cooler than a boy ghost who opens windows!"

"Where'd you hear that?"

"From Michaela," Arch said, pivoting on his crutches to watch Mildred. "While you were in the hospital. The ghost opens the window to get fresh air, because he died of pneumonia in that room. That was where he couldn't breathe. Every once in a while, they see him at the window of what's now the kitchen. He's wearing his little Elizabethan outfit with the ruffled collar, and he always opens the window."

Good heaven, I thought.

"Michaela also told me Mildred doesn't officially exist. When Michaela got real sick after she had Mildred? They evacuated her by helo out of the castle, and the medics saw the baby there with *Michaela's* father, who helped raise Mildred before he died."

The retained placenta mentioned by the flight nurse? Probably. I'd almost forgotten it.

"But Mildred never got a birth certificate," Arch said. "Michaela's going to have to get her one so Mildred can get an official name, and Social Security, and immunizations and all that stuff. Problem is, Michaela will probably get into lots of trouble for shooting out our window."

"I'm pretty sure Mildred will become Mildred Kirovsky," I told my son. "And the way I heard it, Michaela's not being charged with anything regarding our window, as long as she cooperates with the police on the Viv Martini investigation. We're certainly not going to press charges."

"That's good, anyway," said Arch as he bumped away. He was getting awfully agile on his crutches. "The fencing team needs her back before the state meet. Oh," he added as an afterthought, "Howie Lauderdale called and apologized. He said his father offered him a hundred dollars to win the bout with me. He felt really bad, and of course he didn't take any money. I told him I forgave him." He smiled, and so did I.

"Tom called on my cellular," Julian informed me when I reached the refreshments table, "since you lost yours in the moat. He's tying up some loose ends with Boyd and will be here as soon as he can. He says Eliot signed the immunity deal. Eliot has promised to co-operate fully." He served punch to the first three student couples to arrive. "And, uh, it looks like John Richard's probation might have come to an end, although that's being debated, too. Oh, and they're draining the moat, to try to find the stamps."

I smiled. "How about our house?"

Julian grinned. "Saving the best until last. The window's fixed, and so is the security system. You guys can go back there tonight."

The music started. Overhead rotating lights, covered with red cellophane, began to swirl, bathing the gym in a scarlet-tinted, festive air. Arch was hopping back and forth on his crutches. I looked more closely. He was dancing with Lettie, she of the recent breakup. Incredible. But then again, it was Valentine's Day.

The cookies and punch were a hit. Julian served with efficiency and panache. I wished I could have helped him, because just sitting and brooding was making me nuts. I hadn't asked Tom how his meeting with Sara Beth had gone. I hadn't had the heart.

At length, Tom entered the gym. He had a new sling on his arm, I noticed, and a jauntier-than-usual air about him. He made straight for our table.

"Miss G.," he said.

"We should talk," I said nervously.

He held up his hand. "Before you ask, when I left Sara Beth, she told me how much she liked you. I'm...sorry I didn't tell you sooner that she'd contacted me. Like right away, the first of January."

"I'm sorry I didn't trust you," I replied.

Sticks and stones may break my bones, but keeping secrets can....

Fearing he might lose his wife, Eliot had kept Mildred's existence secret from Sukie. Sukie, in turn, had kept her history of cancer secret from Eliot, fearing it would make her look flawed and undesirable. That's why she never mentioned knowing my ex-husband. Viv had deceived John Richard by blinding him with sex, and Andy Balachek's attempts to double-cross his partners had cost him his life.

But now Viv was under arrest, and John Richard was in all kinds of trouble with his parole officer. Sukie had told me that she and Eliot were staying together, no matter what. She wanted to have a relationship with Mildred, and Eliot sheepishly admitted that he wanted to get to know his daughter better, too, no matter how it would tarnish his reputation. Still, Michaela was moving out of the castle, Sukie had added, but only when she and Mildred were ready.

Tom and I, unfortunately, had not done much better than these folks in the full-disclosure department. We stood there, bathed in the crimson lights, facing each other. The first test of honesty in our marriage had ended in about a C+. But we'd survived and remained committed to each other. And wasn't that what counted?

Tom bowed as low as his injury would allow him. "Miss G.... or should I say, my dear Valentine, would you dance with me?"

I allowed him to tug me gently upright. The music had turned slow and romantic. An unexpected thrill darted up my spine. Then the two of us, looking like wounded veterans, stepped onto the dance floor. With infinite care, I put my hands around Tom's waist. My burned arm wouldn't reach to a proper dance position. Tom put his good hand around my waist. We started to move together.

"Sara Beth is on her way back to Vietnam," he said matter-of-factly. "She doesn't plan on returning. Her reality is in another part of the world now. Goldy—" He lifted his hand to touch my cheek. "Thanks for understanding."

I wouldn't go so far as to say I *understood*. Maybe I never would—totally.

I said, "I've heard about guys with gunshot wounds. Apparently, if they're *real* careful, they can make love after five days of healing."

Tom pulled me to him with his good arm, then swung me around. He leaned in close to my ear and murmured, "Oh, yeah? Where'd you hear that?"

And so I danced with my husband, my Valentine. After a few blissful moments, I checked the food table. It was unmanned. Scanning the dance floor, I saw Julian dancing with a lovely, dark-haired girl. An Elk Park Prep faculty member? An alum? Why had I never seen her before? Had Julian just met her? Or were they old friends?

"Tom," I whispered, "who's that girl dancing with Julian?"

Tom pulled me close. "Goldy," he murmured in my ear. Tingles again raced up my spine. "Will you never stop?"

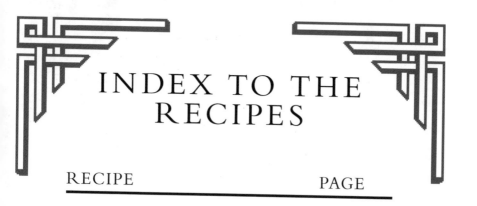

INDEX TO THE RECIPES

ABOUT THE AUTHOR

DIANE MOTT DAVIDSON lives in Evergreen, Colorado, with her family. She is the author of ten bestselling culinary mysteries and is at work on her eleventh.